Part One of the Okal Rel Saga

The COURTESAN PRINCE

a novel by Lynda Williams

EDGE SCIENCE FICTION AND FANTASY PUBLISHING

AN IMPRINT OF HADES PUBLICATIONS, INC.

CALGARY

Edge Science Fiction and Fantasy Publishing
An Imprint of Hades Publications Inc.
P.O. Box 1714, Calgary, Alberta, T2P 2L7, Canada

In house editing by Adam Volk
Interior & Cover design by Brian Hades
Cover Illustration by Echo Chernik
ISBN: 1-894063-28-7

EDGE Science Fiction and Fantasy Publishing and Hades Publications, Inc.
acknowledges the ongoing support of the Canada Council for the Arts and the
Alberta Fondation for the Arts for our publishing programme.

Library and Archives Canada Cataloguing in Publication

Williams, Lynda, 1958-
The courtesan prince / Lynda Williams.

(Okal Rel Saga)
ISBN 1-894063-28-7

I. Title.   II. Series: Williams, Lynda, 1958- . Okal Rel saga.

PS8595.I5622C68 2005   C813'.6   C2005-902176-4

FIRST EDITION
(t-20050404)
Printed in Canada
www.edgewebsite.com

Dedication

To Alison, for being there with me through every draft; to Janice, Richard, Adam and the team at Edge Science Fiction and Fantasy, for their help; and most of all to Edge publisher Brian Hades, for having the courage to be different and the heart to dream large.

Prologue

It began with the Alpha Colonies; the first uninhabited worlds settled by humanity in the late 22nd century. With the aid of an experimental faster than light technology known as "reality skimming", these fledgling colonies settled New Earth, later known as Rire.

Reality skimming however, had unforeseen consequences, with prolonged exposure leading to cellular decay, catatonia, and even death. Cataclysmic accidents were also possible, including one that abruptly severed contact with the Alpha Colonies, leading to economic collapse on a heavily-invested Earth.

In the aftermath of failed colonization a new hope emerged. Self-Evolved Ltd., a global corporation of incredible influence and power, began experimenting with human genetic modification. Despite the long held fears of tampering with DNA, Self-Evolved successfully created a new breed of genetically augmented human beings capable of withstanding the deadly effects of reality skimming. Given the codenames VR and DM, these "super-pilots" became the first in a new line of physically superior humans. Any protests against the genetic aberrations created by Self-Evolved were silenced when colonization began anew, using disposable VR and DM products, who lacked human rights. But dissention still existed, even within Self-Evolved, and a new era began, when a former Self-Evolved geneticist named Amanda Lorel joined forces with a group of renegade pilots, founding a new colony on the remotely surveyed planet designated as G-LN. With Lorel's leadership and scientific expertise, their human allies and liberated VRs and DMs, known collectively as "Sevolites", after the company that had created them, hoped to create a new life for themselves, free from the demands of Earth. G-LN became known as Gelion.

Fearful of further insurrections, Earth declared war on the upstart Sevolite colony. In the resulting clash another cataclysmic shift occurred, which became the symbol of original sin in the fledging belief system called Okal Rel. Earth, the homeworld, was forever lost to Sevildom (exactly as the Alpha Colonist had been) and was believed to have been utterly destroyed.

As the centuries passed, the isolated Sevolite civilization began to grow, and Okal Rel took hold.

Part philosophy, part religion, Okal Rel came to dictate the day to day lives of the Sevolites. Based on a code of ethics using ritualized combat known as Sword-Law, Okal Rel became the dominant political and cultural force on Gelion.

As Gelion flourished however, Sevolites became dominant over ordinary people, known as commoners, and became obsessed with the superiority of their respective bloodlines. The first were the Lorel's, descended from their world's ancestral founder. The second and third were the Vrellish and Demish, the descendants of the original VR and DM superpilots. Only the hybrid family, called Monitum, remained allied with human allies and retained greater knowledge of the past than the rising powers, as Sevolite society developed into a feudal system based of genetic superiority and the tenants of Okal Rel. Years of intermingling between Sevolites and unmodified humans resulted in a mixed population, classified according to the percentage of a person's DNA that was Sevolite in origin. Challenge class was the broadest distinction, and the most important, since membership in one class or the other had significance under Sword Law, and set the upper limits for someone's potential as a pilot. Highborns are the most Sevolite, followed by, nobleborns, Petty Sevolites and commoners. Demish cultures made further distinctions, known as birth ranks, which were greatly important to them but largely ignored by the most Vrellish members of Sevolite society.

But in all cases, highborns were the genetic and social superiors of Gelion, possessing incredible physical strength and the ability to withstand the rigors of space travel. Commoners in turn, were those individuals who were devoid of any of enhanced genetic traits, eking out a sparse existence among the lower strata of Sevolite society. Purebloods, the most powerful and revered rank of highborn, were the elite few whose untainted genetic lineages could be traced back to the original Sevolite founders without any commoner contributions along the way. In time, the inhabitants of Gelion, regardless of genetic rank or political class, became known simply as Gelacks and the aristocratic houses based on the Lorels, DMs and VRs diversified into multiple, hybrid lines.

The Vrellish were represented by the Houses of Vrel, Monitum, and Nersal; the Demish by House Dem, H'Us and Dem'dem. And lastly were the Lorels, who were both respected and feared for their knowledge — and abuses — of the biological science which created the original DMs and VRs. Each House claimed a place on Fountain Court, the political centre of the empire, located on Gelion.

By now, what had begun as a single Sevolite colony had grown into the vast interstellar society known as the Gelack Empire. Ruled from Gelion by a powerful figure known as the Ava, supported by the lieges of Fountain Court, the Empire engulfed countless worlds, controlling vast regions of space known as Reaches which were linked together by a network of reality skimming portals called Jumps.

For nearly a thousand years, Okal Rel has acted as a stabilizing force, preventing the worst excesses of war at the cost of cultural stagnation, abetted by Demish conservatism. Wars break out every few hundred years, reminding people of the terrible cost in lives and far more dire consequences of damage to habitat, which is precious and rare. One such war culminated in the destruction of the Lorel bloodline and an Imperial ban on all Lorel technology, with only House Monitum retaining a tenuous connection with the banished Lorels. Another war expelled the Demish/Vrellish hybrids known as Nesaks from the Ava's court. In the wake of these two, recent challenges to the stability of Okal Rel, peace once more flourished within the Empire until the Sevolites discovered that they were not alone in the universe.

The Alpha Colonies had survived and flourished in forced isolation, creating their own multi-reach, military empire, based on the world known as Rire.

A thousand years after mankind had first ventured into the stars, the two branches of humanity met in a destructive conflict that became known as the Killing Reach War. In the aftermath of the great battles, much of Killing Reach was no longer inhabitable, and regions of it were no longer even navigable due to the wreckage of both Reetion and Gelack ships. In the end, the great Sevolite leader known as Ameron was able to negotiate an uneasy peace, with both sides cutting off all diplomatic relations and retreating within their borders.

So dramatic was the damage done to the military dictatorship of the Reetions, that the "Old Regime", as it is now dismissed by modern Reetions, was felled by an idealistic alliance of Killing Reach survivors, who replaced militarism with a brand new experiment in human governance called compu-communism. Every aspect of Reetion society is now governed by a network of artificial intelligence known as arbiters and Reetions guard against any possible risk from the excess of their own, human pilots, through the use of advance psychological monitoring.

It is now 200 years since the Killing Reach War ended, and Gelion and Rire remain isolated, the last bastions of humanity walking the razors edge between war and peace ...

Pilots Are Uncomfortable People

"Contact?" Ann asked. "With Sevolites?"

She was lounging in a deck chair on a patio. Her recruiter, from the Explorations branch of the Reetion Space Service, perched opposite on a chair, indifferent to everything about her except for her talent as a pilot of faster than light space craft.

"Contact, yes," he told her, "but not necessarily with the beings you might think of as Sevolites. Just ordinary, human Gelacks."

"Naturally," said Ann. "You wouldn't want me to imagine that this mission you're offering me might be interesting, or anything like that." She paused to inhale a lungful of cigarette smoke in defiance of common civility and a lifetime of health education. "So why am I supposed to be interested? Do I get cut loose if I volunteer?"

"You're not exactly tied up," her recruiter pointed out.

Ann had to concede that much. Her group home was set on a white beach on the planet Mega: a sort of holiday resort with built in counseling. But she could not go where she liked or do what she wanted. Not, at least, without a whole triumvirate of counselors giving their fussy approval.

Ann frowned. The recruiter was okay to look at — bit soft in the middle and saggy at the shoulder, but well groomed — and the only company she'd had for a month. All the same he was becoming a bore.

"So," she said. "Why are we so interested in Gelacks again after — what's it been? Two hundred years? I thought we were pretty thoroughly out of touch."

"We were," the recruiter said, "but there have been ... developments. Your job would be to work with an anthropological mission named Second Contact, that will investigate whether there are, indeed, Gelacks on the far side of the Killing Reach Jump. Unfortunately there are limited records from the Old Regime. But what we do know is that First Contact seems to have been rather poorly handled. We hope to avoid those mistakes with the Second Contact mission."

"Rather poorly handled!" Ann repeated, with a laugh. "What would you call the Big Bang? A bit of a rough start?" She sat forward, stubbing out her cigarette. "We got kicked out of Killing Reach down to the last ship — by Sevolites!"

"There are no *Sevolites* in Killing Reach," the recruiter assured her. "No real ones. Certainly, the only Gelacks we've encountered —"

"What?" Ann interrupted; skin tingling as if she had been dunked in a cold bath. "Encountered? As in now?"

"Why, yes!" he exclaimed. "It's on the record."

"I don't like reading when I'm clinically depressed," said Ann.

The recruiter frowned. Such ignorance of current events ought to shame any self-respecting Reetion. "Perhaps you'd like to review the record on your own," he suggested. "Catch up. Before you decide whether you'd like to join the mission. Acquaint yourself with its principle champion, Ranar."

"Ranar?" Ann frowned. She didn't know of anyone called Ranar. It sounded nice though — sort of sensual. Two round, smooth syllables: *Rah-nar*. "Is he a pilot?" asked Ann.

"A pilot? No, no. Ranar is a brilliant young man. A Voting Citizen at seventeen and the youngest member of any netwide council at twenty-four. Gelackology is a bit obscure, to be sure, but —"

"Good looking?" interrupted Ann.

The Space Service recruiter frowned. "You're an intelligent woman, Ann. It's in your profile. And while pilots may be more extreme, emotionally, than most people, you do not have to play up mindless stereotypes."

Ann shrugged. "I have a high libido." She leaned forward, enjoying her ability to make him angry. "That's also in my profile."

Her recruiter resorted to lecturing. "Second Contact is going to be an historic mission, with the potential to make up for a lost opportunity to reunite us with another branch of mankind. You should be honored to be asked."

Ann was no taller than her visitor, and weighed less, but as she rose to her feet it seemed to her as if she towered over him in spirit. "You're not recruiting me for my diplomatic skills," she pointed out. "All you're interested in is my pilot's *grip*. So you'll have to put up with the rest of the package."

"You're a very uncomfortable person," he complained.

"Pilots are like that." Ann said, with a shrug.

"Will you take the deal, as offered?" he asked.

She had already decided. "Of course."

"We'll send someone to collect you in the morning," he said, packing up the few things he had brought with him.

"I can find my own way to a space port," said Ann.

"As you prefer." He took his bag and strode off.

As she watched him go, Ann wondered if looking forward to meeting Ranar might be construed as a little shallow when N'Goni, her lover and mentor, was languishing in a catatonia ward at the nearest Space Service hospital. But how long was she supposed to mourn? It wasn't as if she hadn't tried to warn him either. But oh, no! He couldn't possibly be succumbing to the wear and tear of the faster than light piloting. Not N'Goni, the hot shot exploration's pilot. No "little girl" was going to show him up! Not even if her piloting psych-profile had always been better than his. Ann told herself she had done what she could, right down to socking Lurol for refusing to use an experimental treatment for N'Goni's post-flight coma. The fact that N'Goni had indicated he didn't want such treatment, hadn't mattered to Ann. N'Goni had been showing classic signs of chronic spacer's syndrome in Ann's opinion and Lurol was supposed to be the hot shot space psychiatrist. She should have noticed. The assault on Lurol was the reason she was grounded now, on Mega, instead of out there working. Surely N'Goni himself would prefer that she got on with her life, now. The odds were he would never wake up again. How long was she supposed to be depressed about it?

Ann's primary counselor came out onto the patio from inside the group home. "What does Space Service want?" he asked.

Ann didn't even turn around. "I'm Supervised," she snapped. "Access the record if you want to know."

"I was hoping we could talk about the offer," he began, but gave up when she shouldered past and dove into the common room beyond.

Inside, the big jerk who thought every woman with a high libido must be dying to try his out, hailed her with his usual salute from the common room couch. "Your place or mine?" he bellowed, using a line he had picked up from one of the old Earth movies that Ann liked to watch. Ann did not reply. It just encouraged him.

She went quickly down a short hall to her bedroom, where even in a group home she was out of scope for fellow inmates and the average citizen. Only the ubiquitous surveillance of the AI's known as arbiters applied in a domestic setting, making sure that citizens did nothing to violate each other's human rights. Since Ann was Supervised, her counselors could also check up on her at will, but that didn't particularly bother Ann. Her behavior had been someone else's business all her life. When it wasn't counselors, it was pilot handlers, and before that it had been her parents.

Ann's room contained very few personal effects, which was typical for Reetions and particularly expedient for pilots. Most of what defined her was in digital storage, available from anywhere upon request.

"Stage on!" she ordered, as she entered. Her customized arbiter interface presented itself as a fat middle-aged man, stark naked except for a pair of thongs. His appearance was a composite of nudists she had spied on in her childhood on Rire. Ann had not imbued him with an interactive personality, though. Conversations with an arbiter always worked better if you accepted that it was out to reduce you to a handful of demands with modifiers.

"I want information on a Voting Citizen named Ranar," Ann told the interface. "He's heading up a mission known as Second Contact."

"Ranar of Rire," her nudist told her, "is a social anthropologist who has been exempted from citizenship duties from the age of seventeen in recognition of his intellectual contribution. Ranar is currently twenty-four standard Earth years in age and serving on Foreign and Alien council. He is Rire's leading authority on Gelacks, the humans presumed to share Earthly origins with Reetion civilization, who were first encountered two hundred years ago in the Killing Reach War."

Ann stripped out of her close-fitting yellow sun suit to pull on bright yellow pajamas. She liked yellow — it flattered her light brown skin.

Her stage displayed a reach map that located the world of Mega, where Ann was serving time in the group home. The display showed Mega within a translucent bubble with two exits, known as jumps, located at either end. One jump was labeled *Killing* and the other *Rire*.

"Ranar's got a thing about Gelacks," Ann summarized, pausing to shake out her hair and rub a breast under her loose top. "What else? Any bad habits?"

"No anti-social behavior is on record," said the customized interface.

"He never threw rocks? Lied? There's got to be something." She hesitated. "Maybe he isn't interested in sex."

"Citizen Ranar has registered two relationships since puberty. Both concluded amiably. The first —"

"Skip it!" Ann decided, remembering the jerk in the common room. Ranar might trace requests for his personal information, just as she had, and she didn't want to give the wrong impression. She toyed with asking for a picture but decided not to spoil the surprise.

Ann got onto her bed and drew her knees up. Her morph mattress adjusted under her. "Tell me how Ranar's Gelack mission got launched," she ordered.

"Ranar initiated the process," said the nudist, "based on the discovery of Gelack artifacts traced back to a colony of renegade Reetion pilots living in an abandoned station near the Killing Reach Jump." It indicated the spot on the reach map.

"Renegades?" Ann stiffened, legs sliding down as she sat up. Any pilot who put himself beyond Space Service's control was a hazard to civilization and had to be hunted down by the best pilots that Space Service could field: pilots like N'Goni and herself. "Reference my last mission with my partner, N'Goni," Ann told the arbiter. "We were looking for renegades in the same area."

She paused, almost holding her breath, until the screen displayed proof that the arbiter had the desired context nailed down. "Yes, that's the mission," Ann confirmed. "Are the renegades we were looking for the ones that Ranar found, later?"

"Almost certainly," the arbiter confirmed.

Ann shot up off the bed. "That's not possible!" The feeling of being one-upped raised a flush. "How could he find them when N'Goni and I couldn't? He's not even a pilot!"

"Ranar was able to trace some unique Gelack artifacts appearing in the Reach of Paradise. These artifacts were found in the possession of a pilot named Thomas, and it is believed they had been acquired as trade goods. Subsequently,

Thomas cooperated in the apprehension of his fellow renegades by Space Service and was later deemed fit enough
to be granted exemption from Supervision in exchange for
assisting with the Second Contact mission."

Ann's chest clenched with anger. *Stupid, lawless wipe head!*
she thought. *He gets off. I get Supervised. And N'Goni got worse
than that!*

"Revert to default interface," Ann ordered crossly. "Blank
the nudist."

"This customized interface represents an investment of
two hours," the nudist pleaded its case without a scrap of
concern about the injustice of shooting the messenger. "Are
you sure you wish to destroy this investment?"

"Yes!" Ann flared. "Yes, damn it! Can't you just do what
you're told! Can't anything be simple?"

The naked man became a yellow cube, rotating slowly on
the display stage in the middle of her floor. Ann scrubbed
her face and threw herself down on the bed again.

"Queue me digests on Ranar's investigation of the Gelack
artifacts," Ann ordered.

"Prepared."

"Stage off," said Ann, and the yellow cube disappeared.

Ann hauled up a butler arm fixed to one side of her bed
and adjusted its screen, her legs stretched out beneath it on
her morph mattress, and settled down to read the virtuously
austere digest. Research showed that plain text was less
likely than multimedia presentations to play irrationally on
the emotions, especially when compiled by an arbiter, which
is why knowledge was presented that way. But Ann found
it hard staying engaged. She lingered, instead, over diagrams
illustrating Gelack embroidery that were included out of
scholarly necessity, but even so her eyes began to droop.
After ten minutes she pushed the screen away. "Play me a
synthdrama about Gelacks," she told the stage.

For the remainder of the afternoon and evening she followed the rise and fall of neo-Arthurian empires, populated

by fictional characters with walk on appearances by Ameron, the Sevolite king — although the title used was "Ava" — and a fierce, gray-eyed woman called the Liege of Monitum. Lovers argued on her bedroom stage, Reetion dark and Gelack pale, as Ann walked around them trailing a hand through their solid light projections. Battles were waged on impossible, space-faring steeds capable of faster than light travel by Sevolites waving swords that cracked space stations. All the bad guys plotted against Ameron's desire to spare Old Regime Reetions and were duly thwarted. All the couples paired up to live happily ever after.

Ann fell asleep feeling like she had overdosed on floss candy.

* * *

Her counselor woke her up early.

"There is someone waiting to go with you to the space port," he told her.

"I don't need my hand held," Ann grumbled.

"I know we can't do anything right for you, Ann," he said, "by definition. But there is something I want to be sure you know before you go."

"Flying is bad for my health," Ann said sarcastically.

"Of course, but I didn't mean that." He looked down into his big, gentle hands. "Lurol is one of the mission triumvirate."

Ann was thunderstruck. "Not the same Lurol!"

He nodded. "The same space psychiatrist you assaulted for declining to treat N'Goni." He paused. "Ann, the mission is based on the same station. It is the only one near the Killing Reach Jump." He paused. "Still want to sign on?"

Ann snatched up her clothes in answer, determined to change in front of him if he didn't get out of her bedroom.

"I understand why the mission appeals to you," he lectured. "That's what I am worried about. Just because the modern Liege of Monitum is a man, not a woman — according to Thomas — that doesn't mean he is going to turn out to be

a dashing hero out of a synthdrama, Ann. He is more likely
to be a run-down wreck like Thomas, whether or not he is
supposed to be a Sevolite, to judge by what little we do know
about the modern situation."

Ann froze with her pajama top half over her head, expos-
ing her breasts, and dropped it back again. "I'm going to
meet the Liege of Monitum?" she asked.

"You did not read the digests, did you?" He sighed. "Ann,
you're still a bit depressed. We could veto your assignment
on the strength of that, but —" he added quickly, seeing her
react, " — you are a pilot and you are more likely to improve
under stress than not."

"I want to go," Ann insisted. "Lurol or no Lurol."

* * *

A cheerful woman counselor kept her company on the
public transit ride to the space port. Ann made conversation
like crazy to keep her companion from asking probing
questions. Beneath it, she brooded about Lurol. She should
have guessed the space psychiatrist would still be in the
picture. Lurol haunted high-risk piloting missions hoping for
a chance to test her experimental visitor probe on consent-
ing pilots. The name "visitor probe" was a vain attempt to
make it sound friendly and welcome, but it had the power
to change you, if only for the desirable purpose of restoring
mental health in pilots who succumbed to post-flight catatonia. Physically it looked like a harmless white cylinder
lying on its side and big enough to sleep in. Ann remembered
having to lie in it to establish her baseline. It hinged open for
her to get inside. After that, Lurol's staff had immobilized her
head in preparation. When it closed, and the finely tuned
fields that messed with her brain were engaged, she was left
staring up at a saline drip that kept her eyes lubricated while
she underwent treatment. Some of this was familiar to any
pilot, since the visitor probe was an extension of Rire's psych
profiling technology. But there was one, alarming difference.
Instead of merely reporting reactions to simulated stimuli, the

visitor probe had the power to impose subtle changes. There was a therapeutic reason. Given adequate calibration of a pilot's normal psych profile, the visitor probe could re-impose that profile on a pilot suffering from spacer's catatonia, and in three out of five trials to date, had actually revived the pilot. Ann thought of it as reloading the pilot's own consciousness, to counter the mind-altering effects of reality skimming caused by exposure to what was called the *gap* dimensions.

Like most Reetions, Ann accepted the need for psych profiling, because a malicious act by someone piloting a faster-than-light vessel could be catastrophic. She saw the visitor probe as the next step in profiling development. But N'Goni had refused to consent to the visitor probe. Ann suspected he didn't want to think about becoming comatose, as if planning for the unthinkable might bring it about. And Ann had let the matter drop, even though she suspected he was showing signs of spacer's syndrome.

"I don't want to talk anymore," Ann announced, in the middle of the counselor's carefully weighed responses to one of her throwaway remarks.

The woman did not give her an argument.

At the space port, Ann took a seat on a passenger liner and docked with an orbital space station where she submitted to the usual pre-flight exams, "flight" referring in this case to reality skimming. She argued with the resident psychiatrist about flying cargo, which was pilot slang for being transported out cold in a life-support cylinder. The physical wear and tear of reality skimming was unavoidable but people could fly cargo to reduce the impact of *gap*.

Gap was pilot slang for exposure to dimensions that were ordinarily coiled up in the stuff of the universe. Only pilots with *grip* could contend with it. Arbiter-controlled ships simply popped out of existence, and weak pilots were at much higher risk of disappearing or succumbing to a hazard known as time slip, in which the laws of Einstein's special relativity exerted themselves. Ann wasn't much for following the math. She just knew that *gap* was the enemy and to combat it a pilot needed *grip*.

It was crazy to want to fly conscious when you could be spared experiencing *gap*, but Ann's instincts still rebelled as her handlers put her under, embarrassing her with the memory of last minute, futile resistance when she came around on *Second Contact Station*, hours later. Reality skimming trips never took more than hours, unless someone time slipped.

"Hi," she was greeted. "Have a good nap?" The voice was unusually cocky for one of Lurol's medical staff.

Ann floundered like a landed fish, trying to sit up with the drugs still in her system.

"I don't know why you let them fly you cargo," said the bizarre-looking man to whom the voice belonged. "Any ship I fly in, I pilot. You got that?"

Ann ignored the comment beyond registering that he was a pilot. "Be useful," she grumbled, "and help me up."

His grasp was both strong and frail at once, trembling despite a bite that hurt her arm. He was dressed in stained beige pants with a vest worn over a narrow, naked chest and had piercing eyes set in a face that looked prematurely lined. His hands reeked of stale smoke.

"Thanks," she said, when she was sitting up, and scared up some professional camaraderie. "My name's Ann."

He nodded. "Thomas. Thought I'd tell you in case you haven't looked me up. Gather you don't do much of that." He grinned. His teeth were stained and the gums had shrunk back. Ann, whose many faults included an inclination towards physical beauty, was repulsed.

"You're in pretty good shape for a pilot," he concluded, looking her up and down.

"Can't say the same for you," said Ann. "Who the hell are you, anyhow?"

Thomas whistled. "You really are info resistant, you are."

"I'm depressed," she said tartly. "I don't think you're helping."

He grinned again. "See you at the briefing tomorrow."

The smell of stale smoke he left in his wake was enough to make her think about quitting, which reminded her she had not packed her cigarettes and the station wasn't going to supply them.

As Thomas walked away, she got a good look at the back of his vest and realized the embroidery was Gelack, depicting a sword in the grasp of a well-muscled arm. Then she remembered that Thomas was the name of the renegade pilot excused Supervision in exchange for helping out Ranar. The one who was supposed to teach her how to make the Killing Reach Jump. So far he didn't inspire confidence. Learning how to navigate a jump was a very nearly mystical experience, or in space psychiatry terms a function of dream-like self-consciousness. In either case, it called for sufficient trust to let your guide take over your *rel*-ship's phase-slicing envelope and essentially pilot for you. Not something a girl wanted to do with just any guy and Thomas definitely looked more chewed-up by reality skimming than she was.

Ann passed her post-flight review and was taken to her room by one of Lurol's staff. Promising herself she would study the mission after a nap, Ann lay down to sleep, only to be woken by her bed a whole day later, exactly twenty minutes prior to her briefing with Ranar. Ann dressed in a rush, skipped eating, and pulled on the clean yellow stretch pants and breast band that she found in the closet, pushing her gritty hair off her forehead with the matching headband. She wished that she had time to shower and resolved to expand her lead time on appointments to one hour.

When she walked into the meeting room, an urbane young man interrupted himself to greet her. "Ann of New Beach, I am gratified that you accepted our offer. You are the best pilot Rire has on record."

"Ranar, right?" said Ann, smiling. He was handsome in an understated way, like an Oxford-educated Raja in a British Empire drama from the 20th century Earth repertoire of feature films that Ann indulged in for entertainment. His tunic fell from neck to thigh over matching slacks, a conservative style for Rire redeemed by the exotic addition of a twisted braid motif for decoration. The pattern of the braid never repeated, but tumbled down his body worked in browns and reds evolving through a white phase into solid green dominance.

Ann snapped her fingers and pointed. "That's Gelack!" she remembered. "Green is House Monitum's color."

Ranar's fingers brushed the green threads at mid-chest. "This was copied from images we have of Liege Monitum's vest braid. Of course, fashions may have changed in two hundred years," he added, sounding wistful.

Lurol stood across from Ranar, dressed in the ridiculous white lab coat that was her hallmark affectation. Thomas sat curled up in a morph chair. The room's central stage displayed an idle blue diamond interface.

"The first thing I want to know," said Ranar, "is whether you can work with Lurol."

Lurol stuck her hands in her pockets. She had a wide nose, thick lips and a lanky build with short, brittle hair that was perennially uncombed.

Lurol the brain mechanic, thought Ann, sarcastically. But she said, "My friend, N'Goni, did not give consent to be visitor probed. Therefore Lurol was right to withhold treatment."

"But," Lurol was ruthless, as usual, "I could have ruled N'Goni incompetent on the grounds of advanced spacer's syndrome. I had that authority. But I truly believe he was of sound mind when he declined the visitor probe option. I had to respect that."

"And I did my best to break your face for it," said Ann. "For my part, we're done. You?"

Lurol shrugged. "You work with pilots, now and then you expect the odd assault."

"Good enough," Ranar decided.

"I like this guy," Thomas told Ann, hooking a thumb towards Ranar. "He's driven."

"If you mean that I take this mission seriously," Ranar answered him, "I do. It ought to be self-evident that the black market is an ill-advised way to reopen relations with another human culture. Especially a potentially dangerous one."

"Gelacks aren't dangerous." Thomas lit a cigarette. "They're pathetic."

If he is going to smoke, Ann thought, *he could at least offer me one*. But he did not.

Ranar ignored the rudeness of Thomas lighting up, although his nostrils seemed inclined to pinch closed. "Have you considered," he proposed, "that the Gelacks you have been dealing with may be the dregs of their society, no more representative of their kind than you are?"

Thomas blew smoke at him. "I understand Gelacks better than you. I've traded with them. They're spacers, like me. Without arbiters to make up rules they've got to live by."

"Arbiters only implement our rules," Ranar corrected.

"Whatever," Thomas answered him languidly. Then he perked up and grinned at Ranar as if he had caught him out. "Hoping to find Sevolites, aren't you? Real, live super-pilots who don't wear out flying." He let smoke drift past his stained teeth. "You're dreaming," he gave Ann a meaningful look, "like some kid hooked on a synthdrama." Thomas paused to cough. "Sevolite is just some dumb title. I've met one and he looks worse than I do."

"You met a Sevolite?" Ranar cross-examined him. "Why haven't you mentioned it?"

"I did. He's the *Trinket Ring* station master. My contact. I just didn't tell you that he goes on about being ten percent Sevolite like I should be blown-away awed."

"Ah, yes," said Ranar. "The man who agreed to arrange for me to meet with Liege Monitum."

"Yeah," said Thomas. "After he stopped looking at me like I'd asked him for directions to Earth. I tell you, this

Monitum character's mythical." He blew smoke. "Gelacks
are always on about their gods. There's a whole pantheon
of 'em from some never-never land called Fountain Court.
'Cept Gelacks don't pray to them. They pray for them to
leave 'em alone."

"Including Liege Monitum?"

"Yeah, well, they'll tell you there's been a Liege Monitum,
lives on Fountain Court, since the world began." Thomas
extinguished his cigarette against a callused pad on his left
palm. "Gelacks call themselves Sevolites to make out they're
related to these so-called highborns way, way back. You
know, like Hercules being the son of Allah."

"Zeus," Ranar corrected.

"Whatever." Thomas dropped his cigarette on the spot-
less floor and turned to Ann. "I gather that this station's got
a recreational pool, and I hear Reetion women have taken
to swimming nude since I was hanging around lawful
citizens last."

"Only if they're nudists," Ann told him, still put out because he hadn't offered her a smoke.

"I'll go see if I can convince some of 'em to take it up,"
said Thomas and strolled out.

"I don't like the idea of you risking your life on the
strength of that one's *grip*," Lurol told Ranar, "let alone his
good intentions. Thomas is a dozen trips shy of a medical
discharge."

"I know," said Ranar. "But he won't be psych profiled or
evaluated."

"Part of your agreement," Lurol muttered. She thrust her
big hands in the pockets of her silly lab coat.

"It is my life to risk," Ranar said. He turned to Ann, "And
yours."

Creamy hot chocolate, Ann thought, gazing at him appre-
ciatively. *Well, maybe a little cooled off, but still rich and warm.*

"Ann?" Ranar asked.

"What? Oh, yeah. Sure."

Ranar frowned. "You haven't any idea what's expected of you, do you?" Ranar sighed. "Let's find somewhere more congenial to talk."

Ann thought, *I'm all yours!*

They picked up refreshments from a self-serve bar on *Second Contact's* promenade and sat down together at a table with morph seating that conformed to their respective preferences without needing to ask what those were. Ranar talked about Gelackology's unfortunate tendency to be dramatized in shoddy synthdramas that contributed, in his opinion, to his not being taken as seriously as he should.

"Gelacks," he insisted, "might be what's left of Earth's population. A beta colony that explored in another direction after our jump to Earth collapsed a thousand years ago."

"I thought Earth got trashed in the collapse," Ann said, hoping to sound knowledgeable.

"We don't know that," said Ranar. "In the absence of reliable observations it is impossible to know which maths apply, let alone compute the range of the space-time disturbance on the other side." He went on about the difficulties while Ann listened with her chin propped in her palms.

"I thought you were an anthropologist," she said, during a pause. "You sound more like you study space science."

"I did," he smiled, self-consciously. "When I was a boy."

Ann's chair adjusted as she straightened. "If you are saying we should be leery of poking around in Killing Reach because there might be something nasty in it, I can make sense of that."

"No," he said with force. "I am saying it would be foolish not to make diplomatic contact before informal ones get out of hand."

"You lost me," said Ann, spreading her hands.

"Thomas is not the only one trading in Gelack artifacts," Ranar explained with the air of someone forced to explain the obvious in words of one syllable. "I authenticated other examples, at commercial-economy ports outside arbiter jurisdiction, artifacts Thomas denies ever seeing before."

"Maybe he can't remember," suggested Ann. "He must have a few blank spots between the ears from flying as much as he has."

"The point is," said Ranar, "that the Killing Reach Jump is being used again. Probably by Gelacks. In fact I think Thomas may have learned about it from a Gelack. Someone like his *Trinket Ring* friend, perhaps."

"What?"

"Have you read any of my work at all?" he asked.

"Some stuff about embroidery," she said lamely.

Ranar sighed. "The significance of that is that the work is done by hand, which is typically Gelack."

"How do you know they're not fakes someone manufactured?"

"It can be deduced with a fairly simple analysis. Do you really want the details from me, here, now?"

She scowled. "If you are so smart, how come you took up a subject as obscure as Gelackology?"

"Ah," he sat back, loosening up for the first time since she had met him, as if he was laughing at himself now. "If you really must know, I think I had a crush on Ameron, the Gelack's Ava."

"Ameron?" cried Ann. "But he's a man!"

"Is something wrong?" asked Ranar.

"No! No, I, uh — are you homosexual?" Ann asked.

"Is that a problem?" Ranar asked, puzzled.

"No. I, uh, no! Of course not." She scowled. "Do you think I'm some sort of retro nut case or something?"

"I'm sorry," he said. "You just seemed ..." he lifted a hand in a gesture of uncertainty, "upset," he concluded.

"You're the genius," she told him narrowly. "You figure it out."

He did, but it took a moment. Then he said, blandly, "Oh. I'm sorry. I hope that wasn't a factor in your acceptance of the mission."

"Hell, no! You think meeting sword-wielding Sevolites isn't more exciting than doing time in a group home?" Ann would have claimed a passion for embroidery to change the topic.

"Shall we continue then?" Ranar asked, coolly.

"Yeah. Sure."

He quizzed her on the mission details for an hour. The politics were the hardest to figure out. Foreign and Alien Council was the mission initiator but Ranar, as its champion, enjoyed uneven support. Neither of the mission's other two triumvirs had much clout: Lurol was only on the first expansion of Human Ethics and not a Voting Citizen, and the mission's third triumvir, Jon, was a Space Service executive who happened to serve on the third expansion of the powerful Assembly of Sibling Worlds.

Ranar was anxious to connect with Liege Monitum fast, before his mandate to do so got revoked back home.

"The more clearly I state the obvious concerning the Killing War," Ranar complained to Ann, "the more hotly I am accused of fantasizing threats out of a synthdrama. It did not help at all that Thomas insisted on talking about swords."

"Do they really use those?" asked Ann, perking up.

Ranar closed his eyes. When he opened them, his tone was flat. "We know Gelack politics are neo-feudal," said Ranar. "Fencing might be an elite sport, or swords may be religious symbols. There are ample explanations that fall well short of dueling from horseback in hard vacuum!"

Ann blinked at his vehemence.

He exhaled with force. "I am sorry. It is just that I am sick of people fixating on the damned swords. If the Gelacks are a threat to us, it won't be because of the swords."

"What then?"

"I do not know!" Ranar lost his temper, which upset him more than it did Ann. "If I knew," Ranar told her stiffly, "I could write it up for the record and go home." He excused himself.

Ann sat alone a moment, then went back to her quarters to brood. She considered resorting to a mood lifter, but that always felt like admitting her emotional existence was no more than a by-product of biochemistry. She preferred to feel that she had every right to be miserable.

Instead she invoked her stage. "Has this station got a casual sex roster?"

"Yes."

"Show me."

There were only two entries, both male heterosexuals.

The first was a bit of a production. He had a great body and gave her ample data to prove it. His medical record came complete with links to everyone he had slept with for years. A trophy collector if she had ever seen one.

The second was Thomas. "Needed," his notice read beside a simple picture, "a willing woman." That was it. His medical record was provided by default. The collection of anti-bodies suggested he hadn't been celibate, but her own list of minor risk factors was half as bad. The shock was discovering Thomas was only twenty-five.

Ann shut the stage off without adding herself to the roster or contacting either man. "Show me historical images of Gelacks," she ordered. "Specifically Liege Monitum and Ameron." Both appeared wearing swords.

Ameron, the ruler of the Gelacks at the time of the Killing War, was a pale, lean man with sharp, pronounced features and gray eyes. He was dressed in an embroidered vest laced tightly closed over a white shirt and slacks. The Liege Monitum of his time was a woman, although you had to look twice to be sure; she was so lean and muscular. She had a slightly darker complexion than Ameron, but was still light-skinned by Reetion standards.

Ann listened to one of the few extant recordings which was no more than a snatch of small talk captured, at random, in a corridor. The language spoken was English, the only one that both sides had in common. Ann's stage provided a Reetion translation on a ribbon of streaming text, near the bottom.

Ameron said, "Have you no decent food?"

"Decent?" sputtered an unidentified Reetion of the old, pre-arbiter era. "We're starving and you dare to complain when we provide you with the best we have?"

There was a thud accompanied by sudden movement and Liege Monitum's alto voice ground out, "Speak to him like that again and you will eat your tongue."

Nice people, Ann thought.

She was interrupted by the arrival of a member of Ranar's first expansion. Ann's stage announced her and the door to Ann's room let her in. An expansion was a political unit able to stand in for another political unit when required. Each expansion included a larger number of people than the previous one, but functioned with the same net authority. In Ranar's case, he had brought along a team of anthropologists qualified in First Contact Gelackology, to act in his place as one of the station's three triumvirs while he was away in Killing Reach. In the meantime, they were helping out generally. Ann's visitor was there to make sure Ann was well enough informed to get her safety waiver on record, which meant a review of the mission.

First, she would learn the jump. Normally that took at least three training runs but Ann hoped for fewer. She was talented. Once she knew it, Thomas would fly Ranar through and dock with *Trinket Ring* to make the rendezvous with Liege Monitum. Ann was to act as back up. She was not to dock, just receive transmissions from the sub-arbitorial crystonics unit Ranar would take along with him, which was about the size and shape of a suitcase and was known as the mission box. If something went wrong it was her job to make it back to Rire and report.

After putting her informed consent on record, Ann slept again and turned up on time for the next meeting only to find it already in progress.

"You are out of your mind!" Lurol was dressing Ranar down, her posture belligerent. Ranar looked stubborn. Thomas was enjoying the spectacle. The new triumvir, Jon, had arrived and was listening with a concerned air.

"I need your agreement, Lurol," Ranar pleaded. "If we have a hung vote, it will go to first expansion, and since neither you nor Jon have a complete first expansion on board, a hung vote would bog us down badly. The whole point is to act before the next mail delivery shows up."

Ann took the morph chair beside Jon. "What's up?" she asked.

"Ranar wants to cancel the training runs and go across right now," said Jon. "He didn't like the net traffic that arrived with my flight. The lobby opposed to wasting resources on Gelacks is gaining ground. He's afraid he'll be recalled."

Ranar was saying, heatedly, "It is my life to risk, Lurol!"

"What about the pilots?" she countered.

"It was my suggestion," volunteered Thomas. "I got laid something fine last night — it's good luck."

Ann guffawed.

"The Gelacks I met swear by it," said Thomas. "Before and after. They say it perks you right up if you're space stoned."

"Oh yeah, right," said Ann, cynically. "Have sex with me right now or I'll lapse into a coma. No pressure."

"For the love of reason!" Lurol exclaimed like a disgusted parent. "Enough of that. Ann!" she demanded. "How do you feel about Ranar's proposal? Would you support moving the mission up to the first run?"

Ann shrugged. "Sure."

"You would risk getting stranded in Killing Reach if something happened to Thomas, " Ranar scrupulously pointed out. "Since you won't have time to master the jump properly, beforehand."

Ann shrugged. "I can learn a jump in one pass."

"Space Service recommends a minimum of three training runs in wake-lock with a veteran," Lurol pointed out.

Ann gave her a withering look before returning her attention to Ranar. "I'll do it," she gave consent. "Soon as you want."

Thomas got up and straightened out his clothes. "Let's go."

"Thank you," Ranar told them both warmly, "but it is Lurol I must convince to approve the proposal."

"Submit it formally," Lurol insisted, "or let it drop."

Thomas touched Ann's arm. "Come on," he said. "Let's go suit up." Ann looked back at Ranar as Thomas added, "Either he'll join us on the first run or he won't." Ann fell in, accepting the logic of that.

She was itching to ask Thomas about the jump but knew that would be breaking an unwritten law. In all the years she had flown with N'Goni she had never known how he internalized his jump experiences. It was a pilot superstition not to ask. To her, jumps were like plunging through water, sometimes churned by angry currents, sometimes packed with playful dolphins out to get her lost. Would this one be similar? Or something strange and new?

Thomas crinkled his blue eyes at her. "You checked out my roster entry last night. What put you off?"

"Apart from it being you?" Ann asked tartly, and walked on.

"The record says you've got a high libido," Thomas went straight to the point.

"But discriminating," said Ann.

He lifted a hand and waggled it side to side.

"Looked up all my relationships too, huh?" she asked.

"That what you call your one night stands?"

"The answer is still no," said Ann. Thomas looked exactly like what she didn't want to imagine as a pilot's future: prematurely old at twenty-five with signs of palsy in his hands.

"When we're in that jump together," he predicted, "you'll appreciate my finer points."

To make it through the jump Ann knew she had to surrender herself to his guidance. Some pilots claimed they could sense each other through the *gap* dimensions when their wakes merged, but Ann didn't believe in that. She figured it would have happened between her and N'Goni if it was possible. It certainly wasn't going to happen with Thomas.

Gravity lightened as they dropped toward the station's zero-G hub. A pilot handler — a sort of specialized paramedic counselor trained to deal with post-flight symptoms — met them at the terminus. Ann enjoyed watching the handler fail to convince Thomas to put on a pearly white flight suit that provided at least modest protection from radiation. Thomas preferred his embroidered vest, insisting it was good luck. He also refused to let them put an arbiter persona on his ship. He was still flying the ship he had stolen when he turned renegade, and he had painstakingly overhauled it to rely on algorithmic software alone.

"I let you put a persona in there," Thomas told the flight crew, "and it won't be my ship anymore. Besides, no arbiter nav-persona is going to make it whole through the Killing Jump. No AI has the *grip* for it."

Ann floated in the bay listening with amusement for a moment before shoving off in the direction of her own ship.

Ann's *rel*-ship was a blunt-nosed exploration vessel known as a scout, with a built-in cocoon affectionately known to pilots as the slug, a device that distributed G forces under acceleration and boasted built in life support. She had to take her stretch pants off to benefit from all the hook ups. Her slug irised around her body, sealing her into a cushioned and monitored environment while her onboard crystronics downloaded a flight persona. Ann launched and waited, listening to pop songs as she drifted away from the station.

"Your guide is go for launch," a voice from the station hailed her by radio. "He has Ranar on board."

The next communication was from Thomas. "Okay yellow buns," he referred to her clothing preference, "we're doing it for real the first time."

"Let me talk to Ranar," she asked when they had settled into their distancing run from the station.

"Here," the anthropologist's voice came back.

"When's the last time you flew with your eyes open?" Ann asked.

"Never," he admitted. They both knew it was necessary this time, because they could not count on there being revival facilities on *Trinket Ring Station*, but it surprised Ann to know it was Ranar's first time.

Thomas chimed in. "I'll hold his hand. Listen, once we bite —" one of many euphemisms for transition to reality skimming —"we're only minutes from the jump, so stay close. If you don't make it through with me I won't pop back to find out if it was just because you chickened out."

"Just kick up a wide wake, big mouth," Ann gave him back.

"That's my girl!" said Thomas.

"Fat chance," said Ann.

Their ships did some last minute communicating to make sure their splicing fields were synchronized, then both pierced the skin of the space-time continuum. The transition hit like the insult it always was.

The psychological adjustment was the worst part. The whole concept of existing seemed ridiculous. Ann's ornery streak came to her rescue — there was no way she was going to lose that leering idiot Thomas. He churned up a froth on high shimmer — the physical component of reality skimming — as he screamed toward the jump. Ann pulled ahead, then let him match her mix of gap and shimmer and was enveloped.

Ann inhaled like a kid at the top of a joyride as layers of reality tumbled about, reduced in her mind's eye to the transparent skin of drifting jellyfish. It was definitely jellyfish this time, not dolphins. Then they were out on the other side.

According to prevailing wisdom, jump hallucinations were something the conscious mind slapped over the hole left by *gap* exposure. But they were very real to pilots who made jumps by clinging to their personal internalizations of them. Ann was eager to commit hers to memory. As she snatched at fading impressions, however, she was interrupted by an alarm.

Her flat stage confirmed that her ship's flight persona had been wiped out by the potent dose of *gap*.

"Oh great, just great!" Ann moaned.

She called up algorithmic software, irritated by how fiddly it was just to do that, although she could still rely on voice commands.

Thomas barreled heedlessly on.

"Will you stop!" she shouted, pointlessly. Communication was impossible at faster than light displacements. All she could do was observe his wake signature. At least it was distinct from her own, now. The two ships had slid harmlessly out of wake-lock. She buckled down to follow.

Seventeen minutes into Killing Reach, Ann was getting worried. According to the star map Thomas had put on record, they were about to run over the little Gelack station if they didn't cut out soon, and even a near miss could quake it apart.

Not a polite way, Ann thought, *to open a diplomatic dialog*. Her nerves were on edge by the time Thomas dropped out of skim and she gratefully followed.

Thomas hailed her on the radio as soon as that was workable. "Are we sane?" he asked.

"I am," she told him curtly. "How's your passenger?"

"Out cold!" He sounded merry about it. "Our boy genius doesn't have as much *grip* as he thought. But don't worry. He isn't comatose. Just not laying down memories. He'll come around. I'm going in to dock."

"Stay in touch," Ann threatened.

"Or you'll what? Report me to Space Service?" He sounded smug.

"Damn right I'll report you if you screw this up," said Ann. "You got an amnesty deal for this. That must mean something to you."

"Maybe," he drawled. "Or maybe I want to settle down on this side of the jump.

Ann absorbed that with a cold little shock, but he sent her the frequency that he could be reached on, so she decided he was just trying to shake her up.

"Don't talk to me to pass the time of day, okay, yellow buns," said Thomas, taking charge. "Hearing us talk to each other in Reetion might freak them out."

"You don't want me asking questions," she told him grimly, "you make sure I don't have any to ask."

The silence that followed tried her sanity more than the jump had done. Thomas' ship reached the station and was quickly swallowed up. Presumably, that meant he had docked without incident. She watched the station after that, but there was no external lighting and very little energy of any sort leaking out. She switched from pop music to old Earth vintage and played *The Rite of Spring* by Stravinsky from twentieth century Earth, watching for signals from the silent mission box. The longer she waited the more it nagged at her. She scanned for the expected transmission from the mission box, cursing Thomas under her breath, but the station proved impenetrable.

***

When the data stream from Ranar's mission unit finally came on, it was relayed through what Ann suspected was a specialized communication channel, like a window in the station's hull. The visuals were murky, but other data channels were pretty clear. The mission box sent Ranar's life signs, sounds, air analysis, and echo location schematics of a large room full of bolted-down furniture. English translation capacity had survived in an idiot-savant function of the box, but the voices she heard were not speaking First Contact English. They were using a kind of traders' pidgin, instead. Ann's view was further hampered by dim lighting and thick smoke. Ranar appeared to be drugged, to judge by his medical read outs. Ann made sure her personal log noted that. Thomas was smoking one of the vile cigarettes that fouled the air with something Ann's analysis said was not tobacco smoke. The Gelack across from him sat with a trio of henchmen at his back. At least one henchman looked like a woman and wore a sword. Ann thought the greasy station master wore one too, but couldn't be sure. One of the other henchmen wore something that looked like a hand gun of some sort. None of the details were very clear, at all.

As Ann watched, the woman with the sword flanked Thomas and another henchman picked up the drooping Ranar. Then the mission box jerked up off the floor and Ann's view of *Trinket Ring's* interior went bobbing and swaying through an unevenly lit corridor that seemed to be part of the main promenade around the rim of the station's rotating torus. Pools of light alternated with shadow as the mission box passed. Light was cast by lanterns jutting out from the inner wall that were crammed full of something soft and luminous.

Her party went up in an elevator that opened on a cleaner, brighter floor, and then through a set of double doors. Ranar was lugged into a suite of rooms and dumped onto a bed amid a scattering of dirty clothes.

"Hope you're comfortable, yellow buns," Thomas said, leaning over the mission box. "Looks like it's going to be a bit of a wait after all. You just keep an eye on Ranar here, while I have some fun."

Day in a
Courtesan's Life

Von shot upright out of a perfect landing and dropped his sword, crying, "Eva!"

His den mother, Eva, was bent over, rubbing the heel of her hand, very hard, into a leg cramp. "It's nothing," Eva said through gritted teeth. "Just a muscle."

She and Von had been practicing a sword dance he had adapted to make "in" jokes about recent, well attended duels on Gelion. The changes showcased his own cresting powers, but had challenged those of his thirty-year-old partner.

"That move is too difficult," Von blamed himself.

"It's perfect," Eva said with finality.

She freed her hair from its tie. It fell straight in a cascade of gold that framed classic features, sticking where it touched her damp shoulders. Signs of aging had made inroads about her green eyes, relieved by light touches of makeup, but although she wore a tight fitting dancer's sheath her body was as trim as her young dance partner's.

"Will you spare me a kind word, now and then, when I'm retired?" Eva asked her protégé.

"Eva!" he protested, stricken.

"Let's see if I can walk," she said.

He hovered as she hobbled to the chair where their dancer's drapes waited. Seated, she caught his retreating hand and studied it, stroking her fingers down between the tendons. "You live for today," she said. "It's one of the dear things about you." She looked up into his crystal gray eyes entreatingly. "But soon you'll have to think about the future. You may only be sixteen, but men don't last as long as women in our business. You will have less time than I did to groom your successor."

"You don't have to retire," Von protested.

"I do," Eva rejected the compliment. "And if Liege Monitum doesn't make me an offer soon, I will have to retire here." She smiled. "You would keep me?"

"Oh, Eva," Von despaired, eyes welling with devotion that was frustrated by reasons he could not divulge.

Eva pulled him close, and then eased off, crinkling her nose.

"Vanilla again," she said disapprovingly. "Is Liege H'Us giving you Demoran perfume?"

"It is just the way I smell, all right?" he told her, moving away.

"Von!" Eva laughed at him. "Not even you can sweat per-fume!" She took his face in her hand, smiling. "Must I keep reminding you that I'm not a paying client?"

Von ducked away, irritated that she couldn't see how much the new smell frightened him. He thought it might be an early sign of some disease he had picked up.

They were interrupted by a novice in a white toga, who came dashing towards them from the entrance hall near Eva's office.

"Eva!" the girl cried excitedly. "It's Liege Monitum. He's coming!"

"Di Mon!" Eva breathed the name like a prayer of hope.

The one hundred and third Liege of Monitum, known by the use name of Di Mon, was Eva's best hope for a comfort-able retirement, but Von hated his visits. The grim, Vrellish Sevolite stared at him as if he knew his worst secrets. Von couldn't help feeling jealous of the attention Eva paid her favorite client, either.

Di Mon strode across Den Eva's floor flanked by his niece, Tessitatt, and two household retainers called errants dressed in his livery. He wore the emerald sword of Monitum which Von found less impressive than its literary descriptions, and a sweeping cloak with liege marks prominent at its collars. He swept the cloak off into the arms of a waiting den attendant.

"I would speak with you," Di Mon told Eva, down-speaking her by the five birth ranks between a Sevolite of Highlord birth rank and a commoner.

"Of course, Your Grace," said Eva, and conducted her favorite client to her office, trying not to favor the leg she had injured.

Von focused on Tessitatt Monitum, a capable looking woman who wore Monatese house braids on her jacket, and carried her sword with self-assured confidence. Tessitatt returned him a game smile but apparently was not at leisure. She led the house errants away down one of the spoke-halls that radiated out from the den's Patron Floor.

"Good luck," Von whispered, earnestly, to Eva. Then he headed down a different spoke that led to the novice dorms, where he was always in demand as a storyteller.

He expected a jolly reception. Instead he was greeted by a small boy staring, perplexed, at a knot of girls gathered around the bunk bed of the eldest novice, Sarah, who sat on top crying dramatically.

The boy, who was six, looked up. "Hi, Von."

"Hi, Chester," said Von.

"Oh, Sarah, please come down!" pleaded a nine-year-old named Pam as four other girls hovered, one with a three-year-old boy in her arms.

"Girls are such bawlers," Chester confided. "How do you stand them, Von?"

"Wait a few years," advised Von.

Chester, who was already good looking in a rough-hewed fashion, produced a big, tough-guy frown. "If I try to make sense of girls — real girls — I'll mess up. I'm going to stick to the Vrellish women."

"Uh huh." Von had heard this boast before. He tipped his chin toward the feminine distress at the far end of the room. "You do that?" Von asked.

"I told them Reetions destroyed habitat in the Killing War because they don't have any souls to get reborn. That's why their faces are all brown."

"Ah," said Von. He tapped a thumb on his chin in mock thought, then dropped his arm. "I'm afraid you'll have to apologize."

"But it's true!" the boy protested.

"Do it for the practice in managing unwelcome truths. That will come in useful if you do wind up with the occasional Demish Lady on your hands. And I never *did* say Reetions had no souls."

"You said —"

"Come on," he took Chester by the hand.

Sarah fell silent to watch Von's approach. Pam hung on the side of the ladder that went up to Sarah's bunk and the rest shifted to be sure of a good view.

"The first step," Von told his reluctant pupil, "is to figure out, exactly, what you've done."

"He made her cry," Pam accused.

"I did," Chester manfully conceded, and made to redress the wrong. "I am sorry I told you the truth, Sarah."

Sarah threw a pillow at him.

"See!" Chester stabbed an accusatory arm at her.

"Chester," Von sank to his haunches, put a hand on the boy's shoulder, and pulled their heads together. "Never assume you know what a woman is crying about until you've made a point of finding out."

A couple of the girls giggled.

Von rose and hooked his hands on the edge of Sarah's bed, claiming all her attention. "I know what Chester said, Sarah. Help him out. Tell us why it hurt your feelings."

"I like Reetions." She sniffed, began to wipe her nose, and was deterred by Von filling the offending hand with somebody's volunteered handkerchief. "Reetions live on their own," she elaborated, accepting the correction of etiquette by pausing to blow her nose with the supplied hanky. "But they're not Sevolites. They're commoners."

"Chester said they blew up space stations," said Vivian, an athletic little sword-dancer who was full of spunk.

"Von said so!" exclaimed Chester.

"Reetions did destroy space stations and fire on planets," Von confirmed. The news was met with childish gasps.

"They're *okal'a'ni*," Chester triumphed. "They deserved what they got!"

"Why did Ameron help them?" demanded Pam, fingering the cheap Ameron pendant worn at her throat.

A little girl at Von's side, called Lila, put out her arms. Von swung her up. He said, "I suppose that Ameron saw the good in them."

"But they can't be good!" Sarah's eyes filled with tears once more. "Not if they destroy places to live."

"I haven't had a chance to read the whole *Ameron Biography*," said Von. "Maybe it's all explained later."

One of the den's working female courtesans flew through the door, crying, "Von!"

He put Lila down. The children instinctively moved back.

"It's Liege Vrel!" The messenger paused to swallow. "She is looking for Liege Monitum!" Vretla Vrel was Di Mon's peer on Fountain Court, although she functioned under his tutelage in many things, being much younger and fostered at Green Hearth in her childhood. She was also one of Von's clients.

"Where is she?" Von asked the messenger.

"On the Round," the girl gasped. "I told her I would go look for him. But I didn't! I know where he is — he's with Eva!"

Von began stripping down to his jock strap.

The girl, whose name was Ela, blinked large, blue eyes at him. She was a Demish favorite, as soft and curved as any Demish lady. "Do you think that's going to work?" she asked, incredulously. "I mean I know she's Vrellish but —"

"Just do what I tell you," said Von.

He gave his shed dancer's sheath to Vivian, one of the half-grown novices. "Pretend you stole this from me," he instructed the young sword dancer. "Run toward Liege Vrel, then veer off."

Vivian nodded.

He turned to Ela. "Give Liege Vrel long enough to pick me up and dust me off. Then report that you can't find Di Mon and are afraid to go barging into guest rooms without Eva's say-so."

"There is nobody in any of the guest rooms," Ela protested. "We're closed."

"Just do what you are told!" cried Von.

The frightened woman nodded.

"Go," Von told Vivian.

The girl dashed off. Von pursued. They burst onto the Patron's Floor making for their target.

Vretla Vrel was a tall woman in a long, open vest worked in solid red patterns. She had gray eyes and dark hair, worn short. Her sword sheath hung down her back because her waist was no longer serviceable. She was heavily pregnant, and all of it was carried up front, with little or no generalized weight gain to balance it out. She wore a black body stocking over the pregnancy, proud of her condition.

Vivian slewed around a table, knocking a chair off.

"Children!" The retired courtesan washing the floor tried to warn them, scrambling to her feet in alarm. Vivian flew past but must have got her feet wet as she dodged. She took a spill and skidded to a halt much too close to Vretla Vrel. There was one bad moment as Vretla reached over her shoulder to draw, but she abandoned the gesture.

Following Vivian, Von threw himself into a backpedal, too late to evade Vretla. With strong hands she caught him by the shoulders. It felt like running into a wall.

The jolt was sure to wake the baby! He had spent hours massaging it and Vretla to sleep on occasions when he felt he had earned his own repose.

"L-Liege Vrel!" Von mastered his rattled jaw.

"Never look where you are going unless it's choreographed in advance, eh, Von?" She had a robust, burred voice that he was rather fond of. All the same, he disliked being immobilized and wished that he dared to test his strength against hers. Vretla was over eighty percent Sevolite. He knew that meant that she could grind him to a pulp, but their sexual tussles had given him a sense of physical equality, encouraged by a blind faith in his healthy young body. Besides, she was bruising his clavicles with her thumbs.

"Just can't escape women, can you, Von?" She was teasing now.

"Vivian's not a woman!" he protested.

"Oh?" Vretla hiked both dark eyebrows. "She seems to be on the right track."

He put his hands around her wrists to negotiate more comfort. "It's a prank, Your Highness," he insisted. "We didn't mean any harm. I was going to shower. She snatched my dancer's sheath before I finished undressing and I can't lose it! It's expensive. But I didn't think there would be anyone on the Round."

"Obviously," she said, with a smirk for his state of undress, and let him go. "Taking a shower, hmmm? Have we done that together?"

"Just baths," said Von.

Ela hurried in and bowed. "Liege Vrel," she said, and bowed once more. "No one knows where to look for Liege Monitum, and I cannot find Den Mother Eva to ask leave to search the guest rooms."

"Guest rooms?" Vretla challenged. "The den is closed."

"There are clients sleeping over," Von piped up, not trust-ing Ela to cope.

Vretla Vrel absorbed that with a frown. "Can't find Di Mon, or Eva either?" she mused.

"No, Your Highness," Ela whimpered.

"Then they're probably together, don't you think, Von?" Vretla gave him a slap on one firm, sculpted buttock. "You go see if he's with her. Eva's less likely to bite your head off, unless I am much mistaken about your mutual sleeping arrangements, hmmm? Or is Eva still training you?"

Vretla thought it was a good joke.

Von inhaled to answer.

"Or —" The muscular Vrellish female looked him over again with greater attention to detail. "We could shower."

Von closed his mouth.

"You, girl," Vretla Vrel ordered Ela. "Tell me when Liege Monitum is done. It wouldn't do, I suppose, to offend his precious Monatese dignity. But you find me afterwards, understand? Wherever I am, no matter what I might be up to, you won't embarrass me. True Vrellish are hard to em-barrass."

"Yes, Highness," Ela said hastily and bowed even deeper. *She could have spared herself the effort,* Von thought. Vrellish Sevolites, like Vretla Vrel, were more apt to knock you across the room for overdoing acts of obedience than for failing to be adequately humble. But Ela was a courtesan specializing in Demish men, not Vrellish women.

Vretla hooked a thumb through the waist thong of Von's jock strap. "Now, where are those showers?" she asked.

He slipped his arm under her vest to rub her back as they walked.

"You have strong hands for a commoner," she approved. "Ah, a little lower. Mmm! You can give us both a real mas-sage when we're done." She slapped her rocking stomach lightly. "It is as wild as a swallowed *rel*-fighter. Who would have thought Kertatt Monitum had such lively blood in him?"

"It's your baby, too," Von reminded her.

"Not for long," Vretla said, briefly somber.

The baby was to be the Heir of Monitum. A gift, conceived in payment — Vrellish fashion — for the court education that Liege Monitum had given to its mother. Di Mon's nephew, Kertatt, was the sire: an unremarkable young nobleborn, in Von's opinion, except for the surprising dispatch with which he had made a highborn woman pregnant. Vrellish women normally required a more Sevolite sire, but conception, like duels, could be chancy.

"What do Demish women do with you, Von?" Vretla asked him. "Dress you up like one of their dolls?" She stopped and turned him around, giving him a look that communicated directly with his groin, without checking with his brain on the way down.

Von swallowed. "Demish women ask me about Vrellish women too, you know," he told her a bit huskily. "Would you want me to answer their questions?"

"I wouldn't care," she said. Three hard fingers snagged firmly under the top band of his jock strap.

Not good, he thought.

She pushed him up against a wall.

Oh come on Vretla! he thought, cursing his body for its indiscretions. *Not in the hall!*

She jerked down his strap, proving what she knew, and grinned at him. "Lie down."

I am going to give up Vrellish women, he promised himself, with the good intentions of all thrill seekers at the crest of the next dangerous plunge. *Before I turn twenty.*

They got through the sex, and the shower, without her going into labor or dislocating any of his bones. Drying off in a guest room, he was relieved to feel the unborn child settling down, unharmed, beneath his stroking hands.

"You must have been working this morning before I arrived," said Vretla. "You smelled like a Royal Demish bedroom before we washed." The thought amused her.

"How would you know?" Von forced down alarm at the thought of his odor problem getting around. "I mean about Royal Demish bedrooms."

"I've been in Ava Delm's," she said. "At the palace."

Von sat up, astonished. "You've slept with the Ava?"

Liege Vrel made a rude noise. "Too Demish for me. Besides, Delm hoards his seed like deep-space rations." She grinned. "But then, it is his only asset." She stretched and relaxed, relieved to be free of the pain in her back. "Fountain Court would do better to invite his sister Ev'rel back from exile, bad habits or not. Besides, she was only a girl when she experimented with Rush."

And killed a commoner man with it, thought Von, less forgiving than the Sevolite woman on that score.

Suddenly irritable, Vretla thrust her distorted, but still agile body up off the sunken mattress where they lounged. Von helped her into her body sock and paused to pull on his own dressing gown.

"You still haven't said why you were in Ava Delm's bedroom," he reminded her.

"Oh that." Her mind was elsewhere now. She fetched it back. "I was at some fool party and thought I heard a woman cry out. I went to help, thinking it was a commoner, but it was only the H'Reth woman. You know, the wife of Delm's so-called admiral!" She snorted derisively. "Her husband and Delm treat her worse than a commoner, even though they are both having sex with her regularly. That ought to mean you like a person!" She frowned. "The Demish do everything backwards."

"Lady H'Reth!" exclaimed Von.

Vretla looked impressed. "Do you know everyone?"

"I —" Von spluttered, panicking, "she was my owner. She sold me to Eva's when I was ten."

"Really? Has she been checking up on your progress since?" Vretla burst out in a lewd laugh. "Maybe you've been teaching her how to grace Delm's bed — Demish women have to be taught everything!" She chuckled at her own joke. Von's mouth was dry. Vretla didn't seem to notice. She gave him a hearty slap on the back.

"At least now I know who gives you Demish perfume!"

"About the perfume..." Von began, nervously, wrestling with his conscience over the possibility that it was a side effect of some infection that might harm even a highborn baby. He had just decided he would ask if she knew of any other reasons for someone to smell of vanilla, when the door at the end of the guest room banged open.

"Kertatt," Vretla growled at their visitor.

"I came here looking for my uncle," accused the baby's sire, "and find you, instead, risking the health of the future Heir of Monitum with West Alcove's leading male slut!"

His choice of "you" insulted Vretla by refusing to speak *up*.

"Mind your grammar, nobleborn," said Vretla with a dangerous burr in her tone.

"As if I could defend myself," Kertatt objected, "when you are pregnant with my own child and my family's salvation."

"Yours when it is born," warned Vretla. "Until then, your part in it is done. And you didn't supply anything, except the live fluid, that Von can't do better than you can. Understood?"

I wish, Von thought, *she hadn't said that*.

Kertatt drew his sword. "You like dancers?" he accused Vretla. "Let's see him dance!"

Von dodged Kertatt's flat-of-the-blade swat.

Vretla whooped with laughter. "Do you want me to catch him for you?" she baited Kertatt.

Kertatt got serious. A near miss swept along Von's flank as he dodged. His dressing gown fouled Kertatt's recovery, otherwise Di Mon's nephew would have drawn blood.

Angry now, Vretla swept her sword off the floor with a grunt.

Kertatt was literally out-classed: nobleborn to highborn. She drove him back towards the door, quick and hard. But she was such a large target! All it would take would be one misstep, one accident ...

Von gathered air into his lungs, and screamed, "E-v-v-v-a-a!" When he had finished he found both Sevolites staring at him in astonishment, swords in hand. For a moment he was certain they were going to kill him for presuming to interrupt, then there were running footsteps out in the spoke-hall and Liege Monitum burst in through the doorway.

Di Mon was dressed in his traveling cloak. It settled to a full-length, majestic stillness about him when he stopped. The anger on his lean face was contained but hot. His stare slashed past Von to his nephew, Kertatt.

"What are *you* doing?" His pronoun dropped Kertatt a birth rank, in pointed insult.

"I came to find you," Kertatt told him. "And found Vretla consorting with that courtesan!" He pointed at Von with his drawn sword.

"Is that any of your business?" his uncle asked. "What she is doing with a sword drawn is another matter." He constructed the "she" for Vretla in grammatical peerage. Her expression darkened.

"I am no longer your pupil, Di Mon," she said, with the slow, drunken look about her which could be the prelude to explosive violence. "I am Vretla Vrel, Liege of Red Vrel. Your peer on Fountain Court and Royalblood to your Highlord by birth rank. It is you who taught me about birth ranks on Gelion, in a court steeped in Demish nonsense. I have learned to understand their insults. Be careful how you cast your pronouns."

"I was speaking only in the Vrellish way, and meant no insult," he assured her, adjusting his grammar to the more rigorous courtly standard that distinguished three ranks of highborn: Highlord, Royalblood, and Pureblood. "You, however," he rounded on his nephew, Kertatt, "are another matter. Or is there some hidden sense I do not fathom in exchanging blows with Vretla in order to protect the child she carries?"

Di Mon's thin lips were set in a flat frown, eyes narrowed. Kertatt dwindled beneath his displeasure and left without another word. Vretla stalked out after him.

Di Mon looked at Von, and Von flinched at the scorn that rained down on him. Then the Sevolite's expression unclouded and he left, with a snap of his heavy cloak.

Von waited until his heart stopped pounding, wondering for the hundredth time why Di Mon hated him. Vrellish jealousies were not the same as other people's and unlikely to register a commoner as any kind of competition, so it couldn't be about Eva. Besides, if Di Mon wanted to monopolize her, all he had to do was ask. The thought reminded him that Eva would need him if the meeting hadn't gone as she had hoped.

***

He found her sitting in her office in the dark. There was a bottle on her desk and a drink in her hand.

Von turned on the lights and came to take the drink away from her.

"I am not drunk." She gave him a weary look and took back her glass.

He pulled her out from behind the desk and settled her on the couch in front of the embroidered screen that hid her bed.

"What happened?" Von asked, sinking on his knees before her.

"Nothing." She lay her head back on the couch. "Di Mon does not desire me. That's all."

"Listen, Eva," he took both her hands in his own. "He came here, to you. Was it for nothing? I don't believe that."

She toyed with reluctant hope. "He wants me to host a reception for Prince D'Ander of Golden Hearth."

"Golden?" Von sat back on his haunches. "Di Mon is allied to the Silver Demish, not the Golden."

"D'Ander has appealed to Di Mon in the name of their shared belief in Ameron," said Eva. "So he's agreed to meet D'Ander, but only here, with Silver Hearth invited so Prince H'Us cannot claim he is doing it behind his back."

"Eva," Von enthused, "that's wonderful. It means Di Mon trusts you to host a politically awkward meeting. It might even be a test." He smiled. "Liege Monitum's *lyka* would have to hold her own in any company. And that's what you want, isn't it? To belong to him."

Eva thought it over and surrendered her reclaimed glass. "You are right," she said with rising spirits. "I must prove I can be equal to his expectations."

She took his face in her hands. "Promise me that you will be here? Promise you will dance with me?"

"I don't know, Eva," Von squirmed. "Liege Monitum may not want that."

She released him to sit back, wearing her judgmental frown. "Not more of your nonsense about him disliking you." She folded her arms, long blond hair cloaking her shoulders. "Has he ever done you any harm?"

"No," Von admitted.

"Listen," she said, "you are my good luck. I need you to be there. I always do better with Di Mon when we dance together for the entertainment." She stroked the side of his face with her long fingers.

"All right," he agreed.

"Promise?" she insisted.

"I promise."

He turned her hand over and sensually kissed the inside of her arm.

She stroked his hair. "Don't you have work to do this afternoon?"

"Only for the Princess-Liege of Silver Hearth," Von assured her. "Reading and such."

"I don't know, Von," she said hesitently, but her foot slid up his thigh, sending a thrill through him. He wanted to feel complete in her arms, to make love as if the world ended beyond her office door.

"You should rest that leg," he told her, and rose, swooping her up in his arms.

"If you carry me to bed, my pet," she said, "I doubt I'm going to get much of that."

"I don't know," he said, carrying her around the screen. "I've been entertaining Vretla Vrel. I might fall asleep on you."

Eva stiffened in his arms. "Here? Now?"

"She was looking for Liege Monitum." He set her down and climbed in beside her, feeling playful.

"You did it to give me time," she realized.

It stirred his troubled conscience to see her looking up at him with such affection. It made him wish, with a terrible dry aching, to be worthy of it. Instead he sought the seam of her dancer's sheath with practiced hands and began, with slow determination, to make love.

Eva woke him in time for his next assignation. "It's disgusting," she said, and kissed him again to be sure. "You don't even have morning breath."

"It's not morning," he pointed out.

A Silver Demish car picked him up. There was nothing very special about it despite the Silver Demish crest on both its front doors. It was the sort of serviceable vehicle houses used to run their errands for them up and down the Ava's Way, in South Town, or elsewhere on the palace plane. The pick up car parked in the lot at the steps leading down from West Alcove where Eva's was located, looking ridiculously large and sleek among the rest of the vehicles parked at the moment, but not wholly out of place. It was not at all uncommon for the lot to boast cars belonging to Gelion's top aristocracy. All the cars ran on batteries charged in the act of reality skimming and generated nothing that could foul the air of UnderGelion, which mattered greatly in a subterranean city with ventilation challenges. A couple of Silver Hearth errants were sent along to play escort, and mocked

Von, as usual, over how rough he had it, being a male courtesan who serviced women.

At the other end of the drive they parked near a building called the Market Round. From here they walked draped in traveling cloaks, a strategy that conferred some anonymity because about a third of all pedestrians went about cloaked.

"Tell us a story to pass the time," cajoled the errant captain.

"What sort of story?" asked Von.

"A true one," suggested the junior errant.

"He's a courtesan, Toff," said the captain. "They're not paid for the truth."

"Not by Demish ladies," Toff retorted. "But a man can't lie about what Vrellish women want!" He laughed at his own joke. "I hear Vretla Vrel nearly killed Kertatt Monitum before he finally got her pregnant."

Von wished he was in a position to knock the hot air out of them both, whether Vretla would care much or not.

"A man to be commended, you are," said the captain, thumping Von on the back, "a commoner, able to hold his own in bed with Vretla!"

"What do you figure we could sell him for in the UnderDocks?" Toff joked.

"I'll tell you a story about the UnderDocks," Von said, suddenly. "I heard it from a boy who died there."

The men calmed down.

"This boy," Von began in good Demish literary tradition, "believed there was no stronger force than love. So he flew his sister Mira away to *TouchGate Hospital Station* to learn more than she ever could on Gelion and promised to make payments for her studies, flying freelance. But he was also pretty stupid, so he wound up as a boy whore in the UnderDocks."

"A Sevolite boy!" the captain exclaimed, shocked.

"No." Von's heart was hammering. "A commoner."

"I don't want to hear about boys in the UnderDocks," Toff told him, "I want to hear about Vrellish women."

"Besides," the captain protested, "it's ridiculous. Commoners can't fly."

"Some can," insisted Von. "If they couldn't, why would it have to be against the law? This boy was taught to fly so he could serve the *Gorarelpul* College." He dropped his voice to a conspiratorial tone. "*Gorarelpul* import things that Sevolites don't approve of."

"Likely enough," said the captain. "College teachers should be conscience bonded to the throne, in my opinion. It isn't right to leave people who know as much as *gorarelpul* free to wreck the world with science. But I do not like your story very much."

Toff suggested Von recite an epic poem instead, so he gave them a typically Demish one about lovers who couldn't get themselves reborn again, together, for three generations. The poem got them as far as the great stairs that led from the entrance to the UnderDocks to the levels above.

Von switched to rowdy Vrellish women on the way up, unaffected by the climb that left his escort panting by the time they gained the highborn docks. A Silver Hearth lady of Highlord rank met them, to grant passage, which meant the end of the Vrellish tales. She escorted them through a great, hollow cylinder known as the Palace Shell, and across the Plaza on the roof of a massive structure called the Citadel, to the opening into Silver Hearth, known as Silver Pavilion. Here, they went down a set of spiral stairs, into a room filled with ladies dressed in brightly colored, layered skirts who were playing a genteel game of ring toss, assisted by liveried servants. A hush greeted Von's arrival. He folded his traveling cloak over one arm and waited for the chief lady-in-waiting to come forward and take charge.

"It's this way," she told him, dismissing his escort.

In general, courtesans were not approved of in polite Demish society, except in their role as performing artists, but he was here because his company soothed the ailing Princess-Liege of H'Us — matriarch of the family that managed the Ava's affairs in partnership with Di Mon. Respect for the princess was such that no one viewed her interest in him as improper.

The Princess-Liege of H'Us received him in her parlor.

"Come in," she said a little irritably. A *gorarelpul* was administering a dose of the drug called *klinoman*, used to ease post-flight jitters. She took it to keep her pain under control. "Go on, you two," she told her lady-in-waiting and the *gorarelpul*. "I would rather die holding Von's hand than either of yours."

Her people bowed their way out.

"Come here," she told Von, patting the bed beside her, "and carry on with your reading where you left off."

"Yes, Your Highness," said Von, and steeled himself to breathing as much life as possible into bad English doggerel, even though his client would not understand a word. The book was one of a set from a period when it was trendy to eulogize Earth in a language that only the Monatese still kept alive, among themselves. Von had learned it in his childhood at the *Gorarelpul* College, but told Liege H'Us a Monatese client had taught it to him.

"... as each day ends, and nightfall sings of dawn," Von read seated beside his ailing patroness.

"Dah-wun?" she interrupted. "What is 'Dah-wun,' Von?"

"Dawn," he corrected her pronunciation. "Dawn is morning, on a planet, when the sun comes over the horizon and drives away the cold."

"Ah!" she said. "Dah-wun. It makes a nice sound."

"Dawn," Von corrected again.

She smiled at him. "You are the only one who still thinks it worthwhile to correct me in anything, dear boy. Which is particularly curious as you are also the only one who does not keep telling me I will get well, when I know it isn't going to happen." She fixed him with serious blue eyes. "What makes you do it, child?"

He closed the book and held it in his lap. "If I don't correct you, then you can't learn."

"Must the dying learn?"

"The dying are still alive," he said.

"You say that as if you understood it, child."

I do, Von thought. The better part of him was dead; his current existence was a temporary truce with his conscience that he tried to enjoy. There seemed little harm in that.

"I have seen dawns, you know," the dying Demish princess told him. "Here on Gelion. We used to have parties on the surface when I was a girl. Under a dome, of course, to enrich the oxygen and keep the dust down. We'd go up at night and watch the ships land."

"But you never visited a green planet?" Von asked, incredulously. It was one of his great, unattainable ambitions, like truly being in love.

"No." She contemplated the seamless span of her two centuries. "It was not that I planned it thus. One day just followed the next and I disliked travel."

"You live for today, for this moment," said Von. "I do, too. It is best not to expect too much."

"Such cynicism," she said, "in one so young! I think I will give you the book, just to prove that nice things can happen." She paused, studying her attractive bookcase of doggerel. "Although it would break up the set to make it that one."

He pounced. "Perhaps something less valuable?"

"Well," she allowed herself to be persuaded, "if you'd rather have one of those mismatched one, from the old trunk ..."

He was afraid to trust his luck.

"Go on, go on," she urged him, slightly ashamed after retracting her first offer.

Von scrambled over to the chest that harbored the *Ameron Biography* he had been sneaking looks at. The lid was covered with hand-painted statues of Avas arranged in order from oldest to newest with Ava Delm in front. Von took them off and stacked them in order, knowing Liege H'Us would complain if he put them back wrong. He paused over Ameron's likeness, turning the figure's angular profile this way and that.

"What's that you're looking at?" Princess H'Us asked.

Von held it up. "Did you know him?" he asked.

"I saw him a few times," she said, "when I was very young. My father was against him, of course. Ameron could have led us in conquest of the brown people, the Reetions. Instead, he made friends with them. Can you imagine? Whole new worlds for cultivation, already stocked with peasants. It would have been better for the Reetions, too. Quite a mess he left behind in Killing Reach. Space lanes fouled and ecosystems damaged. Still ..." She reconsidered old opinions in light of modern circumstances. "Ameron was the last Ava worthy of the title. Hurry up there, now. Get what you want."

Von set down the Ameron statue and his hand went directly to his prize: a cheap edition, made with thin plastic, not paper.

"You want that?" Princess H'Us was dubious.

Von nodded, trying to dampen his excitement. She might decide it was too valuable and hold it back.

"Well, if you are sure," said Princess H'Us.

"Thank you!" Von let just enough of his pleasure show to reward her as he slipped the book into a pocket of his traveling cloak. It was a mark of favor that Princess H'Us let him keep the cloak with him, even though she knew he stole apples from her side board, and stuffed the pockets with sugar sticks from sympathetic kitchen staff. After stashing his book away, Von restored the trunk to its former condition and came to sit beside her once more.

"Still no stubble," she remarked, "and sixteen years old?" Usually she teased for fun but today she sounded troubled as if the joke had gone on for too long. "It is not worth it, Von, in the long run: taking Luverthanian drugs to mimic traits you think a client might desire. They can do a commoner harm."

"P-Pardon?" he sputtered.

"Has Anatolia H'Reth put you up to tricks like that?" she said, with a displeased frown. "She has too much influence over you. And not, I think, a wholesome one. "

Von felt so sick inside he could not breathe, let alone defend himself. At the same time it was a relief to believe he would explode and splatter filthy secrets everywhere.

Liege H'Us sighed. "She is a foolish girl, Anatolia ... doing it for her husband, I suppose. Got him an admiralty title. Ah, Delm, you should have been better than other men ... such a pity we lost little Amel." She was drifting into mild delirium, but Von's heart deepened its action as he listened, shaking his rib cage. "Such a vain man ... her husband. H'Reth. And there was something else. That medic, Mira. Do you recall, Von? Quite ridiculous, of course. About you. Just a vain man. And a bit of an idiot. Admiral of Blue Dem!" she muttered in well worn contempt.

Von resisted hearing the words. He tried to concentrate on the smell of apples on the side board, instead. But faces stared out of memory, terrorizing him with the immutability of the past. He could never put it right. Ever. He clutched at the sound of his client's voice as she muttered less and less coherent non-sense. "Such a pretty baby," she said. "Little Amel ... might have made a better Ava. Well, couldn't be any worse than Delm." H'Us mumbled. "Baby Amel ... so young ... to be lost."

"Yes," Von said again with forced solicitude, finding it hard to feel much about a baby mourned as lavishly and long as Amel was, but he could appreciate Liege H'Us' disap-pointment. Her tolerance of the reigning Ava's self-indul-gence was strained by his habit of flaunting his relationship with Liege H'Reth's wife, Anatolia. Such things, if they must happen, were supposed to take place behind closed doors in a Demish court.

Von waited impatiently for his client to fall asleep; checked she was still breathing; then kissed the backs of her fingers, laid down her hand, and tip-toed across the room to help himself to an apple from the bowl on the side board. They were real, orchard-grown apples, flown in on high *gap* to reduce shimmer bruises.

He sank into a big armchair to munch the apple while he enjoyed his new treasure: his very own copy of the *Ameron Biography*, however cheap and well worn. The title page declared it was written by Sela Lor'Vrel, on Monitum. Next came a map of the known reaches, with Gelion in the center. He noted Monitum, the Demish Net, the Knotted Strings, the Vrellish triangle, and fabled but sinister Luverthan. Killing Reach stuck out of the Demish Net, and beyond that, across a fuzzy divide that denoted the unknown, were Reetions.

Von got no further before he heard someone open the parlor door. He stuffed the apple and book into his traveling cloak as he scrambled up.

Lady Anatolia H'Reth slipped in with a backward glance over one shoulder and pulled the door closed. The Ava's mistress was a beauty of the typically Demish sort, her round face studded with blue eyes and her vivid yellow hair entwined with scarves.

"What are you doing here?" Von asked much too tartly for the disparity of their ranks. "If you want to see me, you're supposed to arrange it through Eva."

Bright red circles rose on the lady's cheeks. "We need to talk. Alone." She snatched his hand.

He resisted long enough to get his treasure-laden cloak, then let her lead him deeper into Silver Hearth.

"Someone will see us!" Von hissed at her, alarmed.

"Then let them think the obvious," she hissed back. "It doesn't matter any more — Delm knows."

"Knows what?" Von asked, frightened. "How much?"

Lady H'Reth pulled him after her into a narrow corridor and threw open the first door they came across, startling a servant sleeping on a cot. The man worked in the kitchens to judge by the odor of breakfast spice cakes in the stuffy little room.

"Out!" Lady H'Reth threw the baker a blue honor chip as he blinked at her stupidly.

"It's a bribe," Von volunteered to help him sort it out.

"Shut up!" she cried. Tears of humiliation stood in her brilliant blue eyes, stirring the ashes of Von's sympathy.

He reached to comfort her, saying, "Anatolia —"

"Shut up!" she cried again, and struck at him.

He caught her hand. She pulled away from him with a breathy jerk.

"Don't say anything to anyone," Von told the servant without taking his eyes off the hysterical woman. "It will be safer for you."

Lady H'Reth exploded with venom as soon as the man was out the door. "To think I must let servants think I want to be alone with you!"

Von let her go. "I never forced you," he insisted.

"No," she agreed, coldly. "No, he does that. For both of us."

It doesn't matter if she hates me, Von told himself, fighting the threads of memory unwinding from his inner core. But it did matter. Everything mattered. It always did and it always had.

"I'm pregnant," blurted Anatolia. "I told Delm. He just laughed. He said … he said that he would never be so stupid as to *child gift* to a — to a courtesan-trained slut! I was so upset, I cried too loud. And that horrible Vrellish woman, Vretla, came in to see what was wrong!" She broke down in sobs.

"My Lady, someone will hear us." He touched her shoulder lightly, as if she was a hot pan that must still, somehow, be moved off the stove. "And surely your husband will be pleased that —"

She flung her arms out, fingers whistling by his nose. "It can't be his, either! Don't you see? It must be yours!"

"That isn't possible," Von denied, stunned.

"You told me …" She swallowed. "You told me that there was an accident, once, even though you'd been sterilized."

"Years ago," said Von. "I reacted to the oral treatment Eva gave to all the graduating novices before they became practicing courtesans. I must have thrown up too much of it to do the job. But Eva got a surgeon after that, to make sure." He dropped his voice. "How do you know the baby is not H'Reth's? I mean, don't you ever...when you're alone?"

She shook her head. "He would have to have conceived it straight through you," she said, merciless.

Von nibbled his lower lip as his stomach churned. The tiny threat to his lip reassured him just by being something he could control. Something he could stop before it hurt too much to bear anymore.

"Listen," he told her, "the baby has to be H'Reth's. Somehow. Maybe with the three of us together like that ..." His throat constricted too tightly for him to go on.

"You really think so?" She touched her face, then her neck and chest, hands fluttering. "You're sure that's possible?"

"Of course," he improvised.

"Or maybe," she grasped for a brighter hope. "It is Delm's. I know he uses *ferni* but maybe it isn't strong enough for Purebloods. " She sat down.

They stayed like that a long, cold minute before Von mustered the courage to test her fragile calm.

"Is that all that Delm knows?" he asked. "About me? Just that you rent me out at Eva's?"

"He suspects you helped us rise at court. With information and ... training."

Blood retreated from Von's skin surface shutting him down from the inside out. "But that's all ..." he faltered. "Not...?"

"No. Nothing more."

Von felt dizzy.

"Delm told me to find you and take you home with me to H'Reth Manor," she said, and stood up, looking bleak and destroyed inside. It was the way he felt whenever he was with her husband, H'Reth, and despite himself his heart went out to her. "We are to wait there for Balous, the Royal *Gorarelpul*." She told him.

"Why?" Von asked.

"I don't know." She paused. "Maybe Balous is supposed to end the pregnancy, just in case. Maybe — I don't know!" She broke down over the final words.

Von took her in his arms and they clung to one another in shared misery, too numb even for fear.

Admiral of a Single Ship

Liege H'Reth waited in a crowded ante chamber of the Ava's Palace to be admitted to Delm's presence. It was not the sort of treatment he had come to expect since Delm had appointed him Admiral of Blue Dem. He was getting worried by the time the Royal *Gorarelpul*, a fat, ugly creature named Balous, emerged through the double-doors of the inner sanctum and padded over to him, brimming with smiles.

"Ah, the Blue Admiral!" said Balous, squeezing H'Reth's meaty hand. "Resplendent as usual." He mocked H'Reth's elaborate garb. The winged collar of his admiralty cape jutted higher than that of Liege Nersal's, who commanded Sevildom's most fearsome fleet, and he wore more jewels than a Golden prince. It was questionable whether his sword could be drawn, it was so heavily encrusted with them.

Trying not to think much about Balous, who always made him nervous, H'Reth swept on ahead towards the famous Blackwood Room where the Ava held audience with important visitors.

"Oh, he's not there," Balous said, and gestured towards the stairs that led to a lower level of the palace. "I trust the Lorel Stairs will be endurable?"

H'Reth scowled at the veiled insult. Balous knew perfectly well that the Lorel Stairs did not affect him very much. Personally, he felt their legendary ability to disconcert great pilots was exaggerated. The walls of the Lorel Stairs were black, at first, but warmed to starscapes wherever you let your eyes linger. That was all there was to it as far as H'Reth could discern, although people claimed they played tricks with a Sevolite's instinct to resolve navigational problems the way ordinary people moved around a room without a flight plan. Supposedly you could find yourself believing you were *rel*-skimming through dust fields on the Lorel Stairs, be swallowed up by jumps that could not exist where they appeared, and be harassed by all manner of navigational paradoxes. People said that the stairs, like the floor of the reception room known as the Flashing Floor, had been built by the first Lorel Avas and were powered by the souls they sucked out of pilots they drove mad.

"If you feel it necessary to go around ...?" Balous invited.

H'Reth set his big, square jaw and took the stairs boldly, with no ill effects

Nothing but a parlor trick, he told himself, feeling heartened.

Two of Delm's three paladins stood guard at the bottom of the Lorel Stairs, both of them gorgeously Golden men with pale blue eyes and yellow braids coiled around their heads. They hailed from the Golden Demish heartland of Demora, which was mighty now only in legend, but still extended its artistic influence over the Silver Demish in particular. Blue Demish, H'Reth liked to think, had more confidence in their own aesthetics. Even if there were few of them left.

"Garn H'Reth, Admiral of Blue Dem," Balous announced his arrival.

"His Divinity, Ava Delm, is expecting you," intoned the nearest paladin, down-speaking H'Reth more than their respective birth rank entitled him to. But that was nothing new. Paladins used their own, uniquely Golden Demish rules of grammar.

Ava Delm stood beside a jeweled throne, having just finished standing for a portrait. A freshly planted lawn spread before his feet, strewn with tiny blue flowers, and a cascade of water pumped through an artfully constructed crag to fill an artificial pond in which a pair of pretty children played in wading clothes, trying to look natural. Musicians were just visible behind a screen of shrubs, and the nervecloth lining on the ceiling displayed a convincing simulation of a summer's day. Impressive as all of that was, Delm himself was the most breath-taking. His face was exquisite, if a little marred by its superior expression. His body was well made although a little soft, due to a lack of exercise. He was dressed in long, flowing robes with an exceedingly rare collar of cat fur, cats being extinct within the empire for centuries.

Delm had golden tresses that any Demish princess would be blessed to own, which was a bow in the direction of Golden Demish fashion. At court, long hair was the mark of a male courtesan, but no one was going to raise that awkward comparison with the Ava of the Gelack Empire.

Delm's sapphire blue eyes pleased H'Reth more, because they reflected his Blue Demish heritage. It was Delm's mother who entitled him to style himself a Soul of Light, sacred to all who followed the Golden Demish religion known as *Okal Lumen*, because she had been the daughter of the Golden Demish Emperor. Delm's father had been the last entirely Blue Demish Pureblood, a fact H'Reth considered more important.

H'Reth had to admit that Delm's sheer physical beauty was distracting. But Von's face, in his biased opinion, had the same sculpted lines, though Von's eyes were, admittedly, not blue of any kind. Von also had a bodily vitality that would make him blaze in the sort of clothes Delm wore, not merely glow decorously. Von was H'Reth's antidote to any spell Delm's beauty might cast on him.

Delm remained on his feet until H'Reth and Balous reached his dais, and then sank into his jeweled throne looking as if the mere prospect of dealing with them tired him.

"Dear master," Balous said, "I bring you your very own, personal admiral and captain of the *Vanilla Rose*, as requested."

"H'Reth?" Delm looked him over. "Ah, yes." He tipped his golden head to a waiting page, "Fetch Master Larren."

H'Reth flinched at the name of Delm's number one paladin.

"Do not worry," Delm teased, aware of H'Reth's discomfort, "*Larren* has no quarrel with you." The way he put the emphasis on Larren's name suggested someone else might feel differently.

Larren entered through one of the doors behind the throne, approached Delm and sank to his knees to execute a ritual of reverence. In the middle of it, Delm rose and stepped down from the dais to look at the latest portrait of himself in which he stood languidly contemplating a songbird perched on his raised hand.

"What do you think?" he asked H'Reth. "Is it me to the soul?"

"Nothing can capture you," H'Reth assured him. In this case, it was literally true. The picture portrayed someone meltingly kind which was not Delm by any stretch of the imagination.

Delm waved the painting away, saying, "Dispose of it."

"Please!" Larren interjected. "Let me have it, rather than destroy even an imperfect likeness. For it cannot help but be less than the original."

"You may have it if you like, of course," Delm said, and sighed. "Perhaps I will never find the artist who can capture the essence of my kindness and compassion. Balous," he concluded in a stronger voice, "clear out the ornaments." This included the children and musicians.

Delm retired to his throne, permitting Larren to organize his robes. It was little things like that that made H'Reth wonder if paladins loved the Ava in exactly the same way he loved Von, whether they admitted it or not. He had never found any evidence to prove it, but he had once witnessed something nearly as good as seeing them hung up on Ava's square for the disgraceful death due the *okal'a'ni*, who breeched laws meant for mankind's survival, and the *sla*, who indulged in perversions. He had once seen an angry Liege Nersal, of Black Hearth, slay two paladins, one after the other, in defense of the Golden Prince D'Ander's property rights. Since this took place shortly before Liege Nersal left court, no doubt there was more to it than showed on the surface. But the memory of seeing paladins go down before a better sword could always warm H'Reth's heart when one of them glowered at him.

"Tell my admiral of your plan," Delm instructed Larren, when the room had cleared.

The master paladin stepped forward. "You will take the *Vanilla Rose* to Killing Reach," Larren declared, "to reclaim the world of Barmi II, unlawfully taken from the Blessed Ava Delm by Perry D'Aur, the Blue Demish rebel assisted by the Golden Prince D'Ander."

"What?" Delm spluttered. "Even with a real fleet, instead of just the one ship, that's impossible! The Vrellish endorsed Perry's bastard daughter by D'Ander as a gift child and thus empowered by their own laws to hold title. We could bring Liege Nersal himself down on us! And Vretla Vrel. And even Monitum!"

"You will not, of course, attack openly," said Larren. "You will, instead, master the Killing Jump, defeat whatever Reetions interfere with you, and harass Perry D'Aur and her treasonous rebels from that well protected location."

"Reetions!" H'Reth choked, well versed in the stories surrounding the Killing War. Dark-skinned, and soulless, the Reetion did not abide by the Sevolite rules of war. They destroyed stations rather than meeting in honorable combat, poisoned food, spread disease, destroyed habitable territory and were the personification of every *okal'a'ni* evil.

"You need not worry about finding them," said Larren. "We have found a station in Killing Reach, called Trinket Ring, that has been trading with Reetions, and is willing to be reasonable. *Trinket Ring's* Station Master has already arranged a meeting with a Reetion representative, who will naturally be a pilot. Your job is to convince this pilot to take you back with him through the jump. Once you know the jump, you can take over a station on the Reetion side of it, to use as a base for harassing the Purple Alliance. Even with just the Vanilla Rose, the Reetion shouldn't give you much trouble. They are only commoners."

H'Reth blinked, wondering how they had strayed into such strangeness and how to get out of it.

Delm took up the narrative. "There is one tiny problem. It seems you will have to take on the role of Liege Monitum, since the Reetions have asked for him. I expect they trust the Monatese because they know the ruling family of Monitum already knows the Killing Jump, and has since the Killing War." He frowned. "Much use they have made of it. So," Delm resumed with more vigor, "since I cannot imagine my dear, devoted vassal, Di Mon, being cooperative — " Delm delivered the endearments with pure venom. " — you are going to be the Liege of Monitum, for me, to dupe the Reetions. You have always wanted to rise, at court. You should be very happy."

"Be Liege Monitum?" squeaked H'Reth, grasping at straws. "B-But I don't look Vrellish."

"They are Reetions!" Delm dismissed the objection. "How will they know?"

"But Killing Reach is full of hazards," H'Reth protested, swallowing hard to combat the panic tightening his stomach. "Everyone who is forced to flee civilization for *okal'a'ni* behavior winds up there!"

"Yes, yes," Larren was nodding, "that's why you must trick the Reetions into teaching you the jump so you can base yourself in their territory."

"Wonderful, isn't it?" Delm asked brightly. "And just when *Vanilla Rose* seemed such a failure." Prince H'Us, H'Reth knew, had recently put a stop to Delm's extravagant spending on the flagship's luxurious interior, much to

Delm's displeasure. It was the next biggest quarrel between Delm and his Silver Demish minders, after his affair with H'Reth's wife, Anatolia.

"You are expected at the rendezvous in ten hours," said Larren. "I wish that I was going with you."

"You mean you are not?" H'Reth whimpered. "I am going by myself? Without a highborn?"

"Larren can't be spared, unfortunately," Delm apologized, beaming with false fondness at his quivering Admiral. "You have questions, My Lord Admiral?" he inquired sweetly.

Yes, H'Reth thought, desperately. *What have I done to deserve this?*

But he said, "No," with a gulp.

"Good!" Delm exclaimed, getting up. "Let me walk you to the door then, as a kindness."

H'Reth was so terrified when the Ava actually put his arm across his shoulders, like a friend, that he could not even produce any drivel about being honored.

Larren withdrew. Balous trotted ahead to wait for them by the door which now seemed a long way away across the manicured green lawn and marble tiling.

"I am told," Delm confided, "that you are going to be a father."

H'Reth stopped cold. His heart all but failing.

"It is all right, My Lord!" Delm scoffed at him, clapping his shoulder. "You need not worry. Oh, I confess, at first I was upset to know that I was sharing her." He smiled with indulgence. "But she is your wife, after all. And in any case, I was getting bored of her."

H'Reth's chest tightened. The affair had been his major "in" with Delm, and its success the culmination of Von's many small intelligences, passed on from the bedrooms of neglected Demish wives and discarded mistresses.

"The child is, of course, yours," Delm remarked, and hesitated for effect as if thinking. "Unless it is true what Anatolia says about you?"

"M-Majesty?" H'Reth stuttered, thinking of the Ava's Square, where he had seen at least one man sheath whipped to death for being boy-*sla*.

Delm leaned his golden head closer. "Anatolia said you were impotent."

Impotent! H'Reth boiled beneath Delm's gloating solicitude, but relief was still his dominant emotion.

"So, if it is not you, and it is not me," Delm was saying. He dropped his voice conspiratorially, "You see I take the Lorel infertility drug, *ferni*, to make sure there are not any, ah, accidents."

"Of course, Immortality," H'Reth mumbled.

"You know who the father is," Delm sailed on.

"I do?" H'Reth asked, still stunned.

"Your little informant —" Delm said sweetly, " — the sword dancer. Von, I believe he's called."

H'Reth's throat locked up.

"Apparently you are not the only one who has suffered a surprise of this sort," Delm went on. "There was a certain H'Usian widow named H'Ran, who appealed to Silver Hearth for assistance obtaining an abortion on the grounds the sire was a commoner, but unfortunately nobody believed her. The woman was notorious for taking lovers, and she had to take care of it herself. But it is time, I think, to determine if this Von really is fertile —" he made a fluttering gesture with loose fingers, " — as a service to his other hapless female clients. Oh, and wouldn't it be delightful if he proves to be the one responsible for Vretla Vrel's stomach." The thought brought tears to Delm's eyes. "The look on Di Mon's face when he found out his precious heir-to-be was not his nephew's, would be worth the tiny sting of insult Anatolia has done me by consorting with this sword dancer!"

They had reached the door where Balous waited, making it possible for Delm to appeal to his *gorarelpul* for a second opinion. "Is it possible? Could a Vrellish highborn conceive by a commoner?"

"Most unlikely, your Immortal Majesty," Balous admitted, sadly.

"It would be rich, though," Delm giggled. "Poor Di Mon — so fixated on his precious heir. Ah well." He became brisk. "I have assured your wife," he told H'Reth, "that she will have proof I am not the only possible father. I want to be sure you know exactly whose child you are going to raise as your own."

"My master prefers," explained Balous, "that Anatolia pays for her error in judgment by bearing the inferior child of a sword dancer. And we will, of course, inform Von's other clients. Especially as that will stand a good chance of ruining Di Mon's woman, Eva. There will be some satisfaction in that, whether he cares or not."

H'Reth was having trouble catching all the malice in the revelations Balous and his bond master, the Ava, were pouring out for his inspection, because he was getting off more lightly than he feared he would. He had lost his trump card at court with Anatolia's fall from Delm's favor, but he was not being stripped of rank, only sent on this punitive, crazy mission. Delm might even take him back into his favor if he accomplished its bizarre objectives. Most importantly, Delm knew nothing important about Von. Only the bits to do with Anatolia. H'Reth himself was safe from suspicion of his greatest crimes.

Balous stayed by H'Reth's side when the door to the Ava's improvised, indoor garden was closed. "There are one or two things," the *gorarelpul* said, tapping his pudgy fingers together, "that still leave me feeling unsatisfied."

"What?" H'Reth barked, feeling breathless again in an instant.

"Jarl, your captain of errants," said Balous. "He used to have some very unsavory connections in the UnderDocks. Might have worked there. Selling children, perhaps? I once suspected Von might have come from there."

H'Reth's throat was too tight to swallow. "Mmm?" was all he could said, trying hard to look innocent.

"But," Balous said, with regret, "boys who served such purposes would hardly pass inspection at Den Eva's. Sevolites do not fancy courtesans with unsightly scars. So Von might, indeed, have been a peasant child from your home estate, as Anatolia told Eva. A boy whose exceptional good looks gained your wife's attention. You might, you know, have seen that as a warning sign."

Once again, H'Reth began to relax. "I, uh, really thought it was just as she said, that she had him over now and then to, uh, direct her ladies in some dramas."

"Of course," Balous soothed. "And who can blame her, given your unfortunate problem." He smiled as H'Reth's face grew red. "But the question remains of why, exactly, Von should help you and your wife by divulging secrets learned from clients. A nasty business, using a courtesan as a spy. Not the sort of thing people expect of a place with a repu-tation as impeccable as Den Eva's. What control do you have over him? Loyalty? A thin reed to rely upon. Payment? Perhaps. But always vulnerable to a higher offer. Threats? I can well imagine someone who depends on his good looks for his livelihood might be afraid to spend an hour alone with Jarl. What hold, exactly, do you have over Von?"

H'Reth managed to wet his lips, terrified now that Balous might be onto him and desperate to seem honest. "Von has a family back home," he improvised. "Peasant farmers."

"Ah," said Balous. "Well, you might think of sending him back there fast, except, of course," his mouth spread in an insincere smile, "that would ruin Delm's fun. He will see that Von winds up whoring in the Underdocks, or something worse. Pity really. Such a beautiful and talented young man. But you're best off just letting it happen."

"Y-Yes," H'Reth stammered.

"Good." Balous smiled and patted H'Reth's shoulder. "Anything else I should know about the situation?"

"No. Nothing," H'Reth assured him, fear and outrage making a muddle of his frayed composure.

"All right then. Have a productive voyage," he said, and added with a smirk, "Admiral of Blue Dem."

H'Reth stood fidgeting a moment after Balous left him, then fled through the ornate rooms and hallways of the palace onto the Plaza on the roof of the Citadel. He found his men where he had left them, enjoying drinks and conversation at an open air bar. All, that is, except Jarl.

"Where is my captain of errants?" H'Reth demanded as if Jarl's absence was a surprise.

"Sir!" a young, blond and blue-eyed hand leader saluted. "He said he was going — he said —" The boy looked acutely uncomfortable.

"Jarl went to look up his old haunts in the UnderDocks," said a veteran.

"Damn him!" H'Reth exploded, exchanging his admiralty regalia for a plain traveling cloak.

"Are you going to fetch Jarl back, sir?" the boy asked. "Alone?"

"The UnderDocks are not something I want to expose any of you to," H'Reth said, enjoying the boy's look of admiration, and set off briskly before any of his crewmen could volunteer to come along.

H'Reth brooded on his way down to the lawless district of the UnderDocks, his black cloak drawn tight about him to conceal his good clothes. He was accosted a few times by peddlers offering food, sex, or drugs but there was nothing they had that he desired. He wanted Von. It hurt to know his boy did not reciprocate his feelings. It was always women with Von. That was why H'Reth had brought Anatolia into bed with them, to help Von feel more comfortable, but was Von grateful? Never! H'Reth knew exactly how Von felt about making love to men, in general, and H'Reth in particular. Von hated it. H'Reth had extracted these unwelcome facts from his dear boy with unwise demands for honesty, reducing them both to tears and Von to life-threatening conscience bond attacks when H'Reth

demanded better answers than he got. At least it was not
all bad. H'Reth knew, for instance, that Von could feel sorry
for him. There was hope in that. The rest was a matter of
training and patience. But how could he keep that up, when
he was so far away from court and Von was being ruined
by the Ava? Such thoughts tormented him as he hurried
to the rendezvous Anatolia was supposed to have set up
for him, with Jarl's help, clouding his anticipation of a few
stolen hours alone with Von.

Jarl was waiting for him at a place called the Bear Pit,
where the only bears were frescos painted on the smoke-
stained walls. The public room stank of *ignis* cigarettes and
bad gin, but it was a smell H'Reth associated with excitement. It was here H'Reth had brought the ten-year-old Von
when the boy refused to pay for the loan of a ship with
simple, willing affection. It was here that Von's spirit had
been broken by Jarl, who had worked for the Bear Pit before he joined H'Reth's service. H'Reth regretted that now,
but consoled himself with the belief that Von's suffering
could not have been too bad, since there was not a mark
on him to show for it, now.

It was the middle of the artificial day on Gelion, and
business was slow in the Bear Pit. Only half a dozen patrons
occupied the dimly lit room, most of them looking hung
over from the previous evening's excesses.

Jarl was the only taker at the rail around a stage that
penned a small boy, and had just paid an attendant for a
bucket of pebbles. As H'Reth watched, Jarl chucked the first
stone at the lively boy who dodged as best he could. Jarl
was aiming for the child's head.

H'Reth jerked his captain of errantry's elbow, spoiling
his next throw. "Stop that!" H'Reth ordered.

Jarl turned lazily, a smile sliding over a jagged tooth
below a nose that had frequently been broken. Then he went
back to rock throwing. His next throw clipped the boy on
the ear.

"I never liked that," H'Reth said in a sulky tone. "I never liked killing them."

"He'll live," Jarl said, unconcerned. He flicked his wrist, striking the boy in the ribs. The child yelped. "Sit down and have a drink," Jarl told H'Reth. "I'll be with you shortly."

H'Reth bridled at Jarl's presumptions, including his use of grammatical peerage when he was two birth ranks and one challenge class Jarl's superior, but he decided to let the insult go. Proper grammar, after all, might draw attention. Turning back to find a table, H'Reth bumped into an old woman who seemed to be nearly blind.

"Pardon, My Lord!" she said, her groping hands connecting with the sword beneath his cloak. "Ohhh," she added as if deeply impressed.

H'Reth was afraid she had recognized him. "What is it?" he asked, with alarm.

She stared at him with filmed eyes, apparently overwhelmed, "Oh, to find such a soul fallen so far."

"What are you prattling about?" H'Reth made to thrust her away from him but something in her tone promised things he was hungry to know more about.

"You will do me no harm, I know," she said, speaking up to him as if he was a Royalblood. "I'll go, if you wish, of course. But you must believe my admiration is in earnest, Your Highness."

H'Reth stopped her leaving now. "You had better explain yourself. Do you know me?"

"In this life? No. But I have known you in a clear dream."

H'Reth's thick lips pouted out. He had been deceived more than once by liars who claimed to be able to recall experiences from past incarnations, or at least that was Anatolia's opinion of the expenditures. It was just as possible that he attracted genuine clear dreamers.

"Sit down," he said graciously, so as not to eliminate in her mind the possibility he was a great prince, unjustly imprisoned in his current incarnation for lack of better bodies being available.

"You have lost status through rebirth," she said gravely, still standing.

H'Reth fished out an honor chip. "Tell me more."

"Ah," she said, dropping into the seat to look at the bluish plastic triangle with its invisible single cell of authenticating blood.

"You say you are a clear dreamer," H'Reth reminded her. "One who remembers past lives. Have you seen me in one?"

"Oh yes," she said.

Jarl snatched up the honor chip, startling the old woman out of her seat, which he promptly filled himself.

"I can spare you the rest of it," he told H'Reth. "You will turn out to be the mistreated heir of the last Blue Demish Pureblood, or something of that ilk."

The clear dreamer slipped away, in search of other customers. H'Reth scowled. "They are not all charlatans."

"I'll tell you when I find one of the genuine sort," Jarl promised with no sign of spiritual conviction. "What did golden locks want with you?"

It gave H'Reth a fright when Jarl called Delm names, but it thrilled him, too. He wished that he could be as brazenly irreverent.

H'Reth told Jarl everything about the mission and Anatolia, padding it out with a detailed account of his injured feelings.

"Killing Reach, huh?" Jarl summarized.

H'Reth fiddled with the glass of station gin he had ordered while they talked. "The worst of it is, he'll be glad that I am going far away from him," H'Reth moaned.

"Who?" Jarl's asked.

"Von."

Jarl sneered. "Tell him to lie about it. Tell him to make out he's heart broken."

"It wouldn't be the same," H'Reth protested. "Besides, he might have one of those awful fits of bond conflict and die. I have to be ever so careful with him."

"Von!" Jarl said and spat on the floor. "He gave me this splice in my eyebrow, your sweet Von." He brushed his face to indicate the scar. "He did it defending some girl I was working on." Jarl grinned cruelly. "He likes girls, you know."

H'Reth's ears heated. "Don't."

Jarl let it drop.

"Didn't you tell me that Von can speak English," Jarl said in his sly, planning tone of voice, "and he can fly a *rel*-ship, we known that. That's how you met up. He borrowed a ship to take that sister of his somewhere."

H'Reth was busy fantasizing about saving Von from starvation after Delm ruined his career, and how Von would fall at his feet and thank him for his help.

"We'll take him with us," Jarl said. "To play Liege Monitum."

H'Reth blinked, looking at Jarl squarely again as his fantasy disappeared. "What?"

"Von," Jarl repeated impatiently. "He's a better actor than you are. And from what you've said, we can't really leave him at court. If Delm's going to take a particular interest in him, who knows what he might find out about things like *sla* dens and conscience bonds."

"Yes, yes!" H'Reth patted his hands on the table in excitement. Exile would not be so bad with Von beside him. "He even has gray eyes," H'Reth enthused, "and black hair. He'll make a perfect Liege Monitum."

Jarl scowled. "Just remember not to get stupid about him with the crew watching. Or I'll remove the temptation and you'll be back to playing Monitum yourself and warming your own bed. We can't afford a scandal."

H'Reth shuddered. He knew Jarl would kill Von if he got careless. He was that cruel.

A cloaked figure stopped at their table. Jarl made as if to frighten off another clear dreamer but stayed his hand. "Oh, it's you, My Lady," said Jarl, wielding the title as sarcastically as usual. "Had a rough time rounding up the plaything for his lordship's pleasure?"

Anatolia's round, pretty face looked bloodless, as if with shock.

"You did bring him, didn't you?" H'Reth greeted her eagerly, getting up. "You did bring Von?"

"Yes," she said, bleakly. "And booked the room. I left him in it."

Belatedly H'Reth registered that something was wrong. "Von's all right, isn't he?" he asked.

"I don't know," said Anatolia in a bleak voice. "I am not."

Jarl got up, pressed her into a seat and snapped his fingers at a waiter to order a stiff drink. H'Reth fidgeted, looking past his stricken wife to the passage that led to rooms rented by the hour.

"The toy will keep," Jarl told H'Reth and pointed. "Sit down."

H'Reth complied with a pout.

"Drink that," Jarl told Anatolia. She swallowed once, then put the glass away from her and began to cry. She never did it as attractively as Von could. Her nose ran. His eyes just got shiny like a glaze of warmth over ice crystal and brimmed over in graceful tracks.

"Delm told me to fetch Von, and wait at home for Balous," Anatolia gasped out between sobs. Jarl thrust a grubby napkin into her hands. She dropped it in her lap as if it was a dead mouse, but at least she stopped blubbering.

"Get on with it," Jarl ordered.

Desperately, Anatolia reached across the table to touch H'Reth's hand. He flinched back.

"Von," she said in a defeated voice, "is kinder to me than you are. For less cause." She withdrew her hand, watching as it crept back to her lap to rest on the stained napkin like a wilted flower.

"Just tell us what happened," Jarl prompted.

Anatolia did not look up again. "Balous came with his own palace errants. They told Von to strip and lie down. They tied him to our bed. That was so he couldn't help me, Balous said. Just lie there. Then Balous ordered me to —" she paused to swallow, and continued in a weak voice, " — get a sperm sample."

H'Reth shot up, thinking about Balous saying, 'Pity really. Such a beautiful and talented young man'. "You did that?" H'Reth exclaimed. "In front of Balous? To Von!"

"I had no choice!" Anatolia cried, making heads turn towards them. She sobbed then and covered her face with one hand.

"All went off to the Royal *Gorarelpul's* satisfaction, I trust?" said Jarl.

Anatolia began to cry again, gently this time. "Von told me — he said to think of something else that might help — but I couldn't think of anything but my humiliation, with the servants whispering outside in the halls and Balous there, watching!" She barked a harsh, little laugh. "Von was the only comfort I had, and I think he hated it as much as me, if that's possible."

"I must comfort him," H'Reth exclaimed, and sprang from the table like a child released from some onerous duty.

Jarl's voice spiked through Anatolia's sobs. "Twenty minutes! No more! Understood? And remember we've got a use for him — don't wear him out!"

Ann Meets Beauty

Ann awoke to eerie silence. The slug's embrace of her body felt cloying and her cockpit smelled sweet, in a bad way. She wanted to throw off the feeling of smothering in her own exhalations and run, but space was all that waited for her outside: cold and fatal. She also felt a little lonelier than before. She had fallen asleep listening to the sound of Ranar's breathing and returned to silence.

"The transmission from *Trinket Ring Station*," Ann ordered, "what happened to it?"

Words of apology appeared on the flat screen before her: "Speech interface inoperative. Please use manual controls."

"Oh, fine!" Ann cursed. "Wonderful!" Angrily, she bullied compliance out of her console.

The clip began with a couple of human shapes entering Ranar's dim room. Ann held her breath as they approached Ranar's helpless form on the bed, but they only wanted the mission box. One of them picked it up and carried it out to examine it. In the brighter light of the outer room, Ann could see that one suffered from an eye infection and both of them had dental problems.

Perplexed, they probed the featureless mission box with instruments. That was where the recording ended, making her suspect they had succeeding in damaging it somehow.

Now what am I supposed to do? Ann thought. The jump loomed at her back, but surely it was premature to run. Ranar might wake up. Thomas could be sleeping off a drunk. She decided to stick it out, which was fine for the first couple of hours, then space slowly seeped into her mind around the edges of her resolve, urging her to flee its huge indifference. When she couldn't stand it anymore she hailed *Trinket Ring* on standard Reetion channels. "Thomas? Come in, damn you, you maladapted retrogressive!"

There was no response.

She switched to what Thomas had told them was the local frequency. *"Trinket Ring Station,* this is Ann of Rire. You have two Reetion citizens on board. Please respond."

She was answered with a barked string of choppy consonants relieved by too few vowels to round them out.

"Get me Thomas!" she retaliated. "Or get me Ranar."

More meaningless words rattled back. They were not even speaking English according to the best guess of her crippled on-board systems which showed no signs of being able to repair themselves after the damage they had taken during the jump. Not that English would have helped Ann much — their only surviving translation software had been in the vandalized mission box.

"What about this Monitum person," Ann grasped at a chance to say something that might register. "The Liege of Monitum."

She heard a couple of them shouting at each other in disagreement.

"Stupid retros," Ann muttered, feeling more confident. You didn't catch Reetions yelling and carrying on like bad children. *Well,* she admitted, *except maybe pilots.*

Eventually they did fetch Thomas.

"So, yellow buns, how ya doing?" he drawled.

"How do you think!" she exploded at him. "I'm itchy and hungry and going nuts!"

"Not enjoying the view?"

"Up yours!" said Ann.

"That would be a start."

Against her better judgment, Ann laughed, but then she was lonely enough to have welcomed a lecture from her least favorite counselor just now.

"Did I upset the Gelacks calling down without warning, like that?" she asked contritely.

"Of course, but what doesn't?" He paused to inhale. She envisioned wisps of the evil Gelack smoke drifting from his mouth as he breathed out. "Good stuff they got, this time," he remarked. "They must have scored a deal with someone. In fact this place is all together well off enough to make a person nervous."

"Thomas —" Ann began.

He cut her off. "Look, yellow buns, Ranar will come around in his own time. Just sit tight and don't go freaking out the locals shouting things like Monitum. He's one of their gods from Fountain Court."

"I've heard your anthropological theories," she told him. "I don't think you're as qualified as Ranar."

"Yeah, well, he's still what the locals call slack on *klinoman*. Stuff they claim is good for post-flight problems. But don't worry. When he wakes up, you'll be the first to know." He broke off.

"Wait! Thomas!" But he was gone.

Ann fumed. The enormity of her predicament reasserted itself. If things went sour on *Trinket Ring* she didn't know which way to go to reach another station, even if a Gelack one would let her dock, and she was afraid to try the jump back on her own. She was busy running through her worst vocabulary on Thomas' behalf when she was hit with an outward shiver and a crazy, inward gasp.

A ship had dropped out of skim, very close. A big one.

At least Ann assumed it was a ship, although her instruments insisted it was much too big. Pilots could *bind* mass, in transit, by means of their *grip*. And while different pilots had different radii of influence, Ann had never heard of anyone who had the *grip* to bind something the size of a small space station. Even if such a super pilot did exist, the shimmer stresses on a *rel*-skimming object that large would snap it in half when it tried to skim! It seemed the new arrival was impossible on two fronts. It was also indifferent to Ann's credibility problem. Her instruments insisted it was as big as a space station despite popping out of skim exactly as if it had been a ship, and it showed no sign of being about to shatter. Instead, the newly arrived object lit up in the visual spectrum, showing itself to be a rotating torus-shaped space station. Then the station erupted in a fanfare of audio.

Ann watched her flat stage in amazement as people in space suits popped out of hatches along the blazing, blaring station's hull to stretch out and fasten great sheets of cloth featuring a picture of a jeweled sword sprouting from the stem of a plump white rose.

Ann couldn't have been more delighted if the Gelacks had arrived on horses breathing vacuum. She was so utterly charmed she laughed out loud and clapped her hands.

Trinket Ring Station exchanged signals with the new, *skim*-capable station that Ann spontaneously named the *Rose-and-Sword*. After the first rapid exchange in Gelack there was silence. Then a new voice poured out of her console — the voice of a young man, full of vowels and sweetly modulated.

"Are you the Reetion envoy we're expecting?" he asked.

Ann's flat stage flashed up the words "Language is English" but couldn't do more than guess at a few Reetion cognates for especially stable words carried over from English into Reetion. Ann didn't mind though, she liked the voice.

"Wow, am I ready to meet you!" she responded spontaneously in Reetion.

"I don't understand," he said. "Don't you speak English?"

"English," she repeated, to encourage him. "We need Ranar for English, or at least his mission box, if those wipeheads haven't wrecked it for good."

"You don't speak English," he decided. "Is the language you are speaking Reetion?"

"This is too stupid!" Ann exclaimed in frustration. "Listen, the mission box! Can you get hold of the mission box on *Trinket Ring Station*? Oh damn!"

"Wait," he told her. "I have an idea."

"Hello!" Ann grasped after his vanished voice. "Hey! Are you still there?"

She tried to hail him and got signals probing her capacity for video reception. Within minutes they had worked it out and Ann received diagrams of a ship approaching the *Rose-and-Sword* station to dock.

"Is that an invitation?" Ann asked, both excited and daunted by the task.

Reetions docked at their stations' zero-G hubs, which stayed more or less in place as you approached, but his pictures urged her to overtake an airlock on the rim of the *Rose-and-Sword*. That would not have been so bad if their guidance systems were compatible, but it didn't take long to confirm that she would have to do it all on manual.

The data stream from the *Rose-and-Sword* switched from a series of animated sketches to live video. Her Gelack had turned a camera on his hands where they worked over the soft-covered display surface of his console. At least, she assumed they were his hands — they matched the voice.

He transmitted to her simultaneously on other channels, seeking common ground that they could build on, which turned out to be the written symbols for the digits zero through nine. Once he had written those out on his display cloth Ann was able to supply him with the matching codes her ship's algorithmic software would recognize. They also shared metric units of measurement — further proof of his people's Earthly origins.

If Ranar were awake, Ann thought, *he'd be taking notes*.

For her part, Ann was just relieved the Gelack had found a way to make her systems respond to his navigational corrections. It gave her time to appreciate what she could see of him.

His hands were a rose-tinted cream color. The half moons of his finger nails were pale pastel purple and the tips of his nails were pearl white. Unlike the Gelacks she had seen on *Trinket Ring Station*, his hands betrayed no sign of infection or damage. His skin was as smooth as an infant's: less wrinkled than her own about the knuckles, although she was only nineteen and not yet showing the typical signs of wear caused by exposure to shimmer. His hands were proportioned like a man's, but sculpted for beauty and graceful even in their simplest movements.

Ann's ship passed over pockets in his ship's hull filled with large gray spheres, but if those were supposed to be ship berths, her scout was the wrong shape to dock. Her guide led her to an anomalous berth that his pictures showed locking down small freighters with grapples. Unfortunately, the grapples were not customized to work with her scout.

She was considering how she might ask whether she should get out and space walk, when once again people popped out of the *Rose-and-Sword* Station. Two of them crisscrossed over her, using lines to tie her down. Their suits had strange, bell-shaped hoods that extended into thickened back and chest sections. Once she was secured, they loosed their tethers and vanished back down hatches on either side of the freight dock.

Ann's scout jerked. The landing pad beneath her sank and a door slid over the opening above.

Sensors told her she was in an airless chamber enclosed by a material that defied classification. The way signals bounced around inside this airlock was bizarre.

While the airlock cycled, Ann pulled herself out of her tiresome cockpit slug and cleaned herself off. It was awkward pulling on her yellow stretch shorts in the cramped cockpit, but she was used to that. Dressed, she waited in acute anticipation, taking in deep breaths like an athlete waiting for a starting gun.

The moment that her ship reported the air outside was breathable she popped her hatch. Ann pulled her body half way out into the cool air, surprised to find that the place smelled like a garden. Or on second thought, like an artificially rose-scented space station. A mechanical noise made her start as the wall in front of her slid down, uniting her airlock with a larger space beyond.

Racks of white crates were tied down securely along the far wall of the larger chamber, which made sense to Ann. The G-forces felt in skim were real enough to throw objects around, even if Space Service insisted on calling them "subjective" because they were only proportional to true displacement. Subjective Gs explained why the equipment was secured, but the gate in front gave her an odd feeling because it was locked.

Ann had seen locks in the old Earth movies she liked to watch, but she could not recall ever seeing one in real life. The plain black padlock on the metal grille doors at the back of the larger airlock chamber sent a tiny shiver up Ann's spine.

While she was staring at the lock, four big men in blue and gold uniforms marched in and ranged themselves before her in a stiff line, looking like toy soldiers complete with swords. She rather enjoyed the swords, although the men's jackets were so stiff with braid and embroidery she doubted they could get them drawn. The costume was finished by a white sash worn across the chest with the *Rose-and-Sword* emblem embroidered on it in vivid colors. The men themselves had blond hair, blue eyes, and square chins, their styled hair worn to just below their earlobes.

Ann felt underdressed for the occasion.

"Hi, guys," she greeted the lineup in her best semblance of a diplomatic manner. Nobody so much as twitched an eyebrow.

She looked at the drop to the floor and decided she didn't want to risk spraining an ankle.

Two more men arrived pushing a wheeled frame supporting a huge *Rose-and-Sword* tapestry. One of them blew a fanfare on his little trumpet as soon as the tapestry swayed to a halt, then the second stuck his chest out and announced: "Liege H'Reth! Admiral of Blue Dem and Captain of its flagship the *Vanilla Rose*." All of which was lost on Ann, except the pretentiousness.

The man this production announced had a square face framed in stiff, straw-blond hair and large eyes that were a rich, dark blue in color.

"Liege H'Reth," the herald declared again and bowed.

H'Reth's high-collared cloak tented out as he set his arms akimbo to show off his sword and a breast stiff with strange insignia. There was a pathetic cast to his large, soft features, firmed up by bossiness. It was not a face she felt inclined to trust.

Ann held her breath as she checked out H'Reth's hands but they were chunky, with square ended-fingers, the knuckles peppered with coarse blond hair.

Ann smiled in a manner she hoped would be taken as polite. "Er, hi," she said in Reetion.

Her host answered her haughtily in what she presumed must be Gelack.

"Look," she said, gesturing to indicate the distance between her and the floor. "See? I can't get down. How about doing something to fix that?" She made what she hoped was an enlightening dumb show in gesture of rolling a ramp up.

The puffed-up Gelack struck Ann as none too bright, but he did eventually command the liveried men to deploy a ramp for her. She decided he was in command and they were servants, which made the scene feel like a silly historical synthdrama. With the ramp in place Ann descended decorously to the floor. The room was chilly on her bare limbs and midriff and the cold metallic floor stung her bare soles.

"Brrr," she commented, rubbing her arms.

H'Reth committed a diplomatic *faux pas* by smiling at her. She had experienced more sincere smiles from women trying to steal N'Goni from her in spacer bars.

"Where is the guy who talked me down?" she asked, frowning at her insincere host. "He spoke English," she remembered. "I think that's supposed to mean he was Liege Monitum."

H'Reth grunted something and strode off. A couple of the gaudy guards moved in to hem her around, forming an escort.

Oh what the hell, why not? Ann thought. She wasn't going to fight them for the right to hang around their chilly dock. They passed out of the airlock onto a catwalk connecting berths. Every five berths was a section, separated by a gap in the catwalk where the base of a dull grey wall protruded, matched by a retracted bulkhead above. The sections looked as if they could be isolated in the case of an emergency. *Caused by what?* Ann thought. Maybe Gelacks weren't as confident about their docking procedures as Reetions and had to be prepared in case a ship collided with its dock. *Were they equally apt to be sloppy about reality skimming approaches?* wondered Ann in horror. A reality skimming ship could shake a station apart if it passed too close.

They descended stairs to yet another cold, bare floor and funneled through a second airlock into a staging area where Ann stopped, and muttered, "Wow!"

There was carpet on this floor! The walls were draped in blue and green velvet cloth, the ceiling was entirely covered in pastoral paintings, and the carpet was green as grass and colored like grass, too, with painstaking attention to slight variations in tone. Ann barely had time to take in the changes when she was nudged from the back by one of the toy soldiers.

"Okay, okay!" she snapped.

They herded her to the top of a spiral staircase that dropped straight down through the floor. The golden railing was worked in vine-like decorations. She ran her hand along its cool, polished top as she descended, her bare feet padding down steps that featured details from the worlds, real and imagined, in the ceiling art above. Each step had a different design.

The corridor at the bottom was lined in hanging portraits and *bric-a-brac*. It reminded Ann of a story called *Alice in Wonderland* that she had discovered when she was seven years old.

"Nothing but a pack of cards," Ann said in Reetion, grinning at her toy soldier escort. She imagined her still elusive guide as the white rabbit, his beautiful hands clasping gloves.

They passed a series of carved wooden doors separated by wainscoted walls. Portraits of elaborately dressed women looked down judgmentally from lighted niches.

The fifth door was opened personally by H'Reth, who stood aside to let the rest of them file past. He did not follow.

Good riddance! Ann thought.

Inside, they surprised servants rushing to release soft chairs and polished cabinets from gobs of gossamer, as if a mad spider had spewed it all over the room's interior.

Ann looked to the paintings on the walls for some enlightenment about the people she was now among. The largest one showed a supernatural scene in which translucent figures howled above the outcome of a duel. It was balanced, on a neighboring wall, by the portrait of a man so beautiful it could have been Ann's guide. The man in the portrait had long, golden hair and blue eyes. His lovely hands, so like the ones that had guided her, cupped a single white rose. The nature of his beauty was androgynous at first glance, and then male by virtue of the detail.

Ann was in love.

But when she freed herself of the jeweled eyes and looked beyond the elegant refinement of the penciled eyebrows, she saw an air of arrogance entrenched about the model's nose and mouth. Her misgivings were confirmed as she watched her guards bow to the beautiful visage as they filed passed.

Let's hope he's just a relative, Ann thought.

They passed through a dining room with all its furniture swaddled in the gossamer spider stuff. It created a wintry effect contradicted by the indoor smell of wood polish and fresh linen.

Next came a small parlor with someone inside, tugging the webbing off cushions on a divan. He had his back to them so that all Ann saw at first was the green velvet of his cloak. She thought he was another servant, since he was acting like one. Then he spun around and Ann's heart stopped.

He had the same breathtaking beauty as the man in the portrait. Even his eyes, although they were gray instead of azure, had the same crystal facets and his black hair looked as silky as the portrait's golden locks. But his face wasn't the least bit aloof — he struck Ann as emotionally transparent.

A zing went down Ann's spine, followed by a backlash of moral shock. *He was so young*!

His mouth looked as sweet as an infant's and his remarkable eyes were wide with a childlike astonishment at seeing Ann. He blushed a pale rose as she watched, dropped the gossamer he had in his hands and shook his hair back. Its molten black was echoed by long, curling lashes and his eyebrows were strokes of wet paint on the warm, complex hues of his brow. He vibrated with conflicted emotions like a glorious, wild animal poised on the brink of flight.

Ann did her best to put him back in context as he studied her shortage of clothes with an uncomplicated male interest. He had to be Ranar's Liege of Monitum. He was wearing the right colors and symbols on his clothes.

His eyes rose to meet hers and his eyebrows lifted as his pupils widened with the alchemy of mutual attraction.

Beauty, Ann dubbed him, in her heart: sweet and vulnerable one instant, lustful the next. She liked that.

His expression collapsed beneath her scrutiny so sharply he looked almost ill.

Concern thrust Ann forward, reaching out. "Are you all right?"

He retreated, bumping the backs of his legs into a divan.

Everything about him begged touch, but she held herself back for fear of causing more alarm.

One of the guards made some gruff remark in Gelack. Beauty's gentle intelligence turned peeved and sullen in mild measures, telling her that he had been insulted, which seemed incongruous. Wasn't he the one in power?

Beauty shook it off the minute the door closed on the source of irritation, leaving them alone. His gray eyes spoke a universal language — he liked her.

Well, he likes my body. Ann forced herself to be objective. She wanted to touch him very badly, to see if her hand would pass through his chest and out his back. He was so literally breathtaking she had to remember to inhale before she passed out.

Realizing that made her laugh.

Beauty reacted as if she had stuck a pin in him. His nostrils flared and his eyes widened, a flinch drawing attention to the responsive body buried in layered clothes.

"I won't hurt you!" Ann said, stepping forward. Her hand curled around his forearm, pressing the bunchy sleeve down.

He looked at her brown hand on the white sleeve of his arm.

What am I doing? she thought, and made herself remember that she was probably the first person he had ever met who wasn't Gelack, and a dark-faced alien to boot. With an effort she released his arm.

"This communication thing is hell," she said in Reetion. "Law and Reason! I'm not the anthropologist. All I know about are synthdramas: space knights with magic swords and Ameron!"

At the sound of the name, "Ameron", Beauty lost color, his black eyebrows hiking up.

"Sorry!" Ann exclaimed, stroking the air between them in a restrained attempt to calm him down. "Did I say something wrong?"

He lowered his eyes as they began to moisten.

That's great, just great, worried Ann. Ranar would be so proud!

"You don't speak English, do you?" he said in that language.

"English?" Ann shrugged and shook her head with a smile of apology. "Wish I knew what you were talking about."

He took her hand and touched the back of it in an experimental manner, then checked his own fingers to see if they had come away colored.

"That's right," said Ann, amused, "it doesn't rub off."

He turned her hand over to study her lighter palm.

"You look pretty different to me, too," she told him, feeling odd to be inspected like an artifact. The chill was getting to her. Or maybe it was the contrast between the cool air and the warmth of his touch. She withdrew her hand to rub her bare arms, miming a dramatic shiver. "Don't you people believe in heat, or what?"

He slipped the clasp of his cloak and swirled it around her shoulders in response. It was velvet and very lush. Then he pulled her down beside him on the divan where he promptly reached into the cloak he had just put around her, making her jump. She felt his deft hand glance against her side and didn't know whether she was frightened or glad. But all he was after was a book, stashed in one the cloak's inner pockets. Ann relaxed, content to let him settle down beside her on the divan.

He had trouble with his sword. After a couple of vain efforts to accommodate it, he undid the belt and laid it down on the floor. Then he was able to draw one leg up under him and turn towards her, the book open in his hands. She caught herself following the promising line of his thigh up the dark cloth of his pant leg and gave herself a scolding that snapped her attention back to the book.

Ann knew about books from seeing them in old Earth movies. This one looked like a cheap copy of something grand.

Beauty opened it with reverence to the portrait of a lean-faced, energetic man.

Ann cried, "That's Ameron!"

Tears sprang into Beauty's eyes as quick as thought.

Ann gave him a hug. He did not seem to know how to respond, so she let go, feeling her face warm up, and took the book out of his hands to concentrate fiercely on that.

The next page was, unmistakably, a reach map. But not a familiar one.

"Let's see," she said aloud, in Reetion, and set her finger down on the most heavily connected circle. "Killing Reach?" she asked.

Beauty shook his head and touched the same circle, brushing her hand. "Reach of Gelion."

"Gelion," Ann guessed, "as in Gelack?" She gave the map a harder look. Only eight reaches were known to Rire, and none of those were shown, as far as she could tell, although there were seventeen circles on the reach map. The idea that Gelack reaches might outnumber Reetions ones felt odd.

Beauty pointed to a reach near a nebulous cloud.

"Killing Reach," he told Ann, and moved his finger into the cloud beyond. "Rire?"

"Reach of Paradise," Ann corrected. He looked puzzled.

She stabbed a finger at the page in a series of quick hops, naming the reaches that should go there. "Rire, Union, Gamma."

He was staring at the page, his pastel lips gone colorless.

"What?" she demanded, as a prickly feeling went over her. "Didn't you know there is more than one?"

He had gone as pale as porcelain. Ann took his hand. "Look, it's all right. We're not going to hurt you!" She captured his second hand as well, the book sliding off her lap. "We might try to help you more than you want. Reetions can be like that, but you don't need to be frightened."

He shook his head slightly, eyes welling up with tears that added a warm glaze to the crystal facets of his gray eyes.

"I'm Ann." She tried smiling reassurance at him. When that didn't work she took his hand and placed it on her sternum. "Ann."

"Ann," he repeated, struggling with a constricted throat.

"Good!" She let him go so she could point towards him. "And you are?"

"V —" The sound aborted in a choking gulp. She caught him by the shoulders, her own heart in her throat, but he recovered so fast she had to doubt it had been more than an awkward swallow.

"Okay?" she asked.

"Liege Monitum," he told her in a subdued tone. "I am Liege Monitum of Fountain Court."

The "Monitum" part she understood. "Won't Ranar be jealous," she gloated, tracing the embroidery on his vest where the signature browns and reds of House Monitum's origins evolved towards green at the collar. Beneath it she could feel his heart beating with a steady rhythm.

He caught her hand and put it from him. There was surprising strength in the action. Afraid she had offended him she sought his eyes, but he wouldn't meet hers. He sprang up and fled the room, slamming the door shut behind him.

"Beauty!" Ann shouted, reaching the door as she heard it lock. She had only ever heard the mechanical click of a deadbolt in movies, but it sounded just like one of those and nothing she could do would get the door to open up.

"Hey!" she shouted as loudly as she could, but there was no response.

Baffled, Ann retreated to the couch and pulled Beauty's cloak around her. "He'll come back," she muttered. After staring around the room a little she decided she was tired, and settled down to wait it out.

She was roused by the arrival of a timid young woman flanked by two of H'Reth's toy soldiers. Ann sat up, bemused, to watch as the woman set out food. Instead of livery she was dressed in pantaloons that looked like a full skirted dress, split and anchored at the ankles.

Ann asked after Beauty, remembering to call him Liege Monitum, but the guard ignored her and the woman seemed frightened. On the way out, a guard scooped up Beauty's forgotten sword and book. Ann didn't miss their company when they were gone.

The meal was a work of art. Her plate was filled with fish made of edible patties swimming in a blue sauce that tasted like spiced apples. By the time she had finished eating, Beauty was back with H'Reth at the head of a couple of toy soldiers.

H'Reth had Beauty's book in his hands. He opened it to the page with the map on it and wagged his finger back and forth, asking, "Rire? Rire?"

"Who is this clown?" Ann asked Beauty.

Beauty only looked at her sadly, put out his hand and led her away from the little parlor to another room farther down the hall.

Inside, Ann found a row of comfortably padded seats set in front of head sets and microphones.

"A com room!" Ann realized, and laughed out loud at the quaint, historical oddity of it all. As a Reetion citizen, she enjoyed full access to communications nearly everywhere.

Beauty sat her down and got Thomas on the other end of her connection.

"That you, Ann?" Thomas asked, sounding anxious.

"You were expecting your counselor?" she quipped back.

"Listen," Thomas told her, "something's wrong here. My friends are pushing too hard for us to go back, across the jump."

"How is Ranar?" Ann asked.

"He's still out," Thomas said tersely. "Seems they want this Liege Monitum of yours to come back with us through the jump. Except one minute they seem to be telling me he knows the jump already, and the next I get the feeling that us taking him back through it is exactly what they —"

"Liege Monitum wants to come back with us!" Ann interrupted, excited.

"I've a feeling my bunch have been paid off," Thomas warned, sounding rattled. "I don't like it. I've never seen anything like that *Vanilla Rose*."

The tips of Beauty's fingers ghosted over the back of Ann's neck, behind her. It felt good.

"A flower?" Ann echoed, distracted.

"*Vanilla Rose*," Thomas repeated crossly. "That's the name of the big flying station you are calling from!"

"The *Rose-and-Sword*?" said Ann. Beauty sat down beside her, took her hand and smiled at her. "Tell them sure, we'll take Beauty — ah, I mean Liege Monitum back with us. No problem."

"Beauty, huh?" Thomas said tartly, and heaved a burdened, nervous sigh. "You sure?"

"Sure I'm sure!" said Ann. "We'll be able to talk to Liege Monitum back in Reetion space, via a station arbiter. And Ranar might need medical attention."

There was a brooding silence, and then Thomas said, curtly, "Okay. Can't say I am keen about hanging around. You launch with your Gelack, from *Vanilla Rose*, and I'll go load up Ranar." He signed off.

Ann turned to Beauty with a big grin, "Hey! How about that! I get to take you — what's the matter?" Beauty slipped free and went out the door.

Ann followed. "Liege Monitum?" she called. "Hey, Beauty, stop!"

He looked back over his shoulder, once, then headed off towards the docks, fast enough she had to jog to catch up.

H'Reth blocked her following him into a berth. He smiled so much she thought his face was going to crack, and kept trying to direct her to her own berth, further down.

"Forget it!" she snapped, folding her arms, and waited there, glaring at H'Reth, until Beauty came out, dressed in a flight suit made of leather with a sword at his hip and a green sextant embroidered over his heart. The leather was kinky — it was retro, on Rire, to wear animal products — but she had to admit he looked good! If only he would quit looking so sad.

"Cheer up!" she told him. "You're going to love *Second Contact Station*. Much nicer atmosphere. Showers. And no goofy swords." She grinned encouragement.

H'Reth gave an order and Beauty led her quietly to her ship's berth.

"Why do you let him bully you like that?" Ann asked, but of course he could not tell her. "Maybe it's the feudal thing," she told herself, thinking that was all the more reason to get him back to *Second Contact Station* and clear of H'Reth's influence. With a last arm squeeze and smile of encouragement to Beauty, Ann hurried to her own ship and prepared for launch.

Thomas was already pulling away from *Trinket Ring Station* when she and Beauty launched from the *Vanilla Rose*.

"That Monitum with you?" Thomas asked.

Ann tried one of the channels she had communicated with Beauty on before, and was relieved to hear his voice answer, even if she didn't understand what he said.

"Okay then," said Thomas. "As soon as we are clear of the station, let's boost."

The taxiing seemed to take forever: the gray sphere of Beauty's Gelack vessel, Ann's blunt-nosed Reetion scout and Thomas' modified Reetion ship flying side by side.

"Time to spread out and synch phase splicers," Thomas said, at last.

And then the universe quivered.

Rel-ships! Ann realized, in horror, and boosted instinctively into skim, afraid to be a sitting duck with reality skimming ships churning up space in the area. Thomas and Beauty did the same, but not in synch, and since even a second of reality skimming made a big difference in location, she lost track of them for the time being. She was too amazed to spare either of them a second thought, in any case.

Her instruments registered two groups of incoming vessels, each led by a single, fast ship. They were all doing more than one skim factor. Ann blinked and punched at her console, thinking her telemetry was on the fritz. While she did that she saw more *rel*-ships signatures appear around the *Vanilla Rose*, like hornets swarming out to ward off the attackers.

Attackers? Ann thought, amazed. People didn't fight in the *rel* medium. Just surviving in it for a couple of hours was a big deal. And the number of ships! It was insane! Reetion pilots were taught never to get too close, for fear of being caught in another pilot's envelope, which was extremely dangerous unless both pilots were prepared for wake lock.

Ann screamed, as another ship came up alongside her like a tidal wave, and immediately fell back to a more polite distance.

It was Beauty. She didn't know how she knew it, but she just did.

A clammy feeling crept over her skin.

Her console lighted up with alarms, again. This time it wasn't Beauty. It was two more ships. She thought they were attackers but could not be sure. She had never had to interpret readings like this! That was all the time she got to think.

The universe tried to fall out from under her in all directions as she was flanked on both sides, caught between two different wakes. Ann's initial reaction was fury at such blatant incompetence! Then she realized they might be doing it on purpose, and was unnerved. She compensated with an evasive drop in the direction that was currently serving as "down" and fled towards the jump, flying at the limits of human endurance, with subjective Gs pressing her down into her slug.

The killer ships gained on her. She could feel their intent creeping into her consciousness, paralyzing her with fear. If she was lucky, her ship would crack and spill her into hard vacuum. If she wasn't, eternity would open like a mouth and she would be gone into a future so distant it was ill defined. The physical interpretation of the math governing more than small amounts of time slip constituted every pilot's "great unknown". In her terror she even forgot about Beauty.

But he had not forgotten her.

He cut across the two ships threatening her, looming on her sensors with a reality skimming roar. One of her tormentors peeled off and another stuttered, like a pulsar, before dropping out of skim back into normal space.

Beauty swept back and around, coming up alongside as they reached the jump's edge.

"Come on," she urged him, waiting for him to get into position and afraid at the same time of guiding a pilot who felt so much more powerful than she was! But she waited, and when the moment came, Beauty was there, with her, in wake lock. She experienced his presence like a shout across great distances, miraculously heard. He had never before been in a fight like they had just experienced. He was shaken, and he didn't know the way through this jump, whatever people said. His fear washed through her like a spring storm, as strong as if it was her own emotion.

If they were going to find the way to Paradise it was going to be her job.

I can do this, she decided, knowing it was insane to try and willing herself to go mad if that's what it took. Ann envisioned the roar of the waterfall she had heard before and the shedding onion layers she must fall through, and they were out, on the other side!

Or she was.

Beauty was nowhere in evidence.

She was afraid to stop. If she did, she didn't think she would be able to find the courage to make it back to *Second Contact Station*. So she set off at a half a skim factor, wracked by sobs. She was still crying five minutes later when she picked up a ship bounding towards her.

Fear and hope took her by the throat.

The ship slowed down, pacing her but careful not to wake-lock. She dropped out of skim. The ship followed.

She hailed the vessel on the radio, breathlessly. "Liege Monitum?"

"Ann?" Beauty's voice greeted her! "Oh, Ann, I have been waiting for hours! I thought you were never going to come out! And I didn't know which way to go."

She could not understand his English any better than before, but it didn't matter. "Let's go home!" she announced, and led on.

He would make a damn good pilot, Ann thought, and wondered if N'Goni felt that way when he recruited her.

At a safe distance from *Second Contact Station* Ann and Beauty dropped out of skim and back into ordinary sublight reality.

"This is mission pilot Ann, requesting dock," Ann hailed the station. "I am traveling with a Gelack vessel piloted by Liege Monitum who speaks English but no Reetion. My nav persona blanked in the jump so I'm boiled down to algorithmic software. I'm going to need an upload."

"We copy Ann," answered a controller. "You are cleared to dock. And we'll take care of your guest's language problem."

Ann was able to eavesdrop on the conversation, hearing Beauty's English overlaid by Reetion translation.

"Gelack vessel? This is *Second Contact Station* traffic control inviting you to dock. Understood?"

"Yes. I understand," Beauty said, sounding shaky.

"Follow Ann until we tell you otherwise."

He answered, "I can do that."

He sounded as if he was convincing himself, which made Ann smile. It was easy to dock with a zero-G hub. All he had to do was aim for the middle, slow down, and let a freshly downloaded docking persona take charge. Except his ship was unlikely to support a persona of any sort. She hadn't thought of that until now.

"Control," Ann piped up. "Monitum's ship has no crystronic block aboard."

"We've thought of that," the controller's voice came back. "We're guiding him into an ambulance bay. We're going to cut you out of the conversation now. Must be confusing enough for him and I have an anthropologist at my elbow as well as Lurol."

"Oh, yeah," said Ann. "Of course."

It did not help that she was so much cargo herself once a docking persona was transmitted to her scout's vacant block, but she was able to observe if not contribute.

"Gelack pilot, are you with us?" The controller asked.

"Y-Yes," answered Beauty's voice. His ship was still no more than a large gray marble closing on the hub.

"What is your name?" asked the anthropologist.

"Di Mon," he said, "the Liege of Monitum."

"Are you all right?" the controller interjected. "We have a doctor here to help assess your risk from *gap* exposure."

"Are you feeling vague?" cut in Lurol's voice. "Disoriented?"

"N-No," beauty stammered. "Not that."

There was a brief pause.

"How old are you?" Lurol's voice softened.

"Sixty," he told her. "No, sixty-five."

"Uh huh," Lurol sighed. "Listen, talk to me, kid. Talk about anything."

"C-Can't," he stuttered.

Ann struggled forward in her cockpit's body slug.

"You told us your name was Liege Monitum," Lurol coaxed.

There was no answer.

"Monitum!" Lurol demanded. "Are you with us?" Still silence.

Ann set her jaw. It wouldn't happen again! Not like it had with N'Goni. She would not lose Beauty to *gap*! If Lurol had any legal objections, Ann would put him in the visitor probe herself, even if she had to kill Lurol first!

Field Research

Ranar regained his mind in slow stages. First he heard things, but the sounds had no context. The next time he came around, he realized that the sounds were voices interspersed with the slap of cards. He had no ambition to learn more. His body finally roused him with its determination to throw up. There was nothing to come up except bile but he would have choked on that if the card players hadn't lent a hand.

They made disgusted sounds as they stripped him out of his flight suit, their hands rough and marked with scars. They were all Caucasians. He knew that ought to be significant, but wasn't sure why.

A man with a familiar, darker face was thrust forward, mouth curling at the job of cleaning up.

Ranar put a name to the familiar face, his teeth chattering. "Tuh-Thomas?" he asked.

"Next time someone asks you how you want to fly," said the weathered pilot, hauling a dripping cloth edged in embroidery out of a basin of perfumed water, "tell 'em cargo. Definitely cargo."

Thomas had something to do with Gelacks. Ranar studied Gelacks, but he also knew he had never met one, which did not seem reasonable.

One of the card players yelled at them over his shoulder.

"I don't know your ugly language, you retrogressive wipe-head!" Thomas yelled back in Reetion and tried a string of words in the Traders' Pidgin he used back on Trinket Ring, to no avail.

The Gelack threw a bundle at him. Thomas caught it and jerked free a blanket, spilling clothes. He used the blanket to cover Ranar, then settled down to wipe Ranar's face with the pleasant-smelling cloth.

"Sword-waving barbarians in head-wiping space no less," Thomas grumbled. "Can you process that? I can't."

Ranar's memory began clearing up. They had come to meet the modern Liege of Monitum, but something had gone wrong. He just didn't know what.

When he woke again he felt perfectly clear headed but very weak. The air was cool. His room seemed to be part of a landing screened off by an ornate wooden trellis in disrepair. It had a parquet floor and was lighted overhead by a glowing globe set in a diamond chandelier. Faint domestic noises reached him from an open floor, beyond.

The building seemed to be an abandoned hangar in which the outlines of parked cars and service vehicles alternated with illuminated islands of furniture. Around the edges where the light was weak Ranar could make out piles of dusty crates, and here and there a gilded door.

Turning his head the other way, Ranar discovered an astonishing wall, half obscured by plastic racks. It was covered in embroidered scenes, flowing into each other in a cascade of stories about golden-haired people dressed in elaborate clothes: the women in skirts and the men wearing swords. The detail was mind-boggling, yet here it was, abandoned behind plastic racks, testament to a glorious past.

Ranar dozed off again hoping to be strong enough the next time to ask questions. He was roused sometime later by a woman wearing a purple and white badge on her jacket.

"Perry D'Aur," she announced herself.

"Ranar of Rire," he offered.

Perry was a short, dark-haired woman with a weathered aspect that was contradicted by the life in her dark blue eyes.

She wore a knife at her side as if that was perfectly natural and her clothes were made of leather. She tried to explain herself in Gelack, repeating the word "D'Ander" many times.

"D'Ander," Ranar echoed. He wanted to know everything at once, but had to settle for knowing that his brain was working properly once more. The details of how he got here were gone.

Perry hauled him up with a grunt and, finding him unsteady, set a small but solid shoulder under his arm. Together they navigated the stairs down to the hangar floor and crossed into one of the pools of light around a furnished area. Thomas was already there, seated in an armchair. There was a couch done in a matching floral pattern and a laden sideboard. Four armed Gelacks were waited on by an old man, a boy, and a woman, dressed in white and gold uniforms.

Servants, Ranar decided with a mixture of excitement and abhorrence.

Perry eased him down onto the couch and introduced the leader by pointing him out as she said, "Prince D'Ander."

D'Ander was a wide-shouldered, powerful looking man with a lion's mane of golden hair and light blue eyes. His boldly handsome face, with its cleft chin and high forehead, was frothed in thick eyebrows and balanced by a square jaw. He stood with a hand on the hilt of a dueling sword inlaid with jewels.

There was a second swordsman beside him whose appearance echoed D'Ander's. Ranar nicknamed him Dandy because he was immaculate in contrast to D'Ander, whose classy appearance was compromised by small symptoms of neglect. Dandy would have fit right in with the fairy-tale figures on the embroidered wallpaper.

The rest of the armed people looked more like Perry D'Aur, right down to the badge depicting purple hills against a white background.

"Guess you were right about Sevolite highborns after all," Thomas said and hiccupped. He was jittery, his twitches in full force.

"Blonds," Ranar mused, staring at the golden-haired princes. "I think that means they're Demish. Demish and Vrellish were racial groups distinguished by hair and eye color. The Demish had blue eyes and —"

"I don't care about your monkey studies!" Thomas exploded, startling Ranar with his vehemence. "They're maniacs! All of them!"

Volatile mood swings were a symptom of advancing spacer's syndrome. Before Ranar could answer, Thomas sprang up and made as if to bolt. Dandy intercepted him and tossed him back into his chair like a rag doll where he promptly curled up in a ball.

"D'Ander," Ranar's host introduced himself with a big smile. "Champion of the Golden Emperor of Demora and Liege of Golden Hearth on Fountain Court. Welcome to the planet Gelion, at the hub of the empire."

A few of the words used were English, and Ranar could guess the English cognates of some of the Gelack, but not enough.

"I am Ranar of Rire," Ranar answered him. "Do you understand this language?"

"English," D'Ander said and nodded. "Some. Speak many languages, but English only Monatese now. *Ack Rel*!" he exclaimed in frustration, features reshaping heavily in a frown. "Only House Monitum speaks English, now. Yes? Is the construction better?"

Ranar's ears pricked up. "House Monitum?"

"Know Monitum?" D'Ander asked.

Ranar realized what was odd about D'Ander's speech pattern — he seemed peculiarly loathe to use pronouns.

"Yes, we know something about Monitum," said Ranar. "There was a woman called the Liege of Monitum two hundred years ago. She was always with Ameron."

"Ah, Ameron!" D'Ander's face broke into a wide smile as if Ranar had named a much loved acquaintance. "Go to Green Hearth on Fountain Court? Talk to Di Mon? Di Mon is Liege Monitum, now."

"Yes," Ranar told D'Ander with enthusiasm. "That is what we came for. But maybe tomorrow?" Ranar felt too tired to face anything so vital and envied Thomas, who was sleeping, fitfully, on the couch.

D'Ander wasn't finished with him, however — he wanted grammar lessons. In particular he wanted Ranar to explain English pronouns. Ranar's effort to conjugate the verb "to talk" in every tense his tired brain could muster pleased D'Ander well enough, but the big blond kept demanding more details.

"I talk to you, you talk to me," D'Ander prompted. "Yes? Up or down? By how much?"

Ranar countered by getting D'Ander to tell him what the Gelack pronoun for "I'" would be in the construction he wanted, and was asked for more information. Who was speaking to whom? Up or down? And what were their relative birth ranks?

Saying "I" in Gelack clearly wasn't trivial.

They had been abandoned by everyone except Thomas and the servants by the time Ranar succeeded in conveying he could not continue. D'Ander apologized, still avoiding pronouns, and gave orders in Gelack that sent the servant boy scurrying into the dark.

Thomas had subsided into an unhealthy doze during the grammar lesson. Now that it was over D'Ander snatched him out of his seat and held him up.

"*Pol*?" he asked, using a Gelack grammar term that seemed to mean something like inferior.

Very much awake now, Thomas flailed at the big Gelack and was dumped back on the couch. Ranar prevented the pilot going after D'Ander when the Gelack walked off.

"We could take them all out with one laser," Thomas muttered, hands trembling where they gripped Ranar.

"I could cannibalize your mission box for parts. It wouldn't stop me. It's got no arbiter-smarts."

"Thomas," Ranar took the pilot by the shoulders. "What happened?"

Thomas licked his lips, looking anxious. "They brought us here. D'Ander's bunch. Took *Trinket Ring* and chased away *Vanilla Rose*." The pilot's eyes grew wide. "Brought us here in a ship with no hull. Just nothing but space all around."

"Maybe it looked like that," suggested Ranar. "But we could breath, couldn't we? It must have been some sort of simulation."

"Think you're smart!" Thomas snapped, then just as suddenly began to cry and clutch at Ranar. "I don't like Gelacks. I want to go home."

Ranar did not need Lurol to diagnose encroaching spacer's syndrome. He put an arm around the weeping pilot despite strong personal disinclination.

"What happened to Ann?" asked Ranar.

"Ann," Thomas snorted. "She was drooling all over your fancy Liege Monitum. Beauty, she called him. Guy sounded as if he was still in diapers. They took off together, heading home."

"Liege Monitum?" Ranar asked. "But he's here, on Gelion. D'Ander —"

A couple of Perry D'Aur's people interrupted to take charge of Thomas and marched him off. Ranar stood. The woman servant appeared from the shadows and bowed, which disconcerted him as much as Thomas being forcibly removed. The boy he assumed to be her son fell in beside them carrying a lantern filled with glowing white plastic.

When they reached the door of Ranar's room, the boy grew bold enough to touch Ranar's brown hand and then dashed away as if afraid his curiosity might cause him harm. The incident brought home to Ranar just how alien he was to the Gelacks.

The room he was left in had a bed and other furniture, including a writing desk and sword rack. All were made of old and cracking, but beautifully carved wood. The ceiling was sculpted to resemble glowing clouds.

The door banged open almost immediately, and D'Ander barged in brandishing a book.

Ranar was familiar with books. He had even handled some at a museum on Rire that specialized in Earth artifacts. This one was bound in soft leather, which seemed macabre. On Rire, animals enjoyed a sliding scale of rights based on their emotional intelligence, which precluded the use of most mammals for frivolous purposes. Ranar nearly dropped the book in disgust.

"Ameron!" D'Ander said, stabbing a finger at the book in Ranar's hands and left with a bang that challenged the structural integrity of the walls.

Ranar opened the book with care in case it might prove fragile and encountered the slight resistance of old binding that had seldom been asked to perform. Words leaped off the page at him; English words that he could understand. He closed the book again, faint with joy, sat down at the writing desk, and opened it again, with reverence.

An inscription on the front page read:

> *The Ameron Biography, being an account written on the planet Monitum, twenty years after Ameron's loss, by Royalblood Sela Lor'Vrel. May hope sustain us until Ameron is reborn.*
>
> *Copy 12 of 101 commissioned by the Liege of Monitum, 69 spans of Earth's Sacred Year after the Americ Treaty with the Reetions, and 58 Earth years following the loss of Ameron.*
>
> *Keep this book in token of your spiritual vassalage to Ameron's soul, but if your heart cannot rejoice in his rel, or your own is hard, this book will be redeemed by*

the House of Monitum for its weight in uncut
klinoman. *This we contract by the blood of Sertatt,*
101st Liege of Monitum; daughter of Sela by gift of
Red Hearth; Liege of Green Hearth and all the habitats
and knowledge of the Monatese Oath.

The words *rel* and *klinoman* were anglicized Gelack. Ranar
knew all too well by now that *klinoman* was a drug. It also
functioned as a currency, to judge by Sertatt's offer to redeem
the book. *Rel* was a pervasive Gelack concept, often encountered as the opposite of *pol*. Its use, here, in the sense of "life's
burdens" intrigued the anthropologist in Ranar.

Beneath Sertatt's pledge was a plastic square, framed in
green braid patterns that reminded Ranar of nothing so
much as a slide prepared for an optical microscope.

There was so much to learn all at once, but the first time
that he closed his eyes to rest, he drifted off.

The old servant roused him when he came in with a
meal, later.

"Thank you," Ranar told him in Reetion, relying on a
warm tone to get across friendly intentions. The old man
backed away until he bumped the door, and hurried out.

Ignoring the tray, Ranar went back to the book, trying
to gulp it down all at once. Names were hard to follow. The
same person, as nearly as Ranar could make out, might be
called by his or her personal name, birth rank, family name,
or an assumed title. Ameron, for example, was Ameron,
a highborn of the Pureblood birth rank, a Lor'Vrel, and ini-
tially Heir Gelion, then Ava. People referred to as Demish
used titles such as prince or princess but the author complained of being called a princess by a Demish person.
Vrellish usage, which she favored, used the genderless term
Royalblood for her birth rank. Demish were stereotyped
as blond and blue eyed, like the figures on the wallpaper
in the room where Ranar woke up. The villains in those
same fairy tale scenes correlated with the darker Vrellish

stereotype. Most families, like Monitum, had mixed blood, but identified with one group or the other.

Ranar fell asleep still trying to make sense of it all.

Shouting woke him up. He stumbled out of his room into semi-darkness.

Gelack swordsmen were dashing and slashing about in a dozen pools of light across the hangar like fantastic fish in isolated bowls. Ranar had no idea why they were fighting or even who half of them were, although he recognized Dandy and members of Perry's crew. The scene felt surreal to him. Too bizarre to fit into his sense of reality.

A laser flash lit up the room, showing Thomas bent over the mission box which he had managed to get open and jury-rig somehow. The light produced was hardly a weapon, but it lit up the scene for a moment. Ranar retained an impression of his hosts fighting hand to hand with six intruders dressed in blue and gold uniforms marked with a rose.

Ranar headed towards where he had glimpsed Thomas and stumbled on a body under foot. A child whimpered as he shuffled back. Ranar dropped on all fours, reached out and touched a limp mass which turned out to be the old servant, who lay shielding the body of the boy with his own. The boy was too frightened to move.

"It's all right," Ranar extended reassurance in a language the child couldn't understand. "I'll help you."

The boy began to cry. The old man did not respond. Ranar was steeling himself to find out whether the old man was dead, when something hit him from the side and he sprawled.

Beneath the light of a glow pole ahead of him, Ranar saw Dandy overtake three men in blue and gold uniforms. Two of them were dragging Thomas off. The third one turned back to face Dandy's charge, sword to sword.

Ranar pulled the child free of the old man's body, slipping in blood as he scrambled up. The woman servant took the child from him and dropped on her knees, hugging the boy, as she began to sob. About the same time someone snagged Ranar by one arm and he turned to see Perry D'Aur.

Knife in one hand, Perry thrust Ranar back into his room and slammed the door. Then she drew a second weapon from her flight jacket, loaded it with a bolt and waited with the weapon pointing at the door. It looked like a slender crossbow with retractable arms.

Dandy burst through the door, sword drawn and blood splattered on his immaculate jacket. Perry tried to hide the crossbow behind her back but Dandy saw it, struck her down with a backhanded blow of his left hand and kept her kneeling at the point of his sword.

D'Ander arrived next with a couple of Perry's people at his back, looked at the crossbow, then back up at Perry with a grave look.

Perry scowled.

A rapid-fire argument broke out and engulfed them all until D'Ander interposed himself between Perry and Dandy's sword, extending a hand to help her up. Insulted, Dandy stormed out. Perry muttered thanks, reaching for the weapon that began the row, but D'Ander brought his boot down on it, hard.

Ranar slipped out past them, thinking to get away from the sight of blood and drawn swords, only to see even more. The lights in the hanger were brighter everywhere now, revealing three dead men in blue and gold uniforms and one of Perry D'Aur's. The old servant was dead, too. The boy and the woman knelt beside him, sitting quietly now. The smell of death astonished Ranar.

D'Ander came out, followed by a contrite Perry D'Aur, who was wearing a sword with the crossbow nowhere in evidence. D'Ander bent to pick up the body of the old man, soiling his good clothes with his servant's blood, and carried the corpse away, trailed by the boy and the woman. He returned momentarily wearing a long black cloak and dived into Ranar's room to retrieve the Ameron Biography he had given Ranar the night before. One of Perry's people handed Ranar a matching cloak with a voluminous black hood.

"Go now to Fountain Court," D'Ander told Ranar in his stubbornly pronoun-free English.

Perry's people bundled Ranar into the cloak, tugging the hood forward fussily as if he was a careless child bundling up against a sudden frost. Then they headed off, moving faster than Ranar found comfortable. He couldn't see much either, thanks to the hood, but when he pushed it back Perry D'Aur admonished him in Gelack. He decided that they did not want his dark, Reetion face drawing attention. Why the rest of them went cloaked was more mysterious.

The world beyond the hanger was a huge, indoor cavern full of streets and the outlines of buildings that grew brighter in the direction they were headed. The buildings he could get a look at, nearby, were anonymous boxes disappearing into shadow.

After twenty minutes of walking, on thinly populated streets, a vivid red car roared up from behind, making the lot of them scatter as it careened past. It did a figure eight, hitting a pedestrian, and came crashing to a sideways halt.

"Vrellish," D'Ander dismissed the matter, steering them around the crash.

Dandy had a lot more to say, none of it complimentary to judge by his tone. No one checked to see if the people in the car needed medical attention.

Ranar's nerves were understandably raw when another car pulled up and one of Perry's people jumped out. The driver got out too, a big man with a bludgeon on his hip that, to judge by his battered appearance, was not there for show. But his attitude changed when D'Ander tossed back his hood, revealing his mop of golden curls and ice-blue eyes. The driver went straight into fawning mode. D'Ander stuffed Ranar into the back. Dandy got in the front. They left the rest behind except for Perry D'Aur, who got into the back beside D'Ander.

The passenger compartment of the hired car — if that was, indeed, what it was — was screened off from the street by grimy curtains. A sheet of battered metal cut them off from the driver, in front. Ten uneventful minutes later, amazed it was possible, Ranar dozed off. He awoke when the car stopped.

Dandy shed his cloak, leaving it with Perry and the car. D'Ander left his on, hood back, but adjusted Ranar's for discretion and impressed on him, with isolated words and earnest gestures, not to let his face show and to hide his hands. It felt odd to be self-conscious about his skin color, but Ranar assured his guide as best he could that he did understand.

They were at the far end of the artificial cavern, before a wall pierced by eight entrances.

"Golden Gate," D'Ander said, pointing to one that was gilded in the same, ornate style as the hangar's interior. It looked very permanently closed.

Instead, they turned their steps towards a much busier gate with a bright silver facade, where they immediately riveted the attention of a half dozen men dressed in uniforms bearing a trumpet symbol.

"Silver Gate," D'Ander informed Ranar.

Three blond men barred their way, hands on their swords. D'Ander greeted them airily while Dandy took up a flanking position, drying blood stains on his glamorous clothes. The conversation sounded almost congenial, as if D'Ander was a rival sports hero, although the sense of threat was real, too. To Ranar's relief, only words were exchange this time.

They passed through Silver Gate to a busy concourse on the far side, where workers in a jumble of liveries drove lifts, pushed carts and packed cargo, while vendors peddled their wares to slim, dark-haired Vrellish and larger-framed Demish blonds. Everyone took note of D'Ander as he strode along with his cloak open and his hood thrown back, but no one looked twice at his cloaked followers, including Ranar.

D'Ander led them through an arch and up a flight of
stairs onto a balcony that overlooked a busy floor. At the
far end of the balcony they passed, unhindered, through
guarded doors and into a palatial room beyond.

At this point, Ranar lifted his head to look around, and
felt the point of a sword through his cloak from the back
as Dandy muttered a curt warning in Gelack. Ranar saw
only marble floor after that, but he had other senses to rely
on. The air grew fragrant with the scent of gardens and he
heard the sounds of running water and the whispers of
women moving in long skirts that rustled. They emerged
onto a busy market square well lighted by glow poles and
crowded with stalls. D'Ander leaned towards Ranar to say,
"Close now. This is the Plaza. Fountain Court is below." He
pointed. "Golden Pavilion."

They headed towards Golden Pavilion, which was a large
tent-like structure with a sturdy frame, draped in cloth-of-
gold, frothed in lace and glittering with jewels. Ranar marveled at the dazzling effect, although he was beginning to
suspect gold and jewels were not valuable to Gelacks. Fur
and leather seemed to be rarer.

A group of men wearing the same uniform as those who
had attacked them in the hangar, moved to bar their path
as they approach Golden Pavilion. D'Ander sprang the
clasps of his cloak and let it slump over one arm. Dandy
moved clear of Ranar, drawing his sword.

Ranar held his breath, expectant of more fighting, but
the Blues were joined, at a trot, by a clump of men wearing the livery Ranar had seen at Silver Gate.

Altogether, Ranar counted three Blues and five Silvers,
all of them Demish, with no women among them, which
was all the more interesting because there were equal
numbers of Vrellish men and women in the audience they
were attracting.

The Demish opponents broke out in verbal sallies with
posturing that struck Ranar as a classic male dominance

ritual. D'Ander wished to enter Golden Pavilion, the Blues were against it, and between insulting one another both were trying to persuade the Silvers. After a few minutes of this, the Blue leader slammed his sword back in its sheath in a foul temper and it looked as if the confrontation might end. Then one of the other Blues muttered an insult and Dandy struck the offending man a back-handed blow that sent him staggering.

Swords cleared in a frightening, metallic fugue of voiceless death threats as the Silvers spread out the audience around the three Blues opposing the two Goldens.

Dandy killed his man immediately, running him cleanly through the body, but this left his sword immobilized a fatal moment too long, while D'Ander was tied up dispatching the Blue leader. The third Blue leapt in and out again.

Dandy dropped on one knee, trickling blood that was his own this time. His briefly triumphant opponent lasted only two exchanges with D'Ander before he died, gasping through a pierced throat.

More Blues were pouring in from somewhere outside Ranar's field of vision, but the Silvers closed around the carnage, keeping the violence from spreading.

Ranar's own emotions clashed like duelists. He had just witnessed murder, and found it fascinating. That was awful.

As others in the audience took over the job of damping out more trouble, a couple of Silvers lifted Dandy, who was still alive, and carried him into Golden Pavilion followed by D'Ander, who hustled Ranar down a flight of spiral stairs onto the floor of a large ball room, empty except for the ghosts of a glorious past.

The Silvers laid Dandy on the floor and backed away, offering what might have been condolences. Dandy began thrashing in pain. D'Ander dropped to his knees beside him while Ranar watched, riveted by the drama.

The air stank of opened bowels and groaned with the pain of slow dying. There was no one else around. No servants rushed out of the doors at either end of the big, empty ball room.

D'Ander stroked Dandy's face, talking to him. The dying man grasped at D'Ander's arms.

Then two women came briskly down the spiral stairs dressed in the greens of House Monitum. One wore a sword. The other was old and carried a medical bag. The old one knelt to access Dandy's condition, but Ranar guessed, before the truth blighted D'Ander's expression, that she offered no hope for his survival. She gave Dandy something for the pain, instead, got to her feet stiffly and left.

D'Ander had murdered two people and a man with a serious but hardly impossible stomach wound was being allowed to die right before Ranar's eyes. On Rire, there would have been first responders to help, dispatched immediately by vigilant arbiters. On Rire there would have been group homes and intensive care.

D'Ander held Dandy's hand, tears running down his face, and began reciting something that sounded like poetry in a smooth, rich dialect just barely recognizable as Gelack.

Ranar knelt beside him to grieve his own innocence and knew he would have to study Gelacks for as long as it took to understand them...and himself.

Cultural Misunderstandings

Ann's ship got through its docking sequence as she watched Beauty's craft drift into the ambulance bay, assisted by tugs. She had been debriefed by radio, leaving her free to worry about Beauty with the same open-hearted anxiety she had felt as a child, racing Rire's gentle tides to a box full of fluffy white kittens forgotten on the beach for too long. Beauty made life bright and bearable. He had to survive.

The gray sphere of Beauty's ship touched magnetic anchors in the ambulance dock and drifted off again, refusing to stick the way a Reetion ship would.

"So much for that," remarked an engineer.

"Can you get anything with spectral analysis?" asked a materials specialist.

Lurol tried the radio again. "Can you hear and respond, Liege of Monitum?"

Ann wanted to add her voice but she hadn't been assigned to the response team. She fumed about that while her ship settled alongside a docking spar, looking like one of the buds she liked to pick off saplings back home.

Ann wriggled into her shorts, rotating half curled to avoid the walls, with her attention on her stage as Beauty's ship was coaxed into its airlock. As soon as her ship's airlock cycled, she was out. One bounce off a wall and she was sailing through the puffy joint connecting her spar to the body of the ship and was in the next airlock.

A pilot handler and medic were waiting on the other side, magnetized boots anchoring them to the metal-laced, rubber-coated deck.

"Good to see you safe, Ann," said the handler, snagging her ankle as she floated past.

"Look," Ann said, feeling like a human balloon. "I can't stop now — I have to be there for Beauty."

"For who?" the medic asked.

"The Gelack," said Ann. "You know, Liege Monitum. He knows me," Ann insisted.

"Okay," the handler gave in, "but we'll tag along." She handed over a pair of magnetic boots for Ann to put on.

The ambulance bay wasn't far. Ann argued her way into the control room that looked out on it. Half the response team was there, with the rest in virtual attendance.

"Is that Ann?" Lurol asked from the main stage. She was not physically present. The visitor probe merely projected her image into the lab. That was good, because the lab was where Beauty would be going if he couldn't be revived. "What can you tell me about the Gelack that you haven't put on record?" Lurol demanded.

Schematics on a side stage showed the ambulance bay filling up with air, but the response team was still having trouble getting Beauty's ship open.

Ann tried to think of things Lurol might consider relevant. "Well," she said, "He's got pale skin. A sort of a pinky cream white, except when he blushes."

"Old Earth stock," conjectured Lurol, "based on a much smaller gene pool than ours. We could be dealing with a member of a seriously inbred population."

"He's got amazing gray eyes," Ann continued, "and hair so black you can't tell it's made of strands. His lashes are long enough that you notice. They're silky and they curl back just a little."

"I think we can safely assume his eyelashes are not relevant," said Lurol.

The air in the lock was breathable. Two men were suiting up to try to locate a hatch. A text gloss on the stage explained that the suits were a precaution against undesirable surprises.

"Ship's made of strange stuff," said Lurol. "We have no confidence we can open this package up. See if you can get him to respond."

"Me?" Ann was dubious. Why would Lurol be willing to let her steal her thunder? More likely she was trying to make her look dumb.

"Talk to him," urged Lurol, "if he knows you."

"Can you hear me in there?" Ann ventured, embarrassed. She could just imagine one of her fellow pilots ribbing her about thinking she could talk a zombie out of a coma as if she was a human visitor probe.

On stage, Lurol highlighted a change in Beauty's breathing pattern.

Ann got excited. "You have to open up, okay?" she told Beauty. "So we can get you out and help you." The arbiter translated into English for her, but it did a lousy job of getting her emotions across, which gave Ann an idea.

"Lurol," she said. "I want him to hear me, live, in Reetion."

"He won't understand," Lurol objected.

"You want my help," Ann told her. "You take input!"

"Oh all right," sighed Lurol.

"Hi," Ann tried again, "it's me, Ann. Listen. You took a lot of *gap* making the jump back. It takes you off guard, you know? You hold up in space like a blaze of glory, make it to dock, and-poof! I know. I lost a friend that way. Hey, are you there or what!"

Beauty's wavering voice responded, "A-Ann?"

Exclamations of relief weighed in from across the station.

"Yes! It's me, Ann," she answered. "Welcome to *Second Contact Station* in the Reach of Paradise."

"Ann, I think I'm going to throw up." He sounded mortified. "I think," he said plaintively, "I have already."

"That isn't the end of the world," she assured him.

"I hate this!" Beauty exclaimed, sounding weepy. "My head feels like it's going to explode!" he sobbed. It was a childish, frustrated sound — a threat to her sexual fantasies, reminding her how young he was.

"It's going to be all right," she soothed. "Breathe deeply and then pop the hatch. Do it now."

She heard him inhale. Then the *rel*-ship opened, and Beauty extended a pale hand. The suited pilot handlers floated up to take it.

"Don't pull until you're sure he isn't injured or stuck," ordered Lurol.

An arm followed the white hand, sheathed in his brown leather jacket. He had vomited. Evidence of it mixed with spheres of floating blood.

"Nose bleed?" someone wondered aloud.

Beauty seemed unharmed, his whole body coated in his brown leather flight suit like candy in a wrapper, but blood drifted in fine beads about his head. His face was crimson, his eyes half closed.

"High blood pressure?" Lurol muttered, thinking aloud.

There was a pause as she zoomed in on his eye movements and checked general muscle tone.

"He's nowhere near comatose," she diagnosed, then her mouth tightened. "Get him into higher gravity, now!"

His handlers jetted with him towards a chamber where intensive care capsules waited to rocket critical pilots up to Lurol's lab. Ann was disappointed. She had wanted to greet him in person as he stumbled into her waiting arms.

Ann watched the stage in frustration as Beauty was put into a capsule in preparation for shuttling to Lurol's lab. People all over the ship were commenting on his looks and leather flight clothes. It turned Ann's excitement sour. On his own ship Beauty had been something to make your eyes open wide and the world light up, now he seemed like just another pilot being fussed over and talked about.

Suddenly, one of Beauty's handlers flew away from the capsule, his flailing body knocking supplies off their mounts on the opposite wall.

"What happened?" cried Lurol. But it was already up in instant replay on the stage in the control room that Ann was observing from. Beauty had not struck the man, only shoved. A preliminary judgment excused him on the grounds of post-flight trauma compounded by culture shock. Beauty himself had fainted. The second handler tucked him back into the capsule and sent him on his way to Lurol's lab.

"That's one overpowered cardiovascular system," someone remarked as data began to flow from monitors inside the capsule.

This was how it was with N'Goni, Ann remembered. They had both docked, then N'Goni passed out. By the time she reached the lab he was comatose.

"We should be heading up, too, for your psych exam," Ann's handler reminder her.

"Sure, after —"

"Uh uh," said the handler. "Other way around."

Ann forced herself to be reasonable since it was the fastest way to get clear of her handler.

A medic joined them in the elevator. Standing between them, Ann felt like a sun contemplating going nova with fat, cold gas giants in orbit around her thinking they could stop it somehow. Pilot's ego, people called that. But she didn't think she was better than other people. She could rank herself on every scale of achievement Rire admired as objectively as anyone. What made her different was that she could wad up all she was, in her hands, and stuff it down the universe's indifferent throat. That was what it meant to be a pilot.

As soon as she was done with her debriefing and post-flight examinations, Ann headed straight for Lurol's lab.

Beauty was on his feet and cleaned up when she barged into the recovery room. He was looking everywhere but the stage to find the arbiter.

"It's translating?" he asked in English.

"Don't you have computational devices?" Lurol answered with another question.

"We have nervecloth," he said, noticed Ann, and broke off to smile at her. "Do you really fly like that?" he asked, with a nod towards her state of undress. "Almost naked?"

"Even more naked," Ann said, thrilled to be communicating. "The cockpit slug has attachments for, uh, well ..."

"Waste?" he guessed, and shared her embarrassment with an abortive gesture. "Flight pants are lined with bags down the legs for the same reason."

The simultaneous translations in both directions put a weird strain on the conversation, and the topic hardly seemed romantic, but they were both pilots. They understood each other.

"This is a sick bay?" he asked, looking around.

"Sort of," Ann admitted.

Beauty's dark brows gathered. "Why am I here?"

"Beats me," Ann agreed with him. He did not look sick. He looked radiant standing there, dressed in flight pants and a classy silk shirt embroidered in green leaves and tendrils. His leather flight jacket lay discarded on the bed.

"Young man," Lurol said firmly, "given the antics Ann reported you are lucky to be here at all."

"There were ships on my tail," Ann reminded him. "They would have torn me apart, if not for you. You must have been doing three, maybe four *skim'facs*!" she said with dawning awe, remembering the details as best she could.

"Four!" Lurol dismissed the claim as sheer extravagance. "No one can fly at four skim factors."

Beauty flushed a fetching pink. "Highborns can," he asserted. "And the Liege of Monitum is highborn. Although I don't think, in this case, that I could have really been doing quite that much."

He was lying. That was obvious. It just wasn't clear why, and about what. Lurol reserved judgment behind a thoughtful frown.

Ann grinned at him. "You want a bath?"

His expression opened up in relief, like a flower. He was awfully good at beautiful — he did it in so many variations. "Yes, please," he said. "I would."

"When I have satisfied myself neither of you have leaky membranes, internal hemorrhage, or latent risk of catatonia, you can go steam your skins off if Ranar's anthropology team gives you the chance," said Lurol. "But not until I say so."

Beauty thought it over and decided to look annoyed. "Is your medic also Sevolite, Ann?" he asked.

"Huh?" Ann had forgotten all the anthropology stuff. "Lurol? Uh, no. She's not Sevolite."

"Then why do you let her speak to you like that?" he asked.

"You know, that's a good point," said Ann.

The avatar representing Ranar's anthropology team picked that moment to put in an appearance. It appeared on stage as a genderless yellow manikin. "Can you explain what you mean by Sevolite, Liege Monitum?" it asked.

Beauty's nostrils flared, eyes getting very wide. He took two steps back and asked Ann nervously, "What's that?"

"We are a collective presence," the avatar answered, "representing the mediated input of the five members of Ranar's first expansion. Ranar is the missing station triumvir."

Beauty looked about as enlightened as a spaceborn child to whom oceans were described as lots of water. One thing was clear — whether or not it talked to him, he was not going to talk back.

"Listen," Ann pitched in, "I know I'm just the mission pilot, but he gets along with me, and you are freaking him out. Maybe I ought to do the interfacing for now?"

She moved her hand towards Beauty and he took it. His skin was like silk but his grip was firm.

"I've heard people use the Reetion word persona," he told Ann, getting the pronunciation bang on. "It sounds a bit like the English for person." He nodded in the direction of the avatar. "Is that one?"

"No," she said. His shirt was damp enough to stick in places and he gave off a definite aroma: something breezy and floral over a heavier vanilla base balanced by the lingering smell of leather. Ann swallowed, trying to remember what he had asked. "That's not a persona, it's an avatar."

"Is there a difference?" he asked, shifting closer.

"Oh, sure," Ann said, talking fast. "A persona is a customized function. The station arbiter is always spawning them for this or that. An avatar is a stand-in for a group. In this case, it's standing in for Ranar's first expansion, who are standing in for Ranar. I guess you could say the avatar is generated by a persona, but people don't usually bother about that part. I mean, that's obvious."

Beauty looked blank, but he smelled wonderful. Something in the complex, vanilla musk sent warm shivers flowing down her back.

"What do you smell like!" she exclaimed with a slight laugh.

He demonstrated just how violently he could flush.

Triumvir Jon manifested on stage beside the avatar.

"Can you tell us any more about Ranar and Thomas than Ann has?" Jon's image spoke.

"Thomas might be on *Trinket Ring Station*," Beauty said, shrinking towards Ann, who was glad to put an arm around him. "If he made it to dock."

"Assuming *Trinket Ring* survived that madness," said Ann.

She had not thought it a particularly significant remark, but Beauty separated himself from her, looking shocked and suddenly afraid of them. He said, "It would be *okal'a'ni* to harm the station."

The arbiter flagged *okal'a'ni* as unidentified Gelack but Ann didn't need a translation. She could pretty much guess it meant a big no-no.

"Oh yeah?" she said in Reetion. "I don't remember those berserkers buzzing around us being careful!"

"That's different," Beauty insisted. "That's just ships — a station is a habitat."

"If our people did fall back on the station," Jon asked, "would they be harmed?"

Beauty blinked at Jon's image. "Is he real?" he asked Ann. "Or another avatar?"

Lurol interposed herself between Beauty and the stage. "Talk to our guest a moment, will you Ann?" she asked. Then she turned to talk with the virtual two-thirds of the station triumvirate.

If they were going to confer about Beauty, it was a Reetion transgression to exclude him like that, although he could have circumvented Lurol's tactics simply by accessing their discussion from elsewhere, if he had known.

"Ann?" Beauty sought her attention with a touch.

"It's okay," she told him, sliding an arm around his back. "I'll look after you."

"Look after me," Beauty repeated, in Reetion.

He was picking up vocabulary fast, Ann noticed with a tiny, diamond-sharp shock. Grammar too. She wasn't sure why it should frighten her. It only proved that he was smart as well as beautiful.

Beauty's expression spiraled towards weary desolation. "I have to go back to *Vanilla Rose*."

"Sure," said Ann. "Later. You can't go back right now."

He blinked his long lashes. "I can't?"

"Nobody ever flies twice on the same day," she explained. "You're grounded for at least twenty-four hours."

That took the edge off his tension. As his face opened up in a smile, she had the impossible conviction he would taste like cream cheese whipped with sugar, or maybe white chocolate, warm and firm. She wasn't proud of the thought. Not when he seemed so much like a trusting child.

"We'll let you go when it's reasonable," Ann promised and smiled as platonically as she could. "Still want that shower?"

"With you?" There was no shyness in the question.

She felt her own face warm, wondering whether a twenty-four hour stopover was long enough to inspire a little healthy lust. He would need a nap first, of course, after all the flying they had been through.

Lurol's announcement made Ann jump. "We've decided you should help him settle. Take him to your room. It's as good as any, and he'll need someone to show him around."

Ann considered telling Lurol that might not be such a good idea. Instead she gave Lurol a watery smile and said, "Sure."

"Don't worry about being out of your depth," Lurol misinterpreted her hesitance. "Ranar's team can advise you on anthropological issues. They'll be standing by."

"Thanks," said Ann. She hadn't thought, until then, that interest in Beauty was bound to pierce the usual, near-privacy setting of the Social Transparency Index in private quarters.

Fine, she thought. *There's ways around that*. Only arbiter attention, for example, would actually be with them in the shower, and there were other things two people could do together, as well, that imposed a black out. It would be fun getting up the nose of that many solid citizens simultaneously, quite apart from the main attraction.

"Come on," she said, taking Beauty by the hand. He followed, keeping close. "I really ought to tell you," she said, "about the arbiters."

"Your computers?" he asked.

"Yeah," she said. "They watch us."

He balked.

"It's normal!" she insisted. "We all watch each other, too. Almost everything Reetion is public. Places have what's called a Social Transparency Index — an STI — that combines with what you're doing, or even who you are in special cases. The more political something is, the more transparent. Don't you have anything like that where you come from?"

"We have *gorarelpul*," he said.

"What are those?" Ann asked, the translation being handled by the nearest microstages in the corridor as they passed.

"*Gorarelpul* are people," Beauty said, "but they report everything they know to their bond master. They have to, or they would die. A bond slave is conditioned for that."

Ann made a face. "Is that legal?"

Beauty blanched. "Only if they're declared," he said. "The *Gorarelpul* College is supposed to declare every bonding before Fountain Court."

Ann's door admitted them upon arrival and slid closed; sealing them into what would normally be a people-proof Social Transparency Index of two. Ann's stage showed the STI was higher, of course, due to her guest's importance.

Beauty stood in the middle of the floor, looking around. There was nothing much of Ann's that was personal. She was about to explain that when his knees buckled.

"Hey!" She helped him to the bed set back from the stage in the main living area.

"I have to go back," he said faintly.

"Not yet, though." She held his head against her shoulder. "Tomorrow."

"Tomorrow," he repeated, in Reetion. She stroked his silky black hair and felt him shiver.

He straightened up, avoiding eye contact with her. "I'm all right now," he told her, and climbed off the bed.

Ann watched as he unhooked the top fastening of his embroidered shirt.

"Shower?" he asked.

Ann scrambled off the bed, attention riveted. She took him into the bathroom and showed him how the shower worked. He particularly liked the spray controls. He left the shower on, pelting hot water down, as he pulled off his boots.

"There's a dry cycle, too," Ann babbled, suddenly nervous.

A tug freed his shirt from his waistband.

"When you're finished," Ann said, "you can use my dressing gown." She pointed that out.

His shirt fell beside the boots. Ann swallowed. A soft sheet of Beauty's midnight hair fell forward as he dealt with the complicated fittings of his flight pants, which were intended for waste management. They came off perfectly clean as far as Ann could make out.

I'm staring, she realized as he stepped out of his pants and looked up. She hadn't breathed since the first glimpse of softly curling pubic hair, slick with a clear lubricant. She felt stupid about it, of course, but standing there naked he looked so complete and well balanced: the darkness of his hair matched by his groin, and his torso all smooth, molded surfaces. A lot of men looked clumsy naked. He looked — well, beautiful. He read her interest and the object of her fascination answered.

High blood pressure, Ann thought, and really, really wished she had not. He stepped forward, slid an open palm along her jaw, and kissed her. Then he stopped, leaving her tingling, as whatever evil stalked him once again cast its shadow.

She covered his hand with hers. "What is it, Beauty?"

He shook it off and guided her palm to his parted lips, his breath raising shivers, as the shower pounded away nearby. He supported her against his body and kept kissing her, his strong hands purposefully doing things with her clothes. When he stopped she felt bereft until she realized that he wanted her to come into the shower with him, and did, hungry not to lose skin contact.

He liked her brown skin, but he seemed less concerned about washing it than exploring it thoroughly with his mouth and hands. He was making her a bit crazy before he followed through, right in the shower. How they could be horny after such a flight she couldn't fathom, but their wet skin, his strong hands and her need were intoxicating. It was over before she was ready to stop, despite a very thorough body flush, but even that was worth it for the sake of the endearing way he looked abashed, as if he had done something wrong. Ann attacked him with shampoo, eager to keep her hands on him, and he reciprocated happily, washing her hair and then helping to sloosh the suds down her back and breasts. He carried her out of the shower, wet and naked, to the morph mattress where they made love again, and this time he kept her too off balance to think about anything except his research into what made her body go molten with pleasure. But by the time she was coming down off her second climax, she'd decided he was just a bit obsessive. Her abdomen and thighs felt like jelly. Beauty lay on his back beside her, still erect and apparently content to stop there. It wasn't the first time he had seemed concerned about conserving an erection, either.

Maybe, she decided, *it's some bizarre Gelack custom.*

His skin was warm and flushed over his entire body. She settled on his chest, listening to the subsiding action of his heart. It felt companionable. His vanilla smell had washed off in the shower, but a trace of it was still detectable. She wondered if it was natural. His sex smell was also unusual: a sort of nutmeg spice and musk affair just strong enough to notice. Maybe he took drugs to change his body odor. She had heard of a craze for that on one of the less enlightened worlds governed by the Arbiter Administration.

"I hope I get to keep you," Ann mumbled, feeling drunk on endorphins.

His thumb glided into the soft place between her leg and groin.

"I don't know what you're made of," she moaned, propping herself up to ruffle his hair. "But I'm only human!"

"No more?" he confirmed, conversationally.

"Law and Reason!" she exclaimed with a laugh. "Where did you learn about women?"

He sat up then, and asked, "Are you Vrellish?"

"Vrellish?" she echoed. That sounded Gelack.

"You act Vrellish," he told her in Reetion.

"Oh?" she said. "How do Vrellish act?"

He shrugged and said, "Like you do." She didn't know what to make of that. "But you aren't strong, like a highborn. How Sevolite are you, Ann?" he asked in an apologetic rush, and quickly excused himself by adding, "I can't tell from English pronouns."

"I dunno," she mumbled, and settled down to sleep beside him.

Ann awoke some time later to a whopper of a post-flight hangover. The fact that something as socially sanctioned as piloting left you as trashed as a bad bender always struck her as proof that reality would never conform to the Reetion system of justice, with its finely tuned system of rewards and punishments.

"Finally!" Lurol hailed her from her floor stage.

Ann groped for Beauty, found his place cold, and sat up.

"I hope you enjoyed yourself!" Lurol vented her frustration. The avatar representing the anthropology team was on stage beside her, and so was Jon.

Ann didn't need to worry about being naked. The arbiter would block out any parts entitled to stay private.

"We have been very anxious to speak with you and Liege Monitum," Jon explained Lurol's bad manners. "But the arbiter sustained your right to rest and privacy. We couldn't interrupt."

Lurol snorted.

"What's the matter," Ann asked, arms draped over her knees. "Do you think the arbiter made a *mistake* about that, mmm?"

"Arbiters," Lurol snapped, "are policy implementation and conflict resolution systems. Intelligent, yes, but they haven't any common sense. You should! Damn it, Ann, this is a mission, not a group home for pilots with behavior problems!"

"Lurol, please," Jon admonished.

Lurol stuck her bony hands into her lab coat pockets. *Stupid affectation*, thought Ann. Lurol didn't need a lab coat to operate a psych probe. One day she was going to look up the reason Lurol wore it, so her gibes would be well informed.

"Emotions are high, Ann," Jon counseled. "We are all concerned about our missing people, and naturally there is a great deal of interest in Liege Monitum."

"Where is he?" Ann demanded.

"In the shower again," answered Lurol.

"I want to register a relationship with him," Ann declared, feeling possessive.

"A relationship!" Lurol spluttered. "You bone-headed pilot! This is not just another of your needlessly dramatic affairs! He's a Gelack."

"He's my lover!" Ann fired back.

"Ann! Lurol!" Jon interrupted. "If you can't contain yourselves you don't belong in these deliberations!"

"We concur," said Ranar's team of anthropologists, "but we have no objection to Ann registering their relationship so long as Liege Monitum understands adequately."

"There's something else you ought to know," Jon reclaimed Ann's attention. "According to your ship's clock, you time slipped just under twenty-four hours."

Ann sat bolt upright. "What?"

"It was a contributing factor to the station's decision to let you rest," said Jon. "We're not sure if Monitum did, too, or how much. His ship's controls are incomprehensible."

Twenty-four hours! Ann thought, alarmed. That meant she nearly didn't make it out. Nobody was quite certain what happened to people who time-slipped too far except that the duration of slippage started up a steep, exponential curve as a function of time lost. In the twenty-four hour range, the odds started getting bad.

"It is nothing to be ashamed of," said Jon. "After all, you barely knew that jump. We wondered if Monitum guided you through, in fact."

"He didn't know the way," she said. "But he helped. Somehow he made me stronger while we were in wake-lock. And he time slipped too, I think. But not as much."

Beauty came out of the bathroom wearing nothing but his leather pants. He focused on her naked body, but at the moment that annoyed her. Ann snatched a sheet up.

"You didn't know that jump, did you?" she demanded, daring him to lie.

"His use of Reetion would tend to suggest that he's been here before," said Jon.

"He has said nothing in Reetion that he has not been exposed to, at least once, in simultaneous translation," said the anthropologists through their avatar.

Beauty bolted back into the bathroom.

"You let me deal with this!" Ann told the triumvirate.

"She has proven to be the only effective point of contact," conceded the avatar.

"Is that what you call it?" exclaimed Lurol.

As soon as they dissolved Ann jerked down a storage bin and put on the first clothes she found there: a patterned shift, splashed in greens and yellows.

She found Beauty wedged into a corner near the shower, staring at her out of his amazing grey eyes. He's *freaking out*, she thought, and decided to be thunderously prosaic.

"What would you like, most, right now?" she asked.

He answered tentatively. "Clean clothes?"

"Hey!" Ann grinned. "No problem."

She put out her hand, and led him back into the living room where she drew him down to sit facing her. "I want to declare a relationship with you," she said, and waited out the translation, disappointed when his face retained its strained expression.

"It means we both acknowledge we are lovers and care about each other," she explained. "We could leave it at that, if you prefer. It doesn't have to be anything too permanent or complicated. Not to start with."

When the translation finished he dropped his eyes.

"What?" she asked defensively. "Is there someone else?"

His eyes filled up with tears as he murmured, "Mira."

Ann felt as if a rough stick had passed through her middle. "There is someone else," she guessed.

He shook his head. The tears in his eyes spilled over his lower lids in unison as he blinked.

Damn, she thought, *but he was beautiful*. His face conveyed distress with elegance, and even his pallor had an interesting, opalescent character.

"I would like to acknowledge a relationship with you, Ann," he said. "Really, I would."

"Good!" She grinned. "Because that's pretty much all you have to do. The arbiter is always listening."

His glance flicked around him nervously. It made Ann laugh.

He smiled back with a pained expression. "You are a commoner, aren't you?" he asked.

"Commoner?" Ann narrowed her eyes. "I don't know what you mean by that."

"Even though you are a pilot," he amended. "I always knew it had to be possible for commoners to make good pilots." He looked around as if expecting the walls to fall in on him. When they didn't, he swallowed carefully and went on. "Do Reetions really live without Sevolites, too?"

"Tell you what," Ann set her hand akimbo, "you tell me what a Sevolite is, and I'll explain where ours are."

"I am a Sevolite," he said, getting flustered.

"Are you?"

"I am Di Mon, Liege of Monitum, a highborn of the grammar class Highlord."

Ann folded her arms. "That's not very informative given I know nothing about Gelacks. What's a grammar class?"

It struck her, while he mulled over the depth of her apparently shocking ignorance, that she had assumed being socially primitive would make the Gelacks easy to understand.

"Challenge class is based on genotype," he told her, "although it's really phenotype that matters, unless you are a Demish woman who doesn't have to fight or fly."

Ann made a mental note to look up phenotype and genotype. They had something to do with genetics, she knew that much. "Is that why you thought I was Vrellish?" Ann asked. "Because the other sort of women — Demish women? — don't fly?"

"That too," he said, with a half shrug.

Meaning what, exactly? Ann thought, not sure it was a compliment.

"Was it pushy of me asking you to register?" she asked. "I mean I didn't think, the way things went, that it was your first time or anything like that."

"No, Ann," he said, looking down.

"It's supposed to be important that we both know what we expect of a relationship," she pointed out, and paused, feeling nervous. "It's the part I keep getting wrong — expectations." She rubbed her hands on her thighs, bunching and slackening the printed shift beneath them. "Reetions are supposed to agree about what sex means to both parties in advance. Except I never know and so I get it wrong." She frowned. "Personally I think we do it for the arbiters."

"Have ... sex?" He seemed so worried by the prospect that she had to laugh.

"No, you dope! Register relationships. You see, if we don't tell the arbiters what we expect, they can't figure out who is in the wrong when a complaint is lodged."

"Oh," he said.

"Let me get you some clothes," said Ann. "Then you need to see Lurol. She wants to check you over and you'll need her permission if you want to ship out."

Something about that distressed him.

"Don't worry," Ann assured him. "Reetion law won't let anyone do anything to you that you don't agree to. It's a human right." She smiled encouragement.

He nodded, once. But the fear in his eyes merely took a step back. She didn't have the heart to tell him people could force treatment on you if you got yourself in enough trouble to be designated Supervised, either for your own good or everyone else's. Besides, she couldn't see how that could possibly happen to someone as healthy and nice as him. If he refused examination, the worst that Lurol could do was ground him until he changed his mind, which wouldn't be such a bad thing from her point of view.

"Ask the stage for anything you need while I'm out," Ann said.

He nodded, although she doubted that he really understood.

A woman was waiting in the corridor with an armload of neatly folded clothes.

"Hello," she introduced herself. "I am Alicia, an anthropologist. We thought you might have questions to ask."

Ann popped the one on the top of her list. "What's Vrellish?"

"A racial group as far as we can make out." The anthropologist's mouth tightened. "I'd be careful of letting him decide that you are a commoner. What we've heard so far confirms Ranar's belief that Sevolites comprise a ruling caste. Being labeled a commoner could put you at a disadvantage."

Ann nodded, trying to get her head around that.

"Were you quite sure that you witnessed combat in Killing Reach?" Alicia asked. "Space-faring cultures that indulge in warfare always self-destruct."

"All I know is what I saw," said Ann.

"Perhaps if there were strong constraints in place to set limits," Alicia thought aloud.

"Like that *okal'a'ni* business?" remembered Ann.

"A taboo against station wrecking?" The anthropologist nodded. "But fighting under reality skimming conditions?" She shook her head. "Even if your impressions were accurate, we don't know if what you witnessed was warfare or an outbreak of mass hysteria, brought on — for all we know — by our intrusion."

Ann shrugged, "If you say so." But she remained convinced, herself, that the Gelacks had been fighting one another.

She found Beauty sitting on the bed when she returned.

"I liked your yellow clothes better," he said, nodding at her shift.

"Thanks," said Ann, handing him the clean clothes. "My parents used to complain that I liked to wear things that looked sprayed on."

"You could wear a dancer's sheath if you wanted," he told her. "Lots of people can't pull that off, even if they've worked for it."

"I'm game," she said, watching him pull the tunic over his head. "What's a dancer's sheath?"

"A costume for sword dancers." He stepped out of his leather pants.

"Sword dancers?" This time Ann kept her eyes above waist level. "With real swords?"

"Of course." He seemed uncertain whether to tuck in the tunic or not.

"Sounds unhealthy," said Ann, lending a hand.

The new clothes were nice, although he looked better naked. They stood a moment, staring at each other. Then he said, "You are not a Sevolite. You don't even have a sword."

"Ah, well, not on me right now," said Ann, mindful of Alicia's advice. "Listen, are you going to stay a while?" she changed the subject. "I'd like you to."

He went numb. "I must go back."

"Oh."

"I must ask H'Reth to release your people on *Trinket Ring*," he elaborated. "I mean, *order* H'Reth to do it."

"Whatever," said Ann. It was obvious that he was pulling her leg about something, she just wasn't sure exactly what.

"You can call me Di Mon," he suggested, cajoling now. "If you want."

"Di Mon?" she echoed, wondering what was up.

"It's a use name. There have been a lot of Ditatt Monitums. Di Mon is a personal form." He dampened his lower lip and fidgeted, then rallied, tossing his hair back. "I let my *lyka*, Eva, call me Di Mon," he said with an attempt at *hauteur*, "so could you."

"Your *lyka*?" Ann repeated. An explanation, on stage, flagged the word as intractable Gelack.

Beauty shrugged. "Oh, she's just a courtesan."

That translated.

"Gee, thanks," said Ann.

"Have I said something wrong?" he asked.

"Starting where?"

He fell silent.

Ann rolled her eyes and shook off the peculiar feeling that she was in a poorly acted synthdrama. "Let's go see Lurol," she decided.

She headed for the door. He did not follow.

Ann turned back, arms folded. "If you want to ship out, you have to pass a pre-flight psych exam and physical, and have all your options explained to you, like the visitor probe."

"The visitor probe?"

"We could explain things to each other all day!" she told him crossly. "Come on."

The corridors were unusually quiet. Ann guessed that the anthropologists had asked people to stay clear. She felt annoyed with herself for being short with Beauty and annoyed with him, too. How could he decide to leave as if nothing had happened between them? And then talking like that about his courtesan, as if granting her parallel privileges was supposed to be flattering!

She was actually relieved when Alicia put in an appearance and asked if she should take over. Beauty looked relieved too, and sad, which seemed an odd combination. But Ann was fed up with him being an enigma.

"Courtesan," she muttered, as she watched him walk off beside Alicia. He never even turned for one last look.

Alone in her room again, Ann settled down to do some serious brooding over a snack. Maybe her counselors were right. Rire was enlightened enough to tolerate a wide range of sexual behavior, but did she really want to slot in on the lunatic fringe? She didn't have to go on acting out all over the place. She was really ready to grow up.

She decided to celebrate by checking to see if Beauty was still on board.

"Stage on!" she ordered, and located him in Lurol's lab, getting briefed on the visitor probe.

"It is not a device for controlling anyone," Lurol corrected. "It's for reviving pilots who succumb to post-flight coma."

"But if it can re-integrate consciousness," he said, meshing his fingers and then pulling them apart again with a strangely hopeful look. "Couldn't it rebuild brain patterns? Couldn't it impose new ones or ... or ..."

"Yes?" Lurol prompted.

He went very pale all at once.

"Are you all right?" Lurol put a hand on his shoulder.

Beauty convulsed.

The wrenching feeling in Ann's own chest came as a shock. She leapt up and sprinted for the lab. When she burst onto the scene two minutes later, Beauty was sitting up with Lurol taking his blood pressure. Equipment was on standby and a couple of other medics hovered waiting to pounce if he acted up.

"Hi," said Ann, breathless.

Beauty raised his head. For an instant he was glad to see her. Then he looked as if she had sentenced him to execution just by showing up.

"I wanted to say good-bye," she told him, hurt by his reception.

He went pale again.

"Look, you beautiful dope," Ann said with force, "will you at least think of coming back? Just to visit? Hey, stop it!" Ann interrupted herself. "You're freaking me out."

His eyes brimmed with fatal distress while his face remained ludicrously elegant. "I should have ... before," he whispered, gazing up beyond Ann. "So sorry, Mira." He said it with the last breath he was able to draw, stumbled up, and pitched forward to the floor, in convulsions.

Ann's eyes opened so wide her eyeballs got cold.

Fortunately Lurol's staff were more useful.

"Milap!" cried Lurol. "Prep the probe!"

"We don't have his permission!" objected Milap.

"The arbiter will stop us if we do anything illegal," Lurol decided. "Come on!"

Milap shot Beauty up with tranquilizers. He reacted badly, tearing at the offended arm before the tranquilizers took effect. They forced him into position on the visitor probe slab, braced his head, and positioned saline droppers over his eyes. Then his limbs were chucked inside.

Lurol called out, "Close!"

The probe's outer cylinder closed over him, settled and locked. Organ telemetry and interior visuals filled the large stage at the center of Lurol's lab.

"Stimulate his heart," Lurol ordered. "Respire his lungs. Keep him alive until I figure out what's going on."

Inside his living tomb, a robotic arm slid a thick plastic tube into Beauty's mouth. Ann could see that his eyes were open and looked terrified.

"He's reacting to the tranquilizer!" warned a second medic, named Vera. "Micro-organelles of some kind, right in his arm, are spewing out phagocytes to contain the spread of foreign material."

"Bone marrow and liver activity is picking up," reported Milap. "I'm reading new cells, undifferentiated. Spontaneous cancer? No, they're taking their context from those around them. Law and Reason, even nerve cells, Lurol!"

Lurol did not look up. Beauty's brain lay before her like a star map in which she was hunting a storm. She gestured at displays and muttered commands.

"It's incredible," Milap breathed, his face lit by the physiology reports that he was peering into.

"This is incredible," Lurol corrected, sweeping an arm through the projected model of Beauty's brain function to point out a feature in the display. "He's shuffling memories as if he's a crystronic block running damage control!"

Vera looked up. "His coherence of consciousness rating is dropping off."

"Huh," Lurol answered with a grunt. "It's got a lot farther to fall than most. But yes, of course, we have to calm him down."

"No more tranquilizers!" Milap warned.

They sounded like a pack of children exclaiming over a once-in-a-lifetime toy.

Ann came away from the bed and walked into the midst of the projections on the central stage.

"Ann?" Milap touched her arm.

She pivoted away from him, looking around her at Beauty, vivisected and re-interpreted as data. "Beauty!" she cried, reaching out. Her arms swept through the images as if this was a synthdrama. "Are you still here!" Ann demanded.

"Get her off the —" Vera began.

"Wait!" Lurol interrupted. "He's responding." She pointed at the model of Beauty's brain which was lighting up in an auditory area. "He can hear her on an open input channel. He's awake in there and terrified. Maybe she can calm him down."

"Beauty!" Ann cried. "Can you hear me! What's happened to you! Why did you collapse?"

The brain model flooded with activity. Then the stage came alive in a sense that was frighteningly literal. It glimmered and surged with a patchwork of three dimensional interpretations that were coming out of Beauty through his interface with the visitor probe.

"We've got audio, visual, olfactory, tactile —" Milap looked impressed, " — and parietal data, all feeding back to us." He paused. "But the stage doesn't know what to make of them."

At the center of the new display was a naked shape that radiated color; an inside-out picture of a living being.

"The stage is trying to portray — I think they're memories," said Vera. "Lurol," she gasped, astonished, "he's interfacing with the arbiter in the probe!"

"Reduce the number of sensory channels to ones the stage can reproduce," ordered Lurol.

The confusion coalesced around audiovisual output with other senses reduced to defining Beauty's body in space, making it easy to see what he was remembering. His tactile-shape stood in a dingy little room before a battered metal vanity that was painted to emulate wood. Behind him, a door opened and closed. "Anatolia told me what happened at H'Reth Manor," said a man's voice at Beauty's back, dripping concern and affection.

"He's translating Gelack into English for the arbiter," said Lurol, bent over her analysis read outs. "The arbiter is putting it in Reetion." She straightened, watching the audiovisual display which was getting clearer by the minute. "This is more intense than memory. I'd say that to him, it feels as if it's happening."

"The attack has stopped," announced Vera.

"Because whatever caused it hasn't happened yet," said Lurol excitedly. "He's thrown himself back in time, mentally! Not, I think, as a self-conscious choice," she added quickly. "It was something that the arbiter enabled, provoked by Ann's demand that he explain what caused him to collapse. It's phenomenal!" She sounded like someone having a religious experience.

On the stage, Beauty's molten-skinned self-image turned to face the man who'd spoken, and Ann recognized H'Reth, from the *Vanilla Rose*.

"Are you all right, Von?" H'Reth asked.

"I am undamaged, master," Beauty's self-image replied.

"Call me Garn," H'Reth urged, coming close. "I like you to call me Garn when we're together." He set a big hand on the side of Beauty's face.

"Yes, Garn," Beauty complied.

"I'm going to take you away with me, to Killing Reach," H'Reth told him. "There's something I need you to help me with there."

The bed creaked as Garn H'Reth let them both down on it, Beauty on his back, staring up at the larger man's eager face. "You can exercise all your unusual talents," H'Reth purred, admiring him. "You'll be play acting, and speaking English. You might even have to fly. You remember flying, don't you? It's how we met."

"I remember," Beauty answered in a dead voice. His face was turned aside, the shoulder of H'Reth's jacket the only thing in sight.

"Kiss me," H'Reth said. The perspective shifted, and Ann saw H'Reth's ungainly face bearing down.

In the room on *Second Contact Station* Milap cried, "There! That's the start of the mental disturbance we're fighting."

Ann's lip curled. Surely Beauty would shove the great oaf away from him and run! Or fight back!

"It's definitely a cognitive trigger," said Lurol.

"Relax," H'Reth cooed against Beauty's ear.

The sounds and shifting movement on the stage didn't need much explaining. Beauty was cooperating. Ann felt sick at the thought of the hands touching H'Reth, in the memory, touching her.

She bolted from the lab to cast herself headlong across the first morph couch she encountered. Beauty, her Beauty, had betrayed her trust, and her competition wasn't some lost love called Mira, but Garn H'Reth, the hairy-knuckled, jumped-up jerk with the toy soldiers from *Vanilla Rose*!

As she ran out of tears to cry she promised herself that she would never again make a pass at a man she hadn't looked up and studied at least three days in advance, and she would never take another mission that had anything to do with Gelacks. About the time she had finished crying a new pilot handler showed up: a man, which was a pretty dumb move on someone's part.

"Drop dead," she told him, sitting up on her morph couch in a corridor lounge.

"You've had a nasty shock," he sympathized. "The duty medic's authorized a tranquilizer. Would you like it?"

"Yeah," she surprised herself, still smarting with embarrassment and disappointment. "Yeah, I would. And when I wake up, I want out of this mission. I'll fly the next mail run back to Mega. I want to! You file that!"

"Of course, Ann," he soothed. "If that's what you want."

The Silver Box

Di Mon, Liege of Monitum, strode into his library to collect his sword from beside the chair where he had sat reading the night before, and stopped at the sight of his bonded *gorarelpul*, Sarilous.

She gave him a hard look, standing stiff-backed in front of his reading chair holding his sword in her blue-veined hands as if she did not mean to relinquish it, and wearing the expression that said she did not approve of him exercising native Vrellish recklessness as if he lacked the intellect to know better.

Technically, a word of command from him could kill her. But she had also been his guide and advisor for more years than he ought, by his youthful appearance, to be able to remember. Di Mon was sixty-five and looked timeless. She was nearly eighty and growing frail, although he did not notice any infirmity. She was too much of a fixture.

"I am only going to meet with him, Sarilous," Di Mon told her, impatiently. He held out his hand for the sword, but he would not command her. Not in a matter so trivial.

Sarilous said, emphatically, "The Golden Prince D'Ander is trouble."

"Yes," Di Mon said, briskly. "I think we can agree about that."

Di Mon's niece, Tessitatt Monitum, came in, carrying Di Mon's traveling cloak and wearing her own. She was flanked by her younger brother, Kertatt, in the midst of a petulant argument. "But why can't I come?" Kertatt demanded, clutching the hilt of his sword.

"Let me think," said his sister. "Might it have something to do with that rather Demish stunt you pulled the last time you visited Den Eva's — throwing a fit over Vretla seeing Von?"

"I was not jealous!" he exploded, furious.

"Just suicidal?" Tessitatt said, grinning, "or did you think being pregnant would slow Vretla down?"

"Enough!" Di Mon terminated the banter, took his sword out of his *gorarelpul's* hands and strapped it on with practiced, economical movements.

"But I want to meet D'Ander!" Kertatt persisted. "He's won more duels than —"

"Your liege-uncle has made his decision," Sarilous silenced him.

"Our escort is waiting," said Tessitatt, handing Di Mon his green velvet traveling cloak with its wide, admiral's collar. They turned left out of the Library onto Family Hall, then right, down The Throat — a series of connecting rooms — to the Dining Hall. Here a spiral staircase wound up out of Green Hearth, House Monitum's ancestral residence on Gelion. Three Monatese errants joined them there and together they made good time across the Plaza, where business thrived above the residences of the empire's reigning oligarchy. It was common to travel in fives, which was also the size of a *rel*-fighter strike force called a "hand." Di Mon commanded their formation from the center — as a hand leader would. As a consequence, he was not the first to reach the Ava's Way, a wide boulevard running from the base of the docks, below the Citadel, to West Alcove where Eva's was situated.

Di Mon came upon his lead errant fraternizing with a stocky woman standing in front of a pair of black cars marked with rearing red dragons in two different poses.

She was dressed like a Sevolite — which meant she wore a sword and house insignia.

"Ses Nersal," Di Mon said, discomforted.

"Hiring a car from Ses Nersal was Sarilous' idea," Tessitatt explained to Di Mon. "She says you should be patronizing your *mekan'st's* garage more, especially since she's a birth rank inferior. It's expected, you know."

Di Mon sighed, the beginnings of a headache settling between his brows. Ses Nersal was his only acknowledged *mekan'st* on Gelion. Of course they ought to interact more often.

Di Mon got into the front of the first car. Ses jumped in the driver's seat opposite and headed off before any of Di Mon's people could join them. They went in the second car.

"I haven't seen you for a while," Ses said. "Things busy on Fountain Court?" she asked sympathetically.

"Yes," he said, making a conscious effort to relax. "How long has it been?"

"Six months," she said, casting a crinkle-eyed smile at him.

She was a robust woman with a wide, honest face, grounded from her fleet career by an old wound, taken in a duel, since nobleborns were not regenerative like highborns. An engineer by instinct and training, she now ran a fleet of rental cars on Gelion. There was always a wholesome residue of grease on her hands, and her body smelled of hot metal.

Ses Nersal dropped speed as they cruised through a dark stretch where the glow poles lighting the route had been stolen or burned out for over a month.

"You would think with a Demish Ava, we could at least expect the Ava's Way to be kept in good repair," Ses pointed out Delm's neglect.

"The palace staff are not getting the support they need," Di Mon said.

"I expect not," Ses said in disgust. "It's expensive turning rooms into Demoran gardens. Not hard to understand why my own liege spends his time elsewhere."

Di Mon only barely refrained from pointing out that the company his friend, Liege Nersal, kept these days worried him more than Delm's incompetence. He said, "Any Ava is better than none."

Ses switched subjects, talking about fencing matches she had seen since they last talked, which made for less politically stressful conversation.

"I gather you are hosting a meeting between the Silver and the Golden Demish," Ses said, when they had parked at the base of the steps leading to Eva's. "Be careful. You know what they say about old Demish quarrels."

"That they're as fatal as new Vrellish ones," Di Mon recalled the adage, smiling.

"*Ack Rel*, then," said Ses, "but let me know if you need any back up. My garage isn't far and I've some handy swords employed there." She grinned. "It would be something if you crossed swords with the Golden Demish Champion."

Sarilous, Di Mon thought, *would be horrified*.

"I'll leave you an extra car to send for me, if it gets exciting," Ses offered. "If not, maybe we can make some of our own. You could come see the envoy ship that I'm refitting at the garage. I could use some advice about the nervecloth."

"Possibly," said Di Mon. He had the perfect excuse to avoid her. He had been off *ferni* for months now due to an allergic reaction, which was why he had been seeing only Eva. Courtesans were sterile, but a Nersallian was another matter. Ses would like nothing more than to get pregnant by him and if she did, a lifetime's subterfuge would be overthrown, for Di Mon had claimed, all his life, that he was naturally infertile. That was why his nephew, Kertatt, had stood in for him with Vretla. It was a serious eccentric-

ity, given how desperately he needed a highborn heir to ensure Green Hearth's place on Fountain Court. But he could
never have explained it to Ses Nersal. No one alive, except
Sarilous, knew the truth.

At Eva's, Di Mon was announced to an empty room, but
he had meant to be early so he wasn't displeased at that.

Den Eva's was dressed up for the occasion. Greenery
stood in pots between statues on loan from Di Mon's own
collection; bowls of flower petals lightened the air with
subtle perfume; and the Patron's Floor had been cleared of
everything except one glass-topped table with a ringside
view of the dance floor where Eva and Von would perform.

The thought of Von made Di Mon scowl, but he had to
admit Von *was* good, and it would take something spectacular to distract the Demish from their long-standing quarrel.

Eva came to join them dressed in a dancer's sheath of
green and brown. His colors, Di Mon realized, and wondered why that made him feel uncomfortable.

"You are early, Di Mon," she greeted her illustrious
patron, speaking up five levels of grammar, and gestured
towards the glass table where they were to be seated. "We
settled on Silver Demish chamber music. I decided that was
safer than offending D'Ander with an inferior performance
of a Golden score."

Di Mon nodded, approving her decision. Golden Demish
music, like all of their fine arts, was formidable.

Eva remained standing as Di Mon and Tessitatt seated
themselves at the table.

"I've had Thrisian wine poured," she explained, gesturing to the glass horns seated in ornate silver bases. "A politically neutral choice, since it's Vrellish in origin but acceptable nearly everywhere."

"You've done an excellent job," Di Mon assured her.

Eva deflected the compliment. "Your herald was extremely helpful."

"Where is Von?" Tessitatt asked, looking around. "I hoped he might do his Demish adaptation of *Mekan'stan's Quarrel*. He did it for the Princess-Liege of H'Us' last party and even the Vrellish, who only came to be offended, tried to book him afterwards! Don't tell me Von's booked elsewhere?"

"No." Eva's settled her hand on her throat in a nervous gesture. "I am afraid," she said, "Von's disappeared."

"Not Kertatt again!" exclaimed Tessitatt.

"Oh, no," Eva said quickly, lowering her hand from her neck. "Nothing like that. It's probably one of his regulars. There are one or two Demish ladies who can get a bit possessive." She laughed.

"Are you worried?" Di Mon asked.

Eva never dissembled to him, not when he asked her point-blank. He was not sure why, since he had witnessed her doing it expertly with Demish clients.

She let the truth escape her like a burden she was glad to be rid of. "Yes," she admitted. "But it is true that it won't be the first problem I've had with him, either." She mustered a professional smile. "He took it into his head, once, to hide a pregnant novice who was always getting into trouble. He was gone for a day that time, and came back too battered to work for a week after."

"I will have Sarilous look into what's become of him," Di Mon offered.

Eva shook her head. "That might be very bad for business, especially if it should turn out to be a Demish lady who is detaining him."

"Detaining?" Di Mon asked acidly. It sounded to him more like a simple case of kidnapping. But the Demish were idiotically set on believing that sexual exploitation could only work in one direction. "Very well," he said, loath to injure Eva's interests, "but I will, at least, assure myself that neither Red nor Green Hearths are responsible." By which he meant Vretla or Kertatt.

That was what Eva had wanted. "Thank you," she said, and went on to explain that Von's understudy would perform *Mekan'stan's Quarrel* with her.

"Will you want anything before your guests arrive?" Eva concluded.

"Just the wine," Di Mon assured her.

Eva backed up a few steps before turning to walk away.

"Poor woman," Tessitatt clucked, speaking in English instead of Gelack. "I'll bet she's worried! It would be a blow to lose her *protégé* so near to her retirement."

Eva flinched noticeably, recovered, and bent down as if to adjust her dancing shoes.

Di Mon was intrigued by her reaction. Did she understand English? Von was reputed to know the dead language, now used only by Green Hearth's ruling family, but Di Mon had never taken that claim seriously. Courtesans like Von pretended all manner of nonsense to entertain their Demish clients, and it wouldn't take a clever youth like Von much to mouth plausible sounds out of old books of bad poetry.

"Why should Eva retire?" Di Mon asked his niece in English, while he watched the den mother's back for further proof of comprehension.

"She is getting old." Tessitatt paused. "Haven't you noticed?"

Di Mon had not, particularly, but he said, "Of course."

Eva straightened and resumed her walk towards one of the Den's spokes, which radiated outward from the Patron's Floor.

"Most retirees end up doing laundry and scrubbing floors," Tessitatt continued. "That must be difficult to contemplate after running a place like this one."

Eva's steps faltered.

Di Mon hesitated for a moment, then called to her. "Eva!"

Eva turned around. He watched her face repair itself as she crossed to within a few paces of him.

"Yes, Di Mon?" She exercised her right to his use-name with a thick and emotional hesitance. It embarrassed him to see her vulnerable. It was the competent administrator he admired; her dancer's confidence; her skill at the keys of a piano.

"Tessitatt told me, just now," he explained, as if he had not noticed she had understood the conversation, "that you may soon retire."

"I see," she said, and paused. "Do you think I should?"

"As an active courtesan, possibly. But my *gorarelpul*, Sarilous, is seventy and she is still competent. It does not seem obvious therefore, that aging should reduce a commoner's status. You could manage the den for Von. You show no sign of failing faculties in any —"

"Please," she said a little sharply, and smiled again. "I understand you well enough. Be content that you have promised nothing that you have not honored."

He was sure he had offended her somehow. It struck him that there was a great deal about being a commoner that he did not understand. "Eva —" he began. The entrance door boomed open behind his back and Di Mon spun around.

Prince D'Ander of Golden Hearth strode onto the Patron's Floor shining like a rogue sun. He was as robust as his H'Usian father, with his Demoran mother's golden hair and sky-pale blue eyes. In his full, gold-lined cloak and wearing his jeweled sword, D'Ander overpowered everything else visual in the room.

But it wasn't D'Ander himself who was the surprise — it was the people he had brought with him. One of them was a scruffy-looking woman in a well worn flight jacket, and the other was still completely covered.

An assassin with a concealed power weapon of some kind? Di Mon wondered. No. He distrusted D'Ander's wisdom, not his honor.

A pair of Eva's servants took D'Ander's cloak, which contained enough cloth of gold to require both to carry it away. The scruffy woman refused to surrender her flight jacket, and D'Ander shooed the servants away from the mysterious, cloaked enigma.

Tessitatt violated the usual protocol of leaving introductions to the highest Sevolite present, which in this case would have been D'Ander.

"My liege-uncle, Di Mon," she introduced Di Mon as he came to join them. "Di Mon, you know Royalblood — that is, Prince D'Ander," she corrected herself, allowing for Demish usage. "I don't believe you've met D'Ander's ... *mekan'st*?" Tessitatt introduced the woman. "This is the Midlord Perry D'Aur."

Gods! Di Mon thought, realizing why Tessitatt was being so forceful about her introductions. She wanted to be sure he knew he was in the company of one of the pivotal bones of contention between the Golden and Silver Demish. Perhaps D'Ander planned to surrender Perry to H'Us as a peace offering? That would be practical, but it didn't ring true.

Perry D'Aur returned Di Mon's stare with no sign of trepidation, just cynicism. Her eyes were the azure of the Blue Demish, but her hair was black, declaring her a mongrel with some Vrellish blood in her. She wore a sword like she was used to it, but it was easy enough to wear one, what counted was whether she would live up to the code of limited warfare that it represented. Perry D'Aur's Purple Alliance of rebels and misfits were notorious for violating the constraints of *Okal Rel*.

"I have heard of you, of course," Di Mon told Perry D'Aur, speaking down exactly as their birth ranks entitled him to. He may not trust her, but he would not stoop to exaggeration, as a Demish courtier might have, on the strength of her lack of court status.

Perry answered gruffly. "Nothing good, I'm sure."

Her own address granted him equality with D'Ander, which was mildly flattering, but not uncommon when deal-

ing with a Fountain Court liege, although in this case Di
Mon found it embarrassing.

D'Ander promptly made things worse by likewise granting honorary peerage. "I have told her how the Vrellish live
up to their honor," he flattered Di Mon. "I have told her how
you, in particular, are a follower of Ameron and do not judge
her by the foulness of the liege she was forced to overthrow."

"I —" Di Mon began to answer D'Ander in peerage, but
decided that was apt to come with strings attached. Instead
he addressed himself to Perry, accepting her flattering
choice of address in the first sentence and dropping it there-
after, which was courtly idiom for "thanks, but no thanks."

"Actually, I did consider your case at the time," he told
her. "Seriously enough to research it for my fellow Vrellish
lieges, in fact."

"Research it?" Perry asked, suspicious.

Di Mon wished he hadn't used a word so fraught with
evil, scientific implications. "I, uh, looked into your mutiny," he clarified. "After D'Ander absolved you, of course.
Before that it was strictly a Demish matter."

She grew brittle. "Of course."

"It may interest you to know," Di Mon concluded, "that
we agreed with D'Ander's judgment. You were justified in
turning on a dishonorable liege."

D'Ander beamed, triumphant.

"But we were of two minds regarding D'Ander's gen-
erosity in child-gifting to you so you could lawfully retain
what you took," Di Mon continued.

"Who objected?" Perry asked. "Liege Nersal?"

"No, I did," said Di Mon, and looked straight at D'Ander.
"As a Vrellish solution to a Demish problem, it was politically explosive and untenable."

Perry surprised him with a hearty laugh. "There are days
— uh, Your Grace —" she covered her social backwardness
with a phony cough " — when I agree with you on that
score."

"Fine then," D'Ander told Perry with a touch of pique, "If you don't want my gift-child, I'll take her back!" The child in question was now twenty-five years old. Perry swatted the Golden prince on the shoulder with the back of her bare hand.

Di Mon lifted a thin, courtly eyebrow.

Perry realized her mistake the next moment, and colored, while D'Ander's light blue eyes laughed at her discomfiture.

Were they still mekan'stan? Di Mon wondered. It might explain why D'Ander chose to bring Perry to court. On the other hand, D'Ander was now married to a princess of the Demoran First Circle. Demish marriage, of course, was one thing in theory and another in practice, with most of the hypocrisy on the male side.

Di Mon gave up. It made his head hurt trying to figure out Demish sexuality. Whether they were still lovers or not, he would not know what weight to put on its significance.

"Perhaps," Di Mon addressed D'Ander in a frigid tone, "as we failed to warn Prince H'Us to expect a surprise as unpleasant to him as Perry D'Aur, we might settle your entourage in a guest room, out of sight, before he shows up."

Perry opened her mouth to comment but D'Ander cut her off.

"I had hoped that by coming early," he said, persisting in peerage, "we might conclude our business before Silver Hearth descends at the appointed hour. Then we will have spoken but you can still maintain to H'Us that there was no conspiracy involved."

"I do not play games with my honor," Di Mon told D'Ander, declining the peerage address with finality. "Prince H'Us is my ally."

"Only to uphold a corrupt Ava," D'Ander insisted, "and resist the stale threat of a Nesak war."

"Stale?" Di Mon flared, and had to rein back his temper.

"Besides," D'Ander made a tangible effort to sound worldly wise, "the Nersallians can be trusted to contain the Nesaks."

Unless, Di Mon thought sourly, *they join them*. But he resisted this growing fear too much to share it with D'Ander. Hangst, Liege of Nersal, was still a man Di Mon greatly admired.

"You asked me to meet you in the name of Ameron," Di Mon reminded D'Ander. "I have agreed. But I told you I would do so only if Prince H'Us was also present. We will, therefore, wait to hear whatever —"

D'Ander reached out and yanked back the cloaked figure's hood. The face revealed was a young man's, attractive, and the color of tea with milk in it. Di Mon was speechless.

"I bring you proof the Reetions are in Killing Reach, again," proclaimed D'Ander. "We raided a station called *Trinket Ring* where Reetion artifacts have been showing up, and we found, instead, a Reetion!"

Di Mon caught the Reetion by his wrist. The brown-skinned man blinked at him with large, liquid eyes. He was well made, with intelligent eyes, and seemed remarkably unalarmed. Di Mon turned the hand over to reveal the lighter palm. He rubbed the skin with a thumb. It felt supple and warm. A thin thrill spread up his arm.

Abruptly, Di Mon released the brown hand. "A Reetion," he said, not sure how he felt about it.

"There was a second one called Thomas," volunteered D'Ander, "but he was lost when Delm's men attacked our warehouse."

"I heard about that," said Di Mon. "Blue Hearth claims it was a raid to confiscate an *okal'a'ni* weapon."

"That was Thomas!" D'Ander protested, frowning deeply. "He gave them the excuse. And I have already paid for it, dearly, on the Plaza!"

"Your Golden companion, Arand," recalled Di Mon. D'Ander's eyes filled up. It was a Demoran failing, this too-tangible exhibit of emotions. Di Mon felt driven by D'Ander's palpable grief to extend condolences. "Prince Arand fought with honor, and will soon be reborn."

"It was scarcely a weapon!" D'Ander's eyebrows thickened, mouth squaring in a typically Demish glower. "Just a light flash. The Reetion called Thomas was space-drunk."

"Or just Reetion." Di Mon's attention returned to the brown man who watched and listened avidly. "The Reetions of Ameron's time had no honor," said Di Mon.

"Some of them had!" objected D'Ander with vehemence. "You cannot judge them by one space-drunk madman!"

Di Mon felt his temper warm. "I judge them by the dust-strewn space lanes in Killing Reach that still claim victims; by the disease they spread, on purpose, through misuse of science; by worlds forever spoiled for habitation; and Sevolite blood-lines extinguished, which means the death of souls. That, too, is in the *Ameron Biography*. Or haven't you actually read it?"

"That was two hundred years ago," D'Ander insisted, being stubborn.

"You think they have changed?"

"Why not?" cried D'Ander. "We have. Look what we have on the throne instead of Ameron!"

Di Mon's teeth locked. He looked away to contemplate the Reetion. He had the body of a Monatese archive librarian who turned pages for exercise, and he looked as if getting this far had been an unpleasant experience, but there was no mistaking his interest in what was going on.

He is studying me, Di Mon thought, astonished. The Reetion chose that moment to speak up.

"My name," he said in English, "is Ranar. I am an emissary to your people from my own." He paused. "Are you Liege Monitum? And can you understand this language?"

Di Mon felt as strange as if he had walked into the stables at his home estate on Monitum and been addressed by a cat, a creature long since vanished in the Empire which had — at the best of times — never talked.

"I understand English, of course," Di Mon reacted to the simple absurdity of not being able to do that. "My family keeps records in that language." He paused. "Ranar, you are called? Nothing more?"

"We abjure titles," Ranar answered. "If you kept records from the Killing Reach war, you may think that you know otherwise, but a great deal has changed on our side."

"What is he saying?" asked D'Ander in Gelack.

Di Mon considered lying to him, but D'Ander had the Demish knack for picking up languages. There was no way to be certain how much he already understood.

"Tessitatt will translate for you," said Di Mon, adding a hand gesture for his niece that meant 'keep it basic.' Tessitatt displaced Perry at D'Ander's side.

"The Reetion said his people have changed since First Contact," she summarized.

"There, you see," D'Ander leapt to conclusions. "I told you!"

Ranar shed his cloak, which was making him sweat, and kicked it away from him on the floor. He had a good face, once the shock of its brown color wore off: even features with a wide, high forehead and quiet mouth. His hair looked touchable.

"I am glad to meet someone I can converse with, Liege Monitum," Ranar announced. "I regret I cannot speak your native tongue."

"It would be impossible to speak to you in Gelack," answered Di Mon. "I would not know how to shape my pronouns."

"Pronouns?" the Reetion said, with piqued interest that suggested a previous encounter. "What makes Gelack pronouns so difficult?"

Di Mon hesitated, but could find no objection to explaining something so commonly understood. "Pronouns reflect both who you are and to whom you are referring. For example, the English word 'you' would translate as 'breh' if I am speaking down, and 'bree' if I am speaking up. 'Breh' is the *pol* form and 'bree' is the *rel* one, at least in common gender across most Vrellish dialects. Do you understand?"

"A little," Ranar answered. "More than before. And this is true of all pronouns?"

Di Mon nodded, adding, "It can be contentious for plurals."

Ranar looked impressed and just a bit excited.

A scholar, Di Mon thought, with surprise and pleasure. He had not considered himself one since he assumed his title, but history had been the passion of his youth.

"You said it would be impossible to address me in Gelack," Ranar recalled. "Why is that?"

"What is your birth rank?" Di Mon asked.

Ranar had to think about that. "I am a prominent citizen where I come from," he said slowly, "selected for this work because of my exceptional accomplishments."

Di Mon nodded. "Not all Reetions speak English," he acknowledged.

"Nor all Gelacks," answered Ranar.

I've been put in my place, Di Mon thought, *and very delicately*. It pleased him, somehow.

"You should know," Di Mon told the Reetion, "that Prince H'Us, the Admiral of the largest space fleet in Sevildom, will be arriving soon. He will want to enforce the Americ Treaty we signed with your ancestors after the Killing War."

Ranar said, "I am not aware of the terms of that treaty."

"How is that possible?" asked Di Mon.

"The Old Regime, as we call the space-faring culture that your people fought two hundred years ago, collapsed. Our record of First Contact is extremely poor."

"I see." If true, Di Mon found it exceedingly inconvenient. "The treaty," he told the young Reetion, "entitles either side to execute trespassers."

"That ... explains how we lost contact," answered Ranar.

It was a moment before Di Mon was sure the comment was meant to be sardonic, then he felt trapped. Curse Earth's bored and vengeful gods! He liked the Reetion!

"And this treaty," Ranar asked, "on your side, it is still in force?"

"Of course," said Di Mon. "Why not? There are those who can recall it being signed, most of them H'Usian princesses, who have the most tenacious memories of all."

Ranar looked confused by this assertion, as if he thought his English was failing him.

Who are you, Di Mon thought at Ranar so intensely he almost said it aloud. Physically, he was commoner, but Ameron had accepted a few Reetions as his equals, for diplomatic purposes.

"I will not let H'Us kill him," D'Ander insisted belatedly, reacting to Tessitatt's translation.

"And how would you prevent it?" Di Mon snapped at him in Gelack.

D'Ander cleared his jeweled sword.

Di Mon astonished himself and frightened Tessitatt by clearing his own sword and setting it athwart the Golden Champion's.

"I will not let you duel H'Us over a Reetion," Di Mon said, his teeth gritted, lips pulled back.

It had more effect than it should have. By Di Mon's own calculus, D'Ander was better than he was and had certainly got in more practice, of late, on a challenge floor.

But D'Ander drew back, chagrined, lowering his famous, jeweled sword.

"You would cross swords with me for H'Us?" he asked, crestfallen. "But —" D'Ander shook his head. "I could not kill you! We are oath brothers of Ameron."

"It remains to be seen who would kill whom," Tessitatt told the Golden Champion, differencing her pronouns to suggest a touch of insult.

"Let them calm down," Perry advised Tessitatt. "In cold blood, D'Ander would never harm your uncle, or any member of the House of Monitum, because of your connection with Ameron."

"Gods!" Di Mon exclaimed, despising to be patronized, and mastered his temper sufficiently to sheath his sword. It went into its place with a bang that vibrated through his hand. D'Ander's belief in Ameron was self-styled aggrandizement. He couldn't even read English! Which meant he had read the *Ameron Biography* in translation and very likely one concocted by a Golden Demish poet who dwelt on the relationship between Ameron and the captive woman he had learned about Reetions from, to the exclusion of all political motivations and sheer common sense.

"Ameron meant to re-establish contact with the Reetions," D'Ander insisted, sheathing his own sword and taking a step towards Di Mon.

"You do not know that!" said Di Mon. All that was known was that Ameron met with the Reetions again and was lost as a consequence, although in all fairness it had almost certainly been Gelack treachery at fault.

"I know!" insisted D'Ander, with the vehemence of the faithful. No doubt he thought he had had a vision making a jump and communicated with Ameron's Lost Soul. Di Mon would teach the Demish popinjay a lesson if he tried putting that across, and the odds be damned! A part of him would not believe the odds could be bad. But he knew this was an impulse he could ill afford. Not, at least, until his heir was safely born. He had to tamp his Vrellish temper down.

"The Americ treaty," Di Mon said, tightly, "bans contact with Reetions."

"It was meant to be temporary," D'Ander countered.

"No," said Di Mon.

"All right," D'Ander said, flushed and excited by his failure to prevail with reason. He took hold of Ranar from behind and gave him a shove, right into Di Mon's arms. The unexpected contact shocked Di Mon more than D'Ander's drawn sword had.

"You want to give him to Prince H'Us?" D'Ander challenged. "Fine. Why not kill him yourself, instead, right now! You're as much a signatory of that treaty as H'Us ever was!"

The Reetion gripped Di Mon's forearms to steady himself, and looked up, surprised and faintly alarmed, but not
distrustful.

Di Mon put Ranar aside firmly, wishing he had knocked
back five or six glasses of Eva's wine before D'Ander arrived.
The penalty he paid for inaction was to lock up, inside, in
disabling knots.

"I cannot be swayed by a name," he told D'Ander. "Not
even Ameron's. If he had reasons for revisiting the Reetion
side, he did not share them. Your reasons are your own.
Perhaps you think that trade with the Reetions would make
you independent of the empire. Let's assume it is that, and
not an interest in *okal'a'ni* weapons."

D'Ander actually gasped at the last remark.

"You need a Vrellish court ally," Di Mon continued his
analysis, "for the same reason you needed Vrellish support
to protect you on the Plaza, and Vrellish endorsement of your
decision to child gift to Perry D'Aur. You cannot act entirely
alone. That is what this is about — not about us sharing any
bond through Ameron."

D'Ander had recovered by now. "You think not?" he
asked, suddenly once more light of heart. Then he scooped
Ranar's traveling cloak off the floor and thrust the bundled
cloak into the Reetion's chest until the bemused man raised
his arms to take it back.

"I make a gift to you of my Reetion," D'Ander announced,
flattering Di Mon once more with honorary equality of birth
rank. "Learn from him what threat they pose to the Empire,
and to your Monatese monopolies, too. Because I am your
ally, and I would not see your people harmed by exclusion
from new treaties that would upset your trade in nervecloth
and your brokerage of Lorel drugs from Luverthan."

"The Reetions still practice science, then," Di Mon said
coldly, half-afraid of this all along.

"Ameron believed they could be honorable," D'Ander
countered.

"Ack Rel!" Di Mon exclaimed in disgust and pinched the bridge of his nose where a fierce headache was building up to explode. To be Vrellish and not act in anger could be literally painful.

"I cannot understand what you are saying to each other," said the Reetion.

The unfairness of that struck Di Mon hard. It was the Reetion's life that they debated, and whatever the sins of his kind, he might not be personally guilty of anything more than simply being adventurous.

"Explain it to him," Di Mon snarled at Tessitatt. She translated the gist of the argument.

"I will go with you," the Reetion said to Di Mon, when she was done. He spoke out of that amazing calm of his, as if his consent really mattered to anyone. "I will tell you anything you want to know. Openness is a tenet of Reetion culture."

There was noise beyond the Den's front doors.

Tessitatt exclaimed, "H'Us!"

"Get the Reetion out of sight, and yourself too!" Di Mon snapped at Perry D'Aur and was relieved to find she could obey an order without back talk.

The H'Usian party filled the end of the entrance hall as only an all-male party of broad shouldered Demish princes knew how. Eva's servants made themselves busy taking cloaks.

D'Ander was wearing a grin that Di Mon dearly wanted to rip off. No doubt he took Di Mon's failure to expose Ranar to H'Us as a sign that he had gained ground.

"My thanks for your graciousness to Perry, earlier," D'Ander surprised him by slipping in, double-fast.

"I do not believe she considered me gracious," said Di Mon.

"You do not know her as I do." D'Ander's tone laughed at things he did not say aloud. "Take my word for it — you have restored her faith in courtly honor."

Di Mon gave the Golden prince a sour frown. He had absolutely no intention of befriending Killing Reach rebels of questionable honor and a Golden half-breed with a knack for setting other Demish at his throat. But all Di Mon had time for was to tell D'Ander curtly, "Do not presume too much."

The H'Usians were on the move: five errants, two princes, and their leader, Prince H'us. All of them were male, of course. Di Mon had not really expected to see Demish women because their presence would have signaled that this was, in fact, the social event it strove to portray itself as.

Prince H'Us looked as broad as two men, with his admiralty jacket expanding already wide shoulders. His house braid climaxed in silver at his collar bones, beginning at the hem in threads of blue with the brown thread of the Lorel contribution sketched in much too lightly, particularly in contrast to the emphasis placed on thin infusions of gold across the jacket's breast.

Prince H'Us was not technically liege of Silver Hearth. That distinction fell to his ailing mother, known as the "princess-liege", which seemed to be an honorary title. Di Mon had once assumed this was the style of leadership that Ava Delm aspired to since he left the business of Avaship to his inferiors, but Prince H'Us found the notion offensive. In attempting to explain why, the Demish prince had sputtered on for half an hour about gender distinctions completely lost on Di Mon. Mysteriously, it seemed that equating Delm's style of holding title to that of a princess-liege's was an insult both to Delm and the princesses.

H'Us halted a good few sword lengths from D'Ander and Di Mon to ponder them with a massive frown.

Child novices, barefoot and dressed in white togas, offered them wine horns in up-stretched hands. The glass horns ended in points and could not be put down without a matching stand.

Di Mon took it as a good sign that D'Ander accepted his horn with his sword hand. He took two horns and carried one personally to Prince H'Us, who was glaring at his gloriously Golden nephew, D'Ander, from under an impressive set of bushy eyebrows.

"I will not introduce you," Di Mon told H'Us, nodding towards D'Ander. "I don't believe you have forgotten the child you brought up in Silver Hearth."

H'Us took the offered wine horn from Di Mon. "It is good to see you again, D'Ander," he allowed, and added grudgingly, "it has been too long."

D'Ander said, "We've seen each other uncle. Across the challenge floor in Lion Reach, last I recall. I am glad," he said honestly, "it has not yet been personally, sword to sword."

"D'Ander asked to see me to discuss recent evidence of Reetions in Killing Reach," Di Mon said quickly. "I told him I would do so only if you would attend, as well, out of respect for our alliance and awareness of your differences."

H'Us bristled. "Yes, and here I am, as you see."

"Much to my surprise," admitted Di Mon.

"Hmph," H'Us said, and waved to his errants to deploy themselves around the edges of the Patron's Floor. His highborn kinsmen stayed with him, although he did not bother introducing either man.

"I gather we are going to have Von's Demish adaptation of your *Mekan'stan's Quarrel*," H'Us decided to make small talk as they all drifted towards the table. "It's been a good deal talked about."

"So I have heard," Di Mon said in a tone meant to dry the subject up.

D'Ander set his chair back a little from the glass-topped table and sat down. "Von," he mused aloud. "I have heard there were duels fought over that dancer at a court reception."

"Some Vrellish women showed up uninvited and made a scene afterwards, if that is what you mean," H'Us replied with a glare towards Tessitatt, as if she were somehow re-sponsible for the antics of all Vrellish females. "But it was a very good performance in spite of the nonsense after-wards."

"I am afraid," Di Mon confessed, waiting for Prince H'Us to finish challenging the furniture by seating himself, "that Von has vanished. But Eva tells me that his understudy will perform."

"Vanished?" H'Us took a surprisingly acute interest. But if H'Us had further questions they were postponed. The dance began with a fanfare of music, and the dancers' en-trance from a spoke onto the central performance floor.

The piece opened bravely enough. Eva bobbed around her partner's first attacks, playing up the visual jokes in the choreography. This was the scene in which the lovers meet in an exhibition tournament, the man a Demish prince and the woman a Vrellish highborn. Tessitatt and D'Ander laughed at the contrast of Demish and Vrellish styles, over-laid with sexual innuendo.

But by the second scene, Von's absence was beginning to show. The understudy was reaching for a strength and flu-idity he didn't have, and it impacted Eva's performance. Di Mon had not realized before how much Von extended his strength into his partner's movements, using tricks the understudy's emulation exposed.

"She should retire," H'Us remarked, "before she injures herself trying to keep up."

Di Mon looked at him abruptly. "Eva?"

"Of course," H'Us declined an offered delicacy and fixed Di Mon with a stern stare. "Are you going to provide for her when she does?"

"Am I what?" asked Di Mon, taken aback.

"My uncle thinks one ought to take care of one's discarded mistresses," D'Ander glibly interpreted.

"The Vrellish do not keep mistresses," said Di Mon.

"Well then," D'Ander shrugged, as if it was a moot point, "one's *lyka*."

Di Mon's lips compressed, but at least he understood what was going on now. He was being lectured on his responsibility to a socially inferior sex partner.

"Eva is a courtesan I sometimes patronize," he told the Demish princes. "A *lyka* is more than that. To be *lyka'stan* implies mutual consent and obligation. I have never named her *lyka*."

"Come, man," H'Us objected, "don't split hairs. The woman's yours."

Di Mon carefully coaxed his jaw loose, vexed with Tessitatt for smirking behind H'Us's back, where she had posted herself beside one of H'Us's kinsmen.

D'Ander was enjoying himself, too. "I believe the *lyka'stan* relationship is rather closer to a Demish marriage than having a kept woman," he informed his more powerful, but less flamboyant uncle. "Except you may have more than one *lyka*, and it doesn't interfere with other sorts of Vrellish marriage either."

H'Us gave his nephew a scathing look, "I don't care what they call it. It is a natural obligation to look after the woman."

"Eva is Liege Monitum's business," D'Ander capped the argument. "Not ours."

H'Us let the matter drop and looked back to the dancers, who were struggling for a credible finale to scene two. Eva was making mistakes that were dangerous.

Dear gods, Di Mon thought. *She must have heard all of that.*

"I was sorry to hear about the death of Prince Arand," H'Us spoke directly to D'Ander, ignoring the dancers now.

"I am sure," D'Ander's tone was chilly.

H'Us said, "It is always a tragedy to lose a Golden highborn to the sword."

D'Ander sought Di Mon's eyes as he said, "He fought with honor."

"Goldens are not meant for fighting, D'Ander," H'Us scolded.

The Demoran prince broke eye contact with Di Mon, his eyes flashing clear blue fire under their long, golden lashes and bright eyebrows. "Whereas we are meant for — what?"

"Better things," said H'Us. "Art."

D'Ander handed his wine horn off to one of the hovering novices and leaned forward on both elbows. "On Gelion," he told his estranged uncle, "the artists are all prostitutes."

H'Us' back stiffened. His strong features shifted toward insult, and settled again into bitter disappointment. "You are still young."

D'Ander rolled his eyes as he flung himself back in his chair, struggling with his own anger.

"Oh, yes, I know, you are forty-seven years old," said H'Us. "I was forty-seven long before your father won your mother's Golden heart, and then died of sorrow when she left him to return home!"

"He died," D'Ander corrected, "in space."

"Because he was grieving. He would never have lost his nerve in that shake-up if he hadn't been pining for your mother! Damn it, boy!" H'Us pressed his lips together. "I want you to consider a truce. To begin negotiations with me about all the outstanding issues between us. To reconcile Silver and Golden hearths."

The Golden Champion's eyes widened in surprise, then promptly narrowed. "What do you want that you haven't already got?"

"Does there have to be a reason? You know how we feel about Demora."

"I know," D'Ander returned tartly, "that it has pleased you to exploit Demora's resources, export our culture, and kidnap our princesses to be your brides! But Demora is a proud planet, and we are a proud people!"

"D'Ander, do you seriously believe that we do such things?" H'Us asked, wounded.

"Do I believe that it happens?" D'Ander tossed back. "Or that you see it the same way that I do?"

"While you, who are also part H'Usian, serve Demora's interests with a purer heart?" Prince H'Us laid his big hands on the glass table. "Tell me, D'Ander, do you obey the Golden Emperor? Or do you act in his best interests for his own protection, just as we H'Usian have always done?"

D'Ander's expression locked up.

"If the Golden Emperor is still alive, of course," H'Us gently probed. "He is never seen, now, except by his inner court."

"He is alive," D'Ander said flatly.

H'Us shifted in his seat, looking awkward. "The Golden Emperor is Ava Delm's grandfather."

"Only because," D'Ander warmed to the theme of old grudges, "H'Us looted Demora of its greatest treasure when it forced the Golden Emperor's daughter to marry Delm's Father!"

"No one expected she would die!" cried H'Us in genuine anguish.

D'Ander shot up. "That's no excuse!"

The music stopped. Bird song decorated the silence, the singers hopping from branch to branch of the potted plants, indifferent to the quarrel.

The tension between the two Demish princes had a deep, heavy quality, very different from the hot, quick nature of a Vrellish quarrel. It put Di Mon in mind of the contrast between dodging lightening bolts and living on a geological fault. On the whole, he was more comfortable with sudden storms.

"What if," H'Us wheedled, "we start over? Together we could accomplish much — even usher in a new Golden Age, at court."

D'Ander was completely still for a moment, then he asked, hoarsely, "What?"

H'Us rose, grating the feet of his chair on the floor. Di Mon got up, too, succumbing to the sheer impossibility of keeping still in the face of so much stirred emotion. If the Demish princes had been Vrellish, there would already be blood on the floor.

D'Ander's face had drained white and he trembled with anger. "You want the Golden Emperor," he said in a hushed tone. "You want to bring Him here, to Gelion."

"D'Ander —" H'Us tried to sound reasonable.

"No!" The younger prince retreated, still aghast. "I thought there was still something decent in you, despite it all! I thought you were only blind or stupid!"

"Be careful, boy!" H'Us threatened.

D'Ander shook his golden mane, his face flushing hot. "If you want anything more from Demora — anything — you understand? You will have to take it from me, by the sword, on the challenge floor."

"Wait!" H'Us took a step forward, but D'Ander was already halfway to the entrance hall where servants sprang forward bearing his heavy, ornate cloak. Prince H'Us' attendant princes made to follow, but H'Us called them back.

"Let him go," he told them, with mixed emotions of resentment and pride. "D'Ander could kill either one of you and possibly both at once."

On the dance floor, Eva had called a halt and stood beside Von's understudy, looking as brave as she could. Di Mon met her stare, briefly. Her eyes dropped.

"Go and entertain yourselves," H'Us dismissed his kinsmen. "But keep it light. I won't be long."

"Eva!" Di Mon had to call to her to make her look up. Once their eyes met she grasped quickly that the H'Usians must be steered away from the first pair of guests she had hidden. "Will you see that the H'Usians are made comfortable?" Di Mon asked.

She did, with every symptom of her usual aplomb.

H'Us settled back into his seat. "D'Ander was such a promising boy," he lamented.

"He is an honorable man," said Di Mon. "And a fine sword." Those were the only good things he could find to say about D'Ander right now.

"He's too good a sword!" H'Us gave a discontented grunt. "It will be the death of him, one day, you know." He stopped, and fixed a stern look on Di Mon. "Your message said that he asked you about Reetions."

Di Mon nodded.

"You know what he wants?" H'Us asked rhetorically. "He wants to trade with them! Trade!" H'Us sighed. "I do not know where I went wrong, bringing him up."

"Don't you consider trade honorable?"

"Not with Reetions!" H'Us snapped.

"Perhaps they've changed," said Di Mon.

"Huh!" H'Us grunted and emptied his wine horn. A novice filled it up immediately, but H'Us set it down in its stand and left the refill untouched. "I suppose he asked you to help him cultivate them," said H'Us. "Speak English to them, things like that." He paused. "How did you let him down?"

"I have not yet," said Di Mon. "Not entirely."

H'Us went very still, then said, slowly, "I know that look — you're curious. It's the curse of your Lorel blood."

"D'Ander has already encountered Reetions," said Di Mon. "Wouldn't it be useful to find out what they want? Perhaps they have forgotten the terms of the Americ Treaty. We ought to be sure they are informed of the consequences of trespass."

"Force is all that *okal'a'ni* people understand!" H'Us insisted. "Force and more force."

"Perhaps," admitted Di Mon.

"You need proof?" H'Us fished in his embroidered jacket to produce a slim, silver box and plunked it down between them. Di Mon winced, afraid H'Us was going to crack Eva's glass tabletop.

"What is that?" Di Mon asked.

"It is Reetion. Something they have been selling out in Killing Reach."

"It looks innocuous enough," said Di Mon, trying not to think about Ranar.

"Then watch," said H'Us, and touched the case in a particular spot.

Solid light projections of a brown man and a brown woman sprouted from the box. They were a couple, strolling down a garden path.

Di Mon had never seen such technology before! The tiny brown people were a little translucent, and the scene was hazy at its edges, but on the whole it far surpassed all the imaging capacities he knew of, including his own nervecloth.

The man and woman melted into each other's arms and were transported to a bed inside a bungalow. The transition did not impress Di Mon. One could do such things easily enough. A voice, speaking what he guessed must be Reetion, began a narrative voice-over. Then the focus zoomed in on cross-sectional diagrams of male and female sex organs.

"Instructions for flesh probing," H'Us said with profound disgust.

"I do not ... think so," said Di Mon. The figures, before, had looked realistic. Now the pictures were cartoon-like and the tone of voice struck him as clinical.

"That isn't the worst!" H'Us stroked his hand over the box in the opposite direction.

Suddenly, both lovers were men.

Di Mon sprang up, catching the glass tabletop. His drink crashed. His chair fell back.

"It does another version too!" H'Us exclaimed. "With two women! That is Reetions for you!"

"Turn it off!" Di Mon demanded.

"I know, I know, I only wanted you to see how —"

"Turn it off!" Di Mon stood with his hands fisted at the ends of stiff arms.

H'Us reached over and touched the box on either side, quenching the pictures. There was silence except for Di Mon's breathing, which came harsh and fast.

"I'm sorry," said H'Us contritely. "It spooked me, too, the first time. I should have warned you."

"I would like to study the technology," Di Mon said.

"Keep it!" H'Us told him. "By all means. But I've something to ask in return." H'Us leaned forward.

Di Mon tore his stare from the silver box to look up.

"Von," said H'Us.

"Von?" Di Mon echoed, not sure he had heard correctly. "What about Von?"

"You know about the H'Reths, I suppose?" H'Us said quickly. "How they've both fallen from favor with Delm. There have been disquieting rumors."

"Rumors?" Di Mon echoed again, still numb.

"Things to do with secrets learned in bedrooms and turned to Liege H'Reth's advantage. Von seems to be implicated." H'Us frowned. "Unfortunately, the boy is my mother's best tonic right now. She's fond of him, purely for the sake of his poetry and disposition, of course, but there you have it. And she is dying. I would rather any consequences owed him over the H'Reth business were put off for the time being. So," H'Us finished brusquely, "if you learn anything concerning his disappearance, will you notify me?"

"Of course," Di Mon said, hardly listening.

"Well, then." The big Silver Demish leader got up. "I'll be going. You keep the artifact. And don't let that mad nephew of mine get around you with his talk about Ameron."

Di Mon watched Prince H'Us until he had left the room, unable to get past the shock of the silver box until Tessitatt came back to stand beside him. Collecting himself with force, he took the box from the table before she asked questions about it.

"D'Ander left without Perry D'Aur," he remembered. "Tell the staff to put her up here at my expense for the interim. If she is offended by the locale, being a Demish female," he shrugged, "by all means let her see to her own accommodation. And conduct the Reetion, quietly, to Green Hearth." He paused. "We'll put him in Ameron's room."

Tessitatt was surprised by the last arrangement. So was Di Mon, but it had felt like the right thing to do, somehow.

"I wish to see Eva before I go," Di Mon ordered the servant who brought him his cloak, and was conducted to her office. She turned to face him with a look of fear he had never seen there before.

"You have learned English," Di Mon addressed her in that language, finding the lack of pronoun-differencing odd. The only commoner he spoke English to was Sarilous, and now the Reetion Ranar, of course.

Eva held his stare, although that seemed to strip her of the power to lie. "Yes," she said. "I have."

"Von taught you?" Di Mon guessed.

"I asked him to, Your Grace," she lapsed back into Gelack.

Di Mon frowned. "Do you know that Von may be mixed up in something concerning how the H'Reths gained Delm's favor."

"I knew nothing specific about that, no," said Eva. "But I obtained Von from H'Reth Manor. Lady H'Reth said he was unhappy as a house servant but there may have been more to it. He never told me what." She hesitated, then felt driven to ask, "Do you know what has happened to Von? Whether he is still alive?"

The question took courage. He wasn't sure she ought to feel protective towards her *protégé* just now.

"Did Von teach you English at the H'Reths' request?" Di Mon demanded.

The realization that she might be suspected dawned on Eva with a cruel impact. She sank into an armchair across from where Di Mon stood, interrogating her.

"No," she said, breaking eye contact at last, her shoulders slumped. "I asked him to teach me for my own reasons."

"To impress me?" he asked bluntly.

She looked up, her face desolate. "Yes, Liege Monitum."

"Prince H'Us thinks I should provide for your retirement," Di Mon recalled. "It is, I suppose, a more common thing among the Demish to patronize the same courtesan for many years, as I have done you, and hence a reasonable expectation on your part that I might also behave in a Demish manner regarding your retirement. Is this correct?"

To her credit, she never flinched. "Yes, Liege Monitum."

"But you believed I required encouragement," he decided. "Proof that you could function in my household, where English is spoken. If so, why keep it secret from me?"

She stood. Her face was burning, but her eyes were guiltless. "I am still not as fluent in English as I had hoped. I never will be, now that Von is gone." She paused to shed her blasted hopes. "Foolish, I may have been," she admitted, "and arrogant. But I know nothing about any conspiracy between the H'Reths and Von, and I can not imagine him obliging Lady H'Reth a hair's width more than business required. He disliked her, and I think he was mistreated under her roof. If you don't believe me, it hardly matters. Without Von, or you, I have no livelihood to protect — I am finished. But I would like to be believed, for my pride's sake. And I beg you, take my compliments to the lover who has bested me in your affections. She is a fortunate woman."

Di Mon laughed. It was a cruel sound. Eva stood, frozen, waiting for it to stop. It cut off abruptly rather than fading out.

When he spoke it was incongruously gentle. "You are wrong, Eva. I find you more attractive than most women. And never more so than now."

Her head came up, wearing a puzzled but wary expression.

"I think," he said, "my own pride is your competitor. It seemed to me a courtesan might find me dull. For a Vrellish man, I have a strained relationship with lust."

Very slowly she dared to smile. "I think I can understand that."

"Oh?"

His brittleness drove her on.

"You are a man ruled by reason. To indulge passion you must give up self-control. How can you, when reason is all you trust? It must be frightening."

"You think," he said, amused, "that I am frightened of you?"

"Not me. Of your own needs. I am merely the means of their discharge."

That displeased him. "No, Eva. No one should be that." He inhaled as if against a powerful, oppressive burden, then let his breath out. "Do you still want to become my *lyka*?"

She said, "I do."

"And by that you expect to be kept comfortably on Monitum?"

"The time and nature of my —" she began but sensed that honesty would serve her better. "Yes," she admitted.

His lips tightened. "I will take you to Monitum."

She stopped breathing — it was disconcerting. He reacted by becoming brisk.

"I may bring you back to court with me again, as well," he said, "though not repeatedly. I am sensible of the harm traveling does commoners."

She nodded. He had the annoying suspicion she would have nodded even if the offer included execution should he tire of her.

"You should understand," he said, "what I intend. To be a Vrellish *lyka* is not what you might think of as retirement. I will not put you in a cottage on my property, like an aging Demish mistress, and leave you there to tend flowers by day and sleep by night. I am not demanding as these things go, but I will want you to be available."

"That pleases me."

He smiled cynically. "Let's assume so. There is one other issue."

"Yes?"

"I will require your loyalty."

Eva nodded.

"I want you to think about what I've said."

"That isn't necessary."

"I believe it is," he insisted.

"As you wish," said Eva.

"It must be an honest choice," Di Mon continued. "My *lyka* would be part of my household and expected to think like a Sevolite on occasion and that can be trying for commoners. If you refuse, I will find you comfortable work here on Gelion. I am sure anyone who has managed a den will have no trouble managing inventories."

Eva was clearly overcome. "That is very generous."

"No, it is selfish. I wish you to choose, not be driven."

Eva laughed, then raised her right hand to cover her mouth in horror. Di Mon was puzzled, not offended. He waited with his head cocked a fraction to the right, looking curious.

"Forgive me!" Eva blurted. She relaxed then, and laughed again in a pleasant manner. "Truly, Di Mon, I don't need to think about it."

"I would rather you did," he said firmly. "And in either case there will be things you will need to arrange here. Send word when you are ready, and I will have you fetched to Green Hearth to tell me what you decide. Is there someone competent, here, to take over?"

"Competent?" She seemed dazed. "But — Von may still come back?"

"I don't know otherwise," he told her, truthfully. "But it is unlikely he would be able to run a den unless he is cleared of this association with the H'Reths." He shrugged one shoulder. "Prince H'Us might be motivated to help with that, so long as his mother is still alive when Von turns up."

"Thank you," she said, and then again, involuntarily, "thank you, Di Mon."

He left at once for fear she was going to cry in front of him. Tears were foreign territory to Di Mon. In that, as in so much, he was too Vrellish — his eyes filled only in reaction to an irritant.

He never once thought of taking Ses Nersal up on her offer to come and spend time with her. He wanted to get back to Green Hearth to explore the technology in the silver box. Then he would ask the Reetion about the meaning of the pictures it showed.

If nothing else, Ranar's answers might make it easier to hand him over to H'Us for execution.

Von's Data

"I thought about it all the way back," Ann concluded. "The way I fell for N'Goni; hitting on Ranar; and then thinking I'm in love with a Gelack — it's dysfunctional."

The presiding counselor failed to pounce. In fact, Counselor Ling looked more pained than compassionate. "Do you mind if I get myself a hot chocolate?" she asked.

"Uh, no. Sure," Ann said, getting up. Her hands spread against the sides of her stretch pants. "Bring me one, too," she said, trying to sound casual.

The room she was left in was like every other counselor's room she had ever known, with minor variations. It had some morph furniture grouped around a stage between an arch leading out to the lobby of the building that housed pilots' services, and a completely transparent wall that faced out onto the commons' lawn. The lawn was not covered in grass the way it would have been back home on Rire. Instead, it was a sprawl of mossy ground cover bubbling with tiny purple flowers. All of the planet Mega seemed to be like that.

The odd thing was that two people standing in front of a large tree were staring at her through the transparent wall. The young man actually pointed and said something to the girl on his arm. That was rude!

Ann made a face at the offending youth to scare him off. "Pervert," she muttered, and felt consoled.

Counselor Ling returned with two mugs. "Here you are," she said, handing Ann's over. Ling favored a highly supportive environment. Her morph seating grew a shelf to place her mug on. Ann held hers cupped in her hands.

"I was wondering," Ling began, cautiously, "if you would like to discuss the Reetion vote, in progress, concerning proper treatment of your Gelack."

"He's not my Gelack," said Ann.

"I think," Ling said, "you may be suffering from some factual misconceptions about Von."

"Who?" asked Ann.

"Your Gelack," the counselor told her. "His real name is Von."

Ann shrugged, thinking, *Con artist*.

"I think there's something you should see," Ling told her, turning to her stage. "Reference the Gelack, Von," she ordered, "and display his sexual response profile."

The stage produced a 3D graph.

"If you study that," Ling said, pointing out a valley, "you will see that Von is not the least bit homosexual. That's an aversion response." Her hand shifted, altering the image. "The emotional integration, here, is more typically female than male, but that's shading into general personality, and while this might confuse the issue —" her fingers played through a spiky region, " — it is actually a pan-sexualization pattern, typical in chronic sex abuse victims with an onset in childhood. Subtract the noise and mute the unusual emotional overlay —" her stage did just that. " — and you get sexual triggers that are classic for a male adolescent. A heterosexual male adolescent." She sat back. "In fact, Von is so adverse to homosexuality it is pathological, from a Reetion point of view, however understandable his phobia, given his experiences."

"That's Beauty's profile?" Ann said stupidly, still flummoxed. "Where did it come from?"

"It was included in the data you brought back."

"I never saw it!" Ann protested.

"You never asked to," Ling said simply. "Not on *Second Contact Station*; not in transit; and certainly not since you got back." She signaled the stage off. "I suspect you are so wrapped up in your resentment at his failure to remain the perfect lover that you can't think about him as a person. As the boy you seduced and encouraged to care about you."

"I seduced?" Ann shot up. "Hey! You weren't there!" She pivoted towards the glass wall.

Ling stood, too. "Ann! Wait. That was clumsy of me."

Ann would not wait. She was sick of people telling her to read the record, and irked by Ling taking Beauty's side in their break-up. He had lied to her! Used her to learn the jump! And he had done it all for some great meaty oaf of a Gelack named H'Reth, with his pie-eyes and spectacular nose hair! She walked straight through doors in the glass wall onto the commons, where the hot Megan sun cheerfully tried to cook her in the sweat it instantly inspired. It took a moment to adjust after the air-conditioned visiting room, set to mimic Rire's mild climate. Then Ann set off across the commons at a brisk walk, trying not to think about Beauty's sexual profile.

"Hey! Ann!" A voice shattered her muddled thoughts.

She turned to see a fellow pilot called Josh jogging up to greet her. Josh was always trying to pick her up, and he had even succeeded once, precipitating one of N'Goni's jealous tantrums. Or had it been one of her guilty ones? She wasn't sorry to see him now. Josh was cute, if you could put up with his being a smart ass. A native-born Megan, he was also indifferent to the heat she found oppressive.

"Guess what," he told her. "I am flying the answer back to Lurol. Soon as the vote's in from Rire, I'm off." He grinned.

"Good for you," she tossed back.

"It won't be until tomorrow," he said. "Want to hit the bar with me now?"

"Sure." It was better than anything else she could think of doing.

"You don't know what I'm talking about, do you?" he asked, bobbing along beside her and grinning like it was a good joke. "You really are info-resistant!"

"I sacked out as soon as I passed my post-flight exams, okay?" Ann went on the attack. "Just got up, ate, and went to see a counselor who came over all tutorial, so don't re-play her act."

"Okay, okay, don't be sore." He tossed his loose, curly mass of hair, making her think about Beauty and how — unlike Josh — he didn't flaunt his good looks.

"This will be fun," said Josh, giving Ann a friendly nudge as he took her arm. "I've never dated someone famous be-fore." Being famous wasn't socially acceptable to good Reetions. Prominent in one's chosen field, yes. But famous was a bit crass.

Ann extracted her arm just as they reached the entrance to an underground bunker headed up with a big, archaic neon sign that said "Pilot's Dungeon." Late twentieth-cen-tury warnings about cigarettes were plastered all over the entrance. Josh ushered them in through a pair of quaint swinging doors.

The large open room inside was dim after broad daylight. Ann stood blinking as the funky interior came into focus. Patrons sat huddled around stage pits, drinking and smok-ing, which was normal. The Social Transparency Index sur-veillance strips along the walls were damaged, which was also normal. "Out of Order!" a sign proudly proclaimed.

The noise level dropped as people began turning around in their seats, cued by their neighbors. It wasn't hard to guess why. All the active stage pits were playing scenes with Beauty in them. On one, Ann thought she spotted the sexual response profile Ling had shown her.

"Ann!" an acquaintance called out and waved. "Come join us!"

Other tables erupted in offers, calling things like, "Here!" and, "Yo! Ann!" Ann was sure she had never slept with the man who yelled, "Was he better than I was?" but she yelled back, "Much!" and he laughed.

Josh caught her hand. "I see some people I know."

Ann's eye snagged on every stage pit they passed. The first one showed Beauty being extracted from his spherical ship. The next was full of genetic data. The one of her with Beauty in her bedroom explained her celebrity, even though the display switched to an arbiter summary just as things began to get hot.

The last stage pit she looked at switched its display to "unsuitable for minors" as she went past, but for once Ann didn't mind getting the kiddie treatment. The scene that got censored showed a child-sized self-image of Beauty surrounded by jeering, drunken Gelacks watching him strive to fend off the attack of a grown man.

"What's going on?" Ann hissed at Josh.

"Your Gelack friend," said Josh. "He's quite a show!"

"That's not the official verdict, of course," said the frail-looking man who rose to greet them from the table. His stage-card, a customized graphic keyed to appear on the closest stage when introductions were in order, said his name was Erno.

"Officially," said Erno, "Rire is distressed and concerned by Von's terrible childhood, and not the least bit titillated."

Erno had the forty-going-on-ninety look of a retired pilot, affirmed by the ship on his stage-card. The girl seated beside him was a classic pilot groupie. Her card proclaimed her "Christine!" in an adolescent mish-mash of goofy effects and garish colors.

Christine got two big eyefuls of Ann, and gushed, "You really are her, aren't you? You're *the* Ann."

"Oh, she's Ann, for sure." The last member of the group roused herself to snipe. "Still sleeping with the wrong men."

Ann didn't need to see the woman's stage-card to recognize a contemporary of N'Goni's who had retired when N'Goni should have. Yin was the sort of pilot Space Service rarely got, and wanted more of: the tough, no-nonsense type. Ann had never seen her drunk before.

"So glad you favored us with your company," Erno assured Ann, to paper over Yin's insult. "And rest assured you can speak freely in the Pilot's Dungeon." He winked at her. "They're always having trouble in here with the STI surveillance strips." The display stages continued to sensor displays when a minor walked past, but they were idiot savants, restricted in function. No one counted that surveillance.

Ann sat as far from Christine as she could. Ann disliked groupies — there had always been one or two hanging around N'Goni to complicate her love life.

Yin gestured towards the stage pit. "Look at that!" She waved her hand unsteadily. "Will you just look!"

The image on Yin's stage was a psych graph, but not the graph that Ling had showed Ann.

"Perhaps we ought to turn our stage off, in deference to present company," Erno suggested.

"That's right," said Josh. "Let's protect Ann's exemplary innocence. After all, she is probably the only person in her own update radius who doesn't know we've all been outclassed!"

"What do you mean?' Christine asked, wide-eyed as usual.

"I mean Ann hasn't taken in any of this stuff," explained Josh.

"Go get me a beer!" Ann ordered, and stroked up a menu.

"Uh, sure," said Josh, caught without a snappy comeback. He hauled himself up off the morph seating beside her and went to collect her order from an auto-service bar.

Erno offered Ann a cigarette. She refused him. She could not imagine Beauty smoking.

Yin said bitterly, "The Gelack isn't human."

"How can you say that!" Christine cried, her big girlie eyes filling up with tears. "He's the sweetest man on record!"

Yin slid her elbows forwards, sleeves soaking up beer spilled earlier. "You make me want to puke!" she said, and stabbed an arm at the graph. "Look at that! And think with what's between your ears, not your legs."

It dawned on Ann, suddenly, that the graph measured piloting aptitude. It had been hard to recognize because the scale was compressed in a way that was simply impossible.

"Law and Reason," she breathed. "Is that really — ?"

"Your Gelack boyfriend?" Erno said dryly. "Yes. Remarkable, isn't it?"

She was looking at the specs of a pilot who could fly rings around her. Ann was with Yin. She was scared!

"He's perfectly human!" Christine insisted, sticking out her sensual lower lip.

"That's right," Josh pitched in jovially, plunking down Ann's drink and climbing back into his place beside her. "Way, way too perfectly everything!"

Erno picked up the thread, "Expert opinion leans towards a bioengineering explanation. Von's looks, for example, may have been designed to match a romantic ideal. An obsolete one, now, except in some quarters!" He tipped his head towards Christine. Josh laughed.

"Being bioengineered doesn't mean Von isn't human!" said Christine, her face heated. "There are places in Union Reach where that's done for cosmetic reasons!"

Erno adopted a patronizing manner. "I believe there was much more involved, in this case, than a bit of cosmetic tinkering."

"You don't get change that drastic and complex without doing something unethical," Josh expanded. "Like weeding out whole crops of variants with torture trials over long trips, and then breeding just the survivors."

"Which positively forces one to wonder how they produced the perfect lover," Erno said with mock delicacy.

"Gelacks are bioengineered?" Ann asked, pointedly ignoring Erno. "But they're so primitive!"

"They didn't invent themselves," Josh told her importantly. "Earth did — whipped them up to explore space after losing contact with us. Things must have screwed up on Earth, politically, after the jump collapsed."

"He read that, you realize," Erno remarked. "If Josh ever had an original idea as weighty as that it would squash him flat."

"Then the Sevolites got loose and bred on their own," Josh persevered.

"I believe you did notice that Von seemed capable of that," Erno toasted Ann. Josh spurted beer across the table, unable to stifle a laugh. Ann shoved him off the morph seat beside her.

"Hey!" he protested, scrambling up from the floor. "Take it easy, Ann!"

"We had better be careful," Erno said, with mock gravity. "She may send her boyfriend after us, armed with a pointy sword."

The men began to laugh again, hysterically.

Yin shot up. "Sex and swords! Is that all you young fools can think about?" She pointed stiffly into Von's piloting profile. "Look at that! And think about the fact that he's regenerative, too. Flying won't leave him weak and falling apart." She shot Erno a glare. "He out flew Ann without even finding it stressful, without even knowing that he could. Ann and N'Goni were always the best we had! Don't you understand? It will be the Killing War all over again. And we're doomed!"

There was not a pilot living who did not know that mood swings were a symptom of advancing spacer's syndrome. Yin was N'Goni's past and Ann's future. The whole table fell silent out of respect for that.

"I'm going ... somewhere to sleep this off," Yin muttered, lurching from rage to embarrassment.

"Shouldn't we make sure she gets home?" Josh asked as Yin teetered off.

"There'll be pilot handlers all over her as soon as she shows up on record," said Erno. He raised his glass in salute, "Rire takes care of those it sacrifices to keep the arbiters in synch."

Christine startled Ann by touching her arm. "I think," she said with cloying earnestness, "that Von is wonderful. I'd do anything to help make him better." She actually batted her eyelids.

Ann wished she was drunk enough to slug her. Sober, it just wasn't worth hurting her hand.

"There is something frightening, don't you think," Erno remarked to Josh, "about the way women fall all over men who have suffered, as if they find it stimulating."

"That's disgusting!" Christine turned on him, the red highlights in her hair making her complexion look orange in the mottled lighting of the bar.

"You should have seen yourself watching Von's memories," Erno told her. He tipped his head towards Josh. "I made an illegal copy on off-record media. Works wonders with underage girls itching to get past 'unsuitable for minors.'"

Christine snatched up Ann's beer, which was the fullest, and hurled it into Erno's face. "I hate you!" she cried, scrambling to her feet. "My parents were right about old pilots!" She emphasized the word "old."

"Maybe," Erno struggled to retain his dignity with beer dripping off his thin nose, "but I was right about you, sweetheart. You wanted to know all the gory details."

Ann got up.

Josh caught her elbow. "Ann?"

"Later." She turned to Erno. "That off-record copy you've got. Is it the Gelack's memories? The way they played on Lurol's stage."

"That's right," he said.

"How much is there?"

"About two hours." He smirked at her. "Interested?"

"Not remotely," said Ann. "But I'm going to report you." She looked around the room, suddenly sickened by the smoke and other symptoms of petty pilot rebelliousness.

Erno looked resentful and dangerous.

Josh was startled. "But Ann, you've done stuff like that yourself. With us!"

"Maybe I grew up," said Ann. She turned on her heel and strode out, giving the pseudo-saloon doors of the 'Pilot's Dungeon', which suddenly seemed as childish to her as the bar's inhabitants, a fierce shove.

On the commons it was bright daylight. A couple of pilot handlers in uniform were helping Yin across the emerald lawn.

"Hey!" Ann hailed them, taking a few running steps to catch up as the nearest one turned around.

"Hello, Ann," he greeted her.

She got it all out in one sentence. "Erno's got an off record copy of the Gelack's memories that he's showing to minors for sexual favors."

"Minors like Christine?" the pilot handler guessed. "Thanks, Ann. The bar stages specialize in worrying about who's seeing what, and miss things like that. Of course, we would pick up on them fine if you pilots weren't forever readjusting the bar's Social Transparency Index." He smiled, perfectly aware of the chronic vandalism.

"Are you going to put Erno in a group home?" Ann asked, with the zeal of the newly converted.

"His counselor will certainly be informed," said the handler. "And Christine's parents, of course." He excused himself and hurried to catch up to his partner who was navigating Yin towards the pilot dorms.

By the time Ann reached her own room, she knew what she was going to do.

"Stage on," she ordered, and got the default yellow diamond. "Configure a new interface," she ordered, "based on Von, the Gelack."

"Reference resolved," said the yellow diamond. "Extensive personality data is on record for Von. Specify extent of simulation."

"Just audio visual," Ann chickened out, then relented a little. "But make him capable of conversation."

The yellow diamond winked out and was replaced by Von dressed in the flight pants and sweaty silk shirt that he had been wearing when Ann first saw him in Lurol's recovery room.

"Beauty?" Ann said, with a pang.

"You called me that," the simulation answered mildly. "I also claimed to be Liege Monitum. My real name appears to be Von."

"Von," Ann repeated. "Who is Von?"

"A male courtesan employed at an establishment called Eva's, on Gelion."

"And you're not ... homosexual," Ann ventured.

"I have a strong heterosexual orientation and accept, in general terms, my culture's very negative attitude towards homosexuality."

"What about H'Reth?" Ann demanded.

"H'Reth uses me to satisfy desires condemned by Gelack culture."

"How do you feel about him?" Ann asked, stomach knotting up.

The simulation hooded its brilliant grey eyes. She recognized the pose — it was taken from the record of their time together.

"Sometimes I have violent impulses towards H'Reth," Von's image said. "Sometimes when he touches me I wish I had the courage to die, other times I feel sorry for him."

"What do you mean," Ann began, leaning closer as if she could snatch the trick of light into her arms. She paused to clear a lump in her throat. "What do you mean you wish you had the courage to die?"

"I have an unusually lush nervous system for responding to both pain and pleasure." The stage offered her links to neurological references. "It makes me afraid to die, to lose the pleasure. And it makes me afraid to be hurt again. But this fear betrays all I hold dear. Fear made me betray my sister, Mira. It stopped me fighting Jarl to save a girl I had befriended. Fear would have made me obey H'Reth, and go back to him. I nearly did go back. But then Lurol told me about the visitor probe, and it occurred to me that it might be able to save me, if I rebelled. That way I did not have to betray you. That way I could stay, as well. I hate the things I do out of fear. That is why I sometimes want to die, but I am afraid of that, as well."

"How do we know all this?" Ann asked him, stunned. "Why is there so much of you on record?"

"Tapping my memories was an unexpected side effect of using the visitor probe to arrest my conscience bond attack," explained Von's image.

Ann shook her head as if to get water out of her ears she was so overwhelmed by all the details. "A what bond?"

"A conscience bond," the stage replied in Von's warm tenor voice, "is a hitherto unknown form of aggressive, intrusive conditioning that guarantees obedience to a bond master. If the bond slave rebels, a feedback loop attacks his autonomic functions, resulting in death." A rash of handles sprang up along side Von's projection. "Please refer to references for details."

"You mean rebelling against H'Reth is what caused your attack?" Ann sought her own form of clarification. "And it could have killed you?"

"Yes," the image answered. "Although it did occur to me that the visitor probe offered hope."

"Drop simulation," Ann ordered, and Von's supple form was replaced by the yellow diamond.

Ann hugged her arms to her chest, feeling hollow. "This conscience bond thing," she asked. "Was it something Beauty volunteered for? Some sort of Gelack relationship ritual?"

"The bond was forcibly imposed," replied the yellow diamond.

"When?" Ann barked, her voice rough.

"When Von was a child of ten," the yellow diamond told her.

Blacker and more violent emotions clotted around Ann's memories of H'Reth than had ever affixed themselves to Lurol. It did cross her mind how unfair it was for H'Reth to live in fear for the sake of his sexual orientation, but that was no excuse for enslaving an unwilling ten-year-old! A good man would have found another answer.

"Beauty said," Ann began and stopped herself. "Von said," she started over, "that he betrayed someone called Mira. Who is Mira?"

"Von was raised with Mira, in secret, in a place known as the *Gorarelpul* College, and trained as a pilot in order to import illegal lab supplies for Mira's father. Von smuggled Mira off planet to train as a medic. Von fell prey to H'Reth after that, and Mira tried to save him, years later, when she encountered him working as a courtesan and accused H'Reth of sexual misconduct. But she was unaware of the conscience bond. Backing her up would have killed Von."

"That's what he meant," Ann murmured, "when he said it should have been for Mira. He meant he should have rebelled then and died for her." A warm glow thawed her inside, bringing tears to her eyes. "But he did it for me, instead."

"Von's feelings for you were a contributing factor," the arbiter corrected, "but he was more substantially influenced by a powerful reluctance to return to H'Reth, and an idealized view of Rire in general. His awareness of the visitor probe's potential as a possible means of treatment also contributed to —"

"Stage off!" Ann snapped. She paced the room until the sting of the arbiter's heartless analysis wore off, then called Ling to ask if she could see her again right away.

"I'm going back to *Second Contact Station*," Ann told the counselor, when she barged back into her visiting room. "To be with Von. I love him." Ann dumped her duffle bag on the floor. "I just found out about the conscience bond and all the rest of it."

"I know," Ling assured her.

"I still have a few questions," Ann forged ahead. "Ones I didn't want to ask a stage." She held her breath a second. "Is Von going to be okay? I mean medically."

Ling pursed her lips. "He can't be removed from the probe until the conscience bond is disabled, and Lurol isn't certain she can do that without causing damage. In the meantime he is suffering from total recall episodes which are distressing to him. He thinks of them as 'clear dreams'. That's a Gelack cultural reference. Gelacks believe in reincarnation, you see, and people who claim they can relive events from past lives are called 'clear dreamers'. Von is not reliving a past life, exactly, but 'clear dream' is the closest term he has for what he is experiencing."

"Does he love me?" Ann demanded. "Or was I simply business for him in the shower and afterwards in bed."

Ling frowned at that, but she turned obediently to her stage as Ann waited, trembling a little. "Is the visitor probe data sufficiently detailed to estimate the degree of Von's, uh, personal attraction to Ann," Ling inquired.

"Data bearing on the question is available," the stage declared, and promptly displayed the "unsuitable for minors" message.

"Wait here," Ling told Ann.

Ann waited, pacing the floor. It felt wrong to just ask and be told, even indirectly. But just because Von loathed H'Reth didn't mean he loved other assignments. It made her squirm remembering all the ways he had made sure her needs were met. If she was going all the way back to *Second Contact Station* to be with Von, she had to know what she meant to him.

Ling came back in looking uncomfortable. "Von found you sexually attractive," she confirmed. "But it is difficult to know what else he felt. Love is a hard thing to diagnose by psych profile."

Ann decided she would settle for good, honest sexual attraction.

"Caring about Von will not be easy," Ling warned, guessing as much as she saw Ann grin. "He is larger than life emotionally; a bit of a caricature, like a synthdrama hero. It makes him vulnerable. A normal person gets over falling short of his ideals but Lurol thinks Von rebelled because he can't get over it. He couldn't add betraying you and the rest of the Reetions on the station to his feelings about Mira and the nameless girl he did not help back in a place called the Bear Pit. His rebellion was actually a breakdown. Not even getting rid of the conscience bond will necessarily fix that. At worst, he may never be sane again. At best, he'll be Supervised for years."

Ling's warning settled around Ann like falling snow on a roaring hearth. The problems just didn't matter.

"Will you help me get clearance to go back," Ann asked. She had been flying too much over the last few days and would need the support of a counselor.

Ling looked like she was bursting to give more advice, but gave up with a sigh, "Oh, all right."

They based Ann's case on the relationship she and Von had registered. He was in trouble and she was his lawfully acknowledged sex partner. After hours of appeals and lobbying, and with Ling's help, she was granted a special exemption on compassionate grounds from the usual safety regulations that prevented pilots flying again too soon after their last trip, and was given leave to return to Von on *Second Contact Station*.

Ann received notice of the Reetion vote while she was still taxiing clear. Another twenty minutes and she would have boosted to skim without knowing what Rire had decided. Instead, Ann nearly turned back when she heard Von was going to be flown back to Rire, where a team was assembling to take care of him.

The sensible thing to do was to go to Rire and wait for him, but she just couldn't bear the idea. It would be too much like what had happened to N'Goni, and with luck, maybe it still wouldn't happen. Opinion differed on Rire over whether it was better to expose Von to a long flight in his current, unstable condition, or risk treating him *in situ*. There was some concern that Von's abnormal damage control mechanisms would hinder any attempt to target the conscience bond selectively, but Lurol felt they applied only to preserving memories. Lurol herself was more concerned about re-establishing Von's sanity after the treatment. She suspected that the conscience bond had functioned as an excuse for everything he hated about himself, making his underlying psychological state precarious. But Lurol still favored treatment on *Second Contact Station*. Maybe she would wait for a second opinion from Rire before accepting the first one. It was a slim hope, but Ann clung to it. Especially since it was the anthropologists who had tipped the scales in the end. As terrible as the conscience bond was, went the winning argument, it could not be severed without knowing more about its cultural significance.

Bullshit, thought Ann when she had finished with the audio summaries, reality skimming heartily by now in the direction of *Second Contact Station*. She was certain Von would want the conscience bond out of his head immediately.

A familiar feeling of nausea brought her attention back to piloting just as a *rel*-ship appeared out of nowhere and buzzed by her close enough to dislocate reality. There was no way it could have been Josh! It came at her doing over two skim factors.

Ann's last coherent feeling, before she lost her *grip*, was terror.

Change of Command

H'Reth could not sleep for worrying. He tossed and turned on his bed in the lavish admiralty apartment of his ship, the *Vanilla Rose*, wondering why Von was taking so long. All Von had to do was follow the Reetion called Ann, through the jump, back to where she'd come from; locate her space station; then turn around and come back. He should have returned two days ago.

Half the time H'Reth counted all the reasons why he knew Von must have failed in his mission. His dear boy was only a commoner, after all, and the task assigned him would have been a challenge even for a Sevolite of H'Reth's birth rank. And then, if Von had survived the trip, he may have made the error of landing on the Reetion's station to rest up. H'Reth could not remember giving explicit orders not to do that. He feared he might actually have asked Von to reconnoiter. If the Reetions found out Von wasn't Liege Monitum they might kill him, imprison him, or do something to trigger his conscience bond. Some people didn't take well to conscience bonding and Von was a prime example. He was prone to mistake a stray thought, on his part, for a full-fledged rebellion, and throw one of his alarming fits that forced H'Reth to scream reassurances. What if H'Reth wasn't there when it happened? Finally, even if Von got as far as making it back to the brink of the jump, it was really expecting an awful lot for a commoner to learn a jump after a single pass in the opposite direction. Working his way through the hazards convinced H'Reth, every time, that Von was dead or lost forever in the new jump.

To reassure himself, after such a painful exercise, he thought up antidotes to each cause for alarm. H'Reth knew Von was as talented a pilot as was possible for a commoner — they had met because Von needed to borrow a ship from a Sevolite. And if he did land, nobody was cleverer than Von at being something that he was not. Why, he would positively enjoy playing Monitum! As for conscience bond complications, H'Reth knew that the sexual demands he made on Von were the principle cause of those. How could that be a problem when H'Reth was not even present?

The problem with all such reassurances, however, was the stubborn fact that Von was still not back from his undercover mission on the Reetion side of the jump.

A hard hand fixed on H'Reth's arm, waking him from his fitful dose. He yelped, and flapped about in horror momentarily, until he recognized Jarl.

"Are you courting death!" H'Reth cried, snatched up his dressing gown angrily. "I could have run you through before I recognized you!"

Jarl glanced towards H'Reth's sword, which was resting in a wall brace supported by carved harvest maidens.

H'Reth mopped his sweating face with a handkerchief.

Jarl held up a silver box about the length of his palm. "I got this from a crewman, who obtained it from a pilot stopping over on a travel respite, who got it from a Reetion. In a few hours they'll be selling them at court."

H'Reth tied his dressing gown up. "What is it?" he asked.

Jarl stroked the top of the box and a projected scene sprang forth.

H'Reth might have been delighted by the trick if the pictures had been less alarming. An unflattering version of his own face leered at him from the box's surface, whispering blandishments about love in a wheedling tone. In the background of the projected image, he saw a dingy parlor that he recognized. It was his favorite room in his old place, on the nobleborn docks, before his rise to power.

"That's you, drooling over Von," said Jarl. "Captured in this handy, portable peep show for everyone to enjoy."

"Where did it come from?" H'Reth gasped.

"I was going to ask you that," said Jarl. He stroked the box off, threw it on the disordered bed, and struck H'Reth across the face very hard.

In surprise, H'Reth bumped backward against the bed and sat down.

"What did you do, you fat fool?" bellowed Jarl, dropping all pretense at proper grammar. "Did you strap a camera to his face when you molested him?"

"I didn't!" H'Reth yipped. "I never!" He felt as if he had been upended and swung, dangling, over oblivion. Then a comforting thought buoyed him up. "It's not real. It was never like that. I was friendly. I offered him a place to live. The means to earn money with my ships to pay the bills for his sister's training as a medic with the Luverthanians! That was what he wanted."

Jarl dropped into the servant's chair and scrubbed his face hard.

"This is bad," said Jarl, "very bad."

H'Reth fingered his dressing gown and mumbled, "We have *Vanilla Rose*. We can manage, somehow."

Jarl answered him with a harsh laugh. "You think your crew is going to keep taking orders when they've seen the rest of that?" He stabbed a finger at the mysterious silver box. "They'll see you sheath whipped to death for being boy-*sla*! You haven't seen it all — there is a lot more."

"It's some kind of trick," H'Reth bleated.

"Then it's a damn good one!" Jarl slashed back.

It was a trick, H'Reth thought stubbornly. It had not been like that. He was gentle. It was Von who made everything hard.

"If Von comes back," Jarl spat. "I'll find out where those pictures came from!"

"You will not lay a hand on him," H'Reth exclaimed, excitedly.

"Gods!" Jarl exploded, then continued more coolly. "All right then, tell me what is keeping your pretty boy, if he hasn't found a way to repay you for your love," Jarl made the word drip with sarcasm.

"He'll come," H'Reth defended Von's honor, "as soon as he is able."

"Maybe," Jarl said grimly, "but if he's learned to play tricks around the conscience bond, I'll hold him down for you, the way I used to for the rough trade in the Bear Pit, because I know he hates that more than any thrashing."

"That will hardly be necessary," H'Reth said, disgusted.

"It's nothing but Von with you," complained Jarl, "even with this hanging over us! I say damn Von."

"You are only my captain of errants," H'Reth said. "You cannot give me orders."

Jarl pushed his face into H'Reth's. "I am your backbone," he said, and spat the wad of *ignis* leaves he was chewing on the floor.

H'Reth's eyes bugged, revolted by the insult to his carpet. "Have you no manners!"

Jarl laughed. "Oh, yes, I forget — what you do to Von is polite because you say please and thank you." He huffed again, looking less frightening now and more his usual mocking, obnoxious self. "You are such a priceless hypocrite."

An alarm intruded with an ascending ripple of delightful sound. Jarl looked bemused, having had no occasion to recognize Golden Demish heraldry protocols, but H'Reth knew it announced the arrival of someone on the Family of Light's business.

For one mad moment H'Reth entertained the hope that Delm had been deposed and his grandfather, the Golden Emperor, had sent a paladin to fetch him home to court in triumph, which was the way that things generally ended in Demoran poems.

Unkind reality burst in through the door to his outer rooms in the person of H'Reth's own herald, who bowed and blurted out, "It's Master Larren himself, come straight from court! He wants to speak with you, My Lord Admiral."

"Quick!" H'Reth waved his arms in the direction of the herald. "I have to dress. Go get my valet." He turned in the opposite direction. "Go see what Larren wants, Jarl!"

Jarl lodge himself against a bedpost. "I am not the higher Sevolite." He pitched his pronouns quite correctly. "My Lord."

Coward, H'Reth thought. Not that a highborn like Larren would deign to accept a near commoner's challenge, and of course no one had actually said anything about swords — that made H'Reth feel a bit better.

Servants bustled H'Reth into an admiralty costume. The matching sword was gilded, with a filigree guard that barely fit H'Reth's large hand. H'Reth felt some anxiety about that, and declined it in favor of his usual one.

Jarl raised an eyebrow at the swap. "Thinking of taking on Master Larren?"

H'Reth blushed furiously. "It can't come to that. I'm not in his challenge class."

Jarl shrugged and fell in beside him as H'Reth set off for the bridge at a nervously brisk walk.

"You might consider it an opportunity," Jarl remarked. "If a Golden paladin agreed to kill you, you'd be famous."

"Shut up," H'Reth snapped without looking at him. "There'll be no duel."

"It may be a better way to die than in a whipping frame on Ava's Square at court," Jarl warned him.

H'Reth stopped and spun around in the carpeted, wood-paneled corridor. Sudden tears stood in his eyes. "You want to see me run through? Is that it, Jarl?"

"I'm worried," said Jarl. "What's the paladin here for? Didn't you tell me Delm wouldn't so much as entertain the notion of Larren helping us against the Reetions?"

"Maybe he's heard about D'Ander attacking us," H'Reth ventured. It sounded like a solid explanation once he got it out.

Delm wouldn't send his favorite paladin all the way to Killing Reach just to rub in the results of Von's fertility test, after
all! Besides, it was Anatolia that Delm wished to hurt by making
a fuss about all of that, and she was home on Gelion.

"It's much more likely Delm's discovered that you're boy-
sla," said Jarl.

H'Reth flinched at the word, looking frantically around
to make sure they were quite alone.

"Or he might have found out that you used an illegal bond
slave to help you do your social climbing," Jarl suggested.
"Maybe Balous checked out your story about Von's beloved
parents on your home estates, and found out he didn't have
any. Maybe he traced him to the *Gorarelpul* College."

H'Reth drew his sword and pointed it at Jarl. "Don't speak
of such things aloud," he growled. Jarl said nothing. H'Reth
slid his sword back in its sheath with a satisfying snap, feeling in charge.

Master Larren was waiting on the bridge, a circular room
with an open plan, surrounded by work stations, with a
single chair placed at its center. Vistas of space lined the
walls. Ordinarily H'Reth experienced the room as a place to
bask in his status, but seeing Larren in his chair spoiled that.

The assembled officers of the *Vanilla Rose* understood the
implied challenge, and stood watching in profound silence,
wondering if there would be a duel.

"Greetings, Liege H'Reth," Master Larren said, rising. "I
hope you will forgive me this intrusion, but your mission
has changed. I understand that you brought with you a West
Alcove courtesan named Von."

"V-Von?" H'Reth chattered. "I did, yes. He — you know
he is a special project of my wife's? A, um, young man whose
artistic talents — ah — include acting of a sort. I thought it
would be a fitting thing to use him to —"

"Impersonate Liege Monitum? Yes, so I have been told
by your crew, here." The paladin shifted his feet and cleared
his sword.

The watching circle drew a single breath.

"I am taking command of this mission," said Larren, "by order of Ava Delm, heir to the sacred blood of the Family of Light."

H'Reth gulped although his throat barely worked.

Larren sheathed his own sword after a moment. "I did not think you would have any objections," he said.

H'Reth asked hoarsely, "What do you want?"

"Von," said the paladin. "Give me Von and I will go home."

"But he's only a sword dancer!" H'Reth cried in horror. "What could you want him for?"

"I have not been given reasons," said Larren. "It is enough that this boy's existence pains a soul put in this world to guide us, lest the light of life be destroyed. What is one boy's life set against that?"

"But I don't have him!" wailed H'Reth, finally glad of that.

"I have ascertained," said Larren, "that you sent him across with a Reetion. It seems a mad plan. How can a commoner learn a jump, let alone do it on the strength of a single passage through in one direction?"

"Von is talented for a commoner," H'Reth choked out.

Larren glowered. "Why has he not come back?"

"He might have time slipped," H'Reth admitted.

"More likely," Larren said with frosty superiority, "he has defected to the Reetions."

"He couldn't!" H'Reth exclaimed.

"Oh?" The big paladin arched his manicured eyebrows.

"Th-There is his f-family, you see," H'Reth stammered, terribly conscious of the breathless crowd of onlookers. "B-Back on my Princess Reach es-estate."

"So Balous mentioned," Larren said in a voice like ice. "A bit of evil you seem curiously proud of. He also said he was quite certain, for reasons he could not divulge, that you had lied about Von's parents. He said to kill you if you tried to claim anything even more ludicrous."

Larren sat down in H'Reth's admiralty chair and spoke into the com pickup. "Farin, bring me the Reetion pilot."

Within moments, the ranks of the watchers parted for Paladin Farin, half dragging and half carrying a brown-faced man in an unfamiliar style of pants and shoes, wearing a battered Vrellish vest that was open over his skinny chest. Farin deposited the prisoner on the floor.

"This is the Reetion pilot, Thomas," Larren told H'Reth. "He cannot understand civilized languages, but I do not think that will matter. We are going to let him escape and follow him."

Thomas sat up. He had a facial twitch, and looked half mad. But he put up a token resistance and grumbled when Farin pulled him up again and marched him off.

"You're going to follow *him* through a new jump?" H'Reth marveled, unable to believe his good luck.

"Farin will do that," Larren corrected. "I will await his return to follow in the *Vanilla Rose*, and none of us shall return from the other side until Von has been found and destroyed. He must be destroyed — Delm was very clear about that."

Not in his wildest dreams had H'Reth ever imagined that Delm could be this jealous over Anatolia! The Ava must have planned to kill Von in a jealous rage and been frustrated enough, when he discovered Von was missing, to send Larren and Farin after him.

I have saved you again, H'Reth thought, caressing his hurt feelings. *Will you thank me for it? Will you look at me with love if I risk my life to save you from Larren?* H'Reth doubted Von would. Feeling dispirited, he turned tail and headed back to his rooms, thinking he may as well wait out the nerve-wracking jump Larren threatened in relative comfort.

Jarl was waiting for him.

"Your suite's been taken over by the paladins," Jarl told H'Reth. "You are to find other quarters."

H'Reth couldn't take this in immediately. "What?"

Jarl threw a comradely arm around his shoulders. "Come on." He led H'Reth to the moderately nice receiving room where they had put the Reetion woman while figuring out what to do next. Jarl had already ordered food.

"Eat," he told H'Reth. "You'll feel better."

The food did help a little. The wine helped even more. They ate fast, anticipating a warning to secure for reality skimming, which meant servants would intrude to clear the dishes away and web things down.

"Why destroy Von?" H'Reth asked. "That seems excessive." *It won't happen*, he promised himself.

Jarl snorted. "I agree it is odd," he said. "No one cares that much about a boy whore." He paused to swallow wine. "Except you, of course. But Delm doesn't share your tastes."

"I think it's got something to do with Anatolia's pregnancy," said H'Reth.

Jarl looked as if H'Reth had changed color just to be an idiot. "What are you talking about?"

H'Reth flushed. "You know how Delm thought Von was improperly neutered? Maybe Von is also responsible for Vretla Vrel's pregnancy and Delm wants to blackmail Di Mon over it. Monitum needs a highborn heir. Maybe Delm's afraid D'Ander will convince Di Mon to withdraw his oath and then—"

"Von get a Vrellish highborn pregnant?" Jarl cut H'Reth off with a guffaw. "You are obsessed. That's impossible. It would take at least a Royalblood." He took a slug of wine and shrugged. "Or luck and Kertatt Monitum, I suppose."

"What do you think it's about then?" H'Reth demanded.

They both thought about it for a moment without inspiration. Then Jarl got a funny look on his face.

"What is it?" asked H'Reth.

"I was just thinking how the kid never scarred," said Jarl. He looked up at one of Delm's ubiquitous portraits, half covered in webbing gossamer.

"What?" H'Reth urged, spooked by Jarl's strange behavior.

"Nothing!" Jarl snapped. His expression turned nasty. "I wish I had your pretty boy here, now. I'd beat his secrets out of him."

H'Reth flinched at the idea. "He's my bond slave. He can't keep secrets! Hurting him would be superfluous."

"Not quite," Jarl said snidely. "I'd enjoy it." He hauled himself out of the chair, face still reflecting some disturbing thought that wouldn't settle. "Larren must have decided to see if a day's rest improves his Reetion pilot."

"He did look overflown, didn't he?" H'Reth worried.

Thomas, as it turned out, was too trip giddy to realize he was supposed to escape. They heard it from the servant who came to clean up. Jarl went out to investigate and reported that Larren was waiting impatiently for Thomas to show signs of initiative.

H'Reth drank himself to sleep. In his dreams, he was Hangst Nersal of Black Hearth, slaying paladins in duel after duel to the delight of the empire's most prestigious audience. His dead mother was there with tears in her eyes, cheering for him, and so was Anatolia, holding a deliciously Von-like child in her arms.

Jarl woke him in the middle of the final showdown on the Octagon with Larren.

"The Reetion toy!" Jarl remembered, breathless. "We left it in your bed chamber!" He had been sleeping, too, and his hair stuck up at unruly angles.

H'Reth blinked, adjusting to wakefulness with reluctance. Fear entered his heart in a slow, icy trickle. "Do you think they've found it?"

"Not yet," said Jarl. "Or if they have, they haven't found out how to make it play."

Terror twisted and untwisted in H'Reth's gut. "How can you be so sure?" he demanded.

Jarl's grin looked ghoulish in the dim light. "Because," he said with mocking sweetness, "they haven't dragged you from your bed and beaten you to a bloody pulp. There's a lot more on that thing than the couple of seconds that you saw. Von has betrayed you."

"No," H'Reth whimpered, clinging fiercely to the ever-changing symphony of Von filling space; his unthinking grace; his melting, expressive moods. "No," H'Reth repeated, feeling better every time he said it out loud.

Jarl lay down where he had settled on the floor and pulled his covers over him, grumbling insults.

Imperfect Denials

Ranar woke in a cozy bed under a comforter. Directly above was an elongated S skewed on a diagonal with barbs hooked around either end of its cresting curves, which he recognized as the Gelack *rel* symbol. It glowed, shedding light down on him.

Absolutely ridiculous, Ranar thought. The *rel* symbol had religious significance and to employ it as a lighting fixture was frivolous. Then he remembered he was not judging exhibits at a First Contact Anthropology Convention — this was really Gelion. It served as a crisp reminder not to trust stale academic guesses.

At least his memory had no fresh gaps. He was in a room that had once been Ameron's where he had been put to bed by a woman named Sarilous, who was old but intimidating.

His comforter was made of brown satin embroidered in tangled leaves, with no repeating patterns. Ranar took a moment to enjoy that, and then looked around him in awe. Never in his most extravagant dreams had he imagined waking up in Ameron's bedroom. A portrait of Ameron hung on the wall but not the adult Ameron of the First Contact period. This Ameron was a youth taking time out from exercise to read a book. His discarded gloves and face guard sat on the table top beside his sword. Display cases on the walls contained memorabilia: a leather writing case; a horse's bridle; a chart identified in English as a DNA signature.

An open copy of the *Ameron Biography* was set out on a table under glass. Ranar scrambled out of bed to take a look. The handwritten dedication was in English.

It said: "To Monitum, whose loss has been as great as ours, from Sela Lor'Vrel, 31 years Post Americ Treaty."

If the treaty cited was the one made with Rire, that placed the inscription twenty years after Ameron's failed attempt to reestablish contact, but a letter in the same hand, laying open on the opposite side of the book, was dated 173 Post Treaty, only sixteen years ago. Could the same Sela Lor'Vrel have written both despite the 142 year span? People lived to be two hundred on Rire, but Ranar doubted the state of Gelack medicine was that good.

The letter read:

> *My dear Di Mon:*
>
> *It is sad to see Ameron's line disgraced, but if you believe Ev'rel capable of killing her own child, whoever the father, do what you must. I only wish I could believe Delm was any better than his half-sister.*
>
> *Yours in Ameron's Memory,*
>
> *Sela.*

The dates continued to bother Ranar. Obviously Sela had not written the biography as an infant, but the handwriting matched, making her at least two hundred when she had penned the letter.

"I see you are awake," said a crisp voice. Sarilous stood in the open door. She closed it as noiselessly as she had let herself in and stepped forward.

"Hello," said Ranar and smiled.

She didn't smile back. She was dressed trimly in a plain green suit, her white hair coiled into a harsh knot at the back of her neck. Veins showed through the translucent skin on her lined face but her eyes were a bright, light blue.

Sarilous opened the room's spacious wooden closet. "You have made a favorable impression on my bond master," she announced with her back to Ranar.

"Your bond master?" he asked, intrigued but puzzled.

"Di Mon." She began sifting through clothes. "The one hundred and third Liege of Monitum."

"In what sense is he your master?" Ranar wanted to know.

"I am a *gorarelpul*," she said, selecting an embroidered tunic.

"*Gorarelpul*?" Ranar repeated. "That isn't an English word."

"No."

"What does it mean?" he asked.

"It is a contraction of an older phrase, with elisions, like many such naming words in Gelack. The Monatese believe it derives from a phrase meaning 'the faithful of deep and secret struggles'. If so, the usage predates present law. The only *gorarelpul* tolerated now are those publicly acknowledged as such."

"Forgive my ignorance," said Ranar, "but am I right to assume it is a prestigious title? You seem to be someone of consequence."

"*Gorarelpul* are the only commoners trained in restricted arts," she volunteered, taking slippers out of a drawer. "For that privilege, we submit to the conscience bond."

She turned around, laden with clothes. "But a bond slave is still a slave, for all that. We are capable of disobedience, but not of surviving it. It's a tidy system. Merely being aware of the definite intention to rebel is fatal, by means of a powerful and highly specialized conditioned response. It is delicate work, done only at the *Gorarelpul* College."

"And you are bonded to Di Mon?" said Ranar, finding himself surprisingly resistant to the idea.

"Not precisely," said Sarilous with a prickly air. "I am bonded to the title of Liege Monitum. I served Di Mon's predecessor, Darren, and will serve Di Mon's successor if he manages to secure one." She set the clothes she had picked on the bed. "Will you need a valet?"

"I think that I can manage," Ranar assured her, still bursting with questions that he thought it best to hold back until he knew how to ask.

"Liege Monitum requires that you attend him over breakfast," she informed him on her way out. "Be prompt."

She doesn't approve of me, Ranar decided.

Alone, he applied himself as quickly as possible to putting on his new clothes, struggling not to get distracted by things like the embroidery on the tunic that featured sextants scattered over a stellar map.

He found Sarilous waiting for him in the softly lighted corridor he remembered from the night before. The walls were lined with creeping plants that created a damp, earthy atmosphere, like the inside of a greenhouse. Doors were unevenly spaced along the walls.

"Family Hall," Sarilous named the corridor and pointed. "The Breakfast Room is at that end."

Ranar was too enchanted to feel fear, but he could not hurry either. Every detail along the way made a strong impression on him: the brown and russet mottle of the carpet; a showcase displaying an ancient black typewriter; creeping vines of Earthly greens and a rich, alien turquoise. Light spilled from under the Breakfast Room door. It opened on well balanced hinges in response to Ranar's gentle push and the odor of food wafted out.

Di Mon sat at the massive table inside. He was dressed in a green, quilted vest decorated in vivid embroidery. A herd of horses galloped across his chest, the most prominent foam-flecked and wide-eyed, running from the terror of a gathering storm. He had finished his breakfast except for a parsley sprig tidily put aside.

"Please sit down," Di Mon greeted Ranar.

Ranar took a seat to Di Mon's right, which was the only one set for use. Ranar recognized nothing on his plate but the parsley sprig. There were slices of something red, and a fluffy sculpture made to resemble a berry bush. A drink was included, served in a glass horn with a metal holder. It looked like strained fruit juice.

Di Mon produced a silvery info-blit of the sort distributed at fairs on Rire, and set it down between them with a soft thump.

"What is this?" he asked.

"Where did you get —" Ranar began, reaching for it.

Di Mon's hand retracted suddenly as they touched. Ranar looked up. The Gelack's face matched his vest's gathering storm.

"Prince H'Us obtained it in Killing Reach," Di Mon told him. "It seems they are being traded there. It is from Rire?"

"I think so," Ranar acknowledged. "It looks like an info-blit, a sort of toy given out at —"

"Toy?" Di Mon snapped.

His tone made Ranar uncomfortable. "It is probably instructional," he told his host. "Info-blits are aimed at young people who might otherwise neglect to make the effort to learn what they ought to know. They are handed out at popular events and performances."

Di Mon flicked the blit on with a touch and spoke above the voice of the narrator describing basic male-male sexual hygiene and good conduct. "You teach perversions to your youth!" he accused.

Belatedly, Ranar diagnosed homophobia, which shouldn't have surprised him. Gelacks showed every sign of being socially primitive, but he couldn't believe Di Mon was typical — he had seemed so reasonable about everything else, so far.

"Or are such things normal where you come from?" Di Mon guessed from Ranar's reaction and looked down at the projected lovers, painfully spellbound.

"That depends on what you mean by normal," Ranar said swiftly, with inadequate thought. His mouth felt dry. He

risked a swig of the juice in his glass horn and found it both
sweet and light. It took an effort to put the juice down without rattling the glass horn against its metal holder. "Homosexuality is a minority preference," concluded Ranar.

"But accepted?" asked Di Mon.

Ranar hesitated as he thought how to respond. Reetion
values began with universal access to all information. Lying
wasn't natural, but the truth here might endanger him. In the
end, Di Mon's emotional turmoil compelled him despite that.

"Yes," Ranar told the Gelack. "It is accepted. In fact, it is
my own personal preference."

Di Mon went rigid and then muscle by muscle relaxed
again as Ranar watched, although his tension remained
palpable.

"You have never suffered for that?" the Gelack asked in
a voice that was deceptively calm.

"No. Never," Ranar answered as sturdily as he could. "To
punish someone for their sexual preference is the thing we
would consider perverse, so long as that choice respects the
rights of others."

Di Mon pushed back in his chair. The tension snapped and
vanished as if spent in some internal implosion, although
the bared teeth and rolling eyes of a stallion embroidered
on his chest stared out at Ranar in hot denial of Di Mon's
apparent calm.

"Such things," Di Mon said coolly, "destroy whole lines
on Gelion." He paused. "I would not mention it again to
anyone."

"Thank you for the warning," said Ranar, and swallowed
down a lump in his throat. He also noted the emphasis
placed on the loss of "whole lines."

Di Mon turned the info-blit over in his hand. "The technology in this is impressive. If I dismantle it, will I be able
to learn how it is done?"

"I can't answer that without knowing how advanced your
own crystalline memory systems are."

"Crystalline?" asked Di Mon.

"You don't use crystronic processors?" Ranar surmised.

"Electronics," said Di Mon, "and nervecloth."

Ranar decided not to bring up the antiquity of electronics, to be polite. Instead he said, "I am not familiar with nervecloth."

"It is a Monatese monopoly," said his host, and gestured with the info-blit in his hand. "Can this weather hard flight?"

"It is a simple, non-arbitorial unit," Ranar answered, "so yes, I expect it could cope with the worst any pilot could expose it to. At least three or four hours at one standard skim factor."

Di Mon's thin eyebrows arched. "That is all?" Relief slid quickly into amusement. "Nervecloth cannot duplicate the capacity of this device, but I have personally found it reliable at exposures three times that high, though not as good as living Demish memory."

He's bragging, Ranar thought at first. The next moment he wasn't so sure but stifled the impulse to ask questions. The word "monopoly" raised a warning flag. This was a pre-arbiter culture, which suggested that its leaders could behave criminally in defense of wealth.

"I make you nervous?" Di Mon asked with a sudden smile.

Ranar met his stare frankly and felt the Gelack recoil. "No," he said, and meant it. "Is that an error?"

"Courage is never an error," said Di Mon, a bit sadly, and sighed. "I should explain your position, but first, please, eat your breakfast."

Ranar tried. The food was tasty, but he didn't like eating things he could not identify and he was certain to find Di Mon's steely gray eyes on him whenever he looked up. He soon pushed the plate away and finished the juice.

"Not hungry?" Di Mon asked.

"I find it hard to eat while I am being studied like a specimen of something odd."

Di Mon laughed. "It is hard to remember that you are a commoner."

Ranar took umbrage at that. "That is because I am not."

"I doubt you could convince a single Nesak," said Di Mon.

The *non sequitur* irked Ranar. "What are Nesaks?" he asked.

"Sevolites who exterminate commoners," Di Mon answered casually, "and lesser Sevolites too. They claim that only highborns have souls. Nesaks are the principle reason why I cannot afford to offend my court ally, Prince H'Us, who wants you executed."

He thinks he can intimidate me, thought Ranar.

"How," Ranar asked pedantically, "can these Nesaks be Sevolites — which I understand to be an aristocracy with hereditary rights — without having any commoners to rule over?"

"They do their own work, I suppose," Di Mon tossed off and gestured for a waiter to clear away Ranar's plate. Steaming cups of herbal tea were served next, in cups that looked venerable enough to have come from Earth. Ranar's had been mended at least once and was different than the one served to Di Mon.

"Whether one is a Sevolite," Di Mon resumed their conversation when the waiter had withdrawn, "is a matter of blood, not whom one governs."

"You consider Sevolites to be a race apart?" Ranar surprised himself with his scornful tone.

"Of course," said Di Mon, "although we are running out of Purebloods. Delm and his banished half-sister could not manage to raise a single child, let alone repopulate court. The only other Pureblood we know of is the Golden Emperor, if he is still alive." Di Mon frowned. "And I have no doubt the Demorans would stuff and mount the corpse for ceremonial occasions if he was not."

Ranar let that gruesome little comment pass, guessing it was meant as an exaggeration. He wanted to pursue Di Mon's racism to its roots.

"If you take such a keen interest in genetic heritage," said Ranar, "surely you must know that hybrids are stronger than any result you can get from siblings breeding with each other."

"What you say is true among animals and commoners," agreed Di Mon.

Ranar felt a draft across his heart. *I must stop*, he warned himself. *This could be dangerous.*

"It may be somewhat true of us, as well," Di Mon salvaged Ranar's opinion of him, and paused to frown, as if he had surprised himself with the admission. "But Ev'rel was Ameron's granddaughter, and I wanted to see his line continued." He inhaled slowly. "In any case, inbreeding at some level was the only option for Purebloods unless they were willing to breed down."

"Do you personally believe you are superior?" Ranar demanded as if Di Mon was someone he knew, from home, and not a neo-feudal primitive who could probably order him killed as casually as summoned to breakfast. "Do you think you are inherently better than people who, in your vocabulary, are commoners? I thought you were intelligent!"

Di Mon looked astonished. Then he laughed.

"I have been accused of a lack of faith in the more spiritual aspects of *Okal Rel*," he confessed, with unexpected delight, "but Sevolite superiority is a simple matter. In those things, of course, that we excel in. I have often wondered whether —" He interrupted himself, his high, pale brow constricted, and refocused on his Reetion guest. "Why does it matter so much to you what I believe, Ranar of Rire?"

"I want to respect you," Ranar realized. "You seem to have a good mind. But racism is mankind's oldest error."

"By the mad gods of Earth!" Di Mon exploded. "No wonder your kind provoked us to genocide in Killing Reach! Would you lecture me on mankind's errors? You? Who thought nothing of destroying whole planetary ecologies to save your lives? Who know nothing of *Okal Rel*?"

Ranar blinked. Di Mon catapulted out of his chair. Ranar braced himself for violence.

"Get up," Di Mon ordered.

Ranar scrambled to his feet, alarmed by the sudden energy in his host.

Di Mon took hold of the massive oaken table with both hands and lifted, teeth locked. Two legs of the table came up off the floor. Dishes slid. A spoon clattered. Di Mon set them down again before the antique tea cups crashed to the floor.

"There," Di Mon said, "can you do that?"

Ranar just looked at him, unable to decide whether he was more impressed by the show of strength or the idiotic childishness of the demonstration.

"Ameron valued good commoners more than bad Sevolites," Di Mon told him, "if that is what is nettling you." He clapped him on the back, forcing Ranar to brace himself on the table. "But I will not indulge sheer nonsense. Highborns are highborns."

"Apparently," said Ranar, feeling unsure what to make of that.

"Young, aren't you?" asked Di Mon, now in a cheery mood.

Ranar said, defensively, "I am twenty-four."

"Young." Di Mon smiled at him. "I am sixty-five."

"You don't look a day over twenty-five," Ranar protested, resisting the creeping conviction he was grasping at straws. "And don't pretend Gelacks don't age. I've met Sarilous."

"My *gorarelpul*?" Di Mon persisted in his irksome amusement. "She's a commoner."

Ranar wrestled with his unprofessional resistance to the evidence, but he could not help it. He just did not want Sevolites to be too different from Reetions. Too frightening, perhaps, or just too alien — *for what*? he asked himself. *What am I feeling*?

"I suppose you are going to claim you are immortal," he asked Di Mon tartly.

That sobered the Gelack up. "No, not that."

The change in Di Mon was so sharp that Ranar put his hand out spontaneously to offer comfort. Di Mon started at his touch, looking down into Ranar's eyes. Something electric passed between them.

Oh no, Ranar thought, dismayed, *this is sexual attraction*.

Sarilous entered. Di Mon broke eye contact with Ranar. "News?" he inquired.

The *gorarelpul* gave them both a long, suspicious look before answering. "Yes," she said, "about Von." She sat down and waited while a servant set out tea for her and straightened the disordered table before disappearing again through a swinging door at the back of the room.

Di Mon gestured Ranar back to his chair.

"Is he to stay?" Sarilous questioned his decision, speaking English like her master.

"I do not see why not," Di Mon said casually, and resumed his seat also. "If anything you have to say is sensitive, say it in Gelack." He smiled. "The inverse of our usual rules."

Sarilous sniffed as only a proud old woman knew how. "I do not know what you consider sensitive concerning Eva's star male courtesan," she told her master primly.

Di Mon frowned. "Don't fuss, Sarilous."

She gave up with a final, parting glare at Ranar. "Very well," she said. "First, Vretla Vrel has learned of Von's disappearance."

"So?" said Di Mon.

"Von is her favorite den boy."

Di Mon shrugged. "She'll find another soon enough."

"Doubtless. But she may try to find this one first, so long as she is missing his attention. That could be dangerous for your heir."

"Second?" Di Mon prompted.

"You have asked Eva to be your *lyka*," said Sarilous.

Ranar had to stifle the impulse to ask for a translation of 'lyka.'

"What of that?" Di Mon said.

"It appears that Von assisted the H'Reth's rise to power." She eyed Ranar again, as if he might yet oblige her by vanishing. "Eva might be implicated."

Di Mon leaned forward. He was always restless, Ranar realized. He contained it in a series of frequent but precise shifts. "It does not sit well with me to assume Eva knew. Nor will I condemn her without evidence," Di Mon told his *gorarelpul*.

"I thought not," Sarilous said coolly,

"Is there more?"

"I think so." She glanced at Ranar and resumed in Gelack.

Ranar knew just enough Gelack, from his First Contact studies and what he had been able to pick up from D'Ander, to deduce that Sarilous was telling Di Mon a story about someone called Mira, whom she referred to as a '*medak*' — very likely the Gelack cognate for medic, in English. H'Reth and Von were mentioned more than once, as well as the Princess-Liege of H'Us.

Di Mon listened with a half-bored attitude until the term "boy-*sla*" was mentioned. Ranar noted the term for the sake of Di Mon's sudden alertness and tension. Di Mon listened to a few more sentences, and then shot up in the middle of the next one.

"Enough!" he cried in English, cutting Sarilous off. "Is H'Reth at court?"

"No," said Sarilous, also reverting to English. "Delm sent him off to Killing Reach in the *Vanilla Rose*. Perhaps Delm considered it getting rid of two broken play things at the same time. H'Reth was out of favor, and Prince H'Us had cut off funds for throwing parties in his flagship. It is Delm's subsequent behavior that I can't account for. Delm refused to send a paladin with H'Reth, but Larren left court soon after Delm took one of the Reetion prisoners from D'Ander, and my sources suspect the brown-face went with him."

"Thomas?" Ranar interjected.

"Even more curiously," Sarilous continued, "Balous is no longer stirring up rumors to humiliate Delm's erring mistress. He was making quite a show of proving she was pregnant by Von, and then all of sudden the baby is supposed to be H'Reth's again."

Di Mon settled back, conversing with his *gorarelpul* in the easy way of people long accustomed to each other. "You think H'Reth took Von," he alluded to things said earlier in Gelack. "But if this medic, Mira, was correct as to why —" he shook his head " — is that enough to explain sending Larren into Killing Reach? I cannot imagine Delm being that zealous about punishing the misuse of a commoner."

"It may have been the paladin's idea," Sarilous tried on for size. Almost in unison they shook their heads.

"Larren does nothing but Delm's bidding," Di Mon put it in words.

"Von speaks English," said Sarilous. "You told me he had taught it to Eva."

"Yes." Di Mon rose, unable to stay seated any longer, and stood with his long fingers resting on the top of the table. "You think H'Reth took him to translate for him?"

"I think I might be able to help," Ranar volunteered.

They both looked at him in surprise.

"Have you been in Killing Reach recently, Liege Monitum?" Ranar asked, clinging to his certainty he had something of use to impart.

"No." Di Mon's hard, dark eyes narrowed.

"Yet Thomas told me that Ann met Liege Monitum," Ranar told him excitedly. "Ann was our mission pilot. Thomas said that she was going to take Liege Monitum back with her through the jump, about the time D'Ander's ships showed up."

"Can you describe this Liege of Monitum?" Di Mon asked, annoyingly reserved in his reception of Ranar's information.

"I never saw him," Ranar admitted. "I was unconscious. But Thomas said something about Ann enjoying his company. No, wait." He groped for the words. "I think he was jealous. He thought Liege Monitum was too young for her, or something to that effect. And good looking. Does that sound like this Von person?"

"Oh yes," Di Mon muttered.

"That's incredible!" Sarilous rejected the idea. "Von? Impersonate Liege Monitum? What could H'Reth gain by it?"

"The jump," Di Mon realized. He shifted his stance again, crossing his arms. "Delm has never accepted the loss of Barmi II to Perry D'Aur, and with a space station on the Reetion side, he would have a way of keeping an eye on his lost planet."

"How could Von steal a jump?" asked Sarilous.

"Some commoners can fly," said Di Mon. "It may be significant that H'Reth once ran the sort of hangar that did not trouble its clients to prove they were Sevolites. Find out what you can, Sarilous," he instructed the old *gorarelpul*. "But I will not assume Eva guilty without proof against her, even if her *protégé* has gone so far as to impersonate me."

"I don't understand," Ranar protested. "Why go to so much trouble? We were trying to make contact! We'd have dealt with whoever came forward."

Di Mon blinked at him. "You would willingly have taught the Killing Reach Jump to Delm's admiral?"

"Why not?" Ranar insisted. "There have always been Gelacks who knew it. On that much, the First Contact record was quite clear."

"*Monitum* knows it, yes," Di Mon said.

Ranar's thinking rebounded off his Reetion assumption that all Gelacks would necessarily know what one did. "You purposefully kept it secret? For two hundred years?"

"That was Ameron's wish," Di Mon said.

"Ah yes, the treaty. The reason I have to be executed. Fountain Court may not know it, Liege Monitum," he insisted, "but that treaty has been violated for years by pilots like Thomas and the Gelack pilot who taught it to him, so they could do business on places like *Trinket Ring*. That's why I came — to normalize relations before something goes wrong accidentally. And all Gelack leaders can do is make threats and pretend we can ignore each other for another two hundred years. Secrecy is childish, Liege Monitum."

"Reetion," Di Mon said, in exasperation. "Do you not understand we are a hazard to you?"

Ranar could think of no tactful way to answer that to Di Mon's face. He side-stepped the question. "So you don't think H'Reth could have used Von to impersonate you?" he asked.

"I did not say that," Di Mon corrected. "No, to the contrary, using Von to impersonate me is just the kind of complex and precarious bit of theater that would suit Delm and H'Reth. But if, as you say, they meant to take it so far as to steal the jump, there would be natural limits to how far Von could carry the deception as a commoner."

Ranar repressed an impulse towards impatience at the way Di Mon so crisply distinguished between Sevolites and commoners. It was unprofessional of him, but he couldn't keep Di Mon in focus as a Gelack. He kept wanting to respond to him as a friend.

"There's one more thing we must consider," said Sarilous, "about Von."

Di Mon looked as if the whole thing was giving him a sour stomach. "Go on if you must," he said.

"Is Von really fertile?" There was an awkward pause. Then Sarilous continued. "Anatolia H'Reth is not the only one of Von's clients to have cause for complaint. Lady H'Ran, a Demish widow notorious for her flings with other women's husbands, recently appealed to Delm for access to a silver star medic to perform an abortion for her. She kicked up such a fuss, both trying to keep it quiet and complain at the same time, that it became fairly well known that she held Von responsible. People assumed it was a smoke screen to protect the real father from his in-laws. Delm refused to help and H'Ran wound up taking care of it herself through other channels, but it seems an odd coincidence."

"Or," Di Mon countered, "Lady H'Ran's predicament gave Delm the idea of using Von to shame Anatolia."

"You think Lady H'Reth's child is really Delm's, then?"

Di Mon shook his head. "Delm buys enough *ferni* to neutralize the fertility of a dozen Purebloods. He has no intention of siring any child." He sighed. "I know what is worrying you, Sarilous. You want to believe Lady H'Reth's child is Delm's, because if Von was proved fertile due to some oversight, Vretla might be carrying his child." Di Mon scowled deeply. "I suppose it is remotely possible, even for a commoner. But it is much more likely that her child is Kertatt's, and H'Reth is the sire of his own wife's unborn child."

"Unless the medic, Mira, was right," Sarilous said doggedly. "If H'Reth is really boy-*sla* —"

"It would not prevent him siring a child!" Di Mon snapped.

"But it may," she said, with an air very like accusation, "make him afraid to do so."

The intensity of the ensuing silence dug like a stick in a half-healed wound. Sarilous looked brittle, Di Mon tense. The *gorarelpul* cast Ranar a resentful look shading towards murderous.

"It's all too murky," Di Mon blurted when the deadlock finally broke. "Is D'Ander still at Golden Hearth?"

"Yes, master." Sarilous sounded resigned again.

"Good!" Di Mon rapped out. "Send a herald across Fountain Court to tell D'Ander I'd be obliged if he would accompany me on a visit to H'Reth Manor. He's a Golden prince and that should sit better with a Demish lady than an unexpected visit from a Vrellish highborn."

"As you wish," she replied, frosting up. "If you think that's wise, rather than letting me handle it."

"I will flush out what only a highborn can flush out," Di Mon promised. "You see if you can turn up anything connecting Von with piloting, and especially H'Reth's old hangar on the nobleborn docks before he began moving up in the world. Von is exceptionally good looking, and therefore he might be remembered. Also, if he can indeed pilot, there is a good chance he is at least a bit Sevolite, sired on some hapless servant. There might be a traceable connection."

"Very well," Sarilous said dryly.

Di Mon picked up his sword from a rack by the door, strapped it on, and slid past Ranar with a touch.

Ranar swallowed, feeling oddly vexed, but also reassured. He wanted to follow and knew it would be denied.

"There is a library at the other end of Family Hall," said Sarilous, at his elbow. "You may have some time on your hands. I will show you around."

"Thank you," Ranar answered reflexively.

The library exuded the feeling of quiet hours spent in thought. Books lined one wall before a set of chairs and couches and a globe of Earth stood in a heavy frame by the door, the oceans glistening like molten jewels. This was Di Mon's special place. Ranar felt it instinctively.

Sarilous gestured towards the wall of bound volumes. "You'll find Monitum's history in those, in the hand of 103 lieges. All in English."

While Ranar pondered this miracle, Sarilous went forward, climbed three rungs of a wheeled ladder, and selected a volume not far from the end of the last populated shelf. She climbed down again with the large book under one arm, and offered it to Ranar.

"This one is the one in which my master's reign began, but it begins with his predecessor, Darren, the master I first served."

Ranar took the book. Sarilous gestured towards a chair beneath a well positioned reading lamp. She turned the lamp on.

Ranar sat down, thinking, *It's the record, Gelack fashion*.
The words, "Di Mon, 103rd Liege of Monitum," appeared
beside a date thirty years old. Ranar paged forward, looking for a recent entry, but the volume had been filled decades
before. He opened the book near the front instead and found
the author was now, "Darren, 102nd Liege of Monitum." The
hand was more flamboyant.

Ranar read:

> *Debated the purpose of* Okal Rel *with my cousin,*
> *the scholar. Poor Di Mon! Do I love him in spite, or*
> *because of, his tiresome intelligence? And the way he*
> *goes on about Ameron! Ameron was no martyr to soft-*
> *hearted virtues. His termination of the Killing War was*
> *strictly practical. Reetions are dangerous.*

Darren's style was emotive and personal. In one entry he
described his Fleet Admiral, Mannat, as "the fiercest fire of
Vrellish womanhood." Mannat was Darren's mekan'st, a
term that apparently had no English translation, but whatever a *mekan'st* was, Darren had three children by her.

> *My Liyet toddled into the middle of a grave*
> *consultation about Nesaks and demanded to be picked*
> *up. Who was I to refuse? Mannat was put out by the*
> *indulgence. She would rather hunt Nesaks than bear*
> *children — no wonder they out-breed us ten to one! I do*
> *not think I will train my daughter to the cockpit or the*
> *sword. I will make her a statesman and scholar, and*
> *appoint Di Mon as regent should I succumb to an*
> *excess of character before my time.*

Ranar skimmed the next eight years, looking for references to Di Mon. Most were affectionate, some mocking, but
Darren spoke that way of everyone in his family circle, re-
serving his sweetest praises for his children, Liyet, her
younger brother Dita, and an infant.

Darren's entries stopped suddenly and the next thirty days were undocumented. The log resumed under the heading, "Di Mon, 103rd Liege of Monitum."

There was no mention made of Darren or his children.

Excited and perplexed, Ranar read on, but the log quickly assumed the dry, disciplined character of all Di Mon's entries.

Di Mon himself never had children. He stated bluntly that he was infertile, an affliction that cropped up now and then in the Monatese line. His half-sister chose to commit to an exclusive relationship with an inferior, yielding his niece and nephew, before both parents perished fighting Nesaks. But there were still a few other highborns left in other Monatese families at that time. Families with names like Eversol, Ternova, and Lorm.

"I must leave now," Sarilous said, startling him.

"Oh, yes, of course. Thank you." Ranar told her, astonished to find she was still in the room with him, it had felt so full of characters from the log.

Sarilous levered herself out of the chair opposite, making him wonder if he should offer his help, but although she was old, and even a little frail, there was nothing welcoming about her.

"Do you have any questions before I go?" she asked him blandly.

"No," Ranar said, and contradicted himself instantly. "Yes. Can you tell me what became of Darren? Di Mon says nothing about it or the children, and Liyet was Darren's heir."

Sarilous marshaled herself with a hard, bitter focus. "Their mother, Mannat, killed the children. Darren killed her." She added dryly, "It was quite a duel."

"Killed them!" Ranar nearly choked on the words. "But they were hers!"

"And Darren's," Sarilous noted, clinically. "Darren, you see, was boy-*sla*. He always had been, although he managed to hide it well since he was willing enough to lie with women as well. He got careless that summer and was caught with a couple of peasant boys he had bribed to pleasure him."

"Boys?" Ranar felt nauseous.

"They were willing enough," Sarilous assured him. "Before Mannat burst in on them, tipped off by one of Darren's enemies. He made enemies, my first Liege Monitum but that wasn't his greatest failing. His greatest failing was refusing to believe his enemies were not stupid." There was pain in her voice and an old, petrified anger.

"I understand Gelacks are homophobic," said Ranar, still deeply alarmed. "But why the children?"

"The taint is in the bloodline," Sarilous said.

Ranar felt as if he had come to know Liyet, especially, and her siblings had been so young! The burden of Darren's guilt tried to settle on him like a living thing. He set it aside forcefully. "You said Darren won the duel," he said quietly. "What happened to him?"

"He was lost fighting Nesaks," said Sarilous. "But you'll find nothing about it in the logs of Monitum. Darren ceased to exist the day Monitum learned of his sickness."

Ranar bit back his protestation that it was not a sickness, even though he himself was not so sure about peasant boys paid to give pleasure. Sex with children, under any circumstances, offended Reetion sensibilities.

"It must have been a difficult time for Di Mon," Ranar said, instead.

"Yes, very difficult." Sarilous paused momentarily. "He admired Darren."

A long silence stretched out, in which Ranar framed questions that he was afraid to ask. Eventually Sarilous broke eye contact and left without another word, but he heard the door click after she closed it behind her.

Ranar went back to search the logs for answers.

For Better
or For Worse

Ann fed the banked fire of her identity on scraps, clustered about her like fallen leaves: the beaches of her childhood; her parents' anxieties; N'Goni as a dashing young man; and N'Goni trip-worn and irrational. Her thoughts nudged about grains of guilt, rendered as inert and smooth as pearls. She marveled now over striking out at Lurol. It had been herself she hated, for feeling relieved to be free, and not knowing what to do with the grief that was just as real.

Slowly driving out the older memories were exciting new ones of a vivid young man with too many names — and a demon ship that attacked with consuming self-righteousness. She began to shiver, remembering, and realized that she was adrift in space, but still whole and self-aware.

A quick check revealed that her flight persona was wiped out, again, but there was no structural damage.

The near miss behind her, she boosted to skim again, focused on her goal of reaching *Second Contact Station*.

"Is that Ann?" a controller acknowledged her hail. "Back again so soon with the mail run?"

"I'm not here for the mail run," Ann said, resisting the fear that she had missed Von's departure. "Josh is making that connection. He should have been here ahead of me." She paused. "He's not here?"

"No."

There was an uncomfortable silence in which Ann wondered what could have happened to Josh.

"You have to initiate the info synch," the controller reminded her. "Looks like you've blanked your flight persona."

"I had help!" Ann assured him. "I got wake-rocked by a Gelack on the way here."

"A Gelack?" the controller sounded dubious. "You're sure it wasn't just Josh getting silly?"

"Pretty sure," Ann said, simply. She wasn't going to mention the tidal wave of self-righteous contempt she had experienced. No one had been real receptive to her story about feeling Von's presence in the jump they had made together. "How's Von?" she asked.

"I'm not an info persona," the controller told her. "Synch, and you can spawn one."

"Just tell me, okay?" said Ann. "He's my lover."

"That's right," the controller said coolly. "You declared a relationship based on your appreciation for his courtesan training. Sorry, but he's not much fun anymore."

"I didn't come back for fun," she snapped, stung.

"I'm waiting for your signal to upload," he prompted her. "Or should I send out the tugs and prep the ambulance bay?"

"Oh, all right!" she said, deciding there was no point debating her commitment to Von with some wannabe pilot who would never get closer than talking one into dock. "Give me a second," she said. "It's these damn algorithmics. I have to look up every command."

"Ann?" a voice cut in. "This is Lurol. Have you got the verdict from Rire?"

"Sorry," Ann said. "I'm not the mail run."

"I know that!" Lurol was impatient. "I thought you might have caught the news before you went to skim. So? What did Rire decide? Treat him here, or ship him home?"

Lurol's treatment, Ann recalled, would not take very long. It might be over and done before Josh even showed up. If Josh was going to show up.

Ann suffered a fierce spike of temptation.

"Just a second," she said, sounding guilty to her own ears as she casually wiped out her copy of Rire's decision along with all the other data which had survived in her entertainment buffer. "Sorry," she said. "It's these pesky algorithmics."

She sent the synching signal.

Her ship accepted a new flight persona that took over the docking sequence, and executed a complete exchange of data with the arbiter on *Second Contact Station*, minus what she had just erased.

"Well?" Lurol sounded eager. "Do I cure Von, or ship him home cargo?"

"It was close," said Ann, painfully aware that she had not yet done anything unforgivable, but was about to. She might never get off Supervision for a lie of this magnitude. "The anthropologists weren't sure you ought to do it alone without more background research," Ann postponed her decision, heart hammering. "But the final verdict was to go ahead!"

I've done it now! Ann thought, horrified.

"Go ahead?" Lurol echoed. "You mean treat him here despite the underlying instability?"

"That's right!" Ann groped for details. "It went as far as the third expansion of Foreign and Alien Council," she said, and added in all honesty, "I can't remember how far the expansion of the medical debate went."

"Do it here," said Lurol, sounding challenged, but a bit thrilled.

"Yeah," Ann grasped for something more to make it plausible. "That's why I came out — I wanted to be here for him." She wet her lips nervously. "How is he?"

"Lurol is occupied prepping the patient," an info persona inserted itself into the conversation, and supplied Ann with a text summary.

"Show me Von, now," Ann ordered instead, and was shown the view inside the visitor probe.

Von's head was fixed in place under the hood by rod-like projections of hard morph material. Invisible probe fields recorded and adjusted synaptic flows with an arbiter's genius for detail. He was in an induced coma, but Lurol was letting him surface. His eyes were open and staring. A saline drip, positioned on a slender robot arm, dropped solution into them at intervals, making trails of mock tears down either side of his head.

He came to life with a wave of animation and blinked: a drop of saline catching in his long, dark eyelashes. Ann put her hand out to touch the projection on her ship's little stage, her own eyes prickling. "It will be okay," she said, although she knew he couldn't hear.

She scrambled out of her ship as soon as her airlock cycled, only to be blocked by a pair of new pilot handlers.

"You can't see Von," one of them anticipated her objection. "He's undergoing psychiatric surgery."

"Already?"

The handler nodded. "Lurol had the job all mapped out: how to light up the trigger and then destroy the neural cascade."

She didn't like the sound of "destroy" in conjunction with "neural" but she swallowed down her questions.

"May as well spend the time telling Jon your story," said the other handler.

"Right!" Ann exclaimed, remembering. "The attack. That's important."

"Attack?" echoed the handler.

"Well, yeah," Ann said uncertainly. "I think so. Or else, you know, serious rudeness. He passed me flying way too hard, and way too close."

"You think someone … attacked you. While reality skimming?" asked the handler, sounding more inclined to doubt Ann's sanity than believe in such an incident.

Now she was safely docked and preoccupied with worrying about Von's condition, Ann was half inclined to doubt it herself. Two *rel*-ships encountering each other was a bit like a couple of motorized boats sharing a lake. If you got capsized by a show-off kicking up a high wake, did you call it an accident or an assault?

"Maybe I was attacked," Ann decided, "and maybe not. The pilot was damned reckless if nothing else."

"Josh?"

"It wasn't Josh!" Ann insisted, but could not explain — exactly — why she was sure. "I had better talk to Jon about it," she concluded.

Triumvir Jon listened to her babble about her experience for five minutes before he got a pained look on his face and asked, plaintively, "You don't think it could have been Josh, trying to scare you. Or make an impression."

"I told you!" Ann objected with increasing irritation. "It didn't feel playful. It felt like —" she groped for the fading memory of her encounter. "Contempt. Casual, cold-blooded, dismissive contempt. He didn't even check to see he had taken me out, just kept going. But I bet he did get Josh."

"And you think this mysterious pilot was a Gelack?" Jon's brow furrowed. "How could you possibly know that, Ann?"

"I don't know anything!" Ann insisted, and let out her frustration in a long sigh, stroking her fingers back through her short hair. "Can I go now? This isn't getting us any-where."

The Space Service triumvir agreed, reluctantly, adding, "I hope you are wrong, Ann. Because if what you have described, twice, is actually organized warfare in the *rel*-medium, we have no means of dealing with it. But it is more reasonable, don't you think, to put the first event down to a sort of xenophobic riot in space, and attribute the latter one to hi-jinks. Gelacks do seem quite socially primitive, and Josh has the psych profile for playing tricks. If so, it would seem that he has done himself more harm by it than he did you. Let's hope it is nothing worst than time-slip."

"Yeah," Ann said, wanting to agree with Jon despite her nagging worries. "If it was Josh, when he shows up, can I slug him?"

Jon smiled at her, relieved she had stopped claiming the fly-by had been malicious. "Maybe just this once," he said.

Ann's routine post-flight checkup didn't take as long as her debriefing, but when it was done she found herself stuck, waiting to be dismissed, with nothing but an arbiter persona on the nearby stage to keep her company.

"Do I have to wait here for clearance?" she appealed to the arbiter persona, lacking a human to complain to. "My boyfriend is getting his brain fixed. Can't I go wait where he is?"

"You do not have a boyfriend on record," the persona said.

"Von!" said Ann. "Von's my boyfriend."

"Category violation," the persona objected. "The referenced relationship was extant at the time of your departure, but has ceased to be applicable due to new input."

Ann clammed up, afraid to discover that some dumb isolation malfunction had messed up her claim on Von, because if so she didn't want it coming to the attention of people — like Lurol — who might deny her access to him.

Her parents had once described an arbiter's cognitive core to her as an amoeba, reading and re-ordering its cold stores as it moved through them. The difference was that these amoebas were all one animal, kept in synch by mail runs, and this one was at the extreme range for inclusion in the Arbiter Administration. That integration was crucial to them. The longer a complex, general purpose AI like a station arbiter was cut off, the greater the risk of it becoming what was called eccentric. The visitor probe was run by arbiter class software as well, but as an idiot-savant it was less vulnerable.

Ann waited tensely. The moment her examiner reappeared, she popped off the exam table and bellowed, "I want to see Von, now!"

He looked startled, but said, "If you must."

Ann didn't need help finding Lurol's lab, but her two pilot handlers followed her anyway, much to Ann's annoyance.

In the recovery room outside Lurol's lab, Alicia, the anthropologist, was sitting on a bed looking stunned.

Ann's dread must have showed because the anthropologist quickly said, "Von's alive, Ann. He's just ..." she groped for the right word, "traumatized."

Relief liquefied Ann's bowels. "Hey, well," she laughed again and blurted. "You get over that!"

"Oh, Ann," said the anthropologist, in the way someone does when they're trying to break the news your rabbit got out and was eaten by a neighbor's dog. Ann dodged around her and ran through the open archway into the visitor probe lab.

Inside, Lurol stood with her back to the visitor probe surrounded by a half a dozen pilot handlers who were all looking at a body huddled on the floor in front of them, backed into a corner. There was no mistaking that body — it was Von.

Von was naked and curled into a ball except for one pale leg which described a slow, churning motion as he murmured something sing-song to himself in Gelack.

"Von?" Ann gasped as the cringing creature lurched up, throwing out an arm as if to fend off an attack.

"Clear dream!" Lurol warned. Her team fell on Von as he lashed out with hysterical violence, heaving them along in his jagged dance.

Ann spun on Lurol, her heart pounding. "What went wrong?"

"Nothing," Lurol said clinically. "He's cured."

"That's cured!"

"Cured of the conscience bond," explained Lurol. "There is still the underlying problem." She frowned. "And the clear dreams are a complication."

Von's handlers slowly backed off as he curled up quietly on the floor.

"What did you do to him?" cried Ann, alarming her own handlers enough to make them grab her arms. She jerked free of them and stood her ground.

"He is doing it to himself!" insisted Lurol, rubbery face set in a scowl. "He can't live without the conscience bond to blame for his failings and is too scared to die. A slight adjustment of his personality might do the trick. I've written about the possibility. The biggest challenge is focusing the dysfunction cognitively but he has already organized it, symbolically, around Mira and the girl in the Bear Pit. He can't cope right now because he can't accept that he could have acted differently, and didn't. But he might accept it if I reinforced his sense of his own right to self-preservation, or dampened the competing emotions."

Ann was too preoccupied by her gut reaction to pay much attention to the theorizing. Before her was the body she had dreamed about, and now all she wanted was to run away. It was the same way she had felt about N'Goni, towards the end.

"Can you see if you can get some clothes on him?" one of Von's handlers asked Ann. "He panics when we try to touch him."

Von had stopped trembling now and was looking at them with the patience of a whipped dog.

The handler gave Ann the rejected pajamas.

"I don't know," Ann muttered lamely. "I don't think he recognizes me."

"Try," said the handler.

Just then the central stage spawned a girl in pigtails wearing red shoes. Ann recognized it as her messaging icon, customized to resemble the character Dorothy from an old Earth classic called *The Wizard of Oz*. Dorothy said, "Hi, Ann. Jon requests your input with regard to an unidentified ship, now on its docking run."

Relieved, Ann started returning the pajamas to the handlers, but Von was looking at her from where he rested limply against a wall.

Ann swallowed down repulsion and wiped her free palm on her yellow stretch shorts. "Hi," she said. There was no response.

"Von's your real name, right?" she asked.

He flinched, closing his eyes again.

"He understands Reetion, since his probe exposure," commented a handler. "The arbiter picked up some Gelack, as well. Quite incredible."

Ann got down on the floor like someone trying to coax an animal out of its hidey hole. "Come let me dress you," she said. "You'll feel better."

Von's eyes brimmed.

The Dorothy icon appeared again with an accompanying giggle that Ann remembered putting in as a random variation. "Incoming pilot identified as Thomas," Dorothy reported and clicked her heels.

Von started to his feet, alarmed.

"Stage off!" ordered Lurol.

Von's breath came in jerks, his fine, pastel lips parted.

Right, Ann thought, *first things first.* She selected the pajama pants and held them out.

"We're going to put these on you," she told him. "Okay?"

"Careful," advised a handler, "he could throw you across the room!"

"Maybe," Ann said, sustaining eye contact. "But he won't. Will you?"

His expression dissolved in oceanic suffering. Small wounds left by medical interventions looked vulgar on his white skin. But it was still hard not to look at his groin, so rich and soft and dark against the backdrop of his firm thighs.

"The thing is," Ann bullied, holding out the pajama bottoms again. "You can't go around naked, okay? It's distracting."

He smiled. It was very faint, but it buoyed her hopes.

"I'm glad you're okay!" Ann said, forgetting about the clothes, took his head between her hands and kissed him.

He passed out cold in her arms.

He was heavier than he looked, she discovered, as she tried to hold him up. He clung to her as he came around again. Speaking soothing words, she helped him from the lab into the recovery room, where Lurol and the medics had prepared a bed equipped with a standard psych scanner helmet.

One look at the helmet and Von tore out of Ann's arms like a force of nature, only to collapse on the floor again.

A handler knelt down to confirm he was only unconscious.

"He's scared of the equipment," Lurol decided. "Put him in the other bed."

"What if he needs life support again?" protested Vera.

Lurol shook her head. "Physically, that boy's a powerhouse. It's his psychology that's frail, now. Just keep him comfortable until I figure out what to do about that." Lurol went back into her lab.

Ann followed. Partly, she wanted to find out what Lurol knew about Von's problem. Partly, she wanted to get away, because she couldn't bear the sight of Von in this condition and did not want to think too hard about what that meant. She was rather afraid it meant she didn't care about him when he wasn't exciting company in a good way.

The stage in Lurol's lab was filled with a full-blown simulation of a memory. Ann halted at the sight of a man labeled "Jarl" attacking a little girl. The sound was off, which helped, but not enough. Von's sensory manikin attacked, but Jarl seized him and slammed him against a wall. Pain exploded, white hot, from the head blow.

"One of his focal incidents," said Lurol.

Ann's stomach turned over with a cold thump.

"Von lay and listened to Jarl kill the girl," continued Lurol. "He was afraid that Jarl would kill him, too, if he tried to stop him again."

"Okay," Ann felt nettled. "Okay, but he was only ten! How can you blame him?"

"I don't," Lurol said. "He blames himself." She adjusted the virtual reality controls on her console. "This is the other focal incident," she explained.

They were catapulted into a kitchen where an older Von gossiped with a cook and a serving girl. His reaction to the kitchen maid was skewed in favor of her cleavage, which she made available for his inspection as she leaned over.

Definitely heterosexual, Ann thought and wondered how he felt about her own breasts, which were smaller.

"Something very important happens next," said Lurol.

Von's sensory avatar got up, wiping his mouth, and made his farewells pleasantly. He passed down a homey corridor and out into a fussily decorated parlor where a richly dressed woman waited beside a diminutive girl about Von's age. The girl invoked a tidal wave of feeling.

"Mira," Lurol told Ann. "Von planned to earn enough, flying for H'Reth, to see her through her training as a medic, but things went wrong when he rejected H'Reth's advances. He lost track of Mira, until she turned up as a medic working for one of his patrons. By that time he was conscience bonded to H'Reth to ensure his loyalty. When Mira accused H'Reth to the patron, hoping to help Von, he denied it. Von never found out what had happened to her."

Ann cleared her throat. "Why are you telling me all this?" she asked.

"Because I need your help," Lurol admitted.

"For what?" Ann asked, suspiciously.

Lurol turned the stage off. "Von's conflict is so clearly symbolized! I feel sure I could use that, like a handle, to adjust his emotional balance. It would be the beginning of a whole new field of psychiatric medicine!" Her enthusiasm plummeted. "But I don't think he'll give his permission unless you encourage him. He's phobic about the visitor probe. The experience must have been uncomfortable. But it can't have been too bad! The station arbiter would have stopped me if it was too distressing for him."

Ann shifted, feeling off balance and beginning to worry about what Thomas might be up to, and whether he had been followed. Would Triumvir Jon be cagey enough to question Thomas properly?

Or am I being crazy and paranoid, Ann asked herself.

"So," Ann answered Lurol, tentatively, mind half focused on each of the problems tormenting her. "You want to change Von's personality?" She didn't much like the sound of that.

"I want to make it possible for him to put his own self-interest first when necessary," said Lurol. "Think of it as probe-assisted counseling."

"But it would change his personality," Ann said stubbornly. "Make him less ... nice. Or something."

Lurol glared. "You don't get it, do you?"

"I *get* that you're having way too much fun thinking up new *firsts* for yourself!" Ann snapped at her.

"Listen," Lurol told Ann with strained patience. "This is no boy-next-door you've got the hots for. He's got empathy hard-wired into him the way normal people have survival instincts. He loves people too much! Until he defied the conscience bond, here on this station, he told himself he simply could not do it. That it was not, literally, possible. That was his excuse for failing Mira, and Mira is his big issue. The girl in the Bear Pit is secondary. A symbol, for him, of the moment when he gave up daring to care about someone else. Now he knows he could defy the conscience bond because he did it, once it crossed his mind he might survive with our help. His first problem was, of course, the bond itself. That's fixed now, more or less. But he's stuck with the knowledge he failed someone he loved of his own free will. He can't face what he did, and he doesn't believe he has the strength to do better if he had to make that sort of choice again. An ordinary person would get over it, but he's locked in perpetual crisis and the conflict between fear and love is paralyzing. All I want to do is adjust the balance to his benefit, so he is more like other people."

"By making him less capable of loving others?" Ann asked, dismayed.

"Less driven to self-sacrifice, yes," agreed Lurol. "Or would you prefer we went the other way, and boosted an already abnormally strong sense of empathy to the point that it could dominate his will to live, just so you could really be sure he loved you more than life itself."

"Or we do nothing and wait," Ann said, caustically.

Lurol blew out a sigh and scrubbed her short, dry hair. "I suppose," she said, looking unexpectedly miserable. "I just don't know, Ann, to be honest. That might work. His psych profile is like nothing I've ever seen. Or, for the same reason, he might just be capable of driving himself insane with guilt. What I do know is that he's suffering the way he is."

Triumvir Jon appeared on the stage. "We've recovered Thomas," he said. "He's being brought up to the lab for observation. Says the Sevolites set him loose to learn the jump from him, but claims the ship that followed him into the jump wasn't with him when he came out again."

Neither was Von's, Ann thought, skin prickling. *Because he arrived first!*

"Thomas time slipped!" she blurted. "Just like I did when Von followed me. Thomas must have led through the Gelack who took a swipe at me and might have taken poor Josh out entirely. Someone is out there!" she cried, alarm rising with her voice. "I was attacked. It's real!"

"Why isn't this Gelack here, then, harassing us?" Jon asked, still resistant. "Really, Ann, I am sure there has to be some better —"

Ann's skin was prickling. "He's not here," she said, getting spooked, "because he's gone back to get the *Vanilla Rose*. He's gone back to lead *Vanilla Rose* to us. So they'll have a base to harass us from! Otherwise it would be hard to threaten us. He

couldn't stay out, in skim, indefinitely, and he would have
no idea where else to go. He'd have to ask us, pretty please,
to dock, or else go back through the jump again." She shook
her head, stomach stone cold. "He's gone to get *Vanilla Rose*."

There was disbelieving silence.

"Could Gelacks be a threat to the station?" Jon asked
nervously.

"Culturally, it is counter-indicated," answered Ranar's
stand-in composite. "According to Von's grasp of theology,
damaging habitat is *okal'a'ni* — a potent Gelack taboo."

Ann wet her lips before speaking. "Okay," she said, trying to believe it, then failing. "Okay. What does anthropology have to say about the success rate of taboos holding
up against an enemy?"

"You have something else in mind?" asked Lurol.

"Von," she said, hating herself for the very thought. But
the others had not faced a Sevolite in space. They didn't
understand the way that she did. "Von can fly like they can!
He could help us!"

"You just don't listen, do you!" Lurol lashed out. "Von
is more likely to break out in tears than play hero if you
asked him to do something like that!"

Jon asked her to explain herself and Lurol launched into
it all again, while the rest of the team chipped in with questions or opinions.

Ann backed away from the crowded stage. *Words*, she
thought. *It is all just words to them.*

They had never felt the threat of an approaching Gelack
ship.

Von lay on the recovery room bed in white pajamas. Vera
stood by his head, stroking his fine, jet black hair. She looked
up as Ann approached and smiled with a bemused expression.

"Beautiful, isn't he?" said Vera.

Von stirred, agitated by their voices despite his sedation.
His hand groped blindly and Ann captured it.

"He's going to be okay," Ann said fiercely. "When he sleeps this off, he's going to be just fine again."

Lurol displaced Vera on the other side of the bed. "Don't be ridiculous."

Von's eyes opened and sought out Ann, avoiding Lurol.

Ann gripped his hand more tightly. "Can you understand me? Are you — here?" she pleaded.

"Yes," he said weakly, in Reetion. She could feel him quivering as if just daring to look up at her took a lot of effort.

"You trust me, don't you?" Ann asked him.

"I w-want to," he stuttered, but his attention drifted nervously from her to Lurol.

"There's no need to be frightened," Lurol said stiffly. "I'm your doctor."

He looked as if she had named the hour of his execution.

Jon arrived in person with a couple of pilot handlers transporting Thomas on a stretcher. Von pushed himself up to watch them set Thomas up for limbic stimulation. His grip on Ann's hand hurt, but as soon as she squirmed he looked up, grasped the problem, and relaxed his hold a little.

Jon came over, looking anxious. "Ann thinks your people on *Vanilla Rose* intend to attack us," Jon told Von. "I'd like to know whether you —"

Von vomited. Ann let herself be displaced by a couple of pilot handlers.

"He isn't up to this!" Lurol protested.

"That's for the arbiter to decide," Jon insisted. "It's aware of your analysis and his psych profile. It's been monitoring your treatment. If he truly isn't up to questioning, I am sure it —"

Jon broke off. They had all felt it, a momentary lapse of concentration, unremarkable, perhaps, except that everyone had felt it at the same time. A silence with the quality of thin ice followed.

Ann was the first to speak again. "What was that?" she asked, breathlessly.

The station arbiter answered. "A large reality skimming vessel has dropped out of skim close enough to cause mild psychological side effects on *Second Contact Station*."

"*Vanilla Rose*," Ann whispered under her breath.

Von curled up in a fetal position. Ann spared him a glance and thought, *Do I really love him? Is he what I came here for? To die.*

The arbiter said, "Identification positive. The vessel matches Ann's descriptions of *Vanilla Rose*. The *Vanilla Rose* is sending three reality skimming ships in our direction," it added.

Space Service had protocols about what to do if a pilot flipped out and flew right at a station while reality skimming. They amounted to 'kiss your ass goodbye' in Ann's opinion, or sacrifice a pilot to intercept the nut case. That was a chilling prospect. All the more so because she doubted she could even catch someone like Von if she was willing to try, and there were three Gelack ships out there.

"Approaching ships have dropped out of skim," the arbiter reported.

Ann let out the breath she had been holding without realizing it.

"Incoming radio transmission in Gelack," the arbiter continued. "Stand by for translation."

The resulting Reetion sounded unreasonably harmless as it streamed through the tiny stage at the foot of Von's bed.

"I am Larren," said the message, "Master Paladin in the service of Ava Delm. You have a courtesan called Von who offends the divine goodness of my idol. Yield him, unless you have a highborn who will come to stand against me in an honorable duel. Yield him, and even though you are Reetions, ignorant of honor, I will spare you for the sake of the habitable structure you occupy."

In the silence that followed, Ann realized Von had wet himself where he lay curled under his coverlet.

She looked up to see Jon staring at her. "Would they do that?" Jon asked, incredulously.

Oh yes, Ann thought, and looked at Von shivering in bed, involuntarily weighing him against her own survival.

"No!" Vera put Ann to shame. "We must protect him! Can't you see how frightened he is?"

"It won't be up to us to decide," said Lurol sourly, waving over pilot handlers to clean Von up. "The arbiter won't let us violate his human rights."

"But he is sane?" Jon insisted. "Sane enough the arbiter would accept his right to give himself up if he volunteered?"

Ann kept thinking, *He wet himself. How can I love someone who wets himself in terror and then lies in it, curled up in a fetal position?* But her next thought was, *He's afraid of himself. That's what Lurol was telling me, isn't it? He knows he ought to give himself up. He can't do it, and he can't bear to refuse, either.*

Looked at in that light, Von's reaction was a bit more palatable.

If Lurol's right about all that emotional conflict stuff, Ann thought.

"What will this Larren do if we refuse?" Lurol asked the anthropologist present.

Alicia delayed to check in with her colleagues over a microstage. "We can't be sure," she said. "But if we can extrapolate from that remark about us being ignorant of honor, I'm afraid that we may be fair game."

"So we could be destroyed," said Jon, with a touch of rising hysteria, "by a few mad Gelacks."

There was a long silence broken only by the handlers coaxing Von out of his wet pajamas.

"Can we make them understand that our arbiter won't let us violate Von's human rights?" Jon asked urgently. "That arbiters are designed, at a very fundamental level, to make the very sort of bullying this Larren is threatening impossible."

"I very much doubt we can explain that successfully," Alicia said, looking waxen.

"Then we get him to volunteer," Jon decided. "He might do it, given his psych profile."

Lurol shook her head. "So far it's been two out of two for survival over altruism. And Mira meant a whole lot more to him than we do."

"We shouldn't be talking like this!" cried Vera. "We should be protecting him!"

Easy for you to say, thought Ann. *You aren't the pilot who would have to go out there and try to defend us if we don't give him up.*

Jon appealed to the stage nearest to him. "Hypothetically," he asked, "if the command triumvirate voted to trade the life of one, unwilling person, to save this station from an outside threat such as Larren's — would we be able to implement that decision?"

"External threats may not motivate the knowing violation of human rights in response to acts of reality-skimming terrorism," replied the arbiter, as unmoved as ever. Only Vera had the decency to look relieved.

A siren whooped and all the stages came on, displaying an emergency alert symbol.

"A Gelack ship has violated the station's safety radius," announced the arbiter. "Personnel are being withdrawn from high risk areas as structural damage is possible."

The recovery room erupted in wild babble until Jon raised both arms and cried, "Quiet!"

Jon shoved the nearest handler aside and shouted down at Von, where he lay looking up on his bed. "We'll all die unless you surrender! All of us, including you! It's pointless! You have to tell arbiter you're willing."

Von stared up, tears welling silently. Lurol began to argue there was no point using duress, but Jon just shouted louder. "Don't you understand! You freak!" He seized Von as if to haul him up, then drew his hand back and struck out.

Ann caught her breath as Von's head snapped over. Then she sprang to join the handlers as they hauled Jon off and pressed him down to sit on another bed. Jon put his face into his hands and groaned in shame.

The arbiter was silent.

"I'd say that was assault," Lurol said quietly.

Ann knew what happened in a high surveillance environment, like a recovery room, when you lost your temper. She remembered the restraining foam hitting her while the model of a brain flew the last few centimeters from her hand into Lurol's jaw.

"Jon attacked my patient!" Lurol barked at a microstage, her posture brittle. "Explain your inaction."

"No actionable behavior observed," replied the arbiter. "Assault requires a human victim. Von's classification is undefined. "

"What?" croaked Lurol.

Ann was hit with the familiar dipping feeling of a phase transition. She stayed standing but Lurol stumbled and Jon toppled off the bed he was sitting on.

Ann was the first to recover. "That was a fly-by," she said. "They passed close enough to swipe the station with their wake and perturb the space around us without wiping us both out of existence."

The flying required for such a maneuver was impressive, but the arrogance inflamed her.

The arbiter came back on, reporting damage and the loss of a swarm of its personas that had to be re-spawned from its cognitive core.

One of the pilot handlers queued the stage, moving away from Von's bed. "Why doesn't Von have human rights?" he asked the arbiter.

"Classification of subject Von is undefined since the intake of data during the last half of his interrogation," it answered.

"Interrogation!" exclaimed Lurol, dismayed.

"Our definition of humanity is based on the human genome," said Milap. "And Von's DNA isn't natural. It isn't in our catalog!"

"That wasn't done to exclude someone like Von," Vera objected. "It was done to protect disabled people who might fall outside any particular functional definition!"

Well, thought Ann. *Now I know why the arbiter refused to acknowledge our relationship. Can't have one with someone who's unclassified.* She was getting angry. It felt a whole lot better than desperate and demoralized.

Lurol looked ill. She said, "I didn't interrogate anyone."

Von lay on his side, abandoned by his handlers. Even Vera stood a few steps off, as if his new vulnerability left room for her to shed her sympathy towards him. Ann moved in.

"Look at me," she ordered, shaking him.

Von eased himself onto his back and looked up at her, face as pale as bone and hauntingly beautiful.

"Why just here?" Milap asked. "Why not everywhere Ann delivered Von's data?"

"Von was in the probe for hours after Ann left," said Vera. "That's when it must have happened."

"We don't have time for this," Jon protested.

Von stared up at Ann, and said, faintly, "I am sorry."

If he had clung to her then, if he had begged, she might have managed to reject him. But his acceptance was terrible: Lurol had turned him inside out; Larren wanted to destroy him; Jon had struck him. He didn't understand any of it, but he looked to her for no more than confirmation that another human being might be moved to forgive him for bringing this down on them. He was afraid, but there was no blame in him.

Ann leaned over and kissed his forehead.

"Forget it," she whispered. "You are staying here."

As she drew back a panicky look overtook him.

"We can't just hand him over to be murdered!" Vera was protesting to the assembled triumvirate.

"We can, in fact," said Lurol, shoulders hunched and face like granite. "By which I mean the arbiter will let us. I should have realized," she said, her voice breaking. "I should have thought for myself, not relied on the arbiter. I should have realized something was wrong when it didn't intervene."

Jon's eyes darted from one to the other of his co-conspirators. "What else can we do but surrender him?"

They all looked towards Von. But Ann was there, between him and them.

"No," she said quietly. "I'm going. I'll accept Larren's challenge, but not by going over to *Vanilla Rose* to wave a sword at him. He wants Von? I'll be Von. We've got more than enough data. We can load Von's speech patterns into a custom filter."

"Ann," the anthropologist Alicia warned, starkly, "they'll kill you."

"Maybe." Ann grinned like a mad woman.

"Ann, no!" Von tried to get out of bed and fell. Vera went to help him. Lurol caught Ann's arm, preventing her from joining Vera.

"You know it is probably suicide?" Lurol asked soberly.

"Yeah?" Ann said, glaring at the larger woman. "Well, at least I'm doing something I can live with."

Lurol flinched.

Von interrupted by pitching into another clear dream.

Ann pursed her lips, frustrated to be denied a more picturesque goodbye, but she couldn't waste time on that. She headed for the docks, ordering what she wanted in the hope and expectation that the triumvirate would give her *carte blanche* within permissible parameters. Arbiters did not tolerate weapons, so she was going to have to improvise.

"Good luck," the controller signed off as she pulled away in a standard issue *rel*-ship. She had decided not to take her scout. The cockpit slug was too awkward to get out of quickly once she docked. Instead she wore the pearly white flight suit of an ordinary pilot. Engineering told her it would stop a sword. If they hadn't added that she could still be bludgeoned to death or cooked inside of it, she might have thanked them. Up her sleeve she had a welding laser and if it knew why, the arbiter would have objected.

* * *

"Ann?" Von asked, clutching at the woman leaning over him.

"Ann has gone to impersonate you," Lurol told him, "to buy time."

"N-no!" Von protested, afraid for her. The pounding of his heart shook his chest. The smell of men holding him threatened to raise memories he didn't want to relive. He felt all alone and bewildered.

"You want to help Ann, don't you?" Lurol asked him.

Von whimpered. He did want to help! But something bad would come of it. Something always did. His nerves exploded with remembered pain and a cold sweat broke out over his skin.

Then he was ten years old and lying on a grimy carpet listening to a girl scream. He didn't even know her name, but he knew Jarl was killing her.

Defeat coiled black and leaden in Von's stomach as he told himself lies. It would be different if the girl was Mira. Then he could do it. His head pulsed and pain clung to him in clots. The girl screamed. He closed his eyes tighter.

"What should you have done?" The voice was Lurol's.

He got up. He staggered to where Jarl hunched on his knees over the girl, and hurled him off of her.

The scene changed. He was in the kitchen at Silver Hearth, feeling sad but proud of making Mira believe he had abandoned her on purpose, so she wouldn't get in trouble trying to save him.

"But she figured it out," Lurol forced the fact upon him. "Or half of it, at least. She didn't understand about the conscience bond."

He was standing in the parlor now, with Mira looking heated and confident, commanding him to tell their patron, the Princess-Liege of H'Us, that H'Reth was abusing him. And he was angry with Mira for not letting him protect her, for insisting, as always, that she knew better. He was angry, and not ready to die.

"What should you have done?" demanded Lurol.

He met Mira's eyes one last time, to thank her for his freedom, then he said, "It's true," and his heart stopped beating at the same moment that his breath stalled in his lungs as bond conflict punished him.

And it hurt. It all hurt, more than he could stand. So when his mind filled with star maps he drank the emotionless coolness of them with a fatal thirst. The maps showed him how to find a second jump in the Reach of Paradise where the Reetions came from. One he didn't know how to get out of once he got in.

"If you survive Larren," Lurol's godlike voice impressed upon him, "take H'Reth and his invading Gelacks down that jump. Lose them in it, for all time, and save the lives of innocent Reetions."

Von quailed at this new doom. To be lost in a jump was to be Soul Lost, never to die and therefore never to be reborn. To be lost in a jump with H'Reth raised further objections. It was enough to endure their bodies touching without suffering Garn H'Reth's soul touch in eternal limbo.

But somehow he did have the strength now. He was willing to die, and worse than die, to get this job done. And if he proved, to himself, that he was, then he could regain what he lost when he betrayed Mira. He could have faith in something larger than his own survival, once more.

He woke to find himself in the visitor probe. Its lid opened. He blinked up at the ceiling, tears and saline itching where they had trickled from his staring eyes. He sat up.

Lurol stood with her hands jammed into the pockets of her lab coat. She looked upset, her body clenched with nervous tension. He felt sorry for her.

She said, "There may still be time to save Ann, as well as the rest of us."

He nodded. And then he smiled. "Yes," he said. "I will try."

12

Politics of a Pregnancy

There were times when the lack of good communications in UnderGelion made Di Mon want to become Ava. Maybe then he could get the trunk lines that last functioned under the Lorel Avas back into operation. Instead, every house had its own, limited solution, based on incompatible standards. In open spaces like the Palace Plain, echo-troubled radio transmission was possible, but so vulnerable to interference it was nearly useless.

Thus it was that Di Mon did not learn that he had no state car at his disposal until he and his four errants reached his garage at the mouth of the docks. One car was being serviced, one was signed out to Sarilous and Tessitatt, and the third had been taken by Kertatt with the expressed intention of following Vretla Vrel to Den Eva's.

I will lash the boy if he upsets her again, Di Mon thought.

"If Your Grace would be pleased to wait," his distraught garage manager implored, "we can have a car for you in half an hour."

Di Mon was not disposed to wait, nor was he keen to wind up with Ses Nersal as chauffeur again if he hired a car from her garage.

"We will walk to the Apron District," he announced. "Send a car to H'Reth Manor when one becomes available."

His errants closed around him as they headed off. Their route took them along a boulevard between the Palace Plain and the base of the Citadel, past a water distillery, a hydroponics farm, and an oxygen factory owned by the throne.

Each glowed with light that faded into twilight on the plain beyond, where no one had explicit cause to relieve the darkness of the subterranean shell that contained the empire's capital.

His errants kept their banter to a minimum and did not bother him with questions while they walked. It felt good to be out, and the exercise did Di Mon good. Their destination was the south gate of the Apron District. Spread out at the base of the Citadel, the Apron District was the location of choice for Demish nobleborns residing at court. A crowd of loosely organized guards slowly gathered in a knot behind their captain as Di Mon approached, but they did not close the gate in the high, metal fence at their backs. Since the defenders were nobleborn, Di Mon signaled his errant captain forward to negotiate on his behalf.

"Our greetings to you," said Captain Hesseratt, putting her Demish peer on notice, through her choice of pronouns, that she spoke for Di Mon. "We are here to ask questions at H'Reth Manor concerning a courtesan called Von."

"You may want to come another time, if your business is with H'Reth Manor," said the Demish captain.

"Oh?" Di Mon intruded. "Why is that?"

"Nothing I care to discuss in front of women," said the Demish man.

"Why not?" asked Srain Eversol, a male errant new to court, his manner purely curious.

"What the Demish mean when they say things like that," pitched in a female errant named L'Ket, "is that one of their stifled wives has fallen short of their ridiculous notion that women hate sex, and they're ashamed to let us find out."

Di Mon's male errants, Srain and Tan, laughed at the witticism. L'Ket was sleeping with Tan and out to collect Srain, which was not in itself a problem, by Vrellish standards, though apt to make L'Ket dangerous.

"If you were not a woman —" the Demish captain said through gritted teeth, hand on his sword.

"Pretend I am not!" L'Ket dared him, clearing her own blade from its sheath.

"If you wish to contest my entry," Di Mon decided to make use of L'Ket's bravado, "you may take it up with L'Ket on my behalf."

"I won't fight a woman," the Demish captain opted for a high moral tone. "You may pass."

"Fool words to mask a *pol* truth," L'Ket pushed the issue, disappointed. "I could take you and you know it. That's all."

The Demish guard flushed. A ripple of laughter surfaced here and there through his command.

"L'Ket," Di Mon ordered. "Sheath your sword."

She obeyed with a dramatic snap and pushed forward, glaring at the Demish as she passed.

"Bitch," someone muttered from a clump of guards.

"What's a bitch?" L'Ket asked, looking back.

"A Demish insult," said Tan. He had been born and raised at court.

Srain, who'd had a formal education on Monitum, said, "Literally, it means a female dog. Or an ill-tempered woman."

"Guess he was right then," Tan joked and defended himself from L'Ket's answering slap.

"That's enough!" Hesseratt intervened to separate them. "Tan, take the right scout position; L'Ket, the left flank."

Children, Di Mon thought as they sorted themselves out. The Vrellish could be such destructive children. Sometimes he admired the Demish for their greater constructive powers, but they were no less aggressive merely for being slow and inexorable. Demora did not flourish under Silver Demish rule, despite the worshipful lip-service paid to anything connected with the Golden Emperor. Monatese scholarship would fare no better if Green Hearth lost its place on Fountain Court. Silver Hearth would take over Monitum with all the cloying reverence of a fool for a great book; preferring questions of how best to cite a reference over whether science could be used for good instead of evil, and declaring history heretical to legend.

"We're a novelty," Hesseratt remarked, nodding towards a Demish manor house as they passed, where a half-dozen female faces peered out at them from a bay window. Demish homes were always full of surplus females. To Di Mon they seemed a wasted resource.

Srain smiled and waved at the curious women, who withdrew into the gloom of their parlor, long blue curtains swishing down.

It was unusual for people to see a Vrellish party passing through the heart of nobleborn Demish suburbia, and the Demish didn't like unusual things very much.

They left behind the smaller residences of Midlords for the larger estates of Seniorlord families, which occupied twice as much real estate and were noticeably more ponderous. In Red Vrellish circles such distinctions between birth ranks was rarely dwelt upon — challenge class was paramount, with its clear physical distinctions. In the Apron District, however, Midlord families plotted for generations to become Seniorlords, and never forgot to cite the high water mark of their family's history if their genetic capital should fall.

H'Reth was a downwardly mobile house of the latter sort, supposedly descended from a Pureblood of the Blue Demish line. Di Mon considered the claim fair enough since every Sevolite must ultimately be descended from a Pureblood, unless Monatese scholarship was very wrong. Some houses had simply lost track of their progenitors. But whatever the truth of H'Reth's genetic background, his manor house on Gelion was a recent acquisition leveraged, through marriage ties, shortly after Lady Anatolia H'Reth became Delm's mistress.

H'Reth Manor itself looked sedate and respectable with an ornately pillared porch, green lawns, and a walled garden of *Lor* trees, prized for their high oxygen production and shallow system of roots. Two cars, marked with the Blue Demish Rose and Sword, were parked out front. Delm's errants, wearing matching livery, patrolled the lawns.

"Interesting," said Hesseratt.

The ranking palace errant had taken note of them, too, and realized that Di Mon's presence meant he was out-ranked by a challenge class. He spoke to a subordinate who went through a gate into the walled garden, no doubt to fetch the highborn in command.

Milling about on the lawn, Delm's people looked like a flock of preening birds to Di Mon. He had the feeling he could scatter them just by striding past.

It will be such a relief to be replaceable again, he thought, *after Vretla's child is born.*

"Look!" exclaimed Tan.

A prince in Silver Demish braid came through the gate and halted a polite distance from Di Mon. He had sandy hair and a square jaw so reminiscent of Prince H'Us that the embroidery on his jacket was redundant. Di Mon could not make out the details in the braid, but placed the style. He was a relative from Princess Reach, and to judge by his bearing and expression, unfamiliar with confronting Vrellish highborns.

"Looks like a kid," L'Ket remarked, posting herself at Di Mon's side with a hip cocked. If he wanted someone to exceed the bounds of duty and take on a superior, she was game for it. The edge to her interest might be sexually motivated, but she would happily kill anyone who specu-lated that she was lusting after a Demish genetic superior.

"Do you think he is any good with a sword?" Tan asked.

Hesseratt was studying the young Princessian with nar-rowed eyes. "I don't know," she said. "I've never seen him fight in Demish tournaments here at court."

"Hardly worth the exercise, then," Srain drawled.

"Hush," said Di Mon.

"Good cycle, Liege Monitum," the young stranger greeted him, speaking down the one rank he was entitled to as a Royalblood addressing a Highlord. "I am Taran, nephew of the Liege of HeavenBlessed on the planet Grain in Princess Reach, and husband of Caroleena, daughter of Her Grace Evleen of Blue Dem."

"A venerable lineage," Di Mon said, bowing to Demish opinion in such matters. "Are you acting here for your mother-in-law's liege or your grandsire's Ava?"

"Who are both, of course, the Ava!" Taran exclaimed with delight, and relaxed. "You are quick-witted for a black hair, Liege Monitum, but no less than your reputation."

Di Mon glanced past Taran's shoulder, already bored with the chatter. "What are you guarding?"

The yellow-haired prince looked embarrassed. "To be honest, Your Grace, the Ava's mistress." He sighed. "Even perfection, it seems, finds it hard to be perfect towards women."

Perfection was far from how Di Mon viewed Ava Delm, but he also knew enough about the H'Usians to write the title off as wishful thinking: form again, not substance. Delm was sacred because he was descended from the Golden Emperor, even though the Golden Emperor — according to D'Ander — rejected him.

"Is there some particular reason," Di Mon asked, "why Lady H'Reth has need of such gallantry?"

Taran winced at the sarcasm.

"There have been rumors," Taran said, flustered, eyes flicking towards the strange ambiguity of Vrellish women: hard muscled, dressed just like their men, and wearing swords. "Rumors of, uh, well ... unpleasantness. Concerning the lady's husband."

Di Mon frowned. Demish rumors could spread faster than a flying Vrellish highborn, without ever leaving Demish parlors.

"What unpleasantness regarding Liege H'Reth could require that his wife be guarded?" asked Di Mon.

Taran flushed, then, as if to compensate for so unmanly a reaction, clamped a hand around his sword hilt. "Most likely it is nothing, but all the same, if you don't mind, it is nothing I enjoy repeating."

"I see," said Di Mon. He paused, then continued. "I have cause to put some questions to H'Reth's wife with regard to an investigation."

Taran became very formal. "I hope, and trust, the matter is not pressing."

"What does that mean?" Tan whispered to Hesseratt.

"That he would just as soon not duel," came the answer.

A car pulled up, drawing everyone's attention with its grandiose appearance. It was longer than any state car Di Mon could remember seeing, worked in polished gold and trailing feather streamers. But it had seen better centuries — the gilt was off in patches and the feather arrangement looked hurried. The net effect was remarkably silly from Di Mon's perspective.

Of course it was D'Ander who sprang out of it, acting as his own chauffeur and doorman, but pulling it off splendidly.

"Taran, I think. Isn't it?" The Golden prince greeted the Silver one.

"I am honored that you recognize me!" Taran enthused, executing an odd bow. Di Mon supposed it was something reserved for celebrities; the Demish had more quirks and protocols among themselves than he could catalog.

"I always remember people who cheer the wrong champion," D'Ander assured his young fan. "Your uncle did, I trust, recover from the wound I gave him?"

"Oh yes!" Taran hesitated. "You were right, you know, about the contract under dispute. It wasn't fair to the widow, and that's why I was cheering for you! Not only because you fought a splendid duel!"

D'Ander clapped him on the shoulder and took his offered sword hand. "'Truth is *l'liege* of all,'" he quoted from
some bit of Demish literature. "I hope that you did not come
to any harm for backing me."

"Actually," Taran confessed, abashed, "my mother made
a peasant of me for the haying season. I sunburned something awful."

D'Ander chuckled. "As well she should. I might have
killed your uncle, for all that it was meant to stop at first
blood. Anything can happen in a duel. And it cost your
family a lucrative honor bond. Do you think you could escort us inside?" he asked, changing the subject while he still
had the younger man's attention. "Lady H'Reth might be
more comfortable with you at hand."

"Well, uh, actually," Taran demurred, "I'm here to keep
people out. She's not disposed to social calls."

"Nonsense!" D'Ander told him. "What nobleborn lady
would refuse to take tea with two princes and two Fountain
Court lieges?"

Di Mon frowned at that bit of Demish arithmetic, which
counted D'Ander twice. But it worked — D'Ander already
had Taran headed towards the manor. "See if anyone out
here or in the house will gossip," Di Mon instructed
Hesseratt, "and keep an eye out for our state car."

He caught up to the Demish princes on the threshold.
Servants showed them into an airy parlor.

"My Lady has been indisposed, Exalted Highness," a
lady-in-waiting informed D'Ander, bowing so low Di Mon
thought she might fall over.

"Let her know we're here, that's all," D'Ander told her
kindly, and exchanged useless pleasantries concerning Lady
H'Reth's health and the lady-in-waiting's good family before she left to do as she had been told.

A maid showed them into a parlor. The Demish princes
chatted while Di Mon prowled around uneasily until the soft
swish of skirts in the corridor alerted him to new arrivals.

The lady-in-waiting came in first and curtseyed, followed by a serving man pushing a trolley loaded with a steaming pot of herbal tea and tiny sandwiches.

"My Lady begs your patience," said the woman. "She needs a moment to prepare herself for such an honor. Please, do take refreshment." Her gaze caught on Di Mon as she finished.

Di Mon took a sandwich and ate it in two mouthfuls, but he turned down the tea. He would have taken alcohol but none was offered.

Lady H'Reth came in just before he became impossibly bored.

"I am sorry if we've put you to any trouble," Taran sprang to assure her, bowing, as if make-believe gallantry could compensate for the real disparity of power between Demish genders that lay behind the playacting. "But Prince D'Ander himself wished to see you."

Lady Anatolia H'Reth was a pale-haired woman with a heart-shaped face and swelling bosom. Sarilous had told him she was pregnant, but Di Mon found it hard to tell with Demish women, who were nearly always plumper than Vrellish ones. Presumably it was early enough not to show.

She said, "I'm honored. And glad of the company." As soon as she had said it, her head drooped.

D'Ander leaned closer. "Is something wrong, My Lady?"

Anatolia H'Reth's manicured hands trembled as they worried the embroidered handkerchief she carried.

"I am worried for my husband," she said, insincerely. She was worried all right, Di Mon concluded, but more for herself than for Liege H'Reth.

"What frightens you?" Di Mon asked.

Lady H'Reth blinked at him, startled.

"Forgive me," D'Ander rose to the occasion. "This is Liege Monitum, of Green Hearth. He's Vrellish, but not the most alarming of them."

"We have encountered one another at receptions," Lady H'Reth assured the Demish princes, and turned to Taran with

a surprising show of forthrightness for someone who was
trying to seem timid. "Am I being guarded or kept prisoner?"

"Why guarded, of course!" exclaimed Taran.

"Why do you think Delm would keep you prisoner?"
Di Mon asked, bluntly.

"Prisoner?" her hands fluttered. "Did I say that? You
must forgive me. I've been very nervous lately." Her fingers settled on her abdomen. "It must be my condition."

"Do you know whether Delm or your husband is the
father?" Di Mon asked.

All three Demish reacted as if he had urinated in front
of them. It was maddening! The woman was known to be
Delm's mistress. Even her husband accepted that, since it
had gained him command of the *Vanilla Rose*.

Taran got up stiffly. "My apologies, My Lady, we'll be
going."

Di Mon stood up also. "I am investigating the disappearance of Eva's star dancer, Von," he told Lady H'Reth. "You
were the last person seen with him. Can you tell me where
he is now?"

She stared back, horror stricken.

D'Ander took Di Mon's arm. "Come on!"

Di Mon jerked free of him. "I came here to ask her questions," he insisted.

Lady H'Reth took matters out of male hands by fainting. Di Mon was inclined to haul her back to her feet and
expose the ruse, but the Demish men were taken in entirely.

"Come on," D'Ander deflected Di Mon, after settling
Lady H'Reth on a sofa. "You've done enough damage."

"If word of this gets back to my wife's mother," Taran
fretted as they were shown out by a servant, "I don't know
how I'm ever going to get a day's peace again at home."

"You could challenge Di Mon to a duel to redeem your
honor," D'Ander suggested cheerfully, and slapped the
young man on the shoulder, laughing, when he blanched.

Di Mon was too vexed by their gender-biased blindness to enjoy Taran's involuntary compliment. He shot down the cobbled path from the porch ahead of them.

Hesseratt, L'Ket, and Tan stood waiting at the edge of the lawn. A Monatese car had arrived and was parked at their backs.

"Anything?" Di Mon asked his errants.

"I made up some wild stories about Red Reach orgies and one of the H'Usians coughed this up in gratitude," L'Ket told him, opening her hand to reveal another Reetion info-blit. "He says it proves H'Reth is boy-*sla*. But I can't see how."

"It's for playing recordings," Di Mon told her, and demonstrated how to turn it on.

L'Ket's eyes opened wide at the sight of a miniature projection of H'Reth's face bearing down, eyes soft with passion. The others pressed around. Hesseratt muttered a ward against *okal'a'ni* sciences. Her family was in nervecloth manufacturing.

"Take it into the back of the car," Di Mon told Tan and L'Ket, "and tell me what's recorded on it." The two young nobleborns dived into the car.

Hesseratt wanted to launch into a serious conversation but was forestalled by Srain who came running to join them from the gate leading into the garden.

"My liege!" Srain took two heartbeats to catch his breath before going on. "I was lucky enough to encounter a servant girl who could be bribed with a few kisses." He grinned. "And a bar of chocolate."

Di Mon's errants were forbidden chocolate for the sake of Vrellish sensitivity to caffeine, but Di Mon withheld comment.

"This is how weird it gets," Srain continued, animated enough to make Di Mon suspect he had shared the chocolate with his informant. "Lady H'Reth brought Von back here the day she abducted him from Silver Hearth to meet Delm's *gorarelpul*, Balous, who showed up with a hand of errants."

His eyes got brighter. "And they made Lady H'Reth pleasure Von while they watched."

Di Mon scowled. "I think your servant girl was more
concerned with holding your attention than telling you
anything of use."

"No, no!" Srain protested vigorously. "It's the truth.
Balous made enough of a production of it to be certain all
the servants knew it was to get a sperm sample. Balous took
it back to the palace to be tested. Seems Delm thought Von
was responsible for Lady H'Reth's pregnancy and wanted
to rub her nose in it, good."

"Courtesans are sterilized," Hesseratt objected.

Srain shrugged. "Maybe Eva forgot."

That did not sound like the Eva Di Mon knew. But the
suggestion that she might be untrustworthy touched a raw
nerve. For years now she had been the only woman that he
regularly called upon. Did she know why he feared to sire
children? Could a woman guess, somehow? It was a frightening thought. Di Mon recalled the bright, cool day on
which he had watched from a high window, with a young
Sarilous at his elbow, as Darren crossed the courtyard
headed for the shuttle he would take to join the fight against
the Nesaks.

The last time they had spoken, they had argued. Di Mon
wanted no part of peasant boys in hay lofts. Darren told him
he was jealous and laughed. It was so un-Vrellish to be jealous that the mocking accusation silenced Di Mon. Then,
before the day was out, Darren's heirs were dead, their
mother slain, and Darren gone without a backward glance.

Sarilous had steered her new liege through the months
that followed, telling him to forget what had happened between himself and Darren. He had never dared to wonder
whether Darren had wanted to part without a kind word
or a last touch. The best Di Mon had been able to do for
Darren's memory was refuse to tear his entries from the
Monatese Log.

Back on the porch of the manor, D'Ander broke off his *tête-à-tête* with Prince Taran and descended on Di Mon like a golden avalanche.

"You impossible Vrellish!" D'Ander scolded. "You're incorrigible! Asking a married woman, straight out, if she knows who the father of her child is!"

"The matter seems to be at issue," Di Mon said, unrepentant.

Very quickly, he explained what his errants had learned.

D'Ander's thick, gold eyebrows, hiked up a full finger's width as he listened.

"Boy-*sla*?" he exclaimed when Di Mon was done. "Then, indeed, better the child be the courtesan's. If it is H'Reth's it will be put to the sword the day it is born!"

Di Mon swallowed down the sharpness in his stomach. "Images are hardly proof," he said dryly. "Especially Reetion ones. Delm sent H'Reth off to conquer the Reetions, you'll recall. Perhaps we are experiencing a propaganda war."

"Huh," D'Ander grunted, scowling. "An ugly business, all around."

"An ugly business, yes," agreed Di Mon. "But I think Delm is the threat to his mistress. The child she carries must be his, and he knows it."

"Because Von's a sterilized courtesan and H'Reth is boy-*sla*?" D'Ander guessed aloud.

Di Mon held back the assertion it was possible for boy-*sla* men to sire children. "Because," he said instead, "it would explain Delm's behavior, both in trumpeting Von's role and putting Lady H'Reth under house arrest, now. He wants to pressure her into an abortion. He is very much opposed to reducing his own rarity in the world, and would never do so by a random accident."

"I've heard it said that Delm can't sire," D'Ander told Di Mon. "Or that he's incompatible with non-Demorans, which I suspect is nothing but a H'Usian excuse to pressure us for a compatible bride." He spat, which was not at all characteristic of him.

"Delm must be able to sire, because he takes care to prevent it." Di Mon had no qualms, in this case, about informing on a customer. "He uses *ferni* imported through Monitum. I've toyed with the idea of cutting off his supply. Fountain Court did that once before, during the contract with his half-sister, Ev'rel. But he probably has ways of getting hold of *ferni* from a sympathizer."

"You mean it's possible that Delm sired Amel all those years ago?" D'Ander perked up. "I heard Ev'rel resisted him."

"Ev'rel resisted," agreed Di Mon, "at least at first. Eventually Delm forced himself upon her. More from spite, I fear, than any real wish to honor their child contract."

"Delm raped her?" the Golden prince exclaimed in horror.

"She was not yet fully grown," Di Mon defended her defeat in Vrellish terms, "although, in truth, I never was able to teach her how to fight like an adult."

"She was a woman," D'Ander rebelled with force, "and half Demish!" He snorted in confused sympathy. "The gods know there is no love lost between Pureblood Ev'rel, where she now rules in exile, and my allies in the Purple Alliance. But she was little more than a child when Amel was born!" He shook his head. "Why didn't you accuse Delm of rape at her Honor Trial?"

"Why?" Di Mon asked blandly.

"Why!" D'Ander exploded, incredulous.

"The trial concerned Amel's murder," Di Mon pointed out. "Not whether Delm and Ev'rel fought each other over his conception."

"Fought!" D'Ander struggled, visibly, to get his feelings under control. "The Vrellish lieges might have dismissed it as that, but it would have gained Ev'rel sympathy from the H'Usians."

"Really?" Di Mon's expression soured. "Even though the servants I learned it from were the same ones who corroborated Delm's accusations? Ev'rel did abuse her *gorarelpul*, Arous. He was a commoner, he was bonded to her, and she used him for sexual pleasure even though he was incapable of responding without the use of harmful drugs. Impotence is a common complication of the treatment *gorarelpul* undergo to desensitize them to pain — she should have accepted that."

D'Ander shook his head. "You can't compare her helping Arous, in that way, to rape."

"Helping?" Di Mon echoed, incredulous. Ev'rel had bound Arous to a bed, not because she had to — her wish was literally his command — but because she liked it that way. And in the end she killed him with an overdose of the sex drug, Rush. D'Ander would insist he had died happy, no doubt.

"Gods!" D'Ander exclaimed, in sudden anger. "Delm's a vain fool, but I never thought him worse than that. I never thought a grandson of the Golden Emperor could rape a woman!"

Di Mon locked his jaw against contending with such Demish nonsense. He had spoken with Ev'rel and tried to help her, but he had no doubt she was guilty with regard to Arous. The Demish seemed incapable of grasping that a Vrellish woman was not merely a change of clothes away from becoming one of the foolish, fainting things they so admired.

D'Ander suddenly went very quiet, a stunned look settling over his features. He muttered, "No. Oh, no. You mad gods." His eyes actually glistened with unshed tears. Disinclined to put up with another Demish lecture on gender issues, Di Mon started for his waiting car.

"Wait!" D'Ander called, and took two steps in his direction with a hand outstretched.

Di Mon turned abruptly. "What is it, Demish?"

D'Ander was pale and excited. "Ev'rel is a Pureblood. It isn't likely, is it, that Ev'rel's *gorarelpul* could have made her pregnant, even if she used Rush to overcome his impotence."

"Unlikely, not impossible," Di Mon snapped. "If it could not happen there would be no grammar classes below Pureblood." The argument had come up at the Honor Trial, of course, but without the child Amel as evidence it was Delm's word against Ev'rel's.

D'Ander was developing a glow that was more annoying than his inexplicable moment of shock. "Do you remember Amel?" he asked urgently. "I heard he was a beautiful child, worthy of the Family of Light, except that he was dark-haired and gray-eyed. But then so was his mother!"

"Is there some point to this?" Di Mon demanded, fed up with rehashing the past.

"Von's sperm," D'Ander launched into another *non sequitur*. "Balous took it to disprove Delm's paternity and shame the mother. What if he genotyped it?"

"Why ever would he do that?" Di Mon asked, unable to fathom the use of obtaining the genetic blueprint of a commoner.

If D'Ander did, he was having second thoughts about divulging it. He scratched an ear, looking half embarrassed, then pursed his lips with the look of someone about to explode into words, but merely huffed and muttered, "No, it's too farfetched."

Di Mon resented D'Ander dredging up the Amel business. He had mentored Ev'rel in the same way he had mentored Vretla, only to watch her warp along the fault lines of her half Demish, half Vrellish nature, and he had failed her in a way so personal he could not bear to dwell on it. If he had known earlier about Arous, he could have taught her how to curb unwholesome sexual appetites.

"If Ev'rel had been taunting Delm about how Amel could replace him both as Ava and a Demish idol," D'Ander was saying in a dreamy manner, "and if Delm knew she was sleeping with her *gorarelpul* —"

"She was not merely sleeping with Arous," Di Mon interrupted, nettled. "She was killing him systematically with a banned drug; abusing a bond slave who was utterly helpless to resist her."

D'Ander's heated emotions collapsed in a sheepish look. "I need to think it all through. Do some checking."

On what? Di Mon thought, but declined to ask. He'd had his fill, for the day, of Demish head fluff.

"I am going to Den Eva's," Di Mon told D'Ander tersely. "Have you any message for Perry D'Aur?"

"Tell her she may as well stay there, for now," said D'Ander. "It's as safe and comfortable as anything I could provide, and I dare say she can stomach the embarrassment. And thanks for taking care of her board."

Di Mon wanted to say he had not exactly agreed to take care of her board, nor to feed and house D'Ander's pet Reetion. Somehow he just was.

He felt a headache coming on as he got into the front of his car. They stopped at the gates again. Hesseratt talked to the Demish guards while Di Mon waited with his head down, fingers pinching the bridge of his nose, and tried not to listen to Tan, Srain, and L'Ket muttering over the info-blit in the back. Hesseratt got back in without incident and they headed down the Ava's way toward West Alcove.

Eventually Srain hitched himself forward.

"Excuse me, My Liege," he said, a bit awkwardly. "But the *slaka* in these pictures about H'Reth. It's Von."

Di Mon turned slowly, brushing Srain aside as he looked into the back seat where the info-blit was playing. In the image, Von knelt on a bed, looking at himself in the mirror of a Demish woman's vanity. He was flushed over the whole surface of his sleek, dancer's body, but there was misery in his eyes. A man's voice called to him and he turned, replacing his own image with the sight of Liege and

Lady H'Reth. She appeared resigned, but H'Reth looked smugly self-satisfied.

"Watching that, you can see why the servants think Von is the father!" joked Tan. "Von concentrates on her while H'Reth is working on him!"

"Wouldn't you?" Srain exclaimed, and the three of them burst into nervous laughter.

L'Ket snatched at the info-blit and a skirmish ensued until Hesseratt confiscated the offending object and handed it forward to Di Mon. "You'd better keep this, my liege," she advised. Di Mon accepted it with a nod of acknowledgement. The Reetion thing was at least as bad as chocolate for over-stimulating younger errants. Its content was simply too sexual. He slipped it into a pocket of his vest where it lay pressed against him like an accusation, the memory of Von, flushed and naked, burning through.

"How would anyone record something like that?" Hesseratt asked.

"Some of it happens in the UnderDocks," L'Ket volunteered excitedly. "I recognized the place — a rough den called the Bear Pit."

"Been there have you?" Tan chided.

"I walked through it once, okay?" L'Ket snapped. "It's not my kind of rough."

Hesseratt asked, "How could Reetions have recorded events that took place here on Gelion years ago?"

"I will find out what it means," Di Mon promised, thinking of Ranar. Let him explain *this* as educational!

Teeth locked, Di Mon turned around and faced forward. They were coming up on that dark stretch Ses Nersal had complained about, where the Ava's mandate wasn't being honored. At what point should he intervene to get it fixed, Di Mon wondered. And how often could he do that without draining Monitum's resources, while Delm continued turning palace rooms into Demoran gardens? He could talk to H'Us about it but that, too, felt futile. H'Us would only put pressure on throne servants who lacked the means to solve the problem.

A sword through Delm would solve the problem! Di Mon thought angrily. If they only had a Pureblood who could take his place. But Delm, too, had an heir problem, and liked it that way.

"H'Reth should be sheath-whipped on Ava's Square," L'Ket erupted in the back. "And his wife, too!"

"What about her baby?" Srain asked. "She's pregnant."

"With a *slaka'st's* spawn!" L'Ket said with casual cruelty. "Let it die with her."

"*P'rash*! Are you Monatese or Red Reach Vrellish?" Hesseratt browbeat L'Ket. "Would you pass judgment on the strength of lights from a box? Images can be feigned."

"Feigned how?" asked Tan's voice. "It's too good! So much detail!"

"I say it proves H'Reth is boy-*sla*," L'Ket insisted. "And *sla* flesh corrupts the soul it houses. I say kill him for his own good."

"Enough!" Di Mon loosed his anger in his voice. His errants fell as silent as rebuked children. As silent as Darren's dead children. Di Mon's headache became vicious.

It seemed an eternity before they pulled into the parking lot below West Alcove. Di Mon sprang out of the car and halted at the sight of six neighboring cars parked close together and guarded by a hand of nobleborns. Five of them bore Delm's Rose and Sword emblem and one sported the H'Usian trumpet over a field of grain.

Di Mon stepped back to his own car and leaned down to speak to the driver. "Take this message from me to Ses Nersal," he told the reliable near-commoner. "Tell her that I need back up." There were times when it was very useful to have a *mekan'st* to call upon.

The car pulled out again. Hesseratt formed up the errants around Di Mon and all of them broke into a run. They all knew that Vretla Vrel was in Den Eva's and Vretla was something of a Vrellish icon, being the only Red Reach highborn resident at the Ava's court. They shot up the stairs and onto the West Alcove plaza to find a crowd of Demish milling about outside Den Eva's entrance arch.

Di Mon cleared his sword. So did his errants.

In opposition, Di Mon counted twelve of the Ava's Blue Demish errants led by Thoth, the least impressive of Delm's paladins. A hand of Silver nobleborns stood slightly apart from them, flanking a prince Di Mon had never seen before. The stranger's braid proclaimed he was from Princess Reach, like Taran.

Di Mon went straight for Thoth, but Thoth gave way, swinging back rather than accepting challenge.

"We're trying to help!" the stranger from Princess Reach declared from the midst of his H'Usian errants. "There has been an attack, with *okal'a'ni* weapons."

A shocking sight greeted Di Mon inside Eva's. Bodies lay splayed in ungainly postures on the Patron's Floor, one of them a member of Eva's staff, her dead flesh painted in the melting reds and oranges of grievous burns. Two of the male corpses were sword-slain, the badge of Perry D'Aur's Purple Alliance prominent on their jackets.

The smell of smoke flared Di Mon's nostrils. Smoke lined the ceiling, seeping in from one of the spoke-halls that radiated outward from the Patron's Round. At the same time Di Mon heard sounds through the wall of Eva's office: shifting, coughing, and the whimpering voices of children.

He signaled Hesseratt to check the smoking corridor, turned back himself and kicked open Eva's door. A big Demish captain of errants started at Di Mon's dramatic entrance. Eva shot to her feet from where she had been comforting a crying child.

"Di Mon!" Eva cried.

"Liege Monitum!" exclaimed the captain of errants, who appeared to be charged with keeping Eva's people penned up.

Di Mon wasn't feeling conversational.

Eva pushed forward, shedding the novice who had been clinging to her. "Don't kill him!" she spoke for the H'Usian. "He has been protecting us."

Di Mon hesitated. Then, without lowering his sword, he snatched Eva's wrist in his right hand and dragged her after him back onto the Patron's Floor to see how his errants were doing.

"Down here!" Hesseratt cried from the mouth of the smoking spoke-hall.

"Vretla Vrel and Kertatt are down there," Eva told Di Mon. "Vretla was with a courtesan, so I kept Kertatt out here when he arrived. Our attackers claimed they were Perry D'Aur's people, so I fetched her to see them. But she didn't recognize them. They had flame throwers under their cloaks! Horrible, *okal'a'ni* weapons! She saw it before the rest of us and fought with us when they attacked. She and Kertatt killed those two," she pointed, "then they went down that spoke-hall, after Vretla."

Srain interrupted by calling, "Thoth is coming in after us!"

"Keep him occupied," Di Mon ordered Tan and L'Ket, and went after Hesseratt, who had already disappeared down the spoke-hall. Tan and L'Ket positioned themselves to play rear guard, although by the rule of sword law no highborn was required to accept their challenge. With any luck, the Demish would just argue.

The smoke in the hall thickened quickly, which explained — at least in part — why Toth had pulled out. It burned Di Mon's eyes and lungs. Di Mon suspected Toth had at least one other reason for waiting outside: to obstruct help rather than to provide it. The question was: why?

"Here!" cried Hesseratt, standing by a Demish body slumped against a wall, with a knife sticking out of its stomach.

"Vretla's?" Di Mon asked.

Hesseratt pulled out the knife, turned it over, then handed it off to him as the need to cough overtook her with a spasm. Its hilt was carved with two lines suggestive of hills against a blank horizon.

Perry D'Aur, thought Di Mon, not entirely sure what to make of that.

The dead man was a palace errant, which put him and the D'Aur woman on opposite sides of a Demish quarrel over land, and land was the thing the Demish were most passionate about, notwithstanding all their yammering about love.

Di Mon put the knife in his belt and tried a nearby door that was leaking smoke only to find it locked from the inside. He hammered on it with the hilt of his sword, pausing between bouts to shout, "Vretla! It's Di Mon!" The smoky air burned in his lungs.

"She's busy!" Perry D'Aur's voice cried back.

Kertatt's voice called, unsteadily, "Uncle!"

"Let me in!" demanded Di Mon.

The door opened and Di Mon burst in, followed by Hesseratt. The male courtesan who had opened it fell back. He looked distraught.

The room stank of fire, its mural of field flowers scorched and a heap of cushions reduced to gooey ash. A table had been overturned and its metal frame showed through the fire-damaged wood veneer. One badly charred corpse arched across the toppled table, wearing the remains of a flame thrower harness. The flat fuel tank showed through the ruins of the same sort of leather jacket as the ones worn by the dead invaders on the Patron's Round. This further evidence of a premeditated attack using forbidden weapons set Di Mon's teeth on edge.

The circular bed set into the floor had escaped the fire. A mounded shape lay on it, breathing noisily under a sheet soaked in blood diluted by clear fluid. Perry D'Aur knelt on the floor nearby, her face and hands smeared in gore. One sleeve of her jacket was charred in the right place to suggest it had been raised to protect her face. Kertatt was in a far corner, crumpled over a burned arm.

"Hess!" Di Mon ordered, and gestured to his fallen nephew. Hesseratt went to help Kertatt.

"P-Please don't hurt me," said the terrified male courtesan who had opened the door. Di Mon recognized him as Von's understudy. Vretla must have been using him to console herself over Von's loss.

A second body wearing the Purple Alliance badge lay on its back looking startled, with Vretla's sword sticking out his neck above the sword-proof vest he had on — another testament to the attackers scorn for Sword Law. Over the vest he wore straps securing an unscorched version of the fuel tank they had seen on the charred corpse.

Di Mon looked away again, towards the mass on the bed under the blanket, making snarling, breathy sounds. He knew it must be Vretla. He could not bring himself to accept it, or the blood awash in birth fluids.

"She was shot in the abdomen with a fire thrower, in the act of killing her assailant," Perry D'Aur told Di Mon. "I got the second one with the first one's flamethrower before he could finish her."

Di Mon lost control. He had to attack something or he would explode, and Perry had just confessed to using an *okal'a'ni* weapon, even if it had been to protect Vretla. He dropped his sword first, though.

Perry's small, sturdy form jerked in his hands as he seized her by the jacket marked with the Purple Alliance badge. But he never found out what he might have done.

The bloody sheet on the opposite side of Perry erupted with a mortal roar. Vretla reeked of birth and burns, but she was strong, and incapable of distinguishing friend from foe. She heaved Di Mon bodily into Perry D'Aur, then tried to get up herself and slipped in her own spilled fluids.

The metallic tang of Vrellish fury streamed off Vretla where she lay, half naked and breathing like a bellows, patches of her body sock fused into her burned skin. She had lost the child, but not yet delivered the afterbirth.

Di Mon stared at her, thinking, *My heir is dead*.

"She keeps doing that," Perry gasped, and swallowed. "Attacking anyone who gets close. I think she might be *rel-osh*."

Rel-osh was a physiological condition peculiar to highborn Vrellish that extended performance in crisis, at a steep price. If Vretla had gone *rel-osh*, she would be dead within twenty-four hours, even if her injuries were otherwise survivable. In either case she needed help that could come only from *TouchGate Hospital Station*. The expertise was extinct on Gelion.

Di Mon hauled Perry up. "Take your jacket off," he ordered.

"I am not carrying *okal'a'ni* weapons!" she protested. "If I was, I might have been more help!"

Di Mon backhanded her with a snarl. If he had been Demish, he might have raged or wailed or thrown himself in despair on the motionless lump tangled in the sticky sheet that trailed from Vretla's body, instead he was naked action stripped of the power to reason.

Perry didn't get up, but he was distracted from her by Vretla's next howl. She was trying to tear out her trailing umbilical cord.

Di Mon feared the consequences if the afterbirth was fused to the burned flesh of her womb.

He dove at her, struggling to get her under control.

She narrowed her oval eyes, trying to see through the red blur of her pain as she struggled. She might try to kill him if he let go, and she could probably succeed if she was *rel-osh*. The condition concentrated the victim's remaining strength.

"*Klinoman!*" Kertatt was begging Hesseratt. "It hurts! Give me *klinoman!*"

"I've got it here," Hesseratt told him. "Don't paw!"

Of course! thought Di Mon. "Throw it here," he ordered, still wrestling with Vretla.

Hesseratt tossed her vial of *klinoman*. For an instant, Di Mon feared Vretla would foul his catch, but she went for the umbilical cord again. He snatched the brown vial from the air and forced her body straight to make her stop.

Vretla watched him over locked teeth as he popped the cap off the vial. Then her hand clamped on his wrist, resisting. She probably thought she was going to die, and did not want to do it the *pol* way, slack on drugs. Di Mon levered his right thumb over the open vial to prevent it spilling, unable to let go of her other arm with his left hand and afraid to hurt her in the lower body where she had such grievous wounds. His muscles ached. She snarled like an animal and he was not at all sure she would remember he was a friend if she got him down.

There was a dull crack, behind her, and Vretla relaxed her grip without a sound. Hesseratt had clipped her on the head with the hilt of her sword.

"Thanks," Di Mon gasped, and handed her the *klinoman* to administer. He was afraid he would drop it himself. His right hand swarmed with pins and needles. He drew Perry's knife from his belt in the other hand and severed the trailing umbilical cord as Hesseratt nicked Vretla's inner lip and poured a heavy dose of brown, resinous drug into the cut just in time — Vretla was already coming around.

"Are you sure this was the right thing to do?" Hesseratt asked, handing Di Mon the vial. "It's her right to die as she wants."

"She is not going to die," Di Mon told his captain of errants, discarding the empty vial of *klinoman* with an angry flick of his hand. "We'll get her to *TouchGate* to be cured."

"How? Yourself?" Hesseratt asked. "It will take a highborn. A nobleborn couldn't get her there fast enough."

"Bind her up as best you can," he ordered Hesseratt, looking down at Vretla where she was already struggling to get up again, and flexing his right hand. The feeling in it was coming back. "Then bring her out. Carry her. Drag her. Hit her again if you must."

"If you send her to *TouchGate* and she dies," Hesseratt warned, "the Red Vrellish will hunt you down! Even if she lives, to do it without her permission —"

Di Mon lost his temper. "Do what you are told!" he roared and got no further argument from Hesseratt.

Perry D'Aur stirred and moaned. Di Mon was glad she wasn't dead, but she was not his problem. He was not even certain she was innocent. She and the other Demish could sort it out on their own. He passed her by to haul Kertatt to his feet by his sound arm.

His normally hot-headed nephew groaned.

"*Ack Rel*," Di Mon muttered to him in encouragement, "it won't be long."

He looked only once towards the lump snarled in the soaked sheet near the bed: his heir, dead before he or she was born. Then he headed out, pausing only to retrieve his dropped sword, which was his passport to negotiation with Thoth.

"I ch-chased them from the Patron's Floor," Kertatt chattered, holding onto his uncle with his good arm. "They went for V-Vretla. Had flame throwers under their c-cloaks. The vermin."

The sound of fencing carried down the spoke where Tan and L'Ket stood guard. The Demish could usually be counted on to argue or mess around, matching errant with errant. If one of the Demish highborns had given challenge, Di Mon's errantry could have backed down with honor, except he could not imagine Tan and L'Ket doing that when he had ordered them to hold the Demish off.

He pinned his hopes for their safety on the diffident nature of the dueling sounds. All the same, Di Mon was worried. He handed Kertatt off to Srain, who had stayed in the spoke-hall. Hesseratt was catching up, burdened by Vretla, who made no complaint but a hissing sound.

Hesseratt stiffened, seeing Di Mon's expression. "You mustn't fight, My Liege," she pleaded. "You have no heir!"

Di Mon drew as he ran, outstripping the burdened errants at his back. He burst onto the Patron's Floor and stopped, his fears confirmed.

Tan was down, fallen on his side with blood pooling beside him, sword in his hand.

L'Ket defended the entrance to the spoke-hall. The Demish prince, whom Di Mon could still put no name to, was testing her resolve in a reluctant fashion, as if unwilling to decide whether he wanted to kill a second errant today.

It was a courtesy to accept a challenge from an inferior. As a highborn, the Demish prince could simply have stood back and ordered his nobleborns to overwhelm Di Mon's, at least until Di Mon got there to assert his own right of challenge. So the Demish Champion was probably a man of honor. He had also killed Tan, who was no easy prey despite the disparity in challenge class, and that meant he was dangerous. In fact, he was probably there to spare Thoth the hazard of fighting, just in case an obstacle such as Di Mon's arrival interfered with whatever mission had brought Delm's paladin to Den Eva's on the heels of the shocking, *okal'a'ni* attack on Vretla.

Di Mon deduced all that at a glance, but reason failed there. He was entitled to vent his anguish on the Demish interloper responsible for Tan's death and he meant to do it. He asked no questions, even when the Demish Champion looked up, expectant, hopeful that they might sort out their difficulties with words.

Di Mon attacked, and the Demish prince had no choice but to defend himself or die.

13

Consequences
of Courage

The jump into Reetion space was hair-raising, but soon over. Once *Vanilla Rose* stabilized, H'Reth holed up in the room where Ann had met Von, and a loyal crewman came to tell him they'd discovered Reetions.

"Master Larren is going to crack their station if they don't give up that courtesan you used to play Liege Monitum," the man said, in amazement. "I'll be lost if I see why he's so important."

H'Reth opted for the high ground. "If Larren speaks of cracking stations, he is a man we dare not follow if we hope to be reborn."

"Larren's a paladin," said the crewman. "He knows what's right. He offered challenge."

"Ha!" H'Reth scoffed. "What chance would a Reetion have against Larren in a duel?"

"Then they should surrender," concluded the crewman. "No one would think less of them for that! It's quite proper to decline a fight outside your challenge class, just like you did, My Lord."

When the crew man left, H'Reth wrapped himself in his blankets on the couch. They smelled of his own stale sweat and bitterness — nothing like blankets that Von had warmed. The more he thought about that, the more he convinced himself he must do something to save Von, despite the threat

Larren posed. Inspired, he bolted up and threw himself around the room, pulling his clothing together and strapping on his dueling sword. Then he charged out into the corridor.

Jarl intercepted him twenty paces from his door. "Where are you going?" he asked.

H'Reth gripped the hilt of his sword.

"Oh," Jarl's eyes flicked down to the weapon, "to commit suicide. How gallant."

"Do not mock me!" H'Reth cried. "I have found my courage!"

"Hang on to it then," advised Jarl, "or it may get you killed."

"But Larren wants to kill Von!" H'Reth cried.

"Are there no other boys in all the reaches of Sevildom?" Jarl asked.

No! H'Reth thought. Von ran through his life like a ribbon of silver through dross. When he dressed, he imagined Von in matching clothes; if he enjoyed a play it was because he looked forward to Von's insights when he told him all about it, afterwards. Von was all that made his life endurable!

"I must see Larren," H'Reth said, and shouldered past.

"You won't find him at the command center!" Jarl called.

H'Reth turned around.

"The Reetions are sending Von across," Jarl enlightened him. "He's docking at the same spot that the Reetion woman did." Jarl showed his evil grin. "You'll be just in time to see Larren destroy him. Marvelously melodramatic way to put it, I thought, 'destroy.' So artistic, those Goldens."

H'Reth began to run.

He had no real idea what he meant to do when he reached the docking floor, beyond hoping Von would play some inspired trick. Von was resourceful and even quite strong for a commoner. Perfect all around, in fact! Except for his stubborn interest in girls.

H'Reth burst into the outer chamber of the rim dock making half a dozen heads turn, but the inner airlock was still closed. No Von in sight. H'Reth faltered. Larren and the second paladin, Farin, stood waiting at the center of a company of Blue Demish nobleborns.

"H'Reth is it?" said Larren, without looking around. "Show him the silver box."

Farin took the Reetion projection box out from under his robe. H'Reth's heart skipped a beat. Jarl came in behind him.

"H'Reth knows, I think, what images this evil toy projects," Larren said to those assembled, then turned at last to fix H'Reth with his icy blue stare. "They concern you."

Jarl spoke from behind H'Reth. "They found it," he said, "so I told them about Von."

H'Reth whirled to confront his captain of errants.

"I told them Von must obey you or die," Jarl said, staring at H'Reth as if willing him to exceed his usual thick-headedness. "It seemed important to them to make sure that Von docks. So I showed them that recording you made of having him bonded to you."

"I made?" H'Reth stammered, horrified. Mind churning. Was this betrayal? Why should he be surprised!

"Dishonorable, of course, to harbor a secret slave of conscience," Larren's voice spiked through the rising murmur Jarl's announcement had caused among the guards. "But useful to us just now. The Watching Dead plan better than we know."

The suggestion of supernatural forces at work produced a hush in which H'Reth tried to catch up with what was going on. Clearly Jarl had told Larren about Von's conscience bond. But was that all?

Yes, H'Reth decided. *It's still in Jarl's interest to keep me alive. He just wants to see Von die!*

"The Reetions have forced Von off their station," Larren declared, shaking back his golden locks. "But I was unsure how I might compel him to land until Jarl showed us your Reetion device, documenting what you'd done."

"Incredibly stupid to record a secret conscience bonding," Farin remarked.

Terror began to release its grip on H'Reth's organs. If they were harping on the impropriety of the conscience bond, they couldn't know that he was boy-*sla*. He hoped.

"This is Von," came a voice over the radio, emanating from a speaker panel on the wall. H'Reth's heart jumped. It was Von's voice, sounding a little jaunty for the occasion.

"Von!" H'Reth surprised even himself by rushing forward. "They're waiting to kill you! Don't land!"

Farin heaved H'Reth into the hands of his own erstwhile errants. Before H'Reth regained his balance, Farin's sword was out and held to his throat.

"We know that H'Reth is your bond master," said Larren. "You are, therefore, bound to obey him. But we think he may change his mind about the nature of his orders very soon." He nodded to Farin, who whipped H'Reth's face with the tip of his sword.

H'Reth yelped, and raised a hand to the hot wound.

"Order Von to dock," said Larren, "and you'll be taken back to Gelion to be tried for having an illicit bonding done. Refuse, and Farin will put out an eye."

"High culture comes to Killing Reach," Jarl mocked the Golden reputation for gentleness.

H'Reth shot Jarl a wounded, desperate look.

"I had to tell them," Jarl explained with a shrug. "They threatened torture. You're not up to pain, H'Reth," he finished soberly. "Order the pretty brat down."

H'Reth's eyes were hot. His stomach knotted. But there was nothing he could do! It was too cruel.

"Von," H'Reth said, struggling to side step his choices, "wh — what did those Reetion fiends do to you?"

"Nothing," Von replied by radio, "just detained me. They even bunked me with a woman, Ann. She was really something."

That sounded all too much like Von.

"Von," H'Reth said gravely, "It seems I cannot save you, but you can save me." It was so like an epic poem that warmth swelled H'Reth's chest, pressing on his aching heart. On the crest of the feeling he dared to appeal to Larren who was a Golden prince after all, susceptible to glorious art. "Why must you kill him? He's only a boy. What has he done?"

"Done!" Larren cried as if stung, then his voice dropped low. "It drives Delm mad to live amid the crudity of people like your wife!"

"Ah," muttered Jarl under his breath at H'Reth's back, "Von offended Delm by pleasing Anatolia. That's gratitude, when Von taught her how to please —"

Larren overheard and struck, backhand, connecting with a nasty smack, but Jarl knew how to take blows. He reeled into the guards surrounding H'Reth, breaking his fall.

"Take him out of my sight," ordered Larren, "I've no time to kill him as he deserves now."

Jarl snarled and struggled, but was overpowered. "I know what you are!" he hurled back at Larren as he was dragged out. "Like me! That's what! I'm honest about it! That's all!"

"Tell Von to dock, now," Larren ordered as soon as the commotion died down. "And surrender to me."

"I am sorry," H'Reth said to Von, hoping the tremor in his voice conveyed how upset he was. "I must order you to dock."

There was a long silence. Then Von's voice said, "All right. Where?"

It was only after he heard it that H'Reth admitted he had been holding his breath for fear Von decided he would rather die of bond revolt, out of spite. But he had chosen to obey and trade his life for H'Reth's, instead.

H'Reth's tears mingled with the blood trickling down his cheek. Farin lowered his sword. Larren gave Von instructions by radio.

H'Reth stood rooted as the eager audience inched forward. It was a poignant moment for him when the airlock cycled open, torn between wanting one last exchange of looks with his dear boy and knowing he could not bear to look upon him lifeless. He did not even want to imagine how the paladins might implement the order to destroy Von once he landed.

The wall gave way between the airlock and the freight room; and a murmur of mild surprise followed at the sight of an alien looking ship a little different in design from the one that the Reetion pilot Ann had flown. The twenty-odd people assembled waited for Von to climb out.

"I want to leave," H'Reth whimpered, his courage deserting him.

Farin gestured to a crewman. "Take him to join his captain of errants."

The man touched H'Reth's arm. "If your Grace will come with me?" he asked, apologetically.

H'Reth blinked at the man who just yesterday took orders from him. The man looked nervous, as did most of the crew. They disliked so many changes coming so suddenly. But the simpletons trusted in *Okal Rel's* power to ensure the safety of *Vanilla Rose*, their life raft in the vast hostility of space, so far from home, so long as they played by the rules. They would not help H'Reth get his station back. Not without a proper duel.

The hatch of Von's ship opened.

"Your Grace?" said his hesitant escort, urging him to come. But H'Reth's feet were rooted.

A figure in pearly white clothing climbed out of the Reetion space craft, complete with hood and gloves. A figure with the wrong shape for Von, although Von's voice came from a large medallion it was wearing.

It cried, "Surprise, you retros!"

A crewman shouted, "It's a Reetion!"

The creature raised its arm at Larren, whose clothing and position made him prominent. There was a hiss and a burning smell and Larren fell, writhing on the floor. The creature pointed the wand at its next victim and Farin screamed as he, too, was struck by the *okal'a'ni* weapon.

H'Reth dropped to the floor.

The crew mobbed the stranger as one, incensed by the rule-breaking attack that threatened their survival by threatening to turn the conflict into one in which no holds were barred.

"This is your doing!" Farin cried, spotting H'Reth, and charged with his sword drawn, the shoulder of his other arm giving off a reek of cooked meat, although he looked alarmingly vigorous despite that.

H'Reth grasped that Farin blamed him for the Reetion's sin and screamed, "Jarl!"

He was saved by a darting shape that ran Farin through from behind.

The blade gave H'Reth a bad turn, coming right through Farin's body in front of him. Jarl pulled it out and kicked Farin's body over. Miraculously, they were nearly alone on their patch of floor.

"All right?" Jarl asked, just as if he hadn't betrayed him to the paladins by telling them about Von's conscience bond. He grinned despite his bloody mouth. "Looks like you might be in charge again, Lord-Admiral."

The white garbed Reetion thing was being dragged down, twisting and writhing, the laser wand gone from its hand. The suit contained a woman's body. H'Reth was sure of that much. He had a strong suspicion it was the Reetion pilot, Ann. As he watched, her pearly suit repelled slashing attacks by the crew, who were intent on punishing her with the death of a thousand cuts. Her grunts of pain and protest radiated from the medallion on her chest, still modulated to match Von's tenor register.

"Wait!" H'Reth cried, wanting to keep her alive because she was a link to Von. "Wait! Stop!" Jarl waded through the crowd beside him, buoying up his confidence.

The room smelled of fear and ozone around Larren's body. Someone brought H'Reth the weapon Ann had used, holding it between thumb and forefinger as if it were poisonous.

"Some sort of heat ray, Your Grace," said the disgusted crewman.

"Dispose of it," H'Reth ordered, "and get the Reetion out of that suit."

Jarl dispersed the guards around Ann and knelt on her chest to wrestle with her strange clothes, but he couldn't get them off. People began to close in again almost immediately, dissatisfied.

"*Okal'a'ni*," said a voice from the back.

Other voices picked it up

"*Oh—kal—ah—nee*," the assembled men began to chant.

The Reetion had breached the code of honor that made conflict in space habitats survivable. She must pay, or civilization would come crashing down the way it had in Killing Reach two hundred years before. Places in space that supported life were too precious to waste in any cause — this was the one truth all Gelacks held sacred.

H'Reth understood the crew's mood, but he wanted to ask Ann about Von.

He looked from face to face among the Blue Demish nobleborns and near-commoner crew, wondering if they would obey him if he told them to back off. He was nervous about daring too much. He already had an obstacle to overcome getting them to forget the business about Von being a sort of unofficial *gorarelpul*, which wasn't exactly *okal'a'ni* — like Ann's attack — nor considered as despicable as being boy-*sla*, but was nonetheless frowned upon.

H'Reth agonized, but only watched as the chant in his ears grew more ominous.

* * *

"*Oh—kal—ah—nee!*" heard Ann.

The text translation "prone to destroy what is fought over, anti-life," scrolled across the bottom of her hood's hard plastic visor. But whatever the translation, Ann had no trouble grasping the intent of the mob that hauled her from her ship and went at her with knives and swords, bruising her in their vain attempts to pierce her flight suit. She also recognized the guy sitting on her, trying to get her suit off, as the man called Jarl in Von's bad memories.

"If we cannot stab you, we can crush you," Jarl told her, with relish, hauling her up.

She had always known such people existed — she had read about them. Bullies. Psychopaths. People who relished hurting others, however they were explained and whatever they were called. But it took her by surprise to discover Jarl was frightening in the flesh.

She obeyed his order, freeing her hood first, which made it easier to look around. That seemed incredibly important even though it made her vulnerable. Jarl grinned through bloodied teeth at her. He had a gap in one eyebrow where a serious cut had left a scar and his hands, while powerful, were also damaged: muscle had healed in hard knots and a finger was crooked. She noticed these details with a vivid awareness that was new to her.

"What do you want?" Ann asked, her voice still modulated by the medallion on her chest.

Jarl yanked the output unit off and dashed it to the metallic floor, which had no impact on its wireless connection, but still caused her serious alarm.

"If you break that I won't understand what you're saying!" Ann shouted at him, suddenly more afraid of that than anything, and was reassured to hear her words broadcast in Gelack from the detached medallion, still sounding like Von.

Jarl had a sword. He leveled it at her exposed throat and ordered, "Take off the rest of the white armor."

It isn't armor, she thought bitterly. *It's a space suit*. She wanted to tell him so, as if the clarification would prove that all this violence was plain stupid, but she had just committed murder herself.

"Take it off now," Jarl's commanded in translation through her ear lug. "Or I start by crushing toes and fingers."

Ann slowly eased herself out of her protective flight suit, trying to think of something clever.

Beneath the suit she was wearing her usual yellow stretch shorts and halter top. Her breath came heavily, making her chest heave and her stomach tremble. Jarl grinned and she learned what it really meant to feel her skin crawl.

He said, "I've never had a brown woman." His tone, in Gelack, added brutal overtones to the neutral sounding Reetion translation in her ear.

She almost said "Fuck you", and caught herself — that was just what he intended. Her panic began giving way to anger, which was better, even if she didn't know how to use it yet.

"Pity there may not be enough left of you by the time the crew is finished," said Jarl, and kicked the medallion towards a startled crewman. "Get this thing off the ship. It's Reetion. For all we know it could be a bomb." Then he stepped back and let the crowd have her, crying, "Reetions are *okal'a'ni*! All of them!"

A gang of big men seized Ann as Jarl abandoned her. One slapped her, dislodging the ear lug that was receiving translation from the detached medallion. Now she could not understand what they said anymore! Others bound her wrists behind her so tightly that her hands tingled. She found the grit to smile at how nervous her equipment made the Gelacks as they dumped her suit, medallion, and ear lug in the airlock.

Stupid retros, she thought at them, struggling to maintain her anger. It was better than fear. The airlock cycled and all she had with her of Rire was jettisoned. It was a greater loss than she had expected.

Jarl tied her to the grate at the back of the freight room, with its black metal leaves and twisting tendrils. There were tools inside, locked down for acceleration — tools that might make weapons — but they were impossible to reach.

Jarl slapped her thigh and leered at her, telling her something in Gelack, then turned to make a short speech to the men. Ann looked from face to face in the circle surrounding her. There were guards in fancy dress and crew in plainer clothes, all uniformed. Some were grim, some anxious. A few looked squeamish but not brave enough to protect her, or else too fundamentally afraid of what she had done. All of them were men, and for the first time in her life Ann wasn't proud of her clean, firm limbs, but disgusted by her inability to get them out of sight.

The circle closed in with nerve-racking slowness and stopped out of reach of Ann's legs, which were not bound. Their wariness cheered and surprised her. They didn't seem as certain as she expected them to be that a woman would be helpless in this situation.

Jarl pushed through and went straight for her. She kicked. He caught her foot and forced her knee back into her chest as he closed. He seized her jaw in one hand and pressed her cheeks in between her teeth as he put his tongue into her mouth. It was not a kiss — it was a violent proof of dominance. She jerked with her whole body, disrupting his awkward grasp, but he had made his point — the men were no longer afraid of her.

Ann watched, panting, as the excited men broke into an argument. They shouted and pointed. It was maddening not to know what was being said! But her guesses could hardly be less terrifying than the truth. A group of men wanted to kill her fast, like an execution. Others objected, brandishing knives and raising the *okal'a'ni* chant again that erected her fine body hairs in their follicles. Some of the ones in the slashing camp diluted the religious fervor with suggestions that fetched either gut laughs or disapproving scowls. It helped stave off panic to know that Ranar would be fascinated.

Maybe I ought to be taking notes, she thought.

One of the proponents of rape and knives drew his sword, causing a hush to fall.

Calling the question, Gelack-fashion, guessed Ann. Reetions did that on voting councils when it was necessary to cut debate short. But no arbiter presided over this decision. She wasn't even sure which side she was on — a swift death now, or a little longer to hope while she wished she had died sooner?

The proponents of a quick death wavered and gave up, a few of them fleeing from the room. Now there was nothing between her and the mob. She would have started screaming madly, if the leader of the lynch mob had not made a grab for her and given her something to focus on.

She kicked out, and connected. He backed off, but he wasn't hurt very much. The men laughed. Ann wrenched at her bound wrists. Her hands throbbed. She forgot why she had come. Forgot how much she wanted to prove she could stand by someone she loved. Awareness of the men around her filled her with foulness. She was going to die horribly. And for what? She had never felt so willing to reform, and live a sensible life, but these Gelacks were not Reetion counselors. She wasn't going to get a second chance.

Three men moved in on her fast, snagging her legs when she kicked out, and as she gritted her teeth she swore an oath that this kind of mindless horror must never touch Rire, for Rire had never been so precious to her. Rire was a miracle of decency and reason in a brutal universe.

She thought of Von with anger as bodies shoved in, interfering with each other. She hardly knew him! He had tricked her with his pathetic helplessness and good looks! But she couldn't escape knowing she would never have volunteered if she had known what helpless terror was like, in real life. With a Reetion's equitable logic, she had to forgive him for his cowardice, or condemn her own. That was the acid test of Reetion law: be judged by the same laws you impose on others, as implemented by an impartial arbiter.

"Rire", Ann whispered under her breath, like a prayer, clinging to ideals she had not been aware she possessed.

While the two most aggressive men started a fight over who got first dibs on her, others took advantage of the chance to seize the prize. She kneed the first man. The next one pulled her head back by the hair. There were hands on her! Too many hands! Breath locked in her chest, in fear.

And then she heard Von's voice.

"Ann!" he cried, from across the room, clear and unmistakable. No one else could put so much angst in a single word.

Ann glimpsed him near the door that led out of the docking bay; but her abusers were barely distracted. What could Von do against so many of them? The demise of fresh hope was too much and she closed her eyes with a despairing whine.

* * *

Von started towards Ann expecting to be stopped but unable to do anything more reasonable. It surprised him when the first few men gave way before him, sensing his intensity. It surprised him even more when the two who tried to block him proved no obstacle. He shoved the first man a whole two meters across the floor, knocked the next one down and tore through the rest of the mob, almost hurling himself on Ann in his enthusiasm. His hands gripped the grille behind her. She looked glad to see him. He resisted the impulse to kiss her, and spun back instead to die defending her, unable to do anything less despite his terror.

I've gone mad, Von thought objectively. But he didn't care. He was not going to let someone he cared about get hurt again because he was a coward.

Again? he wondered, suddenly bewildered. *But I stopped Jarl! I stood by Mira! Didn't I?* He knew that was wrong on some level. But a strange compulsion promised he could fix it if he

saved the Reetion station by leading H'Reth away down a
jump neither of them knew how to get out of. The *gorarelpul*
Lurol was responsible. He knew that. But he did not care. He
could fix the past! And H'Reth could no longer command him.

H'Reth was there beside him, quivering with pleasure
at the sight of him, but wouldn't dare to touch him with an
audience of crewmen watching.

"Von!" H'Reth gasped, his face glowing. "You got away
from them! You clever, clever boy!"

"Wonderful," Jarl answered sarcastically. "Now move
away from the girl."

Von reached for the marvelous new invulnerability that
let him trample down fear — and found that Jarl still scared
him. He was disappointed.

"We need Ann alive," Von told H'Reth, instead, forcing
himself to make eye contact.

"She faked your voice, Von," H'Reth told him. "And she
shot two of Delm's paladins. Shot them! With some sort of
laser!"

Von dropped his voice to a whisper. "I know," Von confided in H'Reth, improvising. "I asked her to."

"Von?" H'Reth whimpered.

"To get rid of Larren," Von whispered to his erstwhile
bond master, intoxicated by the proof he could lie to him
without inspiring bond conflict. "For you."

Jarl pushed Von away from H'Reth, roughly. "He can't
keep the girl, H'Reth. The crew is on edge and enforcing *Okal
Rel* will settle them down."

"No!" exclaimed Von. It seemed to him that his rebellious
spirit must be burning like a nova, but H'Reth and Jarl responded to him as they always had — H'Reth's face was
set in a jealous pout, and Jarl looked inclined to beat him
senseless.

"What do you think, My Liege?" Jarl deferred to H'Reth
in a smooth tone. "Should we risk our necks to let him keep
a brown-skinned bed warmer?"

"Wait, please!" Von begged, afraid it might be H'Reth's jealousy that answered. "We have to get out of this reach," he urged. "I know why, and I know how. I found out while I was with the Reetions."

"What does the girl have to do with it?" H'Reth wanted to know.

Von appealed to Jarl. "We can't talk here."

"Fair enough," said Jarl, with a flickering glance over his shoulder toward the hovering crew.

"Von?" Ann asked tremulously from behind him, still bound to the black metal grille.

He wanted to take her in his arms and reassure her, but he knew he dared not, even if they were alone. He was afraid she might turn out to be Mira or the dead girl if he looked at her too hard. That bothered him — his feelings for Ann were explicitly sexual. The girl had died a child, and Mira was his foster-sister. How could he confuse things like that?

For a moment it was unreasonably difficult to hold everything he felt for different people separate, or even to remain aware of the difference between the present, the past, and the false past Lurol had offered him. He reached for the compulsion to lead H'Reth away, again, and held on. If he did that, everything would come out the way he needed it to.

H'Reth touched Von's arm, making him snatch a breath.

"Of course you're telling me the truth," H'Reth cooed. "Or you would be dead. Jarl," he ordered, "bring the girl and follow. You'll be personally responsible for her while I talk with Von in private." His gaze softened with a longing that made organs congeal in Von's abdomen.

"H'Reth —" Jarl began trying to steer from the sidelines, like usual.

"You'll take my orders or I'll have you vented!" H'Reth declared shrilly, not caring if the crew heard. Intending them to, even. "Don't think I've forgotten how you sold me out to Larren!"

"I explained that!" Jarl protested, spreading his hands reasonably. "I only —"

"Just bring the girl!" H'Reth snapped.

The watching crew had gone profoundly silent, cognizant of a power struggle but afraid to take sides; unhappy about H'Reth aborting Ann's execution but not quite prepared to stand up to Jarl.

"Von!" Ann cried as Jarl tore her off the wall.

"It's the best I can do, right now!" Von called back to her in Reetion. "Hang on!"

"You speak their language?" H'Reth remarked, astonished.

Von mumbled, "I picked up a few words." The truth was he squirmed every time he reached for Reetion and found it planted in his brain like it had always been there.

H'Reth touched the small of Von's back.

"It's all right," H'Reth soothed.

Von had to let H'Reth touch him. He knew it. And why not? It wasn't as if this was new. But now he could fight back, and even if he died in the end, just the same, at least he could enjoy the satisfaction of expressing himself thoroughly, first. Would that be just as good as getting H'Reth lost in that new jump? The compulsion said, no.

H'Reth moved up beside him as they neared the room. Von found himself thinking of the day, in the Bear Pit, when he gave up and stopped trying to fight Jarl. He let the girl die because he was frightened, and what good did it do? First he accepted H'Reth's offer of rescue. Then came the conscience bond.

No, he was not afraid to die. Not anymore. It would be a relief to die honestly. To uphold every poem he had ever soared with and cried for; every noble motive that he wanted to believe in. If he could not disprove Jarl's truths, he could refuse to live with them. But dying was not what was required. Not yet. First there would be some span of time alone with H'Reth in a private room. And he did not know if he could reconcile his new found strength with letting H'Reth touch him again now that he had the power to refuse. Not even to obey the new compulsion.

* * *

For H'Reth, having Von back was like clutching at a thorny rose. He was happier than he thought possible, but he suspected Von was taken with the woman and he wanted to have it out with him, alone.

He hurried his sweet boy down the passage to the guest rooms with Jarl pushing and dragging the bound Reetion along behind. At least Von seemed pensive, and did not react to the female's every grunt.

"Take the girl in there," H'Reth told Jarl when they reached the room in which Ann had first been lodged. "Don't kill her until I've heard Von out."

"I'll entertain myself, then," said Jarl.

"No!" Von snapped out of his reverie with a surprising flare of aggression. He nearly went after Jarl and Ann. H'Reth caught him and turned him back, saddened by the wild concern on his boy's expressive features. "You wanted to talk to me," he reminded him.

Von swallowed. H'Reth drew him into a little sitting parlor heavily webbed for travel except for one large couch.

"Now then," H'Reth said, taking Von by either arm. "We're alone."

The way Von wet his lips to speak sent shivers through H'Reth. He had to struggle not to silence him with kisses.

"We will need Ann on the far side of the jump," Von explained in a rush, backing up a step. "The new jump. Without her, we won't know where to go to find civilization on the other side."

Such eyes he has! H'Reth thought, staring into their multi-faceted clarity as he closed the space between them. But it irked him to feel Von growing brittle beneath his touch, like usual. It irked him that Von didn't mention the cut on H'Reth's face, which stung terribly.

Von was getting agitated. "Please!" he urged. "She won't help us if you let Jarl hurt her!"

And why is she willing to help us, I wonder, H'Reth thought unhappily. *Because she's in love with you.*

Von's pulse was jumping in his throat. He trembled with that delicious, isometric tension that welled up from his core to sensitize all his reactions, until he gasped when you stroked him, fainted when you kissed him, moaned if you touched his groin.

"Why can't we stay in this reach?" H'Reth complained, mesmerized.

"It's empty!" Von exclaimed, and caught his breath as H'Reth touched his flank. H'Reth cupped his boy's face, feeling him tremble.

"If we don't leave soon we might be stranded here," Von finished like a runner crashing through the finish line. "Th-the jump we used to get here is unstable. That's why the Reetions and the Monatese haven't used it in two hundred years. And — and there's nothing much here. No planets."

"And this other jump," H'Reth asked reluctantly. "You've learned it?"

Von nodded vigorously, looking pale. "Yes, Ann showed me. The worlds of Rire are on the other side. But I don't know how to find them. She does. Let me go help her!"

H'Reth's ardor was doused by his agitation on behalf of the brown-skinned woman.

"You want her, don't you?" H'Reth accused his dear one.

"I —" Von choked on the word, turning his head aside, his lovely cloak of shivering emotion turning wooden in H'Reth's arms. H'Reth hated that. He let go. His voice became thunderous. "I'm your bond master!" he told Von. "You will answer when I ask you questions!"

"I want her, yes," Von confessed in a gush.

H'Reth's heart sank, then he struggled to be magnanimous. He knew in his heart that Jarl was right. Von couldn't help liking girls. But maybe it would not matter if Von had them, so long as he had Von. He still wanted to strangle Ann, but he could wait until Von lost interest in her.

Von took a handkerchief from H'Reth's own vest pocket, nodding at the cut on H'Reth's cheek. "You've been hurt," he said, trying to force compassion. H'Reth could tell he didn't really care. But the hand holding the handkerchief was as graceful as any Golden lady's, while still unmistakably male; Von's skin was suede-soft and colored like the finest porcelain, but warm and living. H'Reth took the lovely hand in his, making Von drop the handkerchief, and drew Von's palm to his mouth until his lips brushed the mounds below Von's fingers, the fingers straining backward to avoid his touch. To banish the sight of Von's rising tears he let his eyes close. Then he slid his tongue between Von's fingers where the skin was sensitive.

"W-We n-need Ann," Von pleaded. "Let me help her. Let her show us. And afterwards — I will try to love you. Really love you. If you want that."

H'Reth drew back, releasing Von's hand. Von let it fall to his side, holding it away from him a little.

"I've thought about things while I was with the Reetions," Von said with a gulp. "I am bonded to you. So I obey you. But I know you want more. It is a miracle that you have shown me so much patience while I was young. But I'm older now — I can accept the inevitable."

H'Reth's eyes widened. Von filled them, so intense and so beautiful.

"Really?" H'Reth breathed. He couldn't quite believe it. "Do you mean that? Can you love me?"

"I will try," Von backslid just a little. "I can't help liking girls. But I know you are my life now. I will try."

H'Reth was too thrilled to resist kissing him. After so much pain and disillusionment, to finally have what he wanted felt too good to be true. Von endured the kiss as usual, but for the moment at least H'Reth didn't care if he turned into a marble statue without constant nagging and admonishment to relax.

"Maybe," H'Reth murmured, feeling too happy to be niggardly, "we could do something with this Ann of yours, like we did with Anatolia. Until you get tired of her. Then I am sure there will be lots of other brown women available in this new place. But you do know this new jump?" H'Reth fretted, belatedly, knowing he shouldn't take all the miracles Von offered him too much for granted.

"Oh yes," said Von, with conviction.

H'Reth stroked Von's feathery black hair and the shapely head beneath it, not caring that he had sticky blood on his hands. When they were done with the jump and the rest of it, they could take a bath together. Von would tend his cut and he would wash Von's hair with his own hands. Von looked impatient.

"The Reetions have spread terrible pictures around Killing Reach," H'Reth warned Von. "I don't know how the Reetions got them, unless they were somehow in league with Anatolia. Everyone betrays me! But that is just another reason to get one more reach away, since the real Liege Monitum knows the jump that brought us this far. Better not to stay in reach of Fountain Court."

Noises coming from the room next door distracted Von. He pulled away, drawn by the sounds coming through the wall.

"Oh, let Jarl have his fun!" H'Reth scolded. "It won't spoil her for you."

"Master — Garn, please," Von forced a smile. "Let me go now!"

Each expression Von performed was as much a work of art as one of Delm's interminable portraits and transparently eloquent. All H'Reth saw now was anguished concern about Ann. Well, he was not going to let him go running off to save her just like that! Not without proving he meant what he said about trying to love him better!

H'Reth kissed Von forcefully on the mouth, seeking proof of a real change of attitude, but his dear boy was no more responsive than the last time Anatolia had fetched him to the Bear Pit for their rendezvous. He would never change. H'Reth would always have to urge and command his responses. But then, without a word of threat or promise, Von's hands moved to H'Reth's shoulder, and he kissed him back.

Overjoyed, H'Reth would have taken the time to make love, but Von stopped giving back as suddenly as he had begun, pushing H'Reth away with a frightening new show of force.

"Please," Von gasped, his face drained of blood as thoroughly as if he was going into shock, "we'll have so much more time after we have taken the *Rose* through the new jump!"

"How can I believe you?" H'Reth whined. Von's desire to rescue the girl was so palpable he felt that he could all but strangle it in his hands, like a living animal.

"I cannot lie to my bond master!" Von exclaimed, alarmed by a bump in the other room. "I have to do better! And I will! But later!"

H'Reth took pity on him. "All right, Von. Go tell Jarl that I want to see him and make yourself a hero with the wretched girl."

Von tore free like a bolt loosed from one of the big, heavy crossbows used for hunting on the game reserves of Demish lieges.

H'Reth inhaled with a full, but still troubled heart. It would take a long time, but at least he had Von on the right track, at last.

* * *

Jarl hurled Ann onto a couch that was cluttered with used quilts and blankets. He said something mocking in Gelack before he attacked.

Ann drew both her feet up and plowed him in the gut. She wished she had caught him lower, but she thought of that after the fact.

She shouted, "Von!" and scrambled up. Her hands were still bound behind her. It was a serious impediment. Ann backed away, around the couch.

Jarl was up and rubbing his stomach, but he didn't seem put off. Maybe he liked to play rough.

"You could untie me, at least, you sick barbarian!" Ann yelled at him in Reetion.

He positioned himself on the far side of the couch. She backed off. He leapt over it in a bound. They shuffled around the room, this way and that, until he tackled her and she went down with his nails digging into her skin as he yanked down her stretch pants. She sunk her teeth in his ear. She heard, rather than felt, the blow that dazed her in response.

After that she was aware of Jarl untieing her hands and yanking at her clothes, but she could do nothing more than moan and thrash, trying to at least make it difficult. When he had her naked he yanked her up and threw her on the couch.

That helped bring her around. She braced an arm and brought her knees up. He watched with a grin as she tried to struggle up, then caught her and slung her back down.

She drove her fingers towards his eyes but he caught her hands and forced them up over her head where she sprawled beneath him. He had not undressed himself and his clothes were rough on her bare skin. She bit his arm as he shifted to undo his belt, forcing him to let go. She struggled to shove him off, and he hit her. She cried out, astonished by the shock of it. She thought she was tough, but she had no experience with violence like this. Even worse, it was clear he enjoyed seeing her realize that, and he didn't want to spoil the fun by humbling her too fast.

Ann lay still, trying to think. He took the respite to get his pants down, but he didn't take them all the way off.

Good. That would hamper him. She looked around, in swift, sharp glances, seeking weapons.

As he came for her again she rolled off the couch. Jarl grabbed his pants with one hand and dove after her, striking with a thump that knocked her breath out. She fell short of the ornament she had been reaching for, toppling it off the table. She grappled with her attacker, but he expected that. He wedged his forearm underneath her chin beneath her throat. Ann arched her back, struggling to flip him off.

Her resistance proved remarkably effective. Between one second and the next, Jarl was flying off her into a wall.

* * *

Nothing Von had ever done was any harder than kissing H'Reth back, voluntarily, now that he could refuse. The achievement disgusted him, and it made him sick to pity his infatuated tormentor. But redemption waited down the jump to their mutual oblivion, and for that he must retain H'Reth's trust.

He felt guilty about letting things distract him from that greater purpose. Things like worrying about the innocent Blue Demish pilots H'Reth would take with him, and keeping Jarl away from Ann, although he thought his plan was rather clever considering he was mad, because it spared Ann's life without preventing his redemption. All the same, he had the feeling he was spread too thin and out of miracles, which was why he had every intention of doing no more than telling Jarl to report to H'Reth immediately, when he entered Ann's room.

But the room he entered was not the room that he expected. He was in the Bear Pit again, in Jarl's quarters, and Ann was the little girl Jarl murdered. He felt everything just as he had before, except he wasn't the same frightened child now.

Von's hands locked on the back of Jarl's vest in a solid, satisfying manner. In his childhood, Jarl had often knocked him senseless and Von expected nothing better, now. He just didn't care. But when Von braced himself and heaved as hard as he was able, Jarl's body lifted like a doll's and sailed through the air into a wall. Von was amazed.

Jarl shook himself, got up, and grinned at Von, his teeth filmed with fresh blood. He wasn't badly hurt. He said, "I knew there was fight left in you, brat."

Anger coiled up out of Von's past. Behind him, Ann was scrambling for an ornament on the floor. He heard her grunt as she hurled it at Jarl. She would have hit him, too, but Jarl deflected it with one arm.

"Later," Jarl promised Ann, where she knelt, panting, on the floor.

Von struck out with a foot as Jarl came for him. It was a dance move, but the result was wonderful.

Jarl went over, face stamped in a look of shock. Von fell on him, throwing wild, frenzied punches. His hands hurt, but his fist broke Jarl's damaged nose. Jarl's head snapped back. Von straddled his chest, hands together, and whipped his fists back and forth, cutting his knuckles on Jarl's teeth, but not caring. Screams of pain spiked up his arms; the screams of children in the Bear Pit echoed back.

Ann yelled, "Stop!"

Jarl's face was a bloody pulp, beneath him. But Von wasn't finished, there were too many children screaming in his memory to be saved.

"Von!" Ann grabbed his raised fists from the back. "He's dead!"

Von pulled Ann down, trying to complete his blow. She fell across the body and lay hanging onto his bleeding fists, staring up at him as if she didn't recognize him. She was not a little girl, dead or living. She made him think of skin on skin, hers warm and brown and welcoming. He let his locked hands go slack.

Ann smelled of fear, but she moved with confidence, scrambling free of Jarl's body as if it was so much mud. She reached for Von. He veered away and threw up.

He heard her say, "Oh, yuck."

* * *

When Von was finished being sick, Ann grabbed a blanket off the couch to cover the vomit and the disgusting mess he had made of Jarl. She was thoroughly shaken and dressed only in streaks of blood, but Von seemed worse than she was. She was afraid he had snapped. The way he had pulped Jarl was something she was going to have bad dreams about if she lived long enough to enjoy post-traumatic stress syndrome. It took courage to haul him up.

Von clasped her to him with the same strength he had demonstrated moments before, his hands quaking and bloody, and broke into wrenching sobs. She guided him clear of the carnage and settled him on the couch, where he proceeded to cry his heart out. The crying lasted a few minutes but it seemed like a lifetime, with no idea who might come through the door. Ann stroked Von's head, trying to calm him down, saying, "Shh, shh."

She kissed his forehead, and he nestled close, his hand gliding up her side. As he touched her breast he jerked back unexpectedly, whimpering, "Mira?"

"Ann," she told him, touching his face and throat. "I'm Ann."

He kissed her eagerly then, hugging too hard. She eased him off. He sat up, looking puzzled.

"You're naked," he said.

"Gee, you noticed." She was shaking herself, but the wisecracks helped, even if he barely appreciated them.

He looked around him, dazed, still speaking Reetion. "I thought I was somewhere else."

"That would be nice," Ann suggested.

"No," he said, and shook his head.

"What did Lurol do to you?" she demanded.

His expression gained focus, jet eyebrows bearing down. "Made me better, I think," he decided.

"Yeah," Ann bit her lip, "but are you sane?"

"I don't think so," he said factually. "But it doesn't matter."

Okay, Ann thought, *that's creepy*.

"You'll be all right," he said, "after we're gone. I told H'Reth we need you to show us the way to the Reetion worlds. But you don't have to, really. I'm going to make sure H'Reth and I don't come back out."

He's right, Ann decided. *He isn't sane*.

Von shrugged out of his flight jacket and put it around her shoulders. It smelled reassuringly of his vanilla scent. Beneath it, he was wearing a dark green shirt.

"What I'd really like," she told him, "are some pants."

"Take Jarl's," Von suggested.

Ann would rather have skinned lizards with her teeth, but she remembered that the bottom half of Jarl's dead body wasn't the part Von had pulped. She started stripping him, until she realized his bowels had opened in death. That was too much.

Von caught her hand and pulled her up. "Never mind," he said. "We'll find you something to wear."

His jacket hung to her hips. It wasn't decent, but it wasn't her worst criticism of Gelack hospitality so far. They ran along the passage outside to another room. Von yanked her in. The room was lined with wooden closets full of lavish clothes.

Von lodged his back against a closet and marveled at his bloody hands. Ann could see the sick look coming over his face again. She grabbed him by both wrists, making him wince, and pushed his hands down so he would concentrate on her instead.

"It will wash off," she pointed out firmly, referring to the gore on his hands.

"Ann." Von looked distressed. "How did I — I shouldn't have been able —" He shook his head quickly and blurted. "I didn't know I could do that!"

"He deserved it!" Ann insisted.

"But Jarl's strong!"

Ann frowned. "Sooo, what are you worrying about here? Disappointed that he didn't put up a better fight?"

Von shook his head.

"Then what?"

"I don't know!" He didn't try to free himself, but added softly. "Let me go?"

Ann released his wrists. Von remained quiet. She turned from him to pull open a closet, yanked out something too lovely for the purpose, and began to clean Von's bloody knuckles as he watched her with a dazed expression.

"I haven't flown, either," he interjected, in an apparent *non sequitur*. "Not since I was ten. But it seemed ... natural."

"You flew when you were ten years old?" Ann asked, giving up trying to clean his hands without water.

"It wasn't legal," Von said apologetically. "I'm an ordinary person, a commoner, in Gelack." He shrugged. "There's no Reetion word."

"I don't know what you are," she begged to differ, "but there's nothing ordinary about you."

"I meant," he said, "I'm not a Sevolite."

Ann put together what she had witnessed and all the data Lurol had extracted from Von.

"I think you are," she said. "I think you're everything the stories make out Sevolites were."

Tears filled up Von's crystal eyes, making them look like melting ice.

"I can't be a Sevolite," he whimpered. He said it much the way she might have objected to being proven a vampire.

"Look, it doesn't matter," she said. "There's no such thing on Rire as Sevolites or commoners — just people."

He shook his head. "I'm not a Reetion!"

"Maybe not, but you'd make a damn fine one," Ann insisted.

Von looked at his hands again. Fresh blood welled in a crisscross of shallow wounds where he had torn the soft skin of his knuckles.

"My hands hurt," he said, blinking one tear from each eye, to slide slowly down his face.

"Anything broken?" Ann asked, being practical.

He flexed his hand, wincing. "I don't think so," he said.

Ann looked around the room. They couldn't stay here indefinitely and she had no idea when she would be missed or Jarl's body discovered.

"There's a room at the back I can wash in," Von decided on his own priorities. He opened a cabinet to reveal a tiny room with a dainty, painted sink and matching toilet.

Ann made use of the time to find something to put on. The closets of women's clothes were stocked with dresses that looked much too cumbersome. Ann opened closets until she discovered men's apparel and settled on a pair of black satin pants with a drawstring. The buttoned fly hung empty, making her imagine how Von would fill them out. She promised herself that when they made it back to civilization again, she would check it out. The idea cheered her up.

Von reappeared looking chilly and damp. He had rinsed his hair out, also, which seemed needlessly fastidious.

"What's next?" she asked.

He said, "I must lead H'Reth down the jump."

Ann's hackles rose. "The jump you don't know?" she double-checked.

Von nodded. "We will be lost together," he said unhappily.

Ann attached herself to him like a barnacle, hands knotted in his green silk shirt. "Listen up, handsome. You're playing out somebody else's battle plan, and the dumb thing is, it might not even matter anymore! Larren is dead! And to judge by what I saw you do to my unwanted attention, back in that room, I wouldn't be surprised if you could take out H'Reth yourself, with your bare hands. Then who would be in charge?"

"The next highest Sevolite," said Von automatically, and frowned. "But I have to take H'Reth down the jump."

"Damn it, Von!" She struck him in the chest with a thump. He looked surprised, but only took a step back.

"Why are you mad at me?" he asked, incredulous.

"I am mad at Lurol!" Ann exclaimed, and raised a hand to silence him while she thought. Reason wasn't going to get through, but something had to. After all, if he was so hell-bent on playing out Lurol's program why had he detoured to snatch her away from Jarl? And why was he hanging around, now?

For me, she realized, studying the hurt look on his face already melting towards forgiveness. *To save me, he postponed his swan song*. That couldn't have been Lurol's idea. And it gave her a lever to pull on.

"Put on a cloak," he said, "and I'll take you to wait in H'Reth's quarters until someone honorable claims the *Vanilla Rose* — whether that's Liege Monitum or Reetions. I'll tell H'Reth you're in my ship with me. I don't know what will happen to you, for sure, but it's the best I can think of!" He sounded half-hysterical all of a sudden.

Ann stroked him to calm him down. "It's all right," she said. "Breathe, Von."

Could I knock him out and carry him into a rel-*ship?* she wondered, but after witnessing Jarl's death she doubted she could overpower him, and she would need his cooperation if they were going to fly one of the Gelacks' big, gray jaw-breakers. Her own ship was adrift in space somewhere. She might be able to communicate with it, but doubted the Gelacks would let it dock again, given their superstitious attitude. She didn't have a space-suit handy, either, and given Von's reaction to *Second Contact's* zero-G docks, he had to be a poor bet for a space walk anyhow.

Von grew gentle in her arms, exotic as a resting unicorn. She grinned to herself, wondering if that made her an honorary virgin.

"Listen," Ann told Von, still caressing him. "There's no hope for me if I stay here."

He stirred. She held him tighter.

"So I'm coming with you," she insisted. "Down your damn jump."

He pulled away, alarmed. "No, Ann!"

"I know that jump," she told him. "I can get us through it. And maybe then, when you've done what Lurol programmed you to do, you'll be able to think for yourself again and I can take you home. You know? To live happily ever after. That's how all the best fairy tales end."

Von shook his head again, blanching.

"You take me with you," she threatened, "or I'll try to escape myself! Maybe find something else to use as a gun."

Von was horrified. "Ann, you can't do *okal'a'ni* things like that!"

"Too late," she told him. "I already have. If you leave me behind I'll wind up back where you found me, in the middle of a lynch mob. I'm not going to wait around for that — I'd rather go down fighting."

He blinked at her, round eyed, "You'd do that?"

"You bet I would!" It was hilarious, really, threatening him with her own suicide to put herself in a position to short circuit his own.

"Only to be attempted with a Beauty, as a last resort," she muttered to herself for comfort, drawing on her repertoire of 20th century popular culture. "Don't let the kids try this at home on an average guy."

Seeing how well her trick worked made her go gooey inside — Von was paralyzed with worry for her.

"Deal?" she asked.

"But, Ann," Von struggled with her ultimatum, "we can't really lead them through that jump! H'Reth wants to conquer Reetion planets!"

The idea was so absurd Ann nearly laughed, then she remembered the ship that dunked her coming back out to *Second Contact*, and Josh failing to show up.

"Right," Ann had to concede the point. She tried to come up with alternatives and drew a blank, so she settled for grasping at straws. "We can't lead them through the jump, okay, so I won't pilot; you will, just like you're supposed to."

He expelled his breath with relief. "Then you'll stay here."

"I never said that," said Ann. "You get them lost like you planned. Then, when we're sure of that ... well, we'll see what we can do about getting ourselves back out. We made a pretty good team the last time, and I barely knew the Killing Reach Jump. I know the Reetion one inside out."

Anxiety fixed itself on Von's face and shoulders like a clamp. He whimpered, "I can't."

Ann grabbed him by the shoulders. "You are the strongest pilot I have ever known," she told him firmly. "How do you know what you can do?"

He shook his head.

"Come on!" She took his hand and dragged. "You've got to get me into your ship before H'Reth catches on."

He stumbled one step before keeping up. "*Rel*-fighters don't have room for passengers," he objected.

"So we double up!"

"Wait!" He balked at the door, and dragged her back. "You can't go anywhere dressed like that."

He reclaimed his flight jacket and dug out the rest of the lounging suit she had chosen before, which had a rather indecent top half for a woman. It closed across the chest in baggy folds. Von covered the whole thing with a long black traveling cloak.

"People are going to let me walk around in this?" Ann asked. "And not get suspicious?"

"People wear them all the time," said Von.

"Not people," Ann corrected, shifting the all-obscuring cloak on her shoulders. "Gelacks. What a weird custom."

"People wear them when they don't want to be recognized or bothered," Von said, as if that explained it well enough.

"Maybe I should take one home to Rire," joked Ann. "To keep me clear of Supervision."

"Supervision?" Von asked.

"What my culture does to you when you break the rules," said Ann. "I've been through it more than once." Von's sympathetic look amused Ann. She didn't know what he was imagining, but it must have been pretty bad.

The docking berths were not far from the room where they had killed Jarl. They picked one, found it empty, and checked out the next one further along, where they spotted workers inside and ducked back out.

"Hang back," Von instructed. "Then come in and go straight to the ship in the outer airlock as if you're a Sevolite."

Von let himself into the outer airlock. Ann counted to thirty, then she followed.

She discovered Von chatting with a couple of men dressed in overalls. One of them looked up as Ann headed for the airlock chamber. He asked Von a question that Von answered in Gelack. He sounded nervous to Ann, but whatever he made up seemed to do the job.

The inner airlock reminded Ann of an internal combustion engine cylinder of the kind she used to build, in childhood, out of twentieth century technology construction kits; the floor was the top of the piston, fixed at the bottom of its cycle just now. The walls of the short tube were lubricated, and the spherical *rel*-fighter that filled the interior rested in a buildup of thick, brown padding, higher on one side than the other.

Like a marble in a pinball shooter, Ann thought, and wished she hadn't.

She was trailing her hand along the inert gray hull of the *rel*-fighter, wondering how she was supposed to get in, when she heard a raised voice booming from the outer airlock.

"Von!" H'Reth shouted, followed by incomprehensible Gelack that ended in "Jarl."

Oh, oh, thought Ann, her skin prickling with fear again.

Reckless Acts

The Demish Champion met Di Mon's charge with sober courage. He fought right handed, as the Demish usually did, but Di Mon had dueled enough of them in his time not to be put off. His opponent feigned a move to draw him out, but Di Mon did not respond. That worried the Demish prince, who probably counted on exploiting hot, Vrellish tempers when fighting black-hairs. They engaged in a room gone as quiet as space — except for the slash and slither of their blades — and drew back, having tested one another and grown grim.

The Demish Champion began to circle out of range of Di Mon's lunge, or so he thought.

Pent up grief shot Di Mon forward, engaging, rebounding, and whipping a long thin slash in frustration down his opponent's flank. His Demish opponent gave a startled cry but did not lose his concentration. Di Mon was not inclined to stop at first blood, but the strange prince had a strong defense. The only hits that Di Mon landed were harassing ones.

So be it, thought Di Mon. The Demish hurt more than the Vrellish did. He would fray his opponent's wits with distracting pain and his stamina with loss of blood. Di Mon settled with a predator's cunning to the task, and was disappointed when his opponent called the duel off.

"I don't want to fight you!" the man panted, bleeding from three separate cuts. He took a judicious step back as he lowered his sword. "I tried to tell your errant as much, but he attacked."

"You are backing down!" exclaimed the paladin, Thoth, his disapproval measured by a one-rank drop in grammar.

"You fight him if you've cause!" the Demish Champion fired back, nettled, dropping the honorifics owed a paladin in Demish dialect.

Di Mon deduced the champion was loath to take orders without explanation and decided he wanted to encourage that, so he, too, took a step back. The Demish Champion was shaking in the aftermath of Di Mon's attack.

A good sword, but not a blood fighter, Di Mon decided. *A tournament champion.*

"I am sorry I was forced to kill your man," the Demish Champion apologized again, with a dip of his head towards Tan. "We're here to investigate a report of *okal'a'ni* weapons. Nothing more."

Di Mon said, "Get out. Now."

It was Thoth that Di Mon wanted to run through. Thoth, as Delm's surrogate, although he could not rationalize his suspicions and therefore distrusted them.

L'Ket glared at the Demish Champion who had killed Tan. She still wanted blood and that was dangerous. Di Mon's side would be badly outnumbered if a melee broke out.

Thoth stepped forward. "This is completely unnecessary, Liege Monitum," he announced in an official tone. "We both seek justice, nothing more. What cause have you to defend Perry D'Aur?"

"None. You may have her," said Di Mon. "But Den Eva's is under my protection. None of its staff or courtesans will be questioned without my *gorarelpul* as witness. If you accept those terms, I will stand down."

"That seems reasonable," said the Demish Champion.

Thoth was counting up numbers and hoping for a better result.

L'Ket looked too intense for comfort.

I must kill her if she goes for their champion, Di Mon realized. But he didn't know if he could. He understood her desire for vengeance.

Hesseratt emerged from the smoking spoke-hall, helping Vretla, who was on her feet, sword in hand, although just moving took all her concentration.

Thoth perked up. "Liege Vrel's baby?" he asked.

Coldly, Di Mon answered, "Lost."

L'Ket made a low sound in her throat. Thoth hesitated on the brink of some provocative remark, worried by the look in Di Mon's eyes. Di Mon thought, warmly, of Hangst Nersal taking down paladins on the Octagon in defense of D'Ander's hearth right. *One more*, he thought, *would make a nice set*. Silently, he targeted Thoth. He would take him out, personally, if it turned into a melee. The odds were still not good, of course. Highborn advantage disappeared if taking on more than one nobleborn. That was why melees were so hazardous. When there were lots of people involved, it often didn't matter how good you were.

Doors banged open in the den's entrance hall. Through them rushed a dozen Nersallians, some of them still dressed in mechanic's overalls but all of them wearing swords. Ses Nersal plunged through their center and saluted Di Mon.

"Good cycle, *mekan'st ma*," she greeted him.

"Good cycle," he answered, accepting the Vrellish naming word for a friend-lover.

She grinned from ear to ear with her wide mouth. "We heard there might be fighting to watch," she said.

Di Mon smiled back. If he dared to child gift, he'd have offered to do it for Ses Nersal for this rescue. Ses recognized the Demish Champion and looked impressed. The one thing she liked better about court than the Nersallians fleet, from which she had retired, was the chance to watch and bet on duels between Vrellish and Demish champions.

Kertatt began sliding down the wall where Di Mon had left him when he dashed to the aide of his errants.

"Assist Di Mon's sister-son," Ses ordered one of her followers.

Di Mon looked for Eva. "Have you made up your mind?" he asked.

The den mother came away from the wall she had been pressed against, watching. It took a heartbeat for her to grasp what Di Mon meant, then her carriage straightened.

"Yes," she said, firmly. "I will be your *lyka*."

"*Lyka* is it?" Ses said, and winked at Eva. "That's a good sign! Warm him up for me, den mother. He's much too self-controlled to be Vrellish!"

Di Mon frowned, aware he ought to do something to refute the implication he was cold-blooded, but he couldn't — nothing to do with sex felt light-hearted to him.

L'Ket saved him from further embarrassment by demanding his complete attention. She had been kneeling over Tan's body, confirming that he was dead. Now she cleared her sword as she straightened.

The Demish Champion had pinked up a little at Ses Nersal's suggestion to Eva, and wasn't paying much attention.

Di Mon blocked L'Ket's attack with a lunge, driving her sword down. The Demish reacted to the sound, but by then it was already over.

"Assist your captain with Liege Vrel," Di Mon ordered his rebelling errant.

L'Ket blinked, aware that Di Mon could have killed her. He still held her sword down beneath his own, the tension in their arms rock solid. "Tan —" she objected.

"Tan chose to duel?" Di Mon demanded, merciless.

"Yes," she admitted.

"*Ack Rel*, then," Di Mon told her. "I am grateful. Do not shame him with a dishonorable grudge."

L'Ket looked confused, could not sustain it, and came down on the side of obedience.

"We cannot let you remove people from this den until this incident has been properly investigated," Thoth objected with Demish officiousness.

"Why not?" demanded the Demish Champion, who was suffering his bleeding cuts to be bound. "So long as they do not take the suspects, just the victims."

"You are under my command!" Thoth insisted, speaking down sharply.

The champion colored an angry red. "I am here at the Ava's request, as your champion," he told Thoth, sounding splendidly, Demishly stubborn. "There's a difference between that and taking your orders." His pronouns magnified the insult Thoth had offered.

Thoth lead a knot of nobleborns down the spoke-hall where they had left Perry D'Aur and since nothing of theirs still lived in the rooms beyond, the Vrellish let him.

Ses Nersal joined Di Mon where he stood overseeing their evacuation.

"Your work," she asked, bobbing a nod in the direction of the Demish Champion, who was now conferring with his errant captain, the man Di Mon had found guarding Eva's people in the office.

Di Mon felt a little sorry, now, for the ferocity with which he had drawn forth the bright blood spreading into the Demish prince's clean white and silver clothes.

"He has a strong defense," he praised the Demish swordsman to Ses.

Ses laughed, "He should! He's Prince Hendricks D'Astor! You don't know the name? Well," she conceded, "I know you aren't much for the tournaments. D'Astor is a fairly new branch off the H'Usian bush, related by marriage to the Marins, which is about their only court connection, or was, before Marin got run out of the Apron District. Hendricks D'Astor has been tourney champion in Princess Reach for five years running! Delm invited him to compete in the pan-Demish games this year, hoping he would humble D'Ander, I suppose, in case he showed. Although people say D'Astor is too careful — D'Ander wields a bold sword."

Ses saluted D'Astor with a nod as he looked over at her, hearing his name so frequently popping up. It didn't inhibit her at all. "I am sorry I missed the clash in which you bloodied him," she told Di Mon. Ses was one of those lesser

Vrellish forever vexed by their superiors' indifference to
exhibition competitions. She was also betraying her mixed
blood with all her excited chatter. True Vrellish were more
taciturn. But Nersallians were hybrids with some Demish
in them, just as the Monatese were part Lorel. Di Mon's
silence tipped Ses off that she was talking too much, and she
fell silent, plotting — Di Mon was sure — to get the details
of the fight from a witness later.

Feeling weary, Di Mon collected his traveling cloak, and
remembering the Reetion info-blit was still in his vest pocket,
transferred it to a pocket of his cloak. *The things must be all
over court by now*, he thought and found the idea depress-
ing.

On the way out, Di Mon paused to lay a hand upon
D'Astor's shoulder. The Demish prince spun around with
a look of surprise and alarm.

"Your captain of errants?" Di Mon asked, with a nod in
the direction of the man beside him. The errant captain
slowly eased his hand off the hilt of his own sword.

"Uh, yes," D'Astor floundered, at a loss, socially, to be
holding a polite conversation with someone who had been
bent on killing him moments before.

"See he stays in charge until I've sent a *gorarelpul* to witness Thoth's investigation," said Di Mon.

D'Astor's pale eyebrows drew together in a frosty clump.
"You distrust the Ava's honor, Liege Monitum? The Ava to
whom you are sworn?"

"Let's just say I prefer to trust yours," said Di Mon. The
Demish man was still baffled, but conscious of being paid
a compliment. He nodded with a thoughtful expression. Di
Mon followed Ses Nersal out at a jog.

They had three cars, including the one Kertatt had come
in on his own. Di Mon put Srain, Eva, and Kertatt into one
with orders to take Kertatt and Tan's body home and have
Sarilous send one of Green Hearth's younger *gorarelpul* back
under escort. Eva was to brief the *gorarelpul*. Di Mon also

gave Srain a hurried note to be hand delivered to Prince H'Us in Silver Hearth, as soon as possible.

"Vretla's life may depend on it," he told Srain Eversol.

Kertatt's car dispatched, Di Mon joined L'Ket and Hesseratt where they stood guard over Vretla, laid out on a cloak beside Di Mon's car. Ses stood a pace farther off, her garage irregulars deployed to keep watch.

"Thank you," Di Mon told Ses, in grammatical peerage, a compliment implying she had served him as well as any birth-rank equal could have.

She kissed him. It was her due. But he could not share her pleasure. He was preoccupied by Vretla's silent, drug-muted movements, which suggested that the fury of *rel-osh* was still consuming her.

"What are you going to do about Vretla?" Ses asked.

"Get her to *TouchGate Hospital Station*," said Di Mon.

Ses blinked. "That will take hours. Unless a highborn flies, and even then —"

"She will last," said Di Mon.

"You will go yourself?" Ses asked, leery of the idea.

"It seems a bad time to be gone from court," he said. "There is so much still unsettled."

Ses gave a derisive snort. "Perry D'Aur has proved as bad as the other Demish say. There will be no Vrellish opposi-tion, this time, if Delm moves to finish her."

"Which is exactly why I do not think Perry D'Aur was behind this attack," Di Mon said.

"Who then?" Ses demanded.

Di Mon shrugged, unwilling to share his speculations. Ses was his *mekan'st*, but she was also Hangst Nersal's vassal, and he did not know anymore where Black Hearth stood on court politics. It hurt him to acknowledge that. Hangst Nersal had been the strength of Sevildom during the Nesak War and Di Mon's own mentor in the arts of space war.

Vretla rose on an elbow and stretched out a hand, gasp-ing, "Mon!"

Di Mon knelt down. Vretla's bloody, ash-soiled fingers closed in the lace work of his green vest. "No-Lorel-tricks!" she spat, her breath coming like a furnace blast through flared nostrils. "Kill me," she ordered.

She was strong. She knew her dying would be agony. Doing what she said would be sensible, and she would not welcome his attempt to save her. Nor would her people, when they came to court from Red Reach, to learn what had happened to her — the Vrellish distrusted old Lorel powers, particularly the medical sciences still practiced at *TouchGate Hospital Station*.

"No," Di Mon refused. "I will not kill you."

Vretla glared back at him, her teeth gritted. Then she lunged for the nearest sword, half drawing L'Ket's before the Monatese mastered her.

Ses Nersal refused to participate. She caught Di Mon's arm as he rose from helping Hesseratt administer more *klinoman* to Vretla.

"I understand," Ses said harshly. "You mentored her. If you wish it, I will kill her for you."

"I told you," Di Mon said, teeth on edge in a silent snarl, "my intentions."

"She asked for a clean death," Ses reminded him.

"She will live," Di Mon insisted.

"Don't be pig-headed, Monitum," Ses told him. "Red Reach is full of swords. They'll challenge you."

"Red Reach is full of fools," snapped Di Mon, "who will always strike first and starve later, if Vretla does not live to teach them wisdom!"

Ses hoisted thick eyebrows. Di Mon sighed, disappointed with himself for revealing a hidden agenda. Ses would find that disturbingly Lorel, but the fact remained that he had invested far too much in Vretla, and not solely for the sake of obtaining an heir through her.

The car was loaded up and waiting for him.

Di Mon squeezed Ses Nersal's arm. She felt hard and wooden. He wished he could unwind, as other Vrellish males would, and kiss her to cement the trust between them, but it would only go wrong if he tried.

"Trust me," he said instead, and left her.

"Take us to the highborn docks," he told the chauffeur, "but not too fast. Drive carefully." The more time he gave Srain to deliver his message and H'Us to respond to it, the more likely he would have a Demish pilot waiting, to eliminate the need for him to decide whether to fly Vretla to *TouchGate Hospital* himself. During the uneventful trip, Di Mon brooded and even his errants were quiet. The best he could make out was that Delm had staged the atrocity at Den Eva's to blacken Perry's reputation, and Vretla just happened to be there. That made some sense, given Delm's hatred of Perry for occupying territory he considered his own. But he had no clear idea what to do about any of it. He felt as if he had been flying too long, and his will to strive against the bleak indifference of *gap* was faltering.

They found a small group of Silver Demish waiting at the Monatese hangar on the highborn docks, where Srain's note had directed H'Us to meet him, leaving the job of loading Vretla into the waiting *rel*-ship to his errants.

"Heard about the business at Den Eva's," Prince H'Us greeted Di Mon gravely. "Dreadful. What is the empire coming to?"

"I take it that you will loan me a highborn pilot?" asked Di Mon.

H'Us nodded. "A grandson of my great-uncle's line, a good lad. He made three runs to *TouchGate* with my mother, before she refused to go anymore." H'Us hesitated. "Any sign of Von?"

"Nothing except the Reetion recordings linking him with Liege H'Reth, if they can be taken as genuine."

"Huh," H'Us grunted as if struck in the stomach, "that foul stuff. I've heard of it. I hope we can keep it from mother until ... well ... she's dying you know."

"Yes," said Di Mon.

The big H'Usian seemed uncomfortable with the subject of death in connection with his long-lived mother, and the conversation died out.

Presently, H'Us revived it with a question about what the Luverthanians might ask for in compensation, seeing as one of his people would be delivering Vretla.

"I, uh, presume you'll be taking care of it?" asked Prince H'Us.

"I will give your pilot a letter sealed with my blood cipher," Di Mon assured him. "And my niece, Tessitatt, will fly out on his heels to settle up."

The big, sandy-haired prince frowned, an act well suited to his square mouth and bushy eyebrows. "I suppose there's no hope of getting Red Hearth to pay, is there?"

"No," said Di Mon. He declined to add that Vretla's kin were more apt to kill him than thank him for risking her soul to save her body, which was how they viewed the benefits of Lorel medicine. He would just have to convince whoever showed up that things had changed considerably since the Fifth Civil War, over two hundred years ago. If anyone showed up at all. Red Vrellish could be unpredictable. It fact, with any luck, it would only be Vretla herself he would have to convince. Hopefully before she was well enough to challenge him on principle.

The business of getting the ship away with all the necessary cargo occupied the next few minutes. When that was done, they stood watching it taxi off to the highborn chutes as Prince H'Us railed against Perry D'Aur.

"She cannot be a real Demish woman," he insisted. "It must be — if you'll forgive me — the Vrellish blood. She's dark Demish, of course, not a blond. Well," H'Us huffed, "her nest of traitors will regret their faith in her if Red Reach turns on them over this insult! And Vretla pregnant, and all! Not in the way we approve of, of course, out of wedlock. But, well —" Prince H'Us broke off with a mighty scowl. "It's a hard *rel* for you, I know, the child being your heir. I don't pretend to understand how you Vrellish value children, without families —"

Di Mon closed his eyes, willing forbearance.

" — but I understand an heir must matter, particularly in your circumstances. My condolences."

"Thank you," said Di Mon.

H'Us shifted his weight between his feet, unsure about how or whether to carry on, but eager to anyhow. "A pity about your errant, at Den Eva's. Was it Tan?"

"Yes," said Di Mon.

"A fair challenge? That is, Tan agreed to fight out of challenge class?"

Di Mon nodded, wondering how he might politely break the conversation off. He wanted to get out of here and back to Green Hearth.

"Hendricks D'Astor is a good man," H'Us rumbled on. "Bit whimsical, marrying a dowerless Blue Demish girl a challenge class beneath him in blood. But the Marins were once highborn, a good, reputable Blue Demish line. Traders and merchants for the most part, and still had a toehold at court before they lost Marin Manor to H'Reth when he married into a claim to it, and Delm lent him his support."

Di Mon hardly listened to the Demish babble.

H'Us smacked his thick lips and shifted again. "I wanted to thank you for not going harder on D'Astor," he told his Fountain Court counterpart, "over Tan."

"I could not," Di Mon answered factually, "or I would have."

"Really?" H'Us brightened like a child, then looked anxious once more. "You, uh, weren't actually trying to kill him, I suppose?"

"At first?" Di Mon qualified, then added without any hesitance. "Yes, I was."

"Oh." H'Us struggled to shift his mental furniture around, and settled on shared tenets. "*Ack Rel*, then, I suppose," he said. "You were upset I've no doubt. Ugly business — bound to make for tension. But we have the culprit in hand."

"The culprit?" asked Di Mon.

"Why yes, Perry D'Aur!" said H'Us.

Di Mon frowned.

"Except, you see," H'Us pursued, "D'Ander has challenged. I don't suppose you'd like to take him on? I mean, as it was your heir affected."

"Affected?" Di Mon echoed dryly. Then he shook his head. "No, I do not wish to fight D'Ander for the privilege of executing Perry D'Aur."

"That's not very Vrellish of you! I mean, considering it was your heir!"

"Perry D'Aur is innocent of that," said Di Mon.

H'Us was genuinely surprised. "The assassins were wearing Purple Alliance badges," he explained as if all Vrellish were slow-witted children. "And they came to that den to attack Vretla."

"Why?" asked Di Mon.

"Why!" exclaimed H'Us. "Because it's the sort of thing rebels like the D'Aur woman inspire in inferiors too weak to respect the law!"

"No," Di Mon corrected. "Why would Perry's people attack Vretla?"

"Because they hate decent, honorable Sevolites!" H'Us exclaimed as if that were obvious to everyone. "Perhaps they hate you, in particular. Attacking Vretla in her condition was also a blow against Monitum! Maybe they resented your reluctance to acknowledge Ayrium D'Ander D'Aur, years ago."

"But Red Vrellish did acknowledge D'Ander's gift child," Di Mon pointed out.

H'Us shrugged. "The Red Vrellish still raid into Killing Reach," he pointed out. "Vretla never stops them. It might have been over that. In any event, it ought to be between the Vrellish and D'Ander, since he will of course insist on

defending his rebel paramour, Perry D'Aur. So, in case I
didn't find you willing to stand the challenge, given your
heir situation ..." The H'Usian prince grew increasingly
agitated as his explanation dwindled to silence.

Di Mon said, "What have you done?"

"Nothing more than I would expect any Fountain Court
liege to do for another. I sent a highborn flyer out to Red
Reach, to tell Vretla's family what has happened, and that
Perry D'Aur is being championed by D'Ander. In case they
want to put in an appearance."

"And kill D'Ander for you?" Di Mon accused.

H'Us looked disconcerted. "Well yes, or maybe scare him
off."

Di Mon inhaled deeply. A fatalistic cloak of darkness
seemed to be gathering around him. Why did he struggle?
For Ameron, watching from the limbo of souls waiting to be
reborn? He had given up the hope of belief in the supernatural.

He was alone.

Let the Vrellish come, he thought. *I am ready*.

"Spiral Hall would have alerted Red Reach, of course,"
said H'Us. "I just did it faster by sending a highborn out.
This way they'll have a chance of getting here for tomorrow's
duel." He hesitated. "You don't think the Red Vrellish will
attack my pilot?"

"Maybe," said Di Mon, adding a silent, *with any luck*. He
thanked H'Us once more for the pilot he had loaned him,
and headed home on foot, alone, without a word to his escort.

Di Mon walked as fast as he could without breaking into
a run, wanting to get home, and dove down the spiral stairs
of Green Pavillion without acknowledging the salutes of the
errants on guard. It wasn't until he had reached the reception room at the base of the stairs that he let himself acknowledge he had come to see the Reetion. He wanted to ask him
about the new blit, but it wasn't just that. He wanted to see
him for the pleasure of it.

That was terrible.

Tomorrow I may be challenged by a better sword, he thought. *What does it matter if I talk to Ranar?* But it still mattered. Di Mon struggled to resist what he suspected, not even naming it to himself.

"What are you worried about, Di Mon?" Darren used to mock him. "You don't believe you've got a soul in need of ancestral approval to be reborn. It is we who damn ourselves in this life. That's all."

Sarilous entered from the inward door.

"Kertatt?" Di Mon asked.

"Your nephew will be fine," she assured him. "The burns were superficial. Eva is settled in your bedroom. Vretla?"

"On her way to *TouchGate* with a H'Usian highborn for pilot," he replied, feeling brittle. "Tessitatt must fly out after them to settle up."

"It will be done," said Sarilous, searching his expression for unspoken truths. Looking at her he felt the weight of the years which did not show in his own mirror.

I am old, he thought. *The old should have the right to die.* He was heartily sick of himself but not, yet, of Monitum even if it could not offer him a single, extra highborn to be his heir or fly his wounded *protégé* to hospital.

"H'Us has sent word to Red Reach about Vretla," Di Mon told Sarilous, "hoping they will send a sword to stand against D'Ander over Perry D'Aur."

Sarilous reacted as if stung. "Red Reach will be here, then," she said with painful calm, "before Vretla is back to confirm that you had her permission to send her."

"I didn't," Di Mon said, unabashed. He tossed his head back, nostrils flaring. Sarilous felt like the embodiment of the responsibilities he bore.

There was a pause, filled with a strained silence. Then Sarilous said, "You could have dispatched Perry D'Aur in Den Eva's."

"You mean slit her throat? And tell D'Ander that Delm's errants did it?" Di Mon barked a self-mocking laugh. "I would personally kill any errant of Monitum who took orders like that, or stood by to see them done."

"But there would have been no duel, tomorrow, for H'Us to be worried about if there had been no prisoner," Sarilous pointed out.

"There are times when I doubt the necessity of bonding *gorarelpul*," Di Mon told her tartly. "This is not one." He shook his head. "The Demish rebel will not die at my hands."

"You think she is innocent," Sarilous stated, with thin respect for the issue's importance.

"I do not think she is stupid," Di Mon asserted with compensating force. "She needs Vrellish support at court to sustain her daughter's claim despite benefit of wedlock!" Artificially whipped up to begin with, his vehemence swiftly collapsed. He fidgeted, making a throwaway gesture. "But I'll concede that some of her people might be stupid enough, and *okal'a'ni* methods are in character for the likes of those she commands. They might even have meant to get Vretla. Red Reach raiding parties favor Killing Reach for its lawlessness and Red Hearth looks the other way as hard as it can."

Sarilous said, firmly, "You will have to avoid a challenge. Perhaps if you went to *TouchGate* yourself, and waited there until Vretla is —"

"I will fight if I decide to!" cried Di Mon.

Sarilous was an old woman and Monitum was her life's work. She absorbed the force of her bond master's anger silently, then said, in a frail voice, "I must sit down."

"Gods!" Di Mon cursed, angry with her then for being a commoner; angry with Darren for being dead; angry with everyone he loved for their enduring power to command his heart.

He took Sarilous by the elbow and guided her further down the Throat of Green Hearth, a series of connected rooms beginning with the Entrance Hall which ended at the intersection with Family Hall across the back of the hearth. In the first room with suitable furniture, he settled her on a couch. She drew strength from the contact, clutching his strong, unwrinkled hand.

He knelt before her. "I will not be more reckless than I must," he promised. She kept her hand firmly locked on his, her shoulders stooping into gravity. "We have another problem," said Sarilous.

"Oh?" Di Mon urged her gently. "What?"

"The Reetion, Ranar." She raised her head, mouth turning down with unrepentant resolve. "He knows."

"Knows —" Di Mon faltered. He stared into her bright blue eyes, unwavering in their devotion not to him, and not to Darren, but through both of them to Monitum. His heart stopped, then started with a mighty, dizzying pounding bad enough he dared not rise. "You told him," he guessed, in horror.

"I did nothing more than let him read the logs," said Sarilous. "The fact he could deduce the truth from that is proof that I am right — he is too dangerous."

Di Mon staggered up.

"We cannot afford a scandal," Sarilous was merciless. "Whether you live or die."

Lightheaded now, Di Mon turned away, and drew his sword.

"He's in the library still," Sarilous supplied. She did not sound pleased, or even triumphant, only relieved and tired. "You forbade me earlier, but if you want, you could direct me to take care of it myself."

Di Mon didn't answer her. He walked through the rest of the connecting rooms without seeing anyone, lean face set like stone and his sword drawn in his left hand. His heart was still making him dizzy. His ears buzzed. He displaced the *gorarelpul* Sarilous had set to watch the library door and stood staring at the door itself, sword in his hand.

The first time Darren kissed Di Mon was in a library on Monitum. Larger than life and indomitable, his boyhood idol had leaned over his chair one afternoon when they were all alone and kissed him — like a lover — on the mouth. He remembered being shocked by the act, but most of all by his response. Darren looked at him out of confident, liquid eyes ignited by the thrill of the risk he was taking. "I thought so," he said. "Now, do you admit it, or denounce me and destroy the world?"

Destroy the world, Di Mon thought. Darren had not been far wrong.

"See I am not disturbed," Di Mon told the subordinate *gorarelpul* that Sarilous had left to guard the library door.

Di Mon entered the library and closed the door. The room smelled of old books and polished wood, mild illumination warming its earthy greens and browns. Ranar sat reading in one of the armchairs. He put his book down and stood up, expression balanced between a cerebral excitement and his deep, personal calm.

Ranar spoke softly, with compassion. "What is it? What has happened?"

Di Mon was grateful for the status-free grammar of English. He did not want to be forced to speak down. He said slowly, "Sarilous says you know."

"Know?" The Reetion searched the pregnant silence and found what he was looking for. "Oh, yes," he conceded, carefully. "I suppose I do."

"I have to kill you," said Di Mon without apology, feeling he owed Ranar the truth. "Do you want a sword?"

Ranar's eyes widened at the threat but his dark face settled quickly back into its natural mold. "Do you think that would help me much?" he asked sincerely.

"No," Di Mon conceded.

"I think it would help you," said Ranar, "and I don't want to make it easy for you. I think you are a man of honor. Can you kill me for my sexual preference, when it is also your own?"

Passion welled in counterpoint to Di Mon's bleak resolve. "I would rather kill myself, as well," he said. "But I cannot until I have an heir." He swallowed. No force of will could banish the emotion he felt. Lust, yes, but also joy and gratitude! He could talk to this man! He could kill the Reetion with a thrust, then this one threat would be gone but he would be alone with his burden once more. Di Mon closed his eyes to steady himself, hating his affliction: too Vrellish to cry, the need to act boiled in him instead like something flammable.

If the Reetion would only fight back! But instead of attacking, Ranar's warm palm covered Di Mon's hard-muscled hand where it gripped the hilt of his sword. "The crime," Ranar said, "is believing your preference is so wrong."

Di Mon's eyes opened, nostrils flaring. He could not inhale. It felt like falling from a horse at a full gallop. Ranar refused to break eye contact. Di Mon dropped his sword to seize the Reetion's trespassing hand, crushing the circulation out of it.

"Ah!" Ranar exclaimed, finally frightened, and tried to loosen Di Mon's fingers. Di Mon captured Ranar's other hand and spread it out clear of his body without effort, then he forced Ranar down onto the rug.

Ranar resisted, uncertain what was intended. Di Mon himself did not know, explaining only with his body's blind desire, hoping he might kill instead and redeem himself. Once Ranar understood the desire he responded willingly enough, but with less experience than Di Mon had expected. Darren had taught him more than he knew. In the next five minutes, half a century's denial died, but not Ranar of Rire. They made love.

Di Mon lay recovering on the library rug wearing nothing but his open shirt with the Reetion sitting up beside him among the remains of his clothes. As reason returned, Di Mon panicked and shot up, startling his flushed, exhausted lover by once again snatching up his sword.

"You cannot kill me now," said Ranar, his chest rising and falling in unison with Di Mon's, but speaking as if a law of nature stood opposed.

Di Mon blinked, amazed. "I have killed in less necessary causes," he pointed out.

"I know what's at risk," Ranar said very slowly, shifting to get comfortable. "I understood what I read in the logs."

Di Mon's own breath came hard and the action of his heart was so violent it peppered his vision with tiny, bright scintillations. He could still kill the Reetion. He could still wipe out of any living memory of the last five minutes — except his.

Di Mon hurled his useless sword at the bookcase. It struck hilt first. Ranar blinked at it stupidly, as if he couldn't deduce the point of the random act of violence, or was upset at failing to predict it.

Di Mon reached down and hauled him to his feet. "One day," he warned his lover, "I may still have to kill you."

Ranar braced himself in Di Mon's corded arms. "Only," he said with a force of will much greater than his physical strength, "if you think I would betray you."

Every scrap of Di Mon's reason said this was madness, but it couldn't stop him making love to Ranar again, less viciously, reveling in it, until Ranar protested, "No, please! I can't cope with any more right now! Please, wait!"

The Reetion sat up again, folded his arms, and leaned on them, shaken.

"Are you all right?" Di Mon asked, belatedly self-conscious about his own abandon. He wondered if Ranar was hurt. It was hard to spot bruising on his unfamiliar caramel skin, but he was only commoner and Di Mon knew he had been less than gentle. Darren once told him it was nice to have a highborn lover because one had to treat peasant boys ever so carefully for fear of breaking them. But the thought of Darren's peasant boys made the bile rise in Di Mon's throat.

He left Ranar to himself while he pulled on his own clothing. Ranar was shivering by then. Di Mon swept his traveling cloak over the Reetion's shoulders.

Ranar looked up gratefully. "Thanks," he said, teeth
chattering. "I'm just a little ... overwhelmed. Th-That's all.
S-Sorry. I have never been p-particularly physical."

Di Mon helped him up and settled him into the leather
chair where he had first found him reading, bundled up now
in his traveling cloak. Di Mon collapsed onto the couch
opposite, tipped his head back and closed his eyes, managing to think of nothing for a moment.

"I will take you to Monitum," Di Mon decided, after a
long silence. "You will be safe there. I will find a way to visit
you."

I can keep it secret, Di Mon told himself, *if I maintain my
relationship with Ses Nersal, and have Eva with me for cover*. He
could leave a *gorarelpul* with Ranar, to keep an eye on him.
Someone he could trust without question.

"Can we discuss that later?" Ranar answered.

Di Mon sat up. "Discuss?"

"It's very sudden," Ranar said, "but I think I do return
your feelings. And I would respect your problem even if I
did not. But none of that entitles you to take me anywhere
— I am a Reetion citizen."

"I am Liege Monitum," Di Mon reminded him forcefully.

"Yes," Ranar said it as if he had been posed a particularly
awkward problem in Lorel math. "I am aware of that."

They stared at each other, stalemated.

The door of the library opened. Di Mon started and stared,
heart hammering, at Sarilous. The old *gorarelpul* looked at
Ranar swaddled in Di Mon's cloak and her air of harsh
competence collapsed. She sat down on the nearest couch.

"I will take care of it," Di Mon said huskily, "in my own
way."

Sarilous would not look at him. She asked bleakly, "Do
you lack the strength, master, to end this shame?"

Ranar struggled out of his chair, keeping the cloak around him. "You don't need to fear me," he insisted. "Keeping secrets may not be Reetion, but even we acknowledge that some things are no one else's business, and I realize that what has taken place between Di Mon and I would not be accepted, here, as it would be on Rire. But I am not ashamed of anything, nor should your master be. Gelion should be ashamed of what it's done to him."

Sarilous lifted her head to face Ranar, her face alarmingly white and drawn. *She is old*, Di Mon realized, with grief and guilt.

"You have undone the discipline of fifty years," Sarilous cursed his new lover.

"No." Di Mon moved between them. "I have done that myself." He hated himself more than he could ever remember, but he faced down the old woman who had been his conscience since he sacrificed his love of scholarship to take over as liege.

"Keep the Reetion isolated in Ameron's old room," Di Mon told Sarilous firmly. "Take him his meals personally." He turned to Ranar with a closed expression. "Give her no excuse to seek help containing you. If I have to kill a member of my household to protect this secret, you may yet die, for I will not let it happen twice."

"When will we talk again?" the Reetion asked.

"When it is safe," Di Mon dismissed him.

Sarilous was having trouble getting to her feet. Di Mon steadied her. She drew away, but finally looked at him again.

"You will not harm Ranar over this," Di Mon said curtly.

"I am aware of your priorities," she said.

Di Mon's jaw locked. The urge to strike out at her in self-defense was so powerful that he left the library briskly, and went to freshen up in his bedroom, letting his mind fill with the Vrellish peace of complete concentration on what his body was doing, even though the acts involved were trivial and undertaken with more violence than was helpful. He was strapping on his sword, dressed in house colors, when Eva came out of the bathroom, damp from a shower and clutching her robe.

"Is something wrong, My Lord?" she asked.

She had been listening to him banging closet doors, he realized. She looked nervous. Her long hair lay over one shoulder, damp. Her feet were bare on the cool floor. He went to her on impulse, took her in his arms and pushed the fluffy white robe off her slim shoulders. He could desire her, but he would think about Von. Just now that sickened him.

A knock on the outer door spared him a decision. He turned, calling, "Enter."

Srain popped in and smiled at the sight of Eva pulling her robe back together.

"Apologies, My Liege," said the young errant from Eversol, which was one of Monitum's oldest, most aristocratic families. "But Prince D'Ander is here, chomping at the bit to see you. Seems there's been a riot at H'Reth Manor with people going after Lady H'Reth because she's pregnant by a boy-*sla* sire. D'Ander's pretty worked up and I can't blame him. Demish women aren't like other Sevolites, they're more like commoners — they do whatever they're told. And she wasn't girl-*sla*. They should have waited for the baby to be born, first, not killed her!"

Di Mon felt as if he had been kicked in the stomach.

D'Ander was waiting in Azure Lounge, the first room down Green Hearth's Throat after the Entrance Hall. Di Mon came in through the inward door to discover Demora's Champion pacing feverishly. It seemed miraculous D'Ander hadn't spilled ornaments off tables. Perhaps it was some of that legendary Golden grace Demorans were admired for. D'Ander's cape swirled as he spun, eyes bright with a cold fever.

"I know why," he said, enveloped in an aura of awe. "The riot at H'Reth Manor; the attack on Vretla; Larren going out to Killing Reach — it makes perfect sense once you accept the impossible."

"Any conclusion is possible if you start with a false premise," Di Mon answered tartly. "What's the matter with you? You look like you are over-flown and seeing ghosts."

D'Ander surged towards him. "Think about it! Delm sets a guard that fails to save his mistress, and the room where she was trapped is burned — no cells to genotype. Vretla's attackers used flame throwers, and Delm's men were there to clean up after — again, no cells to genotype. What do both women have in common? Can't you see? It adds up. Delm's destroying evidence. And if Larren has gone after H'Reth there's no time to waste!"

Di Mon's eyebrows hiked in a quantum leap at the Demish man's vehemence.

"What are you talking about?" Di Mon demanded.

D'Ander exclaimed, "Von!" Di Mon's stomach contracted, skin prickling.

"Von is Amel!" D'Ander raged on, seizing Di Mon by the shoulders.

Di Mon knocked his hands away violently, stepping back. "Eva's dance partner? H'Reth's *slaka*? The empire's third Pureblood! Are you mad?"

"I hunted up Von's poetry," D'Ander answered, stone-cold sober. "That's why I wasn't at H'Reth Manor when Prince Taran was attacked. I went looking for princesses with good judgment who had watched Von dance."

Di Mon felt as if he had stepped, unprepared, into a Demish parlor game where the stakes were much, much too high.

"Don't you see?" D'Ander counted off points on a big, splayed hand. "Von is a gifted poet, a performing artist —"

Vretla, Di Mon thought dryly, *might agree on that score.*

" — and remarkably beautiful!" D'Ander's voice rose. "He's not blond, but Amel's mother, Ev'rel, has mixed blood. You saw Amel as an infant. Was his hair black?"

It finally dawned on Di Mon that D'Ander was arguing in favor of Von being Amel based mainly on his dance reviews by Demish princesses. "You have lost your mind," he told the Golden Champion.

D'Ander only talked faster. "Think about it for a moment. He's a courtesan. How else would a Soul of Light make a living on Gelion? And Amel would be regenerative. How else could he be getting women pregnant after Eva had him sterilized?"

Di Mon felt a tiny electric shock, thinking about Balous at H'Reth Manor and how the business was so quickly dropped after he got the sperm sample meant to prove Delm's mistress was pregnant by a commoner.

"Then there is Vretla!" D'Ander blazed on. "We've been looking for the wrong connections: things to do with Perry D'Aur or you or Killing Reach. They're secondary! Your nephew didn't get a Vrellish Royalblood pregnant, a Demish Pureblood did it! Amel, son of Delm and descendant of the Golden Emperor! He could be a Soul of Light, and he's alone out there!" D'Ander stabbed an arm outwards towards space, as breathless as if he had run a marathon.

Di Mon scowled at him. "You are making the quintessential Demish error of wishing an ideal into existence. Von is just a talented and pretty commoner. You are forgetting Amel was not sired by Delm. He was Blue Demish and Vrellish, only, through his mother. And I wonder if you would be this inspired to believe if you did not want a contender to champion for Ava, against both Delm and H'Us."

D'Ander drew himself up. "There are Demish who feel more allegiance to me than to Delm," he said, "including ones with palace connections. Von's sperm sample was a great joke in Delm's inner circle of palace staff, at least among the men. Balous ordered it be genotyped so he could give Anatolia the graph, in mockery, even demand she mount it on her wall with the baby picture. It was on everyone's lips. And then, suddenly, no one dared speak of it. Balous told them Delm's sensitive nature was dismayed by their vengeful cruelty on his behalf, and it was never to be mentioned again. But you know him — he's no Soul of Light. That's an act he puts on when it suits him. And in case you still are not convinced, I also know that the technician who did the analysis has disappeared."

"Disappeared?" Di Mon felt cold, and then frightened.

Ev'rel, he thought. *Damn the gods, did she tell me the truth all those years ago when she swore to me Amel was Delm's?*

Di Mon remembered the honor trial surrounding Amel's loss with bitterness. Ev'rel, Ameron's descendant and his fosterling, had proved herself a *slaka'st*. He could not face it. He wanted nothing more to do with her. He would not listen even after she admitted she had abused her *gorarelpul* with Rush when confronted by the evidence. Di Mon had turned away from her as she begged him to find Amel, dead or alive, because any cell of Amel's body would uphold her word over Delm's. He thought Delm weak and childish, but too vain to have sought the life of his own child, and too pampered by the Demish to have any solid motive to fear Amel. But he had not been thinking like a Demish highborn. He had failed to see Delm as a threat because Delm was prepared to act through others and his plans stretched too far back and forward through time. And Amel could ruin Delm now, more than ever, solely on the strength of his genotype, if he was heir to the mystique that Delm traded on.

"It isn't possible," Di Mon objected, aloud, "Von's a courtesan!"

"And worse," D'Ander agreed, looking bleak.

"You have seen the images of H'Reth then, on the Reetion devices," Di Mon said quickly. The revulsion on D'Ander's face burned him like acid.

"I have heard about them," D'Ander said bitterly, tears rising in his bright blue eyes without making him seem any less capable of violence. "Enough to wonder if it is gross selfishness on my part to hope Amel is still alive. If he is Von —" D'Ander shook his golden mane. "No Soul of Light should have had to endure what he has."

Di Mon watched the Golden Champion attempt to hold in mind the intersection of Gelion's worst depravity and Demora's greatest purity, and fail, with a shake of his bright head.

"Better not to think it, then," Di Mon suggested.

I am not H'Reth, he told himself. But he had thought of Von when he made love to Eva; watched Von dance, and hated both of them for his involuntary response. If Von was Amel, his Demish beauty had a vein of Vrellish strength in it that sang in his movements. *Am I just as bad?* Di Mon asked himself and was not sure. He wanted to ask Ranar.

"I will deal with it when I must," D'Ander snapped out of his grisly contemplation. "There are more pressing matters. If I was absolutely certain Von was Amel, it would be clear where my duty lay! I'd go to Killing Reach immediately and hope my daughter, Ayrium, could make it back in time to stand champion for her mother! But bitter gods, whether it is her or I, one of us would still be over-flown tomorrow for the duel! And I am not certain! First, of whether Von is Amel, and if so whether Delm is his father, and if he is Delm's whether he has a Soul of Light within him! I would go, I swear, if I was sure!"

Di Mon frowned, uncertain how to weigh D'Ander's request against his obligations to Monitum. The Soul of Light business was irrelevant to him — not sharing the Demoran obsession with their Emperor's family — but if Von was Amel that did matter. A great deal. How that could plausibly make him responsible for Perry D'Aur's protection, however, remained a mystery. She was not his *mekan'st*, ex or otherwise, and nothing to him or to Monitum. Justice mattered, yes. But not as much as Monitum's need for him to live until he secured a safe, replacement highborn.

"Tell me you will defend Perry," D'Ander appealed, "and I will go to seek Amel should a dozen of Delm's paladins intervene! Or tell me you will take a message about Amel to my daughter and I will turn whole-heartedly to the challenge floor in defense of Perry. But I need a highborn ally! Will you do one or the other for me, in the name of our shared love of Ameron?"

"You," Di Mon warned, narrowly, "do not speak for Ameron."

"I follow Ameron in my heart," D'Ander said angrily. "I thought that you did, also."

Di Mon stared back in anger as D'Ander showed himself out with a flourish, then he whirled and hurried down the connecting rooms of Green Hearth's Throat to Family Hall, seeking the room Ameron had occupied two hundred years before.

Ranar sat cross-legged on the bed, dressed in clothing Sarilous had given him. Di Mon's cloak was laid across the foot of the bed, neatly folded. The info-blit Di Mon had given Ranar was in the Reetion's brown hands.

Di Mon's first impulse was violent until he noticed the Reetion wasn't ogling scenes of Von's degradation. He was studying data marked up in Reetion notation.

"What is that?" Di Mon demanded.

Ranar turned the blit off. "I cannot make much sense of it without an arbiter."

Di Mon jerked him to his feet, snapping the info-blit out of his lap with his other hand and pulled Ranar after him, not letting go until they reached the library at the other end of Family Hall where Di Mon went to his desk and began pulling out and positioning screens of nervecloth.

"I thought there was more than just moving images in these things when I examined the one H'Us gave me," Di Mon explained as he worked. "But I could not decode the data."

"It is meant to be downloaded into a local store for access by an arbiter persona." Ranar said, coming up behind him. "But we may be able to do it, between us, using your nervecloth systems."

They worked together for an hour without speaking about anything but the job. Ranar knew more about information systems than most Monatese scholars and exuded a reassuring calm. It was impossible to feel foul in his presence, although Di Mon was careful not to touch him more than necessary and never let his fingers linger when they wanted to. It reassured him to demonstrate self-control.

I can keep him by me and never succumb again, he thought.

The data coding scheme was unfamiliar, which made Ranar's contribution invaluable. Di Mon programmed the interface, which was easy once Ranar explained how Reetion symbols ought to look when drawn. It helped that the Reetions used a rationalized version of the English alphabet, for which Di Mon already had fonts. At the end of the hour, flows of what Ranar told him were text and scientific measurements played across Di Mon's screens, in Reetion.

"It is a medical report," Ranar told him, frowning at the scrolling words. "All highly technical. It would make a world of difference if I even had subarbitorial crystronics I could program to help with the analysis."

Di Mon postponed questions about the various kinds of crystronics Ranar kept wishing for. "What does it describe?" he asked instead.

"A patient called Von," Ranar said. "The audiovisuals, and much more, were extracted from his memories. It seems it was an accident stemming from some kind of abnormal feedback — this can't be right — but it says that the visitor probe arbiter interfaced with him." Ranar fell silent studying that part again.

"Anything about Von, himself?" Di Mon urged.

Ranar took a moment to adjust the screens. "He's an extraordinarily good pilot, according to his psych profile."

"A pilot?" echoed Di Mon. "Anything else?"

"The data is so detailed it's hard to say," Ranar complained. "Certainly he is abnormal in Reetion terms." He paused, scanning the screen. "Strong reaction to drugs; an over-powered cardiovascular system ..." Ranar fell silent, reading. He pulled a screen towards him, eyes-narrowed, and frowned. "I think this part describes a regenerative neurology." He drew back. "Who, or what, is this boy? Is he human?"

"He is a Sevolite," Di Mon said, "and at least a highborn, possibly a highborn of the highest rank." He felt a headache coming on again. "You spoke of a psych profile. What is that?"

"A technology that allows us to induce reaction patterns in a test subject, to give an impression of how they might respond to complex stimuli. It isn't one hundred percent predictive. There are always variables you can't control for and it isn't ethical to use distressingly intense stimuli. Except in Von's case it seems, unaccountably, as if a good deal of the psych profiling is based on extremely unpleasant and remarkably vivid memories."

"Demish," Di Mon said neutrally. "Amel would have a Golden Demish memory, if he is truly Delm's child." He told Ranar the rest, quickly, including D'Ander's suspicions. "I need to be sure he is Amel," Di Mon concluded, "and not only Amel, but Delm's."

"What would it take to prove?" Ranar asked.

"A gene print," Sarilous pitched in, closing the door behind her as she entered.

Di Mon looked up, acknowledging her right to intrude with a glance. He was glad to see her looking better. She had drugs for her heart and must have taken some.

"You overheard?" he asked neutrally, as if their earlier discussion about Ranar had never happened, and collected her nod before turning to Ranar again. "Does your Reetion data on Von include a genetic breakdown?"

"I don't know," Ranar said, troubled by the whole conversation. "I could look, but I can't be sure I would know if I was seeing one."

"It does not matter, master," Sarilous interjected. "Gelacks will look at pictures and destroy a household as friendless as the H'Reths' on the strength of them, but they will not trust data they are forced to think about. Data can be manipulated, and while your personal honor is good, Monitum's historical associations with House Lorel might weigh heavier. I know twenty *gorarelpul* who could generate a genotype for Amel and half a dozen Sevolites, you first among them." She shook her head. "No proof, except living proof, will be acceptable."

Di Mon was silent for a moment, thinking. Then he said to Sarilous, "Describe a Soul of Light."

She blinked. "It is a Demish idealization of the *pol* virtues of love, self-sacrifice and beauty in, I suppose, a metaphysical sense. Someone so *pol* he is sacred instead of simply being weak. They are said to take only the bodies of members of Demora's imperial family, which means only Delm and the Golden Emperor himself are candidates."

"Can you isolate Von's psych profile?" Di Mon asked Ranar.

"I've seen it," Ranar said uncomfortably. "He seems to be a ... nice person."

"Nice?" Di Mon said sharply. "Elaborate."

Ranar read off a halting summary, his hand drifting down the screen without touching it. "A strong capacity for love and compassion; readily able to see things from another's point of view even when it's personally disadvantageous to do so; derives pleasure from the joy of friends; and is troubled by unavoidable proof of other people's pain." Ranar looked away. "There are some negatives, flagged as probable pathology arising from personal trauma."

"Artistic?" Di Mon pursued.

"Are you trying to deduce this person's paternity on the strength of personality traits?" Ranar asked with acute disapproval. "If so, you ought to be aware that the inheritability of specific behavioral —"

"Do not debate me, Reetion!" Di Mon cut him off.

Ranar folded his arms with quiet dignity. "Then do not ask for my help," he said.

He is not a Gelack commoner, Di Mon had to remind himself. It was still a struggle to live up to the age-old and uniquely Monatese belief that equality with commoners was possible, at least in principle, because it forced him to accept that Ranar both spoke from knowledge, like a *gorarelpul* might, and retained a free will. It surprised Di Mon to find that frightening. He paused to master his anger before answering. "You intended to point out that behavior is complex and not solely dictated by one's DNA or brain structures."

"In essence," Ranar said.

Di Mon nodded. "But you are, naturally, speaking of Reetions, who are commoners and draw on a much larger gene pool than Sevolites, with far more fundamental variability."

"Sevolites are different," Ranar said, growing heated. "Is that your excuse for everything?"

Di Mon raised a hand palm up, as if to hold him off. "I do not have time for this. Suffice it to say that we breed true when we breed true, and I would rather rely on Reetion psych profiling than the opinion of man-starved Demish princesses. So I ask you again, is Von artistically talented?"

Ranar held Di Mon's eyes a moment longer, then slowly turned back to his screens. "Let's see: Von associates high relevance with memorized literature; his movements all draw on his knowledge of dance in some measure, unconsciously. He has what we'd call an intuitive rather than an analytic predisposition for sensory analysis; his skin is highly innervated and integrated with a strong body image. Might he be artistically talented?" Ranar looked up. "Yes. Very."

Di Mon grit his teeth. "I am going to Killing Reach," he decided, "to take D'Ander's message to his daughter."

"At least you will be out of harm's way when Red Reach arrives," said Sarilous. "But Killing Reach is dangerous. Be careful."

Ranar was gazing at him with a strange, absorbed expression, as if memorizing his face. Di Mon was afraid he might do something spontaneously affectionate. But the Reetion proved perfectly reasonable. "If you encounter Reetions," Ranar told him, "let them know I am alive and ... doing field research. Tell them we made contact. They'll be cooperative."

Di Mon nodded. He found himself hesitating, as well, just to look at Ranar a little longer, and lost patience with such foolishness.

"Take care of him," he told Sarilous gruffly, instead.

"Yes, Master," she answered tersely.

When in Rome

Ann watched H'Reth and Von from just inside the inner airlock with her cloak clutched around her, heart pounding, and the great, gray ball of the *rel*-fighter at her back.

The workers who had been talking to Von moved clear when H'Reth started shouting about Jarl and her own escape. Ann recognized only a few words. She checked out the workers' utility belts for weapons as they left, but saw nothing she recognized. Besides, they were out of reach.

Von can take care of himself, Ann told herself, remembering how he had killed Jarl. Unfortunately he seemed to have forgotten how. He let H'Reth back him up against a grille like the one she had been tied to before, touching him and talking in an intimate, wheedling tone.

Explode! Ann begged Von, silently, as H'Reth pinned him against the grille. She could see Von's averted face in profile, his hands locked on the metal bars behind him as if he needed to hang onto something to prevent exactly what Ann hoped for.

H'Reth was breathing all over Von!

"What's the matter with you?" Ann hissed under her breath.

H'Reth took a step back, carrying on hysterically now, as if he was the one whose mind had been enslaved and body slobbered on, vomiting sentences in a voice wracked with a new, growing alarm.

Von's just going to take it! Ann thought in disgust. Nothing mattered more to him than getting H'Reth to lead his fighter pilots down that benighted jump! On the bright side, he wasn't shivering and wetting himself any more. This was willful endurance, not weakness — a determined, inflexible martyrdom. He could not fight back if he wanted H'Reth to follow him into oblivion and no other option would redeem his past by the terms of Lurol's probe-rigged compulsion. But what if H'Reth wouldn't get in his ship and follow them down the damned jump? What if this one sided lovers' quarrel ended with kiss and make up, right here and now? Ann didn't know if she could stomach that.

It occurred to her, instead, that if H'Reth were dead, Von would be forced to rearrange his mental furniture and she much preferred that scenario. How to kill him, however, wasn't obvious.

She had been armed when she had killed Larren. She had nothing like that now and H'Reth's big, robust body, viewed from the back, posed a problem she had not been trained to solve. He was bigger and stronger than she was. She couldn't take him on hand to hand. Von was her most effective weapon but he wouldn't fight back because he was mentally hobbled.

But he had killed Jarl.

She pursed her lips, double-checking her logic. It stood up. Von wouldn't fight on his own behalf, but he would do it to save her despite Lurol's compulsion. Or so she hoped. For all she knew that trick only worked with Jarl, but she had never had any patience with quibbles.

"I really ought to be Supervised," she muttered as she doffed her cloak. Ann hit H'Reth from behind like a small, determined cannonball.

He grunted.

She snatched at his sword hilt as she bounced off, pulling it a hand's width from its sheath before it jerked from her hand. Off balance, Ann crashed to the floor. She took most of the impact on her bottom, but a little too much on one flank. H'Reth threatened her with his drawn sword, spitting Gelack words as he advanced, which were probably overblown insults.

Her stinging bottom made more of an impression on her than his beefy, beet red expression. If she'd had the time, she might have laughed.

The sword was another matter. She had the horrible impression that being run through would feel like swallowing the blade, whole. The thought gave death a cold, metallic flavor.

I'm really going to die, she thought, mesmerized, a second before Von shot between her and impalement.

Ann's eyes opened wide in horror. She had not meant Von to die! She would rather burn down a whole museum full of art treasures!

But Von was showing evidence of healthy instincts, at last. He had blocked H'Reth bodily, but not before locking the wrist holding the sword in his own grasp. The next few seconds were hilarious. H'Reth strained to break free, only slowly realizing he could not. The look on his face when that finally sank in was worth Ann's latest near death experience!

"That's right!" Ann burst out, in Reetion. "Von's got a mind of his own!" Which was not quite true, yet, but at least she had proved that Von could exert himself on her behalf if not his own.

Ann struggled up and nearly toppled over at the unexpected pangs from her abused flank. Von was distracted by the sound of her first, involuntary gasp.

"Ann?" he called over his shoulder, attention divided between her and the man he was inexpertly wrestling.

"Make him drop the sword!" ordered Ann.

Von's grip tightened and H'Reth yelped, still incredulous over the mismatch in strength being demonstrated as his sword clattered noisily to the floor.

The next instant H'Reth erupted into babble once more and Von shoved him away, face contorted by the ugliest expression Ann had ever seen there. H'Reth stumbled and fell down, legs stuck straight out in front of him and looking dumbstruck.

"You're dynamite, you know that?" Ann said, limping up beside Von, who was breathing in quick, hyperventilating gasps. She patted him on the arm.

"Well," she admitted, "maybe dynamite that's slightly damp."

The numbness from her hard landing was wearing off, making it easier to walk. She hobbled over to pick up H'Reth's dropped sword, thinking, warmly, *This is going to be like spearing meat for fondue.* She had every intention of killing H'Reth in cold blood. Her Reetion conscience was thoroughly shocked, but she promised it a long, racking session with a counselor, if they made it back. At the moment she was worried about whether she had the strength to drive the sword through the dense, braided threads on H'Reth's busy dress jacket.

"No, Ann!" Von moved between them just as she was about to go for it with a lunge.

"Are you trying to get killed, or what?" she accused him, afraid she knew the answer. Von had the sad, strained look about him that she was learning to hate a whole lot.

"You can't kill him," he apologized. "I have to lead him down the jump." His eyes brimmed in silence, glistening like a special effect in a synthdrama. "For Mira."

Ann made sure of H'Reth with a glance, then she went for the sledge hammer approach. "Listen, kid, this Mira — your sister? — whatever happened to her can't be undone. It's over! Got that?"

Von's conviction broke up. Despair replaced his aura of incipient martyrdom. He lost interest in everything around him, shoulders sagging as he stepped back. Ann was reminded alarmingly of the wet mess he had been in the recovery room after Lurol took him out of the probe.

H'Reth began edging away from them on his bottom.

"Damn!" Ann spat.

She wanted to shore Von up again with her bare hands, and she wanted to pounce on H'Reth like a mongoose going after an escaping snake. She would have given a great deal for a six-shooter from one of her old Earth cowboy movies, or a portable visitor probe so she could reprogram Von.

H'Reth scrambled to his feet, making breathy, frightened sounds. Ann gave her best impression of a war cry, compounded of all the old Earth movies she had ever watched, and charged.

She got in one good jab at H'Reth's back with the sword, eliciting a gratifying yelp, but she struck too high and lost her balance, surprised by the impact of the weapon making contact with bone. H'Reth fled the room as if pursued by demons.

Ann's bad leg screwed up her recovery and she went down, hurting the hand wrapped around the sword hilt when she failed to let it go. She got her knees under her and forced herself up in time to see the outer airlock close.

This was it then, she realized. *We're doomed*. There was no arbiter to civilize H'Reth's behavior. He could seal them in and capture them like cornered rats, or just depressurize the whole room. She took a quick look at the end of her sword hoping to see lots of blood, but it was hard to tell if she had bloodied H'Reth at all.

"Guess it's harder than it looks," Ann muttered, but she kept hold of the sword. As weapons went it might have been ridiculous, but at least it made her feel armed.

She found Von buckled to his knees and hauled him up by his nearest arm. He rose with a dispirited obedience. Ann towed him into the inner airlock and turned him around to face her, intending to give him a pep talk. Instead, her breath caught in her throat.

Von was Apollo demoralized, Adonis with a heart of gold. He was desolate but forgiving, an inner beauty glowing through his body's stubborn vigor in the face of overwhelming sorrow at his mission's defeat, beyond caring about himself but still responsive to her. First it awed her, then it scared her.

"Listen," she appealed to his madness instead of rejecting it, "if we take off, H'Reth will still follow. Not because he trusts you," she admitted, as if he had raised that objection, "just to get you back."

Von lifted his head, looking hopeful but baffled, and asked, "Why?"

Ann pursed her lips against the drug-like effect of his beauty. "Trust me," she assured him. "I would."

Von's frown took the edge off his eerie radiance. "It will still save Mira?"

"You bet," she told him, not caring what he believed so long as it made him feel better for however long they had to be together, although knowing they were in an airlock made her chest feel tighter with each breath she took.

"If H'Reth would follow ... " Von said thoughtfully, piecing his way through the shattered landscape of his reason, " ... we could launch."

"Yeah," Ann stroked the front of his flight jacket. "We could launch." She huffed out a stillborn laugh. "Like he would help us do that."

"You scared him," Von told her, impressed, as he touched her. "I know him — it will take him a few minutes to get over that."

Ann laid her palm on his cheek, warmed by the way he was melting towards her, as if they were plastic figures heating on the top of a stove. *I am going to die kissing you,* she promised herself as she touched his mouth and felt his breath on her fingers. "I'm glad I scared H'Reth. I want all the time I can get."

"You want to stay here?" Von asked, drawing her hand down, as if he suddenly doubted her sanity as much as she doubted his.

Compassion for him thickened her throat. "Von, sweet-heart," she broke it to him gently, "We're in an airlock and H'Reth controls *Vanilla Rose*."

"But we don't need him to let us out," he said, his fluid black eyebrows waved in puzzlement. "Pilots control rim docks themselves, from the inside. Didn't you know?"

"Law and Reason!" Ann exclaimed and guffawed with a surge of pure pleasure. "You Gelacks really are rugged individualist nuts!" She gave Von a celebratory kiss on the mouth. He responded as naturally as if they had just paused for a view in the midst of a nature walk, looking disap-pointed as she rocked back.

"Let's launch!" Ann cried, brandishing H'Reth's captive sword aloft.

Maybe it was the sword, which seemed to symbolize authority for Gelacks, or maybe the kiss was restorative. Whatever it was, Von snapped into action on her command. She caught up with him as he opened a hatch on the bot-tom of the *rel*-fighter and stood back.

"You're coming?" she double-checked, suspicious.

He dashed off, calling back urgently, "Go!"

Ann nearly grabbed for him, but her nervous lungs held her back — they wanted out of the airlock. She stuck her head up the dark, almost vertical tube leading into the *rel*-fighter. The first question was whether to abandon the sword. She should, that was obvious, but the silly thing was starting to feel like a good luck charm. Ann stuck her wrist through the guard and hoisted herself into the tube, sword and all.

Her bruised flank let her know how it felt about climbing, but so long as everything worked she ignored her complain-ing muscles and groped ahead, finding ridges marked by dim light for handholds. The climb was steep enough she had to brace herself against the tube despite the handholds, and her feet slipped off them more than once. Ann paused to blow hair out of her eyes halfway up. There was nothing to be seen above but darkness that soaked up the dull glow of the handholds.

Ann feared her bruised leg would give out if she rested too long and she wondered, now, why she had brought the sword and whether she should let it fall. The distinct sound of an airlock beginning its cycle made her heart stop.

Von! She thought, alarmed. *He would come,* she reassured herself, afraid to lose him and afraid to be alone. *He is under Lurol's compulsion to lead H'Reth down that jump.* Unless he had figured out it couldn't possibly have any impact on his past and had reverted to cowering in a lump.

Hands covered Ann's bruised buttocks from below, shoving her higher up the tube. She yelped in surprise.

"Sorry!" Von's silvery voice rose from below as his hands withdrew. "I needed room."

"I could get used to it," she told him, feeling better.

She heard the mechanical sigh of a sealing hatch.

"Can you keep going?" Von asked.

Ann looked up. There was no end in sight. She wished she had left the dumb sword outside, especially since it was now pointing down at Von.

"I don't know," she admitted. "I feel all quivery."

The next thing she knew he was sliding between her legs, carefully avoiding H'Reth's sword. His face, in the glow of the hand holds, was absorbed, but he moved with such casual precision that she doubted it took all his concentration for the task at hand. Physically, he was so confident it reassured her somehow, and his vanilla musk, mingled with the smell of his leather clothes, refreshed her spirits like a mild drug. As his hips passed, she repressed the impulse to indulge in a possessive hug. The snug leather of his flight pants felt more exciting than nakedness where they touched.

He climbed past her and vanished into darkness above. She was gearing up to shift her own grip once more, when he reached down from the top. At first, all she saw was his reaching hand, then Von, above, with his feet braced over the opening at the top. The interior of the *rel*-fighter was awash in a pale gray light that came from the lining of its inner hull. He was wreathed in it, like an angel.

Ann sacrificed her grip to clasp his hand. He caught her other hand above the dangling sword and hauled her up as smoothly as an elevator, then he set her on her feet with an arm around her while he reached for an unseen control that sealed the opening they had come through.

He looked excited, but his attention was on the ship's interior except for his hand spread wide against the small of her back. Considering how that made her feel, she was a bit put out that he had eyes only for the ship they were stealing. The *rel*-fighter looked weird and incomplete to her: its interior was filled with a metal cage bracing a single, padded seat at its center and light came only from the curved, interior walls. Everything was made of dull gray metal. To Ann, it looked more like bad sculpture than anything space worthy.

"This is Larren's ship," Von said in a tone that matched his awed expression.

And this is fun to know because ... ? Ann thought, holding him tighter.

"Larren is a *relsha*," Von told her. "That's someone who fights in space, in shake-ups. His ship won't be hobbled. It will let you do *skim'facs* that would kill us both!"

"Oh," said Ann, crankily. "Wonderful." Even perfect men had their flaws.

Von fixed his radiant eyes on her. "This ship could defeat a whole hand of nobleborns — if it had a highborn pilot." His excitement collapsed over this technicality.

"Don't you think we should launch?" Ann suggested.

Von released her. "There is only one sling cockpit," he worried, nodding at the center of the bracing lattice that filled up the sphere's interior.

"We'll share it," Ann decided, even as the implications of a sling cockpit registered. She knew that Gelack ships moved easily in all directions, and she could see that the lattice supporting the sling cockpit was not fixed to the hull but suspended inside of it. The inner frame moved slightly as Von reached to grip a spar of the lattice. "Hold on to me," he said, "and don't let go."

"I can do that," Ann promised him, transferring H'Reth's sword into her left hand.

He hoisted them up onto the inner frame. It gave beneath their feet, slightly, but its resistance seemed to stiffen in proportion to the force exerted. Von guided her to the padded chair of the sling cockpit and relieved her of H'Reth's sword, which he slid into a container at the chair's back.

Designed just for that! Ann realized, and nearly laughed. *Have sword will travel. Gelacks are barking mad!*

Von settled into the contoured seat and pulled Ann up to sit on him, side saddle. She slid off, thinking to give him a chance to get organized, and fell right through the frame structure.

Von caught her by the arms. She hung suspended for a moment, with her face swaying in front of a tank full of holes that gave off whiffs of fresh oxygen tainted with a stale, re-cycled tang. The gray-green organic stuff sticking out of the holes looked like a cross between sponge and tree fungus.

Von pulled her up and sat her on his lap once more. "Are we growing mold?" Ann asked, astonished, and pointed.

"That's ship's moss," said Von. "It recycles oxygen while you're *rel*-skimming. In dock, it's dormant."

"Moss?" Ann leaned over to try for another look, but Von held her back.

"Careful!" he warned. "You don't want to fall into the slip zone between the cage and the inner hull."

Ann didn't ask him for details. She felt like an ungainly child sitting on him, but she could not see what else to do with herself as he checked things out. Von had three kinds of controls in reach of his hands. One was a patch of gray stuff that glowed like the inner hull.

"Nervecloth," he told her, touching it to make it ripple. The cockpit's main feature was a joystick shaped suspiciously like a sword hilt that rose up to a comfortable, two-handed position with respect to the reclined seat. Von's arm and leg rests were contoured and the back and seat of the sling cockpit were likewise padded in a way that made sitting beside him impossible. The seat was clearly meant for a single occupant somewhat bigger than Von. Von was touching things, looking like a kid in a toy store, totally absorbed.

Ann had a nasty thought. "You do know how to fly this thing, don't you?" she asked.

"I flew the other one," Von said defensively. "The one they put me in to follow you."

"That's it?" Ann asked, incredulous. "Tell me you have flown before that!"

"Of course!" he seemed offended. Then he toned it down and added humbly. "I flew for the *Gorarelpul* College when I was younger," he mumbled the last bit, "in a freight hauler."

"But you do know how to fly a *rel*-fighter?" asked Ann.

"I can fly it," Von assured her. "It's just that it's not hobbled. *Rel*-fighters can't have a fixed flight guard because they're used in shake-ups."

"Shake-ups?" Ann echoed, thinking that wasn't a bad description for the phenomenon she had experienced fleeing *Trinket Ring Station*. Shake-ups must be what Gelacks called the purposeful use of reality skimming to war on each other and those they did not consider honorable. Like Reetions. But if this was going to be the last ten minutes of her life, she was not going to waste it worrying about things she could not control and barely understood. She made herself relax, setting her hands palm down on Von's chest and thigh. He felt reassuringly solid but his thigh tensed enough to prove he was not indifferent to her, either. She squeezed back. He put an arm around her on the side where she faced out, casually letting one hand rest in her lap with the other one spread against her back.

"Maybe you'd better learn how to control the ship," he said, his voice low and rich with overtones, "in case I black out under G-pressure."

Ann shifted to be able to look over her shoulder at his face. "You mean in case I crush you?" She frowned. "I'll sit somewhere else!"

"There is nowhere else!" Von insisted. "You'd be thrown around the interior and wind up as jelly on the nervecloth lining of the hull!"

For someone who was so damned kind and sensitive, she thought that was pretty blunt. But if he looked upset and heated, it was on her behalf and she couldn't exactly be angry with him about that.

Her lounging top was hanging open, the folds designed to loosely cover a man's torso. It had also slipped off one shoulder as she changed position. She caught him looking at the curve of one teasingly revealed breast.

"This thing is too big," she said, tugging at the sloppy top.

"You should be wearing something more protective," he admitted, and shifted her forward. She felt him wriggling out of his flight jacket behind her. "Put this on," he said.

She didn't argue, but she didn't fasten it up, either. Thinking leather would protect them against shimmer was sheer Gelack superstition, and she rather liked the way his eyes kept slipping down her sternum to see how much breast might be visible. There was nothing as delicious as distracting a man who was trying to attend to something unrelated. At least it sure beat thinking about her weight crushing him if they were forced to change velocity too fast.

Von positioned her so she was sitting forward, her buttocks across his thighs. She shifted around to get her head positioned on his shoulder, aware she would need to protect her neck and careful not to position a main pressure point against his groin.

"The straps are to help with sling adjustments," he told her as he reached across, fastening wide bands around them both. "I've loosened the harness to cover us both where that's possible."

Ann worried her head might break his clavicle and tried to find a more padded spot to lodge it against him without leaving her spine vulnerable by adopting an awkward position. She tried her legs over his, then between, and put them back the first way. Her arms couldn't reach his rests, so she lay them at her side, brushing his leather pants with her thumbs.

He waited until she stopped fussing before binding the final straps. "Okay?" he asked.

"Yeah, I think so." She tried to sound brave for them both. And that was it. No check list. No countdown. Just —

They launched out of the rim-dock like a stone thrown from a catapult. When her heart had climbed back down out of her mouth they were still too close to *Vanilla Rose* to risk reality skimming, although for the first time in her life Ann wondered if the prospect of taking out the station might be worth it. But mass murder still wasn't her style. The thought alone made her feel creepy. It was exactly what her pilot's training and psych-screening strove to ensure never crossed her mind. Ever. It was the great sin that threatened all civilization and perhaps even life itself.

"I hate this part," Von complained about the zero-G conditions.

Ann ignored his sulky tone. "Did H'Reth know you killed Jarl?"

"No," he said. "He thought that you had."

"Why me?" she asked.

"I told him that you were a Vrellish highborn, despite being Reetion — a hybrid from the first time we made contact. I thought that might help if you were captured again, that he would respect you more."

Ann remembered H'Reth running away from her and chuckled. "A Vrellish woman, huh?"

"You act that way anyhow," Von defended his lie.

"So you've said," remembered Ann.

"I really hate this," Von complained. "I'm going to start cat clawing."

"Cat clawing? What's cat —" Ann began.

She stopped at the first touch of skim transition, alarmed by their proximity to the station. But they weren't under skim. They just dipped and accelerated in real space on the strength of the energy they sucked. It wasn't scary once she grasped what was going on, except that repeated start-and-stop skim transitions were not her idea of fun. She was just getting used to that, when the skin of their *rel*-fighter dissolved into a vista of stars.

Ann screamed and shut her eyes. Von's body clenched beneath hers.

"What is it?" He abandoned the controls with one hand to feel her for an injury. "Shimmer hit?" he asked in alarm.

Ann caught his questing hand and held on, daring to open her eyes again. She could still breathe, so she couldn't really be exposed to vacuum, but the naked stars were still all that she saw.

"The hull," she said, and swallowed. "It's gone!"

"Oh ..." He sounded unsure what to make of that remark. "You mean the nav display?" He guessed. "It's the nervecloth."

Ann tried to concentrate on breathing but it was hard to believe the air in her lungs wasn't getting thin and cold.

"Oh," said Ann. "Right. No problem."

Reetion pilots navigated using psychologically manageable models mediated by the ship's persona. If anything, flying a Reetion ship induced claustrophobia. This view was magnificent — and terrible.

"Riding magic horses flying through vacuum," Ann whispered, remembering First Contact legends. "Bare to space, fighting each other with flashing swords."

Von said, "Pardon?"

"Something everyone thought First Contact observers had got wrong," Ann explained.

"We're clear now," he warned.

The transition to reality skimming was not the shock it usually was. If they had really been astride a vacuum-treading stallion, it would have been like leaping from a walk to a gallop. The stars began to shift position with nearest ones turning red or blue. What Ann recalled of Paradise Reach constellations hinted that the blue ones were getting closer while the ones that were receding reddened. She blinked a couple of times, wondering if she was imagining the colors like that because she knew that Doppler shift shortened the wavelength of an approaching light source and lengthened the wavelength of a receding one. But a *rel*-ship skipped the space between manifestations and behaved like an ordinary object during each brief, in-phase period, which meant any virtual Doppler shift effect would have to be calculated based on a series of in-phase measurements, instantly made and knitted together, in the same way as a pilot's subjective experience of *rel*-skimming. Not even an arbiter could perform a feat like that.

Nervecloth, she decided, *might be worth studying after all.*

"No one's coming after us," Von fretted.

"They will," Ann promised. "In the meantime, since we can't accelerate hard with me sitting on you, I think we ought to get a head start."

That alerted her to the next problem.

She knew the constellations of the Reach of Paradise as seen from Mega, and she knew the way the stars looked around *Second Contact Station*, near the Killing Reach jump, but without a computational aide, she couldn't tell where they were headed.

"How do you navigate?" she asked.

"By sight," he said, sounding so matter-of-fact it was clear that he thought it a surprising question.

Ann let her breath out, staring ahead into the increasingly altered arrangement of color-enhanced stars.

"I can get us there," Von said, sounding like a child challenged to prove he could find his own way to a friend's house. "Lurol showed me how it looks, she put it in my brain somehow. But H'Reth isn't following us, Ann!" He was getting hysterical.

"What are those for?" she asked, pointing at controls above his console.

"Mix," he said. "Ann, H'Reth knows I can disobey him, now. He won't trust me to lead him down the jump."

"He'll come," she insisted. "The controls. Come on, talk to me, Von."

He hesitated. She listened hard, afraid to hear him start obsessing about H'Reth once more.

One step at a time, she thought. If they reached the jump alone, she could pilot them through, and the Reach of Rire was more heavily populated than the Reach of Paradise. There were plenty of stations around the jump. There would be people on them who could help her with his mental problems.

"You told me I ought to know how to fly, just in case," Ann reminded Von.

"The toggles and sliders are backup for the nervecloth panel," said Von, "in case it takes shimmer damage."

Ann smiled encouragingly. "How fast are we going?" she asked.

"I don't know how to read that," Von admitted, nodding to the nervecloth panel. "It's all in Demoran symbols I don't recognize. But I'll know if we're going too fast, won't I? I'll feel it."

Not before I do, Ann thought. He was a Sevolite. Ann would stake her life on it. She probably had.

Which led her to a brand new worry: never mind them accelerating too hard for him, what about him sustaining a higher *skim'fac* than she could endure?

Von was drawing breath for his next, fretful sentence when a patch of space blanked out in the upper left quadrant of the nervecloth lining their hull, to be replaced with a blob of blazing blue orbs.

"Five of them," Von said, at a glance. "A hand." He boosted speed, adding excitedly, "You were right, Ann!"

Ann was pressed back firmly, but bearably, into Von. On the nervecloth she could see H'Reth's party shrinking, their blue color easing up as their shapes became smaller, each of them separate and distinct now.

"Are they ahead of us?" Ann gasped.

"Behind us," Von answered her. "Opposite where they're showing in the delta patch."

"The what?" Ann was getting vague. *Gap*, she thought. *I bet we're doing more than one skim'fac.*

"If there's a rapid rate of change in a section at the rear," Von was explaining to her, "it's projected as a delta patch on the far side of the ship's diameter, so it's still in the pilot's line of sight without the cockpit slinging." He pointed at another new jigsaw section. "And that's a cascade effect. It happens when what's covered by the delta patch is also interesting, and displaces something in the pilot's view that ranks lower." He paused. "I think. I've only heard about *rel*-fighters that delta patch and cascade."

"Real-time display?" she asked, academically, aware that she should be more dismayed, and that it wasn't a good sign that she wasn't.

"You have to anticipate a little," Von admitted. "But mostly real-time. There's no central processing. Nervecloth is a distributed medium, using cell to cell effects for communication based on threshold stimuli. It'll function even if sections of it get killed by shimmer."

Somehow it wasn't surprising to learn nervecloth was alive in some sense, since Ann was already breathing air kept fresh by something called ship's moss. She had the eerie thought the whole ship was a living thing that had swallowed her, and she would die in it, dissolved by the *gap* that functioned as digestive juices.

Hallucinations, she thought, and stammered, "How hard are we sk-skimming?"

He searched the forward display, and his control panel, brow furrowed. "I'm not sure of this dialect, but I think it says two *skim'facs*."

"Can we stick," she asked giddily, "to something survivable?"

"I must be reading it wrong," Von protested. "I'm a commoner. And this doesn't feel like much of anything."

"Listen, Von," she began to explain, "you're not — what's it? — oh, yeah. Nothing common about you, kid." She sounded drunk, and it was getting hard to think properly. She imagined shimmer stress peppering her cells and knew she ought to be worried about taking damage, but *gap* washed her fears smooth and blank. She forgot what she was saying but that was all right, she was safe with Von, getting digested inside a gray marble.

* * *

"Ann!" Von exclaimed, feeling her body slacken against him. They were close to where they could lead H'Reth down a jump and never come out, except he had Ann with him, pressed against his own body in a way that he couldn't ignore, and he was flying harder than was possible without a trace of impairment!

And now Ann was in trouble. He had been flying on high *gap* to reduce the odds of a fatal accident in unfamiliar territory, but now he reduced *gap* exposure without raising shimmer, cutting their net *skim'fac*. To prevent taxing their straps — and Ann — he slung the inner shell of the cock-

pit about. The deceleration felt as if someone huge was standing on his thighs and chest where Ann's weight pressed
hardest. It took an effort to expand his lungs, but it was possible.

"Ann!" he pleaded, freeing a hand to feel her throat and
face. She was breathing.

Von blinked at the delta patch. He had half expected to
be swiped into oblivion as they were overtaken but instead
H'Reth had shed speed to match them. Maybe he wanted
to go through the jump after all, believing Von knew it and
was trying to escape from him, expecting Reetions to be easy
conquests, or even believing Ann had kidnapped him and
determined to get him back from her. Could H'Reth be that
stupid? The idea was unbearably exciting. Make the jump.
End the pain. Fix everything. They were coming up on the
lip of the jump area.

"Ann, please!" Von begged, his hand moving down her
body to clasp hers. "This can't be right!" he cried. "You are
so much more *rel* than me!"

He slipped his hand inside her loose top to reassure himself her heart was beating, and was moved by the tactile
reward of cupping her small, firm breast. "Ann?" he begged.
"Oh, Ann, why did you have to come with me!"

She answered him with a moan.

The blue blobs on the rear patch of his nervecloth dimmed
as H'Reth matched pace.

"Get ... me back ... to Lurol," Ann said thickly. "To the ...
visitor probe."

Tears started from Von's eyes, hot and useless. *Why do I
always cry?* Von asked himself bitterly. *Crying never did any
good!*

He had to go down the jump although he knew he
couldn't navigate it. The obsession was too hard to fight.
Once, he would have died proudly for Mira and nothing
could have stopped him taking Jarl on. But his flesh had

learned to cringe, and his heart had learned to doubt that love meant anything. Lurol had given him the means to put that right!

But Ann was on his ship with him, in his lap, warm and living, not a ghost or a bad dream. He heard himself cry out in anguish, his feelings for Ann arrayed against his horror of accepting his past as it was.

"Go down your damn jump!" Ann rallied, coming to life again to clutch his arm to her chest. "Go in, lose H'Reth, and get me back to *Second Contact* when you climb back out again, on *this* side!"

H'Reth was in position, cruising at the same mix and *skim'fac*, in phase with him. Von could almost feel him, waiting. Gently, Von slid his hand between the folds of Ann's open flight jacket to cup her breast beneath her beating heart, for courage, and tipped them both down the jump.

Follow me, he thought at H'Reth, with more will to seduce than he had ever felt toward him before, *and you'll never hurt anyone again*.

Liege Monitum in Killing Reach

Di Mon encountered pirates halfway across Killing Reach. They swarmed out of a battlewheel positioned near the only passage through a debris field two hundred years old, leaving Di Mon the choice of retreating or taking them on. The hand of ships arrayed themselves in a flower formation, waiting for a signal from their leader.

Di Mon dropped speed to give them more time to consider. He was not escorting freight and hoped they might disperse spontaneously when that dawned on them. But they didn't.

Fine, Di Mon thought angrily, and sprang for the hand leader, sending a flanking ship reeling. Instinct brought him into wake-lock, their ships merging envelopes as pilots vied for dominance. The pirate was a woman, and Vrellish enough to respond with greed at the prospect of landing a highborn male. Fear of the harm he could do her came second. She was space drunk and hunting for thrills. The foulness of her soul-touch made Di Mon exalt as her *grip* weakened, but his fierce joy was followed by black fear as their fading connection threatened to reveal more than he wished anyone to know about him.

He reached for Darren's soul to give him courage, one of the Watching Dead his mind did not believe in but his heart could not reject in its need, and the pirate was no longer with him. The leaderless formation broke and Di

Mon sprang ahead, hoping that the path he believed to be clear had not become fouled since last report by mindless pirates.

As he sped on, risking death, he felt the echo of Darren's soul mocking him. Darren believed such things proved the soul's existence, while Di Mon argued in vain about the hints in Lorel math of spatial overlap or weird, temporal echoes. Now it felt as if Darren was with him, laughing off questions as he had years ago in the library, on Monitum, when Di Mon asked how he dared to believe in Watching Dead when he was boy-*sla*.

"I am sure death is a broadening experience," Darren had scoffed at that objection. "What have they to complain of where it matters? I have given them three highborn children. Host a soul, and quell a critic."

I have got to slow down, Di Mon realized. He had settled to averaging two *skim'facs* when a flock of ships burst, blue, onto his forward display, doing nearly four. He touched six *skim'facs* avoiding them, dunking one despite neutral intentions and sending another ship reeling into its neighbor. Both shattered, wakes interfering with each other.

Di Mon arched clear as a cloud of slower ships diverted around the crack-up and decided to look for their station of origin to find out what had caused them to flee from it, en mass.

As a youth, he had played the game of skimming outward from space stations to observe their transmission histories farther and farther into the past. In Killing Reach, intelligible Gelack signals dissolved into a Reetion buzz beyond a two hundred year radius of light travel time, but the signals themselves could still pinpoint a station if it had been around that long. Gelack battlewheels were another matter, because they could move.

After a little unsuccessful signal hunting, and equally futile consultation of his latest Killing Reach chart, Di Mon decided simply to backtrack and soon spotted a trio of guard ships twinkling red and blue as they whizzed around the invisible challenge sphere of a station. It was normal for at least one guard ship to be out on patrol, but three seemed a little extravagant for locals who were short of trustworthy pilots to do the job, and the warding dance had a suspiciously disciplined air to it without being overtly repetitive: to the contrary, the difficulty was avoiding ruts and wake traps when ships cooperated.

Nersallians, Di Mon realized, not sure if he was pleased or alarmed. Nersallians expanded by swallowing up others who offended against *Okal Rel* and could be overzealous about it, sometimes.

As Di Mon hovered, a warding ship broke off and sped to greet him.

"House of Nersal," it danced with assertion, writing the skim-signature of the Dragon House in jagged shapes and sharp transitions of color on the inner lining of Di Mon's hull, purely by means of jerky movements transmitted through the skin of space itself, stretched out between them. There was no other means to communicate in what pilots called, euphemistically, the *"rel*-medium", across distances great enough to make light itself too slow a messenger.

"Liege of Monitum," Di Mon answered, in kind.

They were close enough for shivers of soul-touch to leak through their shimmer dances. The stranger's will was frank and clean.

Di Mon danced the pattern that meant, "You go your way and I'll go mine."

He was answered with a request to dock, which Di Mon declined, indicating his business was urgent. The Nersallian made a kin-offer of assistance on the strength of their mutual Vrellish ties, warning of hazards ahead caused by shakeups.

"Ack Rel," Di Mon accepted, and moved off again towards the Reach of Paradise Jump, wondering how he would get rid of the Nersallian once they arrived. It was either that or

risk his escort wake-riding, and he was uneasy about the prospect of Nersallians having access to Reetions with the info-blit as yet unexplained and so offensive. But accepting their help proved a wise move. Twice the Nersallian shimmered a warning of what spacers called bad weather and diverted them around the treacherous resonance of recent shake-ups with their spreading clouds of hullsteel slivers. Even better, Di Mon's guide left of his own accord after he had seen him through. It took Di Mon only a few more minutes to locate *Trinket Ring Station* where D'Ander had told him to expect to find Ayrium D'Ander D'Aur.

Di Mon dropped out of skim obediently after dancing Liege of Monitum when challenged by station defenders. After a brief conversation in normal space, in which he proved to their satisfaction that he came at the request of Ayrium's father, D'Ander, he was invited to get close enough to converse with the station by radio.

"Welcome to *Trinket Ring*," a woman's voice greeted Di Mon cheerfully. "I am Ayrium, Protector of the Purple Alliance."

Di Mon frowned at the title, which had no precedent in history except as an old Golden Demish idea. In either case it rubbed him the wrong way. Ayrium should simply be Liege of Barmi, not Perry D'Aur's excuse for also hanging onto other bits and pieces of the self-proclaimed Purple Alliance.

Di Mon replied, "I am Ditatt, one hundred and third Liege of Monitum, known as Di Mon."

"We are not exactly prepared to host a peer of the empire," Ayrium continued with a touch of chagrin. "But if you are here on my father's business, you are nonetheless welcome."

"I bring a letter from D'Ander," Di Mon corrected her, offended. "My business is all Sevildom's, not solely his."

The ill humor he felt was also partly due to suffering zero-G.

"Court business, is it?" came Ayrium's excited reply. Transparency of feeling was a Golden trait which she seemed to have inherited from her sire. "I, uh, don't have a lot of court experience," she added awkwardly. "Is it okay to be addressing you in *rel*-peerage? I mean, since we're both Highlords and everything."

"Your grammar," Di Mon told her sourly, "is accurate. But I have news of both your parents and my time is limited. May I skid in to *Trinket Ring*?"

"Oh," said Ayrium.

The tedious business of making a sub-light speed approach tried Vrellish patience, but that didn't negate the fact that done improperly, skidding in could be fatal for all concerned. A skid-in was extremely impolite without the permission.

"All right," Ayrium decided. "But you'd better take it easy, this station isn't exactly up to Nersallian standards for structural integrity."

"Understood," Di Mon agreed. He cut it close enough to leave him only fifteen minutes worth of coasting and cat clawing to make it to dock.

Ayrium stood waiting for him when he left the inner airlock. She looked like a Demish woman except for her clothes, breasts and hips packed into snug flight leathers with the jacket worn open to the sternum, probably to help her cool down. She had an undershirt on beneath. There was sweat in her hair line, and her hands were soiled with grease from some equipment she had been working on. But she carried herself with a sword fighter's confidence despite her unVrellish deployment of body fat, and her large hands looked strong. Her Golden Demish inheritance shone in her eyes' sky blue brilliance, undiminished by the tell-tale facial mask of travel bruising under the eyes, at her temples, and around her mouth. Her short-cropped hair reflected glints of gold.

In addition to her dueling sword, she also wore a projectile sidearm of some kind holstered under one arm. Di Mon's attention fixed on the gun, with instant distrust and alarm.

"Is that an intended insult?" he asked in his most urbane manner.

Ayrium flushed pink. "Sorry!" she said, slipping the holster off to send it skidding away from her across the floor. "I forgot I was wearing that." She sealed up her flight jacket and wiped her hands. "We've had some trouble with the local population," she explained her *faux pas*. "*Trinket Ring's* occupants haven't all proved to be, uh, totally honorable."

"I see," said Di Mon. "I hope you executed all the offenders."

"Ah, well, pretty close," said Ayrium, scrubbing her cropped, blond hair with one hand. "That was a sweet skid-in you performed," she praised Di Mon's delicacy. "You learn that doing court receptions?"

"In the Nesak War," said Di Mon.

"Before my time," she said. Ayrium was only twenty-five.

Di Mon looked around him with a frown. The dock was grubby and half the equipment brackets on one wall had snapped and never been repaired. His chiseled nostrils quivered as he cataloged traces of stale *ignis* smoke and human urine.

"We haven't had a chance to clean up," Ayrium excused the bad housekeeping. "Like I said, some of the locals contested our occupation with tactics worthy of the Killing War." She gave a nervous laugh. "You know. Poison gas. Damaged docks. Power hand weapons."

Reetion tactics, Di Mon thought with a pang. It was ridiculous to feel concern for Ranar's honor, but he could not help it somehow.

"You are an unusual creature," Di Mon concluded, "for a female Demish highborn."

Ayrium grinned at him. "You're not what I imagined, either."

Di Mon frowned, prepared for anti-Lorel prejudice.

"I thought you'd be a lot more arrogant," she told him, "and way stuffier. I mean, being Monatese and an Old Sword, you know?"

"I see," Di Mon said, dryly, unsure whether he had been insulted or flattered.

"So what's this letter from Dad about?" asked Ayrium.

Di Mon pulled D'Ander's letter from his flight jacket. "Your mother's execution," he told her, "and Pureblood Amel."

Ayrium blinked at the double whammy, but she didn't babble questions like most Demish. She snatched the letter out of his hand, flicked it open, and sucked the words off the pages. Once she exclaimed, "No!" and later, "Good gods!"

There were not, to Di Mon's knowledge, any 'good' gods. The gods of the *Okal Rel* pantheon were all sadistically mad. Nesak priests believed them to be the Great Souls of extinguished lines, still obsessed by the doctrines that had been their own downfall. Monatese scholarship suggested they were remnants of old Earth religions. Most people thought of them as dangerously bored demons of uncertain origin. But if any line of Sevildom would be prone to insist on a good god, it would be the Golden Demish one.

When Ayrium looked up, she said, "My mother's innocent."

Of very little, Di Mon thought with a frown, but he said, "I do not believe she wished Vretla harmed."

"You lost your heir," Ayrium realized, with a sympathetic impulse.

"If D'Ander is correct," Di Mon said, stiffly, "the child that Vretla lost was more likely Amel's than my nephew's."

"Amel," Ayrium breathed the name like poetry, and shook her head. "My father would like to believe that," she followed up soberly, "but Monitum has a reputation for using its head. Could this Von really be Amel? It seems like a bad joke on the Golden Demish, or maybe more particularly on my father, since Amel would also be descended from Ameron through his mother, Ev'rel."

"I am sure Von is highborn," Di Mon insisted carefully, "with a personality that parallels the Golden Demish notion

of a Soul of Light." He raised a hand before she could protest. "Your father's Reetion showed me how to extract hidden data from the Reetion device."

"And you trust him?" Ayrium asked.

"I trust the data," Di Mon told her, "yes. And my *lyka's*
information about Von — she was his den mother."

Ayrium lowered her hand, the letter clenched in it. "I
should go to court to defend my mother."

"Your father can take care of that," said Di Mon.

Her head came up sharply as if she had been insulted, but
she laughed instead. "Sorry!" she said. "I thought you meant
because I'm a woman — but you aren't Demish. And you
are right — my father is already at court, and I am here. He
needs me to rescue this kid who just might be a Soul of Light
for him. Where do you think this Amel-prospect is?"

"On the *Vanilla Rose*," Di Mon guessed, "if he is still alive."

"Which is in the Reach of Paradise," Ayrium said, and
sighed. "Well, we know there are Reetions who make the
jump. They've been popping in and out with increasing
frequency over the last eight or nine months. That's why I
was clamping down on spots like *Trinket Ring* that run their
contraband and father got involved when he found out. He
said he wanted to take proof to court, to reopen the question of Reetion contact." She shrugged. "But he took the only
Reetions that we ever captured with him to court. My people
don't know the jump."

"I will teach you how to make the jump," said Di Mon, "in
exchange for the support of Purple Alliance fliers. H'Reth will
not have any highborns, himself, except the paladins and if
they fly against us you and I will have to take them out."

He was half afraid she would balk at the prospect of fighting paladins, who were revered by Golden Demish. Her
father was something of an unofficial paladin himself in the
service of the Golden Emperor. But if she revered the calling it did not extend to paladins in Delm's service, like
Larren.

"The jump to the Reetion side has been a Monatese secret for two hundred years," she noted, instead. "Why would you be willing to share it with me, now? If Amel is a Pureblood, he's a mostly Demish one: a Blue and Golden Demish cross. I'd say that made him more my concern — on both sides of my parentage — than yours."

Di Mon didn't have the time to explain that he had settled for Delm, when Ev'rel disappointed him, solely because any Ava was better than none, or that proof of Amel's existence was important to him for the sake of vindicating Ev'rel. Instead he said, simply, "Believe me, in the name of Ameron."

Ayrium bit her lip and looked down at the letter again, in her hand. "You ought to know," she said, shifting her weight, "that father charges me with hanging onto Amel for him, not surrendering him to you."

Di Mon was not entirely surprised. "D'Ander," he said, "would like to be the power behind the throne."

In the silence that followed both pondered their reactions to that prospect, and their doubts about each other. They had different interests, but Di Mon believed that Ayrium was honorable, which was all it took for *Okal Rel* to make cutting deals possible.

"*Ack Rel*?" Di Mon suggested, "We cooperate to gain him, and then settle possession through a duel."

Ayrium grinned as if he had offered her a compliment, and said, "Done."

"I would suggest," he amended, "to first blood."

"You're on," she agreed at once, happy to play by Demish rules. "Amel alive and working as a courtesan!" She shook her head. "Dear gods."

Di Mon got back into his *rel*-fighter to wait for Ayrium to organize her people rather than deal with the gawking stares of the Purple Alliance staff assisting pilots to get ready. He launched with Ayrium. It was difficult to coast in the discomfort of zero-G, waiting to get clear of the station, but *rel*-fighters did not carry auxiliary fuel. All they needed was power for their phase splicer and once in skim it was a case of trying to prevent the energy they swam in from drowning them, metaphorically speaking. *Grip* was an act of holding back, to remain in the world as you knew it. Letting go was to surrender to the currents unleashed by a phase splicer's first, thin incision into the living flesh beneath the surface skin mankind knew as three dimensional space plus one temporal dimension.

Ayrium fielded two hands of nobleborn *rel*-fighters.

"I will come through with you, accompanied by three volunteers," she told Di Mon, by radio, as they cleared *Trinket Ring Station*. "If there are clear skies on the other side, I'll go right back to lead the next bunch through. I've instructed the first wave to follow your lead while I'm gone."

"Agreed," he said simply.

"That's the nice thing about you Vrellish," she told him. "You almost never talk too much." Her good humor wavered. "Do you think Delm would kill Perry before the trial?"

"He needs a scapegoat," Di Mon assured her. "A public one."

"Thanks," she said, still sounding anxious about her mother.

Conversation ended with skim transition. One of the PA pilots started seconds late but caught up without losing them, since they were following a straight line to the jump.

Ayrium and her volunteers jumped with him in fearless trust. Di Mon himself felt more trepidation because to him it was a terrible and hollow one, filled with the ghosts of the Killing War. He headed for the light that was Ameron — as if Ameron could still be felt in the jump that claimed him nearly two hundred years before, in a ship that had been piloted by Di Mon's ancestor.

They emerged on the other side without losing anyone. Two stations were present. A Reetion one and the *Vanilla*

Rose, still lit up like an Ava's Way floor show — neither had warding ships out on patrol. The lack of activity felt ominous.

Ayrium signaled she was going back.

Di Mon made for the Reetion station at half a *skim'fac*, leading Ayrium's three nobleborns. He dropped out of skim well clear of the station's challenge radius, conscious of the threat posed by a highborn approaching a station of commoners, and cat clawed to sustain a half-G thrust. Only one of the PA ships proved able to manage the technique and keep up. The rest coasted, less troubled by low gravity than Di Mon.

"This is Di Mon, Liege of Monitum," Di Mon transmitted using the protocols Ranar had provided. "I bear greetings from your kinsman Ranar of Rire, who tells me you can understand English. Please confirm."

There were sputters, in response, but it was no good. He had to stop cat clawing to sustain contact. As soon as he did, a thick stream of material not meant for human comprehension flowed over his nervecloth. The incident revved up his blood pressure as he worked to block it off, worsening his zero-G intolerance. He spoke through gritted teeth when he was ready to get back on the radio.

"My ship cannot communicate with your arbiter," he told the Reetions. "Our technologies are not compatible."

It was an educated guess, but it seemed to register. A woman's voice responded, deep and forceful, speaking in what Di Mon judged to be Reetion. It was quickly replaced by an English translation that sacrificed most of its color.

"This is Lurol," the Reetion said. "I am the last non-collective member of our command structure. The collectives have suggested I be spokesman. You said that you bring word from Ranar?"

Di Mon did not understand much except her last remark. "Yes," he told her, as his head began to pound. "Ranar told me to assure you he is doing field research on Gelion. Excuse me for a moment, my head is aching."

There was a long pause in which Di Mon indulged himself in a quick "solar flare" maneuver. He looped between the stations and the jump, keeping to less than two *skim'facs* and avoiding unknown territory.

The Reetions communicated as soon as he had settled back into a zero-G coast.

"We can't surrender," Lurol's bland, translated words sounded at odds with the distress suggested. "We cannot force a station arbiter to disregard Reetion law. You must understand that."

"What are you talking about?" Di Mon asked, bewildered.

"That display you made, just now. We're aware that your kind can exceed a single skim factor. We know we can't defend ourselves. But surrendering just isn't in our station's repertoire, in fact, arbiters have deep directives never to be coerced by acts of terrorism."

"I have not asked you to surrender," Di Mon exclaimed in astonishment. "And I was not attempting to coerce you."

"Then why did you do that loop maneuver," Lurol asked.

"I was restless," said Di Mon, feeling mildly ridiculous. There was a long pause.

Di Mon lost patience and hailed the Reetions. "Station Master Lurol," he addressed her by the only title he could think of that might be applicable. "I am seeking a young man known as Von. He is a Gelack, not a Reetion. Von is all I want."

"Von again," Lurol answered. "Law and Reason!"

"Explain," Di Mon demanded.

"I don't know if I can. I don't know, entirely, what's happened!"

Di Mon sighed. "Do you have docks?"

"Yes. At our hub. We'd like to talk if you would come on board."

"No thanks," said Di Mon, well aware of what hub docks implied. He had had all the zero-G he cared to stand.

A new voice took over, its inflection in translation only somewhat different from Lurol's. "I am Alicia," it said. "An anthropologist in Ranar's first expansion. Ranar is my liege, after a fashion. My mentor."

Di Mon wondered if she was trying to humor him.

"You are the real Liege of Monitum, aren't you?" asked Alicia.

"Yes, I am real," said Di Mon, with thin patience.

"Von claimed to be you when he was on board," she told him. "We had contact with him. But he's gone."

They are not telling me everything, Di Mon decided.

A torrent of words erupted, in Reetion, over the open connection. None of it translated. Di Mon cut them off, fed up, and boosted to a *skim'fac* to cruise in a loose figure eight pattern until his ears stopped ringing from high blood pressure. In the middle of his second pass he spotted Ayrium arriving with the rest of her PA irregulars. He paced her, and they dropped out to claw-walk in tandem, close enough to pick up each other's light transmissions if they transmitted in bursts.

"Amel was on the Reetion Station," Di Mon transmitted. "But he is not there now."

"Do the Reetions know where he is?" Ayrium asked, in the same fashion.

"I can't tell."

"Shall I try?" she asked.

"Please do."

She left him in command of both hands, out beyond the challenge sphere. He shimmered basic deployment signals at them in the oldest of universal shimmer codes, and hoped their shared vocabulary would be enough if fighting broke out. Ayrium was back within fifteen minutes.

"They're a little nervous, that's all," she told Di Mon. "Delm's Master Paladin, Larren, threatened to crack them if they didn't surrender Von." She paused to overcome a catch in her voice. "Von volunteered, which might prove he is Amel. Or at least a decent human being," she said huskily. "But it probably means he's dead, as well."

"Are you prepared to help me take the *Vanilla Rose*?" Di Mon asked her.

"Yes," said Ayrium, with a steely spring in her rich, Golden Demish voice.

The pair of them boosted to skim again, Ayrium signaling her nobleborn entourage to stand clear until they were called upon. In a pincher formation, the two highborns swooped around *Vanilla Rose*, just crossing the rim of its challenge sphere.

Two hands of ships shot out like disturbed hornets as the intruders soared clear again. Ayrium shot through an anti-highborn formation before it could form, scattering the nobleborn defenders for her pilots to chase down on equal terms.

But no highborn ship launched from the station.

Di Mon executed a flashy spike at six *skim'facs* and dropped into a slow loop around the station while Ayrium danced a Blue Demish signature, followed up by the complex and quite beautiful pattern to which her father's blood right entitled her, and ending with a simple PA signature.

Behind her, her PA irregulars fanned out in formation. None had been lost in the scuffle, and resistance was nonexistent. Now was the time for Larren to contest Ayrium's right of challenge if he so intended. Instead, the surviving defenders signaled their surrender and made for their docks again.

Ayrium dropped out of skim to communicate. "Think we can both risk going down?" she asked.

"No," said Di Mon.

"That's a Blue Demish station," said Ayrium, "I intend to land on it and claim it honorably, by the sword."

The idea of the scruffy PA inheriting Delm's monstrosity of a luxury battlewheel rather appealed to Di Mon, especially since he was too far from his own base of power to make any other plan workable.

"*Vanilla Rose* is yours," he told Ayrium. "I'll cover you in space when you go down. But I still expect a chance to challenge you for Von."

"*Ack Rel*," she acknowledged, and kept her channel to him open as she gave instructions to her nobleborns. The usual approach was to secure the docks using subordinates, or arrange an exchange of hostages to keep both sides honorable. With an allied highborn in flight however, able to punish any breeches of protocol, Ayrium could afford to cut corners.

Di Mon looped and prowled around *Vanilla Rose* for half an hour before he was signaled by a PA *rel*-ship, dropped out of skim and spoke to Ayrium, who told him she was standing on the floor of the great, open bridge, from which H'Reth commanded when the *Vanilla Rose* was at rest, under rotation.

"Come on down," she invited. "I'll leave a couple nobleborns on challenge watch."

A Blue Demish crewman bobbed a bow when Di Mon climbed out of his ship. "The Lady-Liege of Barmi II, daughter of D'Ander, awaits you on the bridge, Liege Monitum," he announced, with a second, nervous bow.

Di Mon paused to strap on the sword held in his hand. He felt more relaxed than he had expected to. *Okal Rel* seemed safely in ascendance on *Vanilla Rose*.

They passed quickly through Delm's ridiculously fussy corridors, servants and crew bowing every time they crossed his path. Di Mon spotted a portrait of Delm mounted amid Golden Demish spider-webbing and resisted the impulse to slash the over-refined, handsome face with his sword. It would be so much more satisfying to find Amel and bring him back so he could rub Delm's nose in his son and heir's continued, inconvenient existence.

Ayrium stood at the center of the operations floor, the great dome of nervecloth overhead casting a convincing blue sky full of moving clouds. Crewmen waited at their workstations, some of them actually down on their knees looking up at Ayrium, who stood at the center, confident and pleased with what she had won. A few of the ship's senior officers knelt before her with their swords laid flat on the floor.

"Ah," said Ayrium, hushing the stream of Demish babble pouring out of an obsequious informant. "Well met, Liege Monitum."

"Von?" Di Mon asked.

Ayrium heaved a sigh that swelled her breasts inside her flight jacket. Some of the bridge crew, who were all male, stared at her, unabashed. The rest seemed unsure where to let their eyes settle. They were not accustomed to being under a woman's command.

"There's no corpse to report," Ayrium assured Di Mon, "but the news isn't exactly good." She dismissed her erstwhile informant with a kindly touch, saying, "Later, thanks."

Di Mon surveyed the congregated stationers. They were Blue Demish according to the braid on their uniforms, and none of them more than a Midlord, like Perry D'Aur.

"I take it your claim went unchallenged," Di Mon remarked, in a matter of fact tone.

"Larren was here, but he's dead," said Ayrium. "Shot by a Reetion who docked claiming that she was Von. Liege H'Reth took off chasing Von and the Reetion woman, taking his best hand of fliers, and we took out anyone else with a will to defend Delm's right to the *Vanilla Rose*. They think the Reetion woman was a Vrellish hybrid. Word is she beat H'Reth's errant captain to a pulp, probably while he was trying to rape her, so I can't cry too hard."

"Where is the body?" asked Di Mon, feeling skeptical.

Ayrium's informant led them through more busy Demish passages to a little lounge near a rim dock to find Jarl lying where he had died, reeking of opened bowels.

Di Mon lingered just long enough to convince himself no Reetion commoner had done that kind of damage with her bare hands, and while it wasn't inconceivable that the Sevolites of Ameron's time had a child or two with Reetions, it seemed unlikely to him given the prejudice of the times.

"Well?" asked Ayrium, when they were clear of the foul smell again.

"Our Golden Demish Pureblood has a temper," Di Mon said, wearily.

"Then Amel could be no better than his father," said Ayrium.

Di Mon shook his head. "I knew him as Von," he said. "His den mother is now my household *lyka*. On the whole, I think she'll tell you he was gentle. But given what is on the info-blits, he had ample cause to pulp Jarl."

Ayrium drew her arms about her with a shiver.

The crewman who had been trailing her, eager to be helpful, spoke up from the doorway. "Amel?" he said, a quaver in his tone. "Amel is ... Von?"

Ayrium and Di Mon turned.

"I talked to him," the crewman said, eyes widening. "I told him where to find the brown girl, when he docked. I mean, she did deserve killing, yes, but a girl — well, a girl is...a girl. You know." He bobbed his annoying bow in Ayrium's direction again, eyeing her unfeminine sword. "Uh, err, well."

"Never mind," she told him, patiently, "go on."

"Well," he let out a breath in a whoosh and inhaled again. "I didn't like the idea of abusing her. Death was good enough, I thought, for what she did to the paladins and all. But I wasn't going to get myself killed for her! Then Von showed up asking for her."

"What happened to Von, here, after you saw him," asked Ayrium.

"He ran off to help the Reetion woman," said the crewman. "And you think he's really Amel?" His eyes were growing wider in his head with ever word. "Oh, no," he said suddenly, in horror.

"What is it?" Di Mon snapped eagerly. Even bad news would be better than uncertainty.

The thunderstruck Demish man whimpered, "I called him a whore. I said he was a lucky whore to escape from the Reetions. Amel! The grandson of the Sacrifice!"

Di Mon's patience expired. "If you learn anything useful, let me know," he snapped at Ayrium. "I will wait in my *rel*-fighter."

He slashed at Delm's painting on the way back but it did not help as much as he had imagined.

Waiting to launch, he faced the prospect of confronting Delm at court without Amel, living or dead, for evidence. It seemed futile. But now that he was convinced himself, he had no choice but to do his best to bring Delm down. He owed that much to Ev'rel, whose perversion was — perhaps — no worse than his own, and who in other ways had been so promising. H'Us, of course, would think he had gone mad, and D'Ander would inflame the rift between Golden and Silver Demish. The Red Vrellish would be in no mood to listen and Hangst Nersal was getting much too friendly with his Nesak cousins to be interested in stabilizing Fountain Court. There were no more Lor'Vrellish, like Ameron, to keep Fountain Court together — chaos and destruction would descend and consume them all. On top of all that, he was still Monitum's last living highborn — and gods — there was Ranar! How was he going to deal with that?

Di Mon rested his head against the back of his sling cockpit and wondered if it was too much to hope for more competent pirates on the way home.

Ayrium brought him news in person, climbing up the access tube of his *rel*-fighter.

"Best I can make out," she said, "Amel took off with the Reetion woman and H'Reth followed. They headed for the jump on the far side of the reach, which Amel claimed he knew how to make before things went sour. H'Reth chased him with a hand of *rel*-fighters. A couple of them chickened out and came back, which is how we know as much as we do. They're claiming they knew it was wrong to chase Amel, now." She snorted her disgust. "Too bad they weren't enlightened by their ancestors a little earlier."

Di Mon looked down at Ayrium's head and shoulders, propped up in the mouth of the access tube. Her eyes were as bright as ice crystals. Her expressions brought a vivid, child-bright life to her strong features. He knew he ought to find her attractive. If she knew he had found Von attractive, would she kill him for it he wondered? He wouldn't blame her.

"Amel went down the jump," continued Ayrium, "and H'Reth after him. But according to the Reetions I spoke to, Amel didn't know the jump. They set him up, somehow, to lead H'Reth off. I'm not certain about the details." She locked her jaw briefly, but lost the struggle to remain silent. "You know more about Lorel science than I do," she appealed to Di Mon. "Is it possible to extract and record Demish memories? Or program a highborn like nervecloth? Can the Reetions have done things like that?"

"I don't know," Di Mon said stonily.

"I think you do," said Ayrium, sounding more guarded than before.

"I see no point in waiting," Di Mon told her. "I will return to court."

Ayrium withdrew from his access tube.

Di Mon was relieved to launch. *Vanilla Rose* had felt more Demish by the minute as it mourned Amel. The Demish loved dead heroes. Di Mon could envy Amel for that. Dead, he would be useless to Monitum.

Amel

Soul touch swallowed Von in the new jump. Ann was a warm mass in his chest, welcome to shelter there, but a jolt of recognition froze him as he felt the grasping touch of Garn H'Reth.

There was nothing physical about the strange communion between souls felt through the *gap* dimensions. There was no time in *gap* either. The mind constructed the experience as it was disposed to do, no two minds doing so in exactly the same way, despite some measure of communication.

Von's experience, like Von, was body-centered. He was clinging to a mountain top, beset by icy winds. Ann sheltered inside him, safe. H'Reth wanted desperately to get in. He pressed, like an infection, against Von's skin, penetrating barriers as Von was driven to compassion for his misery, despite the revulsion he felt. H'Reth coalesced into a body by his ankles, hands sinking into his flesh as he climbed up Von's leg, trying to take shelter from the cold wind.

The Ann thing in Von's chest roused itself at this intrusion and became a small, hot fire. It hissed and popped as H'Reth burrowed. H'Reth's hands began to slip. H'Reth pleaded with his emotions, babbling in wordless awe as if Von was the sun that warmed him and the air that he needed to fill his lungs. It moved Von with dreadful pity he did not desire. But the Ann-fire was not willing to share. She swelled, re-structuring Von's strength. And H'Reth screamed and sloughed from him.

Detached, H'Reth failed to fall away. His beefy face stared up from a meter below Von's feet, suspended in the chilly winds that slashed at both of them.

"I can't," Von shouted to him over the storm, tears streaming down his face, whipped by the wind. "I can't bear you! I'm sorry it hurts you, but you never cared if you hurt me, or Anatolia, or anybody else in your whole life!"

And finally, miraculously, Garn H'Reth got the idea. He could not help it. Von might have helped him then, because his own *grip* on the mountain had grown firmer. The ice-laden wind still roared, but Von's feet sunk into the mountain the way H'Reth's hands had sunk into his flesh, and he felt Ann, safe inside of him, weakened but confident of his power to protect her from the storm. It was so peaceful, in that moment, that Von could have found it in him to forgive the self-deluding, spoiled child that was Garn H'Reth. Not completely. He could never forgive him completely for all the pain he had caused. But enough, at least, to spare him the ill-defined fate of becoming a lost soul.

It was H'Reth who could not take Von's outstretched hand, because to take it demanded he see himself through the eyes of his savior, once, thoroughly. He could not find the courage to bear that.

H'Reth shook all over and began to blur, as Von watched. "No," H'Reth denied the mirror held up to him, inextricably bound up with the help being offered. "No. Impossible."

And H'Reth began to fall apart, as if he was made of leaves the wind was scraping off, first one by one and then faster and faster until there were only scraps of him left, still fixed in place against the pressure of the cold wind.

When the last leaf was gone, Von might even have mourned. The soul he had experienced was as pathetic and sad as it was heartless and self-absorbed. But there were others nearby who were also unraveling in the jump. People he did not know. One he frightened and could do nothing for. But the second accepted his outreached hand, making

Von laugh, in his *gap*-induced dream, at the awe inspiring image of himself that was reflected back.

"No, no," Von told this new soul. "You are not insignificant. You are Ron D'An, a good man of the Blue Demish line. And I am just a boy, not a big, warm sun."

He didn't know how he knew the man's name was Ron D'An, or anything else about him. It had all simply been handed to him, like a gift of complete trust. The experience left him feeling intoxicated. In fact, he might not have worried about completing the jump if it weren't for Ann, curled up about his heart and growing weaker. He wanted her to be strong and separate from him again. A woman in his arms, in a *rel*-ship. To have that, he knew he must back out the way he had come, and return to the Reach of Paradise.

Von came to himself with a gasp, in his sling cockpit, and shivered at the thought of actually trying to help H'Reth! That *really* had not been the point of the exercise! Whatever had come over him? The intoxicated feeling was gone, too. His skin was clammy with a cold sweat. But he recognized the stars surrounding them. They were back in the Reach of Paradise. Von laughed and clutched Ann to him.

But she was much too still.

"Ann?" Von begged, shifting her. Her pulse was steady but she lay in his arms, inert.

No, he thought, *no! I protected her!*

A ship popped out of the jump. Von broke away from it, panicking, and swiftly cut speed again, afraid for his passenger. Ann seemed to be comatose. He undid her harness bindings so he could cup her against his chest, and bent his head to nuzzle her. "Don't be catatonic," he begged. The material of her Blue Demish lounging pants slid in folds against her warm skin as Von boosted her limp weight up higher against him, careful to make sure her head was secure.

Get me back to Second Contact, she had said. To Lurol.

A flash of clear dream fractured Von's reality and for an instant he was back inside the probe again. He gasped, and pressed Ann against him, still navigating by sight with his hands on the flight controls.

Ann murmured and shifted.

"Ann!" he cried, wild with relief.

She slid a hand across his chest over his green silk shirt decorated in the heraldry of Monitum and shifted her leg, straddling him with her knees bent. Then she subsided like a sleeper, her breath warm on his neck.

"Ann?" he asked, abandoning the mix control.

She made a comfy, snuffling sound and shifted her hips, settling against his with an extra wriggle.

Von cleared his throat. "Uh, Ann, can you talk to me?" Sensual behavior was a good sign, in its own way, but the suggestiveness of her movements was starting to make him uncomfortable, dressed in snug flight leathers.

Ann mumbled and squeezed him gently with her thighs.

She must be space drunk, he thought anxiously. That was better than catatonic, but still not safe. Space drunk pilots needed stimulation. Eva said that was why they started fights, but pilots also claimed that sex was good insurance against wiping out in your sleep after a wicked flight and if it was a choice between that and fighting her, Von knew which he preferred.

Of course he had never heard of people making love in a sling cockpit under skim, but he figured he could control the ship with one hand, since he didn't feel anywhere near catatonic himself. In fact if Ann didn't stop what she was doing, he was going to have to loosen his pants!

Undressing in a sling cockpit proved a lot harder than he had anticipated, due largely to Ann's participation. Still in her *gap*-giddy stupor, she responded with clumsy enthusiasm, giving him a scare the first time she nearly lurched out of his grasp. He also had to keep his eyes on the display.

Von was rapidly reaching the conclusion that this was a really stupid idea, when Ann reared up, opened her eyes, blinked down at him with a wide, reeling grin and said, "This is a wild dream!"

"Ann?" he asked, unsure whether she was making sense.

She came down on him with her mouth and lower body simultaneously, and he lost control of the ship, confirming, for future reference, that it really was a stupid idea. He just managed to fall out of skim before something fatal went amiss, and plunged into zero-G with the roar of his blood pressure exploding like a nova in his head.

He came around feeling mildly ill, and very silly, with a nasty low-G headache. Both of them had come loose from their moorings in the sling cockpit, so it was extremely lucky they had not been hurt.

Ann floated out of reach, her lounging top completely open under his flight jacket and the matching pants adrift on the far side of the ship's interior. Embarrassing balls of fluid drifted lazily between them, with a swarm of red gems clustered about his head that proved his nose was bleeding.

Teeth gritted against the headache, Von batted away the blood that made a fluid impact on his silk shirt and quickly pulled his clothes together, overcompensating and misjudging everything. He wasn't used to zero-G and he decided that he never wanted to be.

He hooked Ann's pants without letting go of the cockpit frame. Next, he retrieved her. Ann felt like a big, limp doll in his hands as he struggled to get her pants back on, and then pulled her down with him into the sling cockpit so he could secure them both again. His face burned the whole time with an embarrassment augmented by his powerful blood pressure. He might have felt all right if it had worked, but Ann was unconscious again. Maybe his pilot clients had been wrong about sex as a curative.

Ann needed help, and only the Reetions who terrified him had the expertise to give it to her. Refusing to dwell on what that might mean for him, he boosted back up to one skim factor, heading for the help she had told him she would need.

He got as close to *Second Contact Station* as he dared before he dropped out of skim and hailed them on a Reetion
frequency.

"I've got Ann!" Von blurted in Reetion, upset by the
horror of repeatedly discovering his brain knew how to speak
and understand it. "She's unconscious. She said the visitor
probe could help her." Just naming the demon thing unnerved him.

"Message understood," began an arbiter, only to be displaced by Lurol. "We'll take care of you both," she promised him. "We'll dock you in the ambulance bay again." Her
voice faltered as she hesitated. "We want to help."

"I'm docking," Von told her breathlessly, trying not to
think of anything else.

He nearly fainted twice. A Reetion voice he did not recognize kept talking to him soothingly, but he paid it very
little attention. He held Ann as the ambulance bay filled with
air, and thought about the sword they'd brought with them.
Did he have that kind of courage? He wasn't sure. A voice
on the radio startled him.

"This is Ayrium D'Ander D'Aur of the Purple Alliance,
calling the Gelack known as Von," said a woman's voice in
Gelack. "Von, if you can hear me please respond."

She addressed him *rel*-to-*pol* without differencing, which
was extremely flattering coming from a Highlord like
Ayrium D'Ander D'Aur, infamous in Demish court circles
as a woman who acted like a man. Princess H'Us said she
was a pirate. But at least she was Gelack. Von waited for his
heart to slow down after its spiky reaction to the new voice.

"Von, are you there?" she asked again.

"This is Von," he transmitted back, carefully avoiding a
pronoun that might commit him to a position with regard
to her condescension. The only explanation he could think
of was that she was hard up for entertainment this far from
court. People said she acted Vrellish despite her Demish
looks, but on the other hand, presuming that a Demish

woman's interest was sexual could be disastrously presump-
tuous, whatever the truth of the matter.

"Hello, Von," Ayrium answered, sounding relieved and
so delighted that it made him blink. "What is your situation?" she followed up practically.

He had to decide how to address her or start sounding
silly. He opted for using the proper differencing suffix. "I
am in a Reetion dock," he said, "but my ship is still sealed."

"Don't open it," Ayrium ordered him.

He wet his lips. A lump rose in his throat at the hope
Ayrium offered him.

"I have to open it, Your Grace," he said respectfully. "I
have a Reetion pilot with me who needs her people's help."

"Keep her with you," Ayrium advised him. "I am in
possession of *Vanilla Rose* now. You can bring her to me."
She hesitated before adding, "I have spoken with the pilot
you saved from the jump on the far side of this reach. A jump
you did not know when you went into it, but had both the
grip to survive and the compassion to extend your help to
an enemy. Have you thought about that?"

Von's brow furrowed, too confused and scared to dis-
semble. "Maybe it was Ann," he said. "I don't know, Your
Grace. Nothing makes sense."

Ayrium's voice softened, kindly. "The pilot said you soul
touched him."

"A little," Von said. He could not, honestly, remember it
well. He had been swamped with Ann and H'Reth's feelings.

"He said you glow in soul touch, like a light," said
Ayrium. "I'd like a chance to get to know you better, to
decide if I agree."

Von flushed at the compliment, but at least he knew where
he stood, and it was familiar territory. "I'd be honored," he
said, "b-but I'm afraid the Reetions won't release me." He
kept his pronouns scrupulously precise, too intimidated to
accept familiarity.

"Open your hatch," Lurol ordered suddenly.

Ayrium's voice countered, "Don't do it!"

Von inhaled and held it. He could not obey Ayrium while Ann needed her own people, not even if she might offer him protection. He kissed Ann, who remained inert, sprung the hatch and pushed her through it into the hands of waiting Reetions.

Then he triggered the hatch closed again. One of the Reetions barely got his arm clear in time, causing Von a spasm of sympathetic alarm. Safe again, he felt bereft. Ann was gone. He already missed her.

"What's happened?" demanded Ayrium, sounding vexed.

"I gave them Ann," he said. "Now I'm sealed in again." He knew it wasn't wise to admit to disobedience, but he could not think up a clever excuse. A cloud of fluid spheres touched his face. He swept them away with a stifled sob, sickened by the sordidness of his existence.

"Von," Lurol said firmly, "open your hatch."

Von pulled himself back into his cockpit and fastened one piece of the harness across his waist.

Ayrium seemed to have gone away, but he lacked the strength to wonder about that. He closed his eyes and was ambushed by a clear dream with Jarl in it. He opened his eyes, tired of cringing, made himself straighten his limbs and lay still, not knowing whether to hope for death, or rescue, or simple abandonment. He wanted to get out into space. But Reetion docks were not like Gelack ones. He needed the Reetions to release him.

"Let me go," he pleaded.

"Von?" It was Lurol's voice, sounding genuinely anguished and concerned. "Please, open your hatch again. I'm sorry about ... it was ..." She broke off, and said desperately, "Just let me help!"

"Is Ann okay?" Von asked, voice wavering. Why did he always have to wilt like a cut flower! Mira used to tell him that he cried too easily. The thought of Mira hit like a fall on the dance floor.

He had lost H'Reth down the jump but the past was still immutable. Only the compulsion had left him. He hugged himself, rocking back and forth as the Reetions kept yammering away at him, while the zero-G was making him light-headed.

"Help Ann!" he worked himself up to order Lurol. "I won't listen and I won't talk to any of you again until I hear her!"

There was an abashed silence. Then Lurol said, "That may take some time, at least a half an hour."

"Fine!" he said.

"All right," said Lurol, sounding nervous. "If you promised you won't do anything silly. Just rest."

"Fine," he said again, sulkily. Heartsick and dizzy, he drifted in and out of bizarre dreams in which Mira advised him on how to commit suicide.

He was so sure the Ayrium alternative was obsolete that it gave him a bad start when her voice intruded.

"Hi, Von," she said, sounding cheerful. "Sorry about the long silence there. Took me a while to convince your hosts to quit jamming me, but a buzz around their station made them friendlier. You see, they aren't at all convinced we know how to conduct ourselves honorably."

"Pardon?" Von echoed, bewildered.

"You know your Demish poetry?" asked Ayrium.

Poetry? Von thought. But one did not argue with a client's eccentricities.

"Some," he said cautiously, not wanting to sound boastful. He had memorized every line he had ever been exposed to.

"What did Liander tell Prince Farsil about the virtues of potential misbehavior, act one, scene three, in Larthin's *Comedy of Desires*?" asked Ayrium.

Oh-kay, Von thought, *whatever else she is, she really is Demish.*

He mustered the quotation readily. "Liander says: 'To commit an act that is *okal'a'ni*? Indeed, that is quite fatal both to lady's love and thine own, manly honor, but seeming — '"

"Whoa! Stop there," said Ayrium. "You're hired."

Von was taken aback, the rest of the quote stalled on the tip of his tongue: — *but seeming can fetch those results that doing might preclude enjoying.*

"You're going to engage your *rel* drive in dock," Ayrium instructed him.

"I'm what?" Von spluttered.

"Or would you rather stay put until you expire?" asked Ayrium. "This way, if they won't let you go, at least you'll take them with you!"

Von was horrified. Only an unspeakable, *okal'a'ni* maniac would do something so terrible! It would be soul-death for a Sevolite. He wasn't sure what the rules were for commoners but that hardly mattered. There were so many people on *Second Contact Station* and so many more yet to live on it!

He twitched his head away from a drifting string of blood gems as the quote played through his head again, then it struck him — bluff! That's what Ayrium was telling him!

"Let me go!" he declared in Reetion. "Or I'll engage my *rel*-drive. Right here. In dock. I'm warning you!"

"Really?" Lurol answered him with chilly skepticism. "You want me to believe you would destroy this station after bringing Ann here for treatment?" She added more compassionately, "You wouldn't even kill me, and you've got better motivation for it."

Von gasped, and was suddenly a child again in the baiting ring with leering faces slashing past him. He regained the present with the sound of Lurol's voice, cajoling. " — didn't extend human rights to you. It should never have allowed me to do what I did. I stand by my decisions but I meant you no harm. I will do all I can to correct the damage."

Von slammed the heels of his hands to his temples, teeth gritted. He did not want Lurol in his head again. The idea made him shake all over.

"I will, too!" he cried. "I'll skim out of here! I don't care if it kills everybody!"

Reetion voices babbled in a collage of emotion inter-spersed with the calm voice of an arbiter.

"That boy," Lurol's voice cut through, "will not destroy a populated station. There is no way. It's just not in his psych profile. He's making threats because he's frightened."

Von thought about the sword in the back of the chair again.

"I'd be more worried about suicide," said Lurol. "If, that is, he had some means to do it that was painless."

She was right, he thought hopelessly. *He couldn't!*

A clear dream struck. He thrashed in his flight harness, uttering noises appropriate to a beating. He came to him-self blinking spots out of his eyes and listening to the roar of his own blood in his ears, feeling exhausted. In a poem, this would have been the right time for the hero to pass away gracefully, but Von suspected he would last a long time even if he managed to overcome his squeamishness enough to open veins with the sword. Sticking it through a vital organ, he felt pretty sure, was beyond him. Then he remembered the ship's moss would stop recycling oxygen in dock. He wouldn't have that long to wait after all. But he wasn't opening the hatch to any Reetion.

"Don't listen to Lurol!" Ann's voice fetched his attention.

Von perked up, warm relief inspired by the vigor in her voice over the radio. At least coming back had been worth something.

"I've flown with him," Ann's disembodied voice weighed into the argument. "He might have been what Lurol thinks, but that's before she messed with him. He's dangerous now! He's gone mad!"

Von's lips parted to assure Ann he was not that crazy, really, and closed again. Maybe she, too, was bluffing, to help him. Still, he wished he knew whether she really believed what she was saying.

"We could release him," Jon said, anxiously, "It's not a core governance issue. He isn't our responsibility. And if he *is* crazy —"

"He's not dangerous!" Lurol objected, her voice intense with her own emotional imperatives. "Von is more likely to sacrifice himself for us than kill us, even if the compulsion has spent itself! He needs to be treated. He's a hazard to himself the way he —"

Von heard a loud crack, a quick series of smacking sounds, and Jon's astonished voice exclaiming, "You hit her. You hit Lurol!"

"Let the crew vote!" Ann cried. "It's debatable! Go to a referendum!"

"Ann!" Von surged up against the restraint of his flight harness.

"Spare not opportunity!" Ayrium's voice quoted at him.

He knew that one, too. A lady friend said it to Princess Demora when she feigned an injury in order to preoccupy the company so Demora could exchange words with her true love. Demora nearly blew her chance worrying about her friend instead of taking advantage of the moment, as intended.

The radio was gabbling away again. Von tried to isolate the voices and found streams of code that linked with what he instinctively imagined as the living thoughts of arbiters. It frightened him, but apparently this was how Reetions made decisions.

The station notified him that he was clear to go.

"Thank you," he said simply, disbelieving.

"Your release from dock is undertaken counter to the recommendations of medical staff concerning your well-being," said the arbiter, "with sixteen reservations on record by members of the Foreign and Alien collective."

Von wet his lips, heart in his throat, concentrating on his breathing.

"Release is authorized by virtue of a station referendum, which passed with a 70 percent majority. Threshold, under natural disaster protocols, was 45 percent in favor with no more than two reservations, with simple majority standing. Stand by for instructions."

The ambulance bay air flushed into vacuum. Von waited, fearful of spoiling the miracle, but unwilling to go without knowing whether Ann would suffer.

"I want — may I speak with Ann?" he summoned the courage to relieve his anxiety.

"Request being negotiated," answered the arbiter.

Von had no idea if that was good or hopeless. Instructions intervened. He worked at doing what the docking persona told him without panic.

The station ejected him with a blast of forced air the way it had last time. The acceleration was light, but he still felt better momentarily. Then he was weightless again, drifting away from the Reetion station.

"Hi, Beauty," Ann's voice greeted him over the radio. "Guess I'm going to be Supervised a long time." She paused. "It was worth it."

"Will they let you go if I surrender?" he asked, committed to making the sacrifice if necessary, but mortally terrified.

"It's okay," she answered with difficulty. "They won't actually hurt me. Just ... come see me sometime, will you?"

"I'll — try," Von promised, meaning it and knowing it would not be possible. He promised whole-heartedly anyway — even the powerless had the right to swear to their intentions.

"Don't forget me," Ann said plaintively.

How could I possibly? Von wondered.

Lurol's voice cut in. "I want to help you."

Von ignored her and engaged enough to start cat clawing, feeling the pounding in his head diminish as he gained acceleration. Ayrium D'Ander D'Aur was waiting at the edge of the challenge sphere.

"Can you fly?" she asked. "Safely?"

He knew she meant reality skimming. "Yes," he said, "I think so."

"Let's go then," she told him. "I'll lead. You follow."

He decided to enjoy the trip, since he would probably never be allowed in a cockpit again, and certainly not in a ship like Larren's *rel*-fighter. Apart from missing Ann, he slowly realized that he might be looking forward to improvements. There were worse things than having a pirate for a patron, and while there were people he would miss at court, being rid of H'Reth was such a miracle he couldn't entirely take it in. And how bad could Ayrium be if she enjoyed Demoran poetry enough to memorize it?

While his airlock was cycling, after docking with *Vanilla Rose*, he devoted himself to a critical review, professionally. His shirt concerned him. It was decorated to imply he was Liege Monitum. It was also bloody, and smelled of his ridiculous vanilla odor. He didn't want Ayrium thinking he used women's perfume. He whipped the shirt off and used it to swab his armpits before upending himself to stuff the incriminating garment into the tank of ship's moss, for lack of a better disposal option.

There was dried blood on his scuffed knuckles but the best he could do was to rub off the crumbly parts without starting the deeper cuts bleeding, and use his fingernails to clean each other. He considered, but balked at, cleaning his nails with his teeth, because he had never liked the taste of blood. He ran his fingers through his hair and shook it out. He was sure that he still looked a mess by court standards, but after all this wasn't court. Maybe he would pass.

Ann had his flight jacket, but he knew his dancer's physique would stand up to inspection. He had more qualms about the flight pants, but greeting Ayrium stark naked would probably not be appropriate, however unusual she was for a Demish woman. Besides, she already knew he had trespassed on Sevolite privilege by impersonating Liege Monitum, but with luck there would be people on *Vanilla Rose* who would confirm that H'Reth made him do it to deceive the Reetions.

His worst fear was that she would find out what else H'Reth had used him for. If she did she was bound to reject him at the very least, and he found that he wanted her to like him. She had saved him from something that he feared worse than death, and he liked her forthright confidence.

The airlock finished cycling and there was no further excuse not to slide down the access tube and get out. Von landed and sprang to his feet in the inner airlock chamber, the air cool on his bare chest. The door to the outer airlock chamber was still closed.

I can do this, he thought, staring at the door that led to Ayrium. *And who knows? If I stay in the Reach of Paradise I might see Ann again one day after all. She might visit. Ayrium might lend me to her.*

His ears burned imagining what Eva would have to say about his professionalism, and hoped things had gone well for her with Di Mon. The door between airlocks began to open. *I can do this*, Von told himself, more convincingly, ready for anything —

— but not a roomful of excited Demish stationers who inhaled as one when they laid eyes on him.

The fine hairs on the back of his neck stood on end. All he could think was that they knew he had been H'Reth's *slaka* or else they had discovered that he had killed Jarl, or maybe they were simply out to make up for the lynching he had deprived them of when he saved Ann.

If he wasn't dancing, Von was terrified of eager crowds. They reminded him of the Bear Pit, in this case so vividly that he felt a clear dream coming on and thought, *No, not now!*

A nobleborn pushed forward, moving bodies clear to either side. He was wearing flight leathers, his sword strapped on his hip and a starry look in his dark blue eyes. The people he disturbed moved aside gently, staring at Von. He recognized some of their faces, but they looked at him as if they had never seen him before. He was afraid to breathe for fear some error on his part would turn them into a mob.

The advancing nobleborn stopped and drew his sword.

I am going to faint, Von realized with disgust. Heroes in classic poems never fainted when offered an honorable way out! Of course, he was only a courtesan, not someone any poet would bother to write about, and he also suspected that few real Demish princes lived up to the standards of their literary counterparts. But if he had to die he would really rather do it with some style despite his birth rank.

The nobleborn sank to his knees, holding out his sword in both hands. "Pureblood Amel," he intoned, "grandson of the last Blue Demish Pureblood; great-grandson of the living, Golden Emperor; descendant of Ameron and wronged son of the reigning Ava, I beg you to accept the oath of Ron D'An, a Midlord hitherto of Liege H'Reth's oath, whose life you saved and whose soul you have blessed with your touch."

Von found inhaling out of the question. All he could do was spring back, close the airlock in the face of the worshipful man, and lodge up against the side of Larren's berthed *rel*-fighter. When he finally had to breathe, he hyperventilated, palms against the comfortingly solid hullsteel at his back.

He had heard about Amel, of course. But impersonating Di Mon had been bad enough! He wasn't up for playing Pureblood Amel, not even for Ayrium.

The airlock opened and a large, handsome woman stepped through, wearing a sword and dressed in flight leathers. She had short blond hair, a clear complexion, and bright blue eyes.

"Are you okay?" she asked, speaking up to him with the two step differencing suffix a Highlord owed a Pureblood.

His stunned look fetched a hissing sigh out of her. "Are you all right, Von?" she tried again, reverting to the indistinguishable *rel*-to-*pol* address she had used with him over the radio, which was confusing enough since she should be down-speaking him by five ranks. "Oh, please," she urged him anxiously, "say something."

"Are you Ayrium D'Ander D'Aur?" he asked, with proper commoner-to-Highlord grammar.

She grinned. "That's right. Yes."

He murmured an appreciative, "Wow." Ayrium dressed roughly for a Demish woman, but she was stunning when she smiled. He couldn't fathom why she would need a courtesan.

Ayrium gave him a pained look, "I didn't realize this was going to be so hard!" she complained aloud, and stiffened, seeing Von react. "Don't faint! Okay. Just don't."

He pulled himself together, face flushed. "The people in the outer airlock," he asked. "What's that about?"

Ayrium inhaled deeply, swelling her chest which Von found irresistibly interesting. He had never met a Demish woman of her rank, or build, who tried to fit herself into flight leathers. "You made quite an impression on Midlord D'An," she said. "Saving him after he was sure he was already lost."

Von waited for his brain to turn over, grateful Ayrium seemed prepared to give him time for that. "I hope he'll be all right," Von said, at last.

"All right?" Ayrium echoed puzzled.

"Well, he seems a bit dazed. That is, he said he thought that I was —" Von made a spinning gesture with one hand.

"The missing Prince Amel?" prompted Ayrium.

Von bit his lower lip until it hurt enough to stave off a clear dream or more tears. "Please," he said, "I've just been through pretending to be Di Mon and that wasn't my idea, either. Please don't say you really want me to pretend to be Prince Amel. That would be loads worse. I mean, there are people on this crew who know me, and Amel was a Demish prince, wasn't he? I've got gray eyes and black hair."

"Actually," Ayrium said, circling closer as Von turned, "so did Amel. He had gray eyes and silky black hair, as a baby. Just like yours."

"He did?" Von bleated.

"Yes," said Ayrium. She folded her leather clad arms. "Amel has some Vrellish blood through his mother. People thought Demish coloring would be dominant, which was one of the reasons the Demish, particularly, were easy to convince that he couldn't be Delm's son. Sometimes a superficial detail like that can blind people to the obvious. For example," she smiled at him, "you're beautiful."

Von managed a mumbled, "Uh, thanks," feeling no more secure about anything than he had before she brought it up.

"You look a lot like the Golden Emperor," said Ayrium. "That is, to go by some very old pictures of him. Dad's never let me actually lay eyes on Fahild for fear I'd frighten him too much." She set her arms akimbo, pulling his stare into her waist and out over her hips and thighs. "Or set foot on Demora, for that matter," she said, and gave a rough laugh. "We hybrids have it rough."

Von experimented with an encouraging smile.

"Look," Ayrium firmed up, shifting her stance to set a hand on her sword. "This is ridiculous — I can't keep talking to you like you were a commoner."

Von thought that over, trying it this way and that. Then he blurted, stumped and getting desperate, "Why not?"

"Because you *are* Amel! You got that?" She was speaking up to him again with two-level differencing suffixes, which felt like being stuck with sharp pins. There were only two known Purebloods in the empire, not counting Fahild on Demora, and whatever might be running around uncatalogued in Red Reach. He felt as if he might be struck down by one of the Watching Dead any minute for insulting all of Sevildom.

"I thought it was incredible myself, at first," she went on, jarring him with every pronoun. "But looking at you, I can't understand how Fountain Court could be so blind!" She threw up her hands. "I mean, dear gods! There you were performing for them in a dancer's sheath, right under a portrait of Delm in all likelihood!" She shook her head. "You are Amel. And you are Ava Delm's son."

Von was speechless.

Ayrium spread the fingers of one large, shapely hand, counting points off. "One, Ron D'An experienced a Soul of Light. Two, you fly pretty well for a commoner."

Amel flushed with pleasure at that, and then blanched again.

"Three," she said. "There's Jarl."

"Jarl!" Von exclaimed, in alarm.

Ayrium grinned at him. "Good job."

Von blinked, incredulous. "It was?"

Ayrium barreled on. "Four, Liege Monitum claims he's got physiological data from the Reetion gadget that confirms you must be highborn."

"Reetion gadget?" Von echoed.

Ayrium scowled. "Let's skip that part for now." She dropped her hand. "Believe me, dear Von, you are Pureblood Amel, lost in infancy and raised as a commoner on Gelion. I'd bet my beating heart on it. You are, like it or not."

Liking it isn't the issue, Von thought. *It is coping with a patron who is stark, raving mad.*

Ayrium looked at him soberly and asked, "What did you think I wanted you for?"

"Uh ..." said Von, not at all sure there was a right answer to that question, "to provide entertainment. I'm a sword dancer."

Ayrium looked him over with the first real, patron-like interest she had demonstrated thus far. "And I bet you are very good," she told him.

"I am," he said, sure of his ground for the first time in the conversation.

"*I am,*" she corrected his grammar in the direction of implying he was Pureblood, then gave up and rubbed her nose. "Okay, I can see this is going to take time. So try this on: I'm a nut case, and I want to celebrate capturing this station with a little fancy dress up gala. With me so far?"

Von nodded slowly, feeling dubious.

"Everybody out there," said Ayrium, pointing towards the outer airlock, "has been told to act as if you were the real Pureblood Amel, on pain of getting booted out to take a space walk. Understand?"

Von nodded again, although he didn't think that she believed a word of what she was saying.

"So," said Ayrium, "your first assignment in my employ is to get through that crowd with me, to my quarters, playing up the role of being Amel." She winked at him as lewdly as someone with her robustly sunny disposition could. "Do it just to put me in the mood. Think you can do that?"

"Yes, Your Grace," Von agreed. There didn't seem to be any other course, and maybe if he stuck it out as far as a shower and a night's sleep, he could figure out why she still believed that he was Pureblood Amel.

He touched his naked chest, "I'm underdressed for the occasion."

"Kid," said Ayrium, "don't worry. I suspect you would look like a Demoran idol dressed in greasy overalls. Besides," her cheeks dimpled as she flashed her wide smile, "it'll add a touch of realism. See, the way the story goes you've just been rescued from one hell of a mess." Her tone softened. "Working as a courtesan, kidnapped off Gelion, captured by Reetions."

Von shivered.

"Sorry," Ayrium said quickly.

"It's all right." Von faltered, and tossed his hair back. "It's your story."

She continued to look sympathetic. "I wouldn't have written it like that, Amel, believe me."

He averted his eyes, afraid she knew he had been H'Reth's bed boy.

"Come on," she said, stepping in to take his hand and give it a reassuring squeeze. "Stick close." He overcame his shame enough to look up and smile faintly. Whatever she knew, she didn't seem disgusted by him. Ayrium led him into the outer airlock.

Ron D'An was still kneeling where he had been rejected. He lifted his head as they appeared, hope in his face and the tracks of tears beneath his dark blue eyes. He didn't move as Ayrium led Von towards him.

"Immortality?" D'An asked uncertainly, gazing up into Von's face.

"He accepts your devotion," Ayrium told him. "He's just a bit — shy."

Shy? Von thought, looking at her, offended. *Courtesans aren't shy!*

Ayrium gave his hand a little tug. "Come on."

People bowed as they made room, all eerily quiet. Von wondered at their strange expressions. The crew of *Vanilla Rose* had never struck him as a repository of such serious acting talent.

They believe this! Von realized with alarm. *They really think I am this Pureblood Amel!* He held Ayrium's hand a little tighter.

A cry of anguish made them both start. Von recognized the source immediately. It was a nobleborn he was slightly acquainted with whose name was Arl. The last time he had seen Arl was when he had docked on Vanilla Rose looking for Ann. Now Arl came stumbling through the bodies lining their path to collapse at Von's feet, clutching at the bottom of his flight pants.

Ayrium jerked Von back, looking annoyed. She had her sword half drawn in her other hand, but shoved it contemptuously into its sheath again as the distraught man fell forward on his face in a deep bow.

"Forgive me, Soul of Light," he wept with heart-wrenching sincerity, "I meant no wrong."

"What's the matter with him?" Von hissed at Ayrium, not taking his eyes from Arl.

"He's harmless," she assured him. "Just a Family of Light devotee. Seems he called you something less than dignified last time he saw you."

"He said I was a lucky whore," Von recalled. The prostrate man struck his forehead on the ground. He reared up, tearing at his hair with both hands and issuing piteous moans.

Von flinched. "Does he have to do that?" he whispered to Ayrium.

She said, "You could stop him." The "you" said a lot in Gelack. *You who are my superior by two birth-ranks. You could make him stop.*

Von's brow furrowed, but the noise Arl was making was too heart-rending to ignore. He knelt and coaxed Arl up, taking him gingerly by the elbow, still instinctively expecting to be hit for the presumption.

"Please don't?" he asked him mildly, and let Arl go, sustaining only eye contact. That was unsettling enough.

"You forgive me?" the Midlord blurted in a warm gush, using a "you" that not only accounted for their respective birth ranks, but added something Von recognized from his fondness for poetry — an honorific reserved for the Family of Light.

The cloying, sticky need in the words made Von too uncomfortable to quibble. He muttered, "Yes, of course, sure," and was grateful to feel Ayrium take charge and start them forward again.

"Nobody said," she muttered under her breath, "that babysitting Souls of Light set loose in a nasty universe was going to be easy work."

He trotted to keep up with her brisk pace. "You're angry with me," he fretted, forgetting to speak down to her in his contriteness. He didn't know what he had done, but he was sure it was a mistake.

"Just smile, and nod, and try to stop talking like a commoner," Ayrium instructed through her teeth.

"Okay," he promised.

They made it through the crowd in the outer airlock, through a couple of crowded landings, and into beautifully empty corridors kept that way by posted guards who followed Von with their eyes as he walked past.

He was grateful when they finally reached the suite of rooms where Ayrium had set up housekeeping. Ayrium posted guards at the door with orders to see to it that they were left alone.

Inside, she threw herself down on a couch in the forward lounge. "I need a drink," she said. "How about you?"

He spotted a liquor cabinet webbed down with Demoran gossamer and willingly sprang to wait on her. Ayrium gathered her breath to protest, but gave up and just smiled, even answering his questions without insisting on Pureblood Amel grammar. He served her a mixed drink with a stir stick, topped with a square of fruit preserve and sat down near her, feeling much better.

"Thanks," Ayrium said, looking at him in a fond, wistful manner.

"Can I do anything else for you?" he asked her. "I know how to massage post-flight pilots."

Ayrium reached out a long, work-roughened finger to sweep a few strands of silky black hair clear of his crystalline gray eyes. "Don't tempt me," she said. "Dad would kill me."

She put down her drink and got up, squaring herself to look down at him. "This suite should have a comfortable bed and shower," she explained. "If you're hungry, ring. I picked the least excitable servants I could find to assign to you. I'll be available if you need me for anything, at least until we've jumped back into Killing Reach and I've settled *Vanilla Rose* down as the Purple Alliance's latest acquisition." She grinned. "On your behalf."

He let that pass. What registered was that she was going to leave. "These aren't your quarters?" he asked.

"They're yours," she said. "I hope they suit you. I didn't think you'd want to use the admiralty suite."

"You aren't staying?" he repeated, alarmed.

"Come here," Ayrium said, and put her arms around him in a firm hug. When she let go she set her large, competent hands on his shoulders. "I'm not angry with you, or dissatisfied, or anything like that." She looked him in the eyes. "Got that?"

"No," he said, honestly.

She ruffled his hair. "You will," she said. "Eventually. You think I'm bad? Wait until dad gets hold of you! He'll be dumping a whole freight-load of High Demoran culture on you." She laughed a little. "I'd relax and rest up while you're able, Immortality."

Von resisted the urge to whimper at the Pureblood title.

Ayrium laughed again. "You poor kid! Listen, I'm your friend. Okay? Believe that."

His heart lightened a little at this reassurance. He believed her. He had never met anyone so much like a Golden Demish prince — except she was female. But that was a bonus to him. "Okay," he answered.

"Got to go now," said Ayrium. "I've got work to do. You need a doctor?"

Von shook his head. She smiled again and really left this time.

He looked around him in amazement at the lush drapery on the walls, luxurious upholstery and soft, floral carpet that were all his, just to relax in and enjoy, alone. It felt too good to be true.

Ayrium stuck her head back in again. "And another thing," she told Von, as he spun around, "you have the Family of Light's own exclusive body odor. How's that for proof?"

Von blushed violently over his whole exposed skin surface. Ayrium laughed again and closed the door.

The first thing I do, Von thought, *is shower*!

Ayrium opened the door and leaned in again, hand on the knob. *"Vanilla Rose?"* she prompted, "and the Demoran taste in perfume, which influences H'Usian court fashion? Think about it."

Von's ears were radiating in mortification.

"Oh, I give up!" exclaimed Ayrium and slammed the door.

Just about the time Von had decided it was safe to look for the bath, she made her last appearance. "And it smells very nice," she told him, "so you can stop going pink when I mention it." The door closed without slamming this time.

Von sat down on the couch, picked up Ayrium's abandoned drink, and stared at it, waiting for the turmoil she had caused in him to settle down.

It didn't, so he drank the cocktail so fast it made him cough.

Okal Rel

Ranar lost the jury-rigged connection to the medical data on the info-blit and sat back to straighten aching shoulders. The blit reverted to displaying Von's perspective of his conscience bonding at the age of ten but the sound was off so Ranar barely noticed.

It must be nearly morning, he thought, *or whatever passes for it in UnderGelion*.

A woman's gasp made him look up to see Eva, dressed in pajamas, and probably expecting to find Di Mon in the library. But it was the direction of Eva's stare that raised a prickling feeling across Ranar's back. Slowly, he turned around to find Sarilous behind him, leveling a weapon that looked something like a spring-loaded version of a crossbow. Ranar has not seen her enter and had no idea how long she had been in the room. Her face was stark with hatred, but she seemed ill; perhaps even about to collapse.

"Bond conflict!" Eva said breathlessly, speaking English. "Sarilous, no!"

"I am bonded to the office," Sarilous repeated like a mantra, sweat showing at her hairline, "not the man."

"But Di Mon is Monitum!" Eva cried in alarm.

"Go back to his bedroom, *lyka*," the *gorarelpul* ordered.

She wants to kill me, Ranar realized. Based on the Monatese logs, he guessed the weapon that Sarilous held was a needle gun. Its bolt was too narrow to kill unless expertly delivered, but it was common to augment its efficacy with a chemical payload. It was also a dishonorable insult; an assault outside the bounds of Sword Law.

On the blit's display, Von was about to be dragged from the office of his foster father to be conscience bonded, shouting hysterically — in silence.

"Sarilous," Eva pleaded, "don't do this! He needs you! Whatever the problem, I will do my best to influence Di Mon to see reason!"

"Influence him?" Sarilous barked, harshly and narrowed her eyes. "You have no idea, woman."

Ranar turned on the blit's sound.

"Why!" Von's recorded voice shrieked. "What have I done!"

Sarilous' attention flickered.

Ranar meant to swing Di Mon's chair at her weapon but he underestimated its weight. All he managed was to get it between him and the silver bolt that shot from her gun. It was blind luck that the poisoned needle stuck in a slat.

"It is not what you've done," the dispassionate voice of the college dean spoke out of Von's captured memory. "It is what you are."

Sarilous crumbled.

Eva stared, fixated by the distress in Von's familiar voice coming from the little silver box. Ranar turned the sound off. Eva dropped down beside Sarilous.

"She's dead," Eva reported, still in English, looking thunderstruck.

A heart attack? Ranar wondered. *No. The conscience bond. She tried to disobey Di Mon.*

"Why?" Eva demanded. "Why did she want you dead?"

I must lie to her, Ranar realized. It was a novel thought. Telling lies was not a skill one practiced much beneath the scrutiny of arbiters. All Ranar could manage was, "I mean no harm to Monitum, and certainly not to Di Mon."

Eva's wide-eyed stare shifted from the dead *gorarelpul* to the blit playing silently once more upon the table. Ranar turned off the projection. Eva staggered up off the floor.

"I could use a drink," said Eva, with a nod towards a liquor cabinet.

Ranar obliged without thinking what it might mean, socially, to wait upon her. She reciprocated by becoming imperious about directing how he mixed the drink. To establish he wasn't a servant, he poured a drink for himself, as well.

"What are you doing in the library?" Eva demanded when she had taken a few long sips of her stiff drink. "The library is allowed only to family and intimates."

Ranar found he did not like what that implied about Eva, especially as he knew Di Mon would much prefer to love a woman. The discovery that he could be jealous disconcerted him.

"Di Mon required my assistance with the info-blit," he said as neutrally as possible.

"Blit?" Eva nodded towards the table. "You mean that thing with Von's voice on it?" She fingered her drink nervously, studying Ranar. "The Lorels used to force secrets out of Demish prisoners with science like that and turn Vrellish ones against their own kind. That's why people distrust *TouchGate Hospital*, even though some continue to rely on the connection Monitum maintains with *TouchGate* for medical services." She clutched her glass tighter. "Why is Von's voice coming out of it!"

He told her all that Von, himself, had been able to divulge about H'Reth and the conscience bond via the record on the info-blit.

Eva never once asked a question until the end. "Von's in Killing Reach, then?" she asked. "On the *Vanilla Rose*?"

"More likely on *Second Contact Station*," said Ranar. "It is my people who cured him of his conscience bond, and extracted the data on the info-blit."

"Reetions are Lorels, then," Eva said with a shudder, looking past him towards the body of the old *gorarepul*. Her eyes filled up with tears. "I should be angry with Von! Conscience bonded! And helping the H'Reths' rise to power while he worked out of my den!" She pressed a hand over her mouth, and held still a moment until she dared to lower it again. "He tried to warn me, I think," she said sadly, "from time to time."

Eva needed a counselor. Sarilous needed to be taken care of. It was indecent to leave her body laying there. On Rire, first responders would have shown up by now to do all those things for him. But there was no one but him to take care of it.

Ranar floundered. "Di Mon has gone to Killing Reach to look for Von," he offered.

"What?" Eva asked, baffled. "Why?"

"Di Mon thinks Von might be someone of significance, politically," Ranar explained. "A child who went missing in infancy and is being hunted by his father now that he has come to his attention. I am not sure I understand all the details, but I understand the attack on Den Eva's was to eliminate Vretla's child, because even such a child would be enough to prove Von is this missing infant, Prince Amel. You don't believe me?" Ranar finished, worried by Eva's blank stare.

"No," she said, in stunned quietude. "I do believe you. It makes ... a hideous kind of sense." She broke eye contact, shaking her head. "Von was so beautiful; so strong. He learned so effortlessly. He was even starting to smell of — " She broke off, looking like a woman condemned to death. "Gods," she exclaimed in a dull staccato. "I had him sterilized. Twice. The grandson of a Soul of Light! I will be flogged to death on Ava's Square!"

Ranar knelt in front of her.

"Do Sevolites expect their courtesans to be sterilized?" he asked gently, aware he was asking her a question about herself that was painful and personal, or ought to have been. She nodded, still looking stunned with dread.

"Then you did nothing wrong, by your own standards," said Ranar.

She swallowed slowly, staring at him, and finally said as if the weight of it should quash his careful reasoning, "But he's Amel!"

"What is so important about being Amel?" Ranar retaliated with a touch of impatience.

"Of course," she said, briskly, with the aplomb of a true survivor. "You're Reetion. You have been out of touch with civilization for two hundred years."

That is not how I'd put it, Ranar thought.

Eva put her glass away from her. "Von didn't like me drinking too much," she said, blinking rapidly.

"It is important to Di Mon we prove that Von is Amel," Ranar told her. "Is there anything you know that could help?"

"Me?" Eva scoffed. "Convince Fountain Court?" She laughed as if he had made a joke at her expense. "Blood and swords make truth on Gelion, Reetion. And without blood proof, I don't thing even Di Mon's sword will make the Demish listen. Delm matters too much to them and Von too little. You need living proof, that can't be called a Lorel trick."

Of course, Ranar thought ruefully. *I, of all people, should understand that proof must be culturally meaningful.*

"Is it possible there is another child?" Ranar asked, feeling strange to be pursuing such a subject. Children did not get misplaced on Rire, or used as evidence in criminal trials.

"Let's see," said Eva, "there's Vretla and Lady H'Reth — we know what happened to them. Before that there was Lady H'Ran's complaint. She's an old favorite Von kept seeing even after he racked up two Fountain Court lieges as clients. We all assumed H'Ran got pregnant by a Sevolite lover and was simply trying to blame Von. But H'Ran had an abortion, even though Delm refused to give her leave to do it."

"I see." Ranar envied Eva her detachment. "Any ... others?"

"Let me think," said Eva. "Commoners can get sterility drugs for free. It's policy, to reduce births among servants on Gelion. The first time, I used those on Von. But the second time I had him surgically sterilized. He had trouble from time to time after that, which I thought was just the usual infections and treated accordingly." Her expression hardened. "Gods. He was probably at risk for regenerative cancer. But his body must have reabsorbed the false starts until it took properly. He can't have been fertile long. What does that leave, apart from the women I've mentioned? He didn't work as much once he established himself as a star. There might have been a space drunk Vrellish pilot, now and then, who took off again the next day, killing anything Von might have started. Or maybe a besotted servant girl who wasn't —" Eva caught her breath suddenly. Then she exclaimed, "Kath!"

"Who?" asked Ranar.

"Kath was a novice," she explained, breathless with excitement. "She and another girl got pregnant while Von was bed training them for Vrellish customers. That's how I found out he was fertile the first time. I thought he had palmed his drugs. I was so angry with him." Eva swallowed, banishing distracting qualms now she knew that she was speaking about a regenerative highborn. "One of the girls was a dancer and eager to accept my help securing an abortion. But Kath was determined to have her child and Von helped her. He was gone for a day. When he got back, I had him surgically sterilized."

"Would people at Den Eva's know about Kath's baby?" Ranar asked, alarmed.

"Some of them, yes," Eva admitted. "But Paladin Thoth was asking about recent clients. They might not think to mention a novice who ran away two years before."

"I don't think we can afford to count on —" began Ranar.

A commotion broke out in the hall, spiked with shouts that pierced the library walls.

"The Vrellish," Eva cried, in alarm. "They're in Green Hearth."

"How did they get in?" Ranar asked, disconcerted. He had felt oddly safe in Di Mon's library.

"Through Green Pavilion," Eva answered. "There is no highborn at home to deny them entrance."

Okal Rel again, thought Ranar, with an odd thrill. The whole system was based on trust but was bent on enabling murder. *Time to start working with it*, he decided.

"Will an honorable highborn kill a commoner?" Ranar asked.

"Sometimes," said Eva, and frowned. "If the commoner acts very foolishly."

"You will have to translate for me," Ranar instructed.

"Pardon?"

"Unless you have a better idea?"

"Better than what?" demanded Eva.

The voices in the hall were getting louder.

"Just translate for me," Ranar ordered, and pulled her through the open door after him.

A knot of people with drawn swords blocked the corridor outside Kertatt's bedroom. Kertatt himself stood with his torso wrapped in bandages, holding his sword drawn in his left hand. He was flanked by Green Hearth errants. Elsewhere, faces peered through doors, held ajar, or watched from the opening of the Throat where a bunch of them were lodged in one fleshy lump. All servants, or lesser Sevolite guests and retainers, Ranar surmised. People who were not expected to risk their lives by the prevailing social rules.

Confronting Kertatt were two of the most extremely Vrellish-looking Sevolites Ranar could imagine. The leader was more muscular than Di Mon, but definitely female to judge by the contours of her prominent genital mound and small, firm breasts. She wore an embroidered vest open over bare skin in exactly the same style as her male companion, whose pants were also generously filled out. He had a healing wound along the ribs that looked angry enough to have bared bone, a beaded headband and tinsel strands of shiny color tangled in his black hair.

The female fixed her attention on Ranar the moment she spotted his dark face. And glared.

"Who is she?" Ranar asked Eva.

"Liege Sert of Red Vrel," Eva whispered, "Vretla's clan mother." He could feel her shaking and suspected she was wise to be afraid. But the Red Vrellish struck him as magnificent! Sert seemed equally intrigued with his brown skin. She said something bold in Gelack, addressing him.

Kertatt answered her, using the word Reetion and snapped orders at Eva.

"We have to go back to the library," Eva translated, tugging Ranar in that direction.

"No!" Ranar stepped forward, sustaining eye contact with the Vrellish leader. "I need to talk to you," he declared.

Kertatt flushed angrily. "Take him away," he ordered an errant.

L'Ket stepped forward to obey, and was blocked by the Red Vrellish male who heaved her up and backward into Srain. The two of them went down with a lot of noise, smashing into a table.

Kertatt attacked. Sert grabbed his blade with her free right hand, yanking it out of his grasp. Then she backhanded him into the bedroom and left him sprawled across the doorway with his legs sticking out into Family Hall, moaning with the pain of his burns.

The Monatese are leaderless now, Ranar realized, *and it is my fault for interfering when I barely know what's going on*!

Sert barked something in Ranar's direction.

"Tell her I am Ranar of Rire," Ranar instructed Eva, "an explorer brought here by the Demish and the house guest of Liege Monitum." As an afterthought he added, "Don't use commoner pronouns for me."

"What?" said Eva.

"Refer to me as her equal."

"Are you mad?" Eva exclaimed in horror.

"I need her to listen to me," Ranar urged. "Do what I ask."

Eva inhaled bravely and turned to speak to the Vrellish hearth invader.

Sert listened. Then she stepped closer, put out a hand towards Ranar then lowered it with a frown.

"She wants to know if your color is contagious," said Eva, "if you are here to spread disease or other *okal'a'ni* evils."

"Ask her if Liege Monitum would have me as his guest if I was *okal'a'ni*," Ranar suggested.

Eva looked at him with trepidation, but she did it and reported back again. "Liege Sert says she is here because she doubts the honor of Liege Monitum." Eva told him, shaking.

"Tell her she is here because she is angry," said Ranar. "Tell her Liege Monitum shares her anger. Ask her if she wants to catch the person responsible for hurting Liege Vrel, her — what did you say she was? — clan daughter?"

Sert listened to Eva's halting translation with a deepening scowl and then interrupted, throwing out an arm for emphasis in a style that made the people watching from door jambs pull their heads in.

"Tell her," Ranar spoke over whatever Sert was saying, "that I know she still respects Di Mon's honor. If she did not, she would not be here with a sword to settle their differences. She would have attacked in space. Tell her that Di Mon will oblige her with a duel when he returns, if that is still her pleasure. Tell her, also, that we need her help to solve the crime committed against Vretla."

If Sert had not encouraged Eva to continue, Ranar doubted she could have made it all the way through his script. A silence ensued when Eva finished. In it, the Vrellish male helped up the Monatese errants he had knocked down and transitioned seamlessly to flirting with L'Ket. Srain objected and got casually elbowed into a wall, spilling a potted plant. L'Ket snapped at him as he struggled up and slugged him across the jaw, lightening the mood among the watchers who seemed to take this as a spectator sport. Even the Red Vrellish male laughed his approval.

Sert sheathed her sword.

"*Ack Rel*," she said boldly, to Ranar, and followed up by smacking her male companion on the arm. "This is Kan. A *mekan'st*."

Eva translated *mekan'st* as lover.

There will be time to study the nuances later, Ranar promised himself, excited by the prospect of a lifetime's raw material for Vrellish anthropology. *If I live*, he reminded himself.

Sert swept Ranar and Eva back with her into the library where she immediately spotted Sarilous, took note of the needle gun and grunted something harsh that might have been "Good riddance!" before laying into Ranar again in Gelack.

"I don't understand," Ranar told her in English, resisting the urge to back away.

"Sert wants to know why you aren't wearing a sword," supplied Eva, recovering her wits.

"Tell her I ... did not bring one with me from Rire," Ranar improvised. "Tell her I did not foresee the need. My people settle our differences peacefully."

Eva relayed that and was asked something else. "Yes?" Ranar prompted when she hesitated. Eva sighed and gave it to him literally, "She wants to know what you taste like."

"She wants to eat me?" Ranar asked, incredulous.

"Not in the nutritional sense," the courtesan assured him. "It's a common slang for sex among Vrellish women. She wants to know if brown men taste different."

"Oh," said Ranar, completely unprepared, and looked at Sert again. "Tell her that we haven't got time," he recommended, "then explain about Von being Amel and how we have to find Kath and her child before Delm."

While Eva launched into that, Ranar dropped into a chair to sort through his emotions. He was impressed with himself, but afraid he was likely to wind up dead before the day was over. Five minutes later, Eva left Sert prowling about before a wall full of books in leather bindings and came to find him.

"She'll help us," reported Eva, and added bleakly, "but only until Di Mon returns — she still intends to fight him over sending Vretla to be treated by Lorels."

Ranar shifted forward. "Even if we can prove that Delm was responsible for the attack on Vretla?"

"I don't know!" Eva said fitfully. "To be honest, Di Mon worries me as much as Sert does."

"What do you mean?" Ranar asked.

"Just that I think he would like to cross swords with someone over something. He's so ... tense." She clasped her arms trying to shake off disquieting thoughts that Ranar shared with her, except he knew exactly why Di Mon might be inclined to be reckless — he knew what he was trying to avoid.

Sert and Kan collected them and swept them out of Green Hearth, across the Plaza and down the stairs to the floor of UnderGelion. There were rather a lot of stairs, Ranar found. He made a valiant effort to keep up.

On the floor, Sert commandeered a car by the simple expedient of pulling the Demish driver out. The H'Usian she picked on declined to take the matter up. Kan drove. The best Ranar could say of the experience was that Kan managed not to actually kill anyone, despite intentionally veering at least once to amuse himself by frightening sword-wearing Demish pedestrians. Eva, who seemed able to take this in stride, gave directions.

"We're here," she told Ranar as they pulled up across a wide boulevard and piled out of the car. She pointed across the street to a boxy looking complex with a big enclosed yard. "That's the H'Ran hydroponics farm."

The yard contained tanks of growing vegetables, barely discernable beneath uneven night lights that cast eerie shadows out onto the boulevard. It was towards the end of night cycle and everything seemed peaceful except for a couple of early rising chickens scratching about in the yard.

Sert and Kan started forward, then stopped and turned their heads to listen.

"What?" Ranar hissed at Eva, but she didn't answer. Kan reached back into the car to turn their headlights on.

What do they use for fuel, wondered Ranar. The cars made no exhaust and had no tracks to run on. Everything seemed to operate on some kind of internal battery power. He found himself wishing for Lights Up because the dimness of the artificial night felt strangely hostile. Then, as if in answer, he saw headlights looming larger and heard approaching vehicles.

Eva exclaimed, in fear, "We've been followed."

Two cars pulled up across the boulevard, blocking their way back, while another two swerved around them to block their escape on the other side.

Thoth sprang out of one of the lead cars, backed up by a dozen errants getting out of the other cars. The Vrellish turned to meet him and Sert drew her sword.

But she's hopelessly outnumbered, Ranar despaired, *even if they stick to using swords!*

Neither Sert nor Thoth seemed aware of that. Sert took a step forward and Thoth fell back, arguing and waving his hands.

Combat ritual? Ranar wondered, remembering D'Ander's fight outside Golden Pavillion. *Are there rules?* If so, he wondered how they got enforced because the further Thoth drew Sert in the direction of his errants, the more tense her *mekan'st*, Kan, seemed to get. All at once, Kan frowned and moved back towards his car.

Maybe he plans to use his car against the Demish if they gang up on Sert, Ranar speculated, almost breathless with excitement and ashamed to be so interested.

Suddenly a trio of new cars arrived, marked with heraldic devices other than Delm's rose and sword. *Gelion doesn't have arbiters*, thought Ranar, *but people here certainly take a keen interest in each other*. Prince Hendricks D'Astor led the Demish contingent of spectators, and Ses Nersal the other, shadowed by very two Vrellish looking men wearing bright red claw marks on the breast of a black uniform. "Nersallian highborns," Eva whispered, nodding in the black-clad men's direction.

The sound of bodies pelting up against the mesh fence of the farm made Ranar turn around to see children jostling for places as floodlights from a couple of the new cars lit up the stretch of boulevard Sert and Thoth occupied. The boys pointed, the girls stared, all dressed in clean overalls or aprons. Some adults stood further back, watching with less enthusiasm, but the farm people seemed to know they were immune from any violence they might witness and were not afraid, just interested.

Okal Rel again? Ranar wondered. Eva touched his arm, startling him.

"That's Kath!" she pointed at a young woman standing two rows back in the troughs, staring back at her. Kath had a lively black-haired toddler in her arms who was distracting her by struggling to get down. One good look at Eva and the young mother mastered her child forcefully and bolted.

"Is there a back entrance?" Ranar asked Eva.

"This is it," she said. "There's a lawn out front with a patio entrance."

Ranar took her hand. "Come on."

The insignificance of commoners protected them even when Ranar's hood fell back as he ran, to reveal his brown skin. Everyone was focused on the possible excitement of a duel.

Ranar and Eva made it around the building in time to see Kath darting across the front lawn with the child on her hip and a hastily stuffed bag over her shoulder. Eva gave chase. Ranar bent over with a stitch in his side.

Eva faltered. "Are you —"

They heard a shout behind them. Six palace errants had taken note after all.

Kath stopped to open a gate, gasping and struggling with it and her burdens.

"Go!" Ranar shouted to Eva, forcing himself to straighten. She was an athlete. He wasn't. "Go — get her!" Ranar ordered. "Explain! Take her back — through the building."

"But —" Eva protested.

"Safer in public!" Ranar got out, and gave Eva a shove.

She took off like a bolt from a needle gun while Ranar turned to face the palace errants charging at him with drawn swords.

I am going to die, he thought, feeling that was horribly unfair when he had managed so cleverly, thus far.

A soft buzz, like a swarm of well-mannered insects, filled Ranar's ears and he wondered if he was going to faint before he died, but the noise was not internal. A blur of movement cut between him and the errants and became a small, decorative motorbike. D'Ander hopped off the gilded motorbike with fenders painted in romantic scenes of splendor. He handed the bike to Ranar and cleared the sword he carried slung down his back. The discarded sheath was pretty but the blade looked wicked: a sort of narrow straight-saber sharpened down the top third of its length to a very business-like point. It was a dull gray at the top, glinting in gold gilt further back, and bejeweled about the hilt. The gilding on the end looked like it had worn off.

The gloom of twilight lifted. Not all at once, but still suddenly. D'Ander's golden hair seemed to glow.

Lights up, thought Ranar. It was morning in UnderGelion.

D'Ander frowned. "I've an appointment to keep at Fountain Court," he told the men arrayed against him. "So let's be fast. I give you leave to step beyond your challenge class. Come nobleborns, step up! And be the first to go down!"

This is impossible! Ranar thought, struggling to grasp at Gelack he didn't really understand. *He's outnumbered six to one!*

* * *

Di Mon did not call down from orbit. He made a quiet landing, declaring only his challenge class to the Ava's control tower, and taxied down the highborn docks where he was recognized by the gatekeepers and passed on. He was met at Green Hangar by a messenger who gave him a letter from D'Ander, written in gold ink.

"My contacts in the palace report that Delm is watching Eva," Di Mon read. "I will do what I can if something comes of it. But I must be back to stand challenge for Perry D'Aur. If I am held up, I do not expect you to fight that challenge. But I do expect that you will make them wait!"

Di Mon crumpled up the message in his hand. How dare D'Ander presume to give him orders? Perry D'Aur meant nothing to him! Besides, all D'Ander wanted was Demora, free and clear, very likely by means of Amel, now, if he could get hold of him. Gods! The Golden Champion might even want to use Amel to claim the throne! Di Mon would not be party to that.

At the same time, if he let Perry D'Aur die, Ayrium might be disinclined to honor the agreement between them to duel for custody of Amel if he turned up.

Di Mon wanted to scream in frustration. He had tried — Gods! How he had tried! — to be worthy of Ameron. Now he felt lost. He did want to be honorable, yet he did not believe in *Okal Rel*, not like others did. Not literally, as the laws that mediated re-birth. And he had fallen in love with a man, again — and a Reetion.

He closed his eyes, wondering how a person knew when he had gone mad.

An errant, out of breath with hurry, stopped before him and went down on one knee. It was Srain, from Green Hearth.

"My liege," the young nobleborn blurted, "the Vrellish came while you were out. They took Eva and the Reetion to go look for evidence." He dropped his eyes. "Sarilous is dead. She was found with a needle gun in her hand. We're not sure what happened."

It was like taking blows to the chest. The Vrellish here. So soon! Ranar and Eva taken! Maybe dead? And Sarilous.

She tried to save me from myself, Di Mon thought.

He wished he could believe in ghosts. He wanted to tell Sarilous that he ought to be dead, instead of her. He should never have succumbed to the comfort Ranar offered: the physical relief, the companionship of sharing his curiosity and doubts.

Vrellish tantrums seemed a trivial matter compared to the despair in his heart.

"I would like to rest, here," he told Srain, wearily, "until Lights Up."

The young errant rose slowly, embarrassed. "It is already Lights Up, my liege," he said haltingly.

Di Mon looked around him. The hangar was always lighted up to guide ships into berths but never as fully lighted as living areas. But it was true, there was light elsewhere, all around, if he had only paid attention.

"That isn't possible!" Di Mon snapped. He was highborn and he knew it was two hours before Lights Up. Unless ...

"I have time slipped," Di Mon realized in shock. Srain said nothing.

Di Mon struggled with shame. The flight back had not been arduous. If he had time slipped, he could blame only himself for the *pol* feelings of disinterest, despair, and depression that had brought it on.

"Get me a car," he ordered, as he strapped on his sword. "I have to get to Fountain Court, now."

Whatever else was true he knew that Perry D'Aur was innocent — that much was simple, and he was tired of backing down.

* * *

D'Ander's confidence made a *rel* impression. None of the nobleborn errants charged.

I ought to do something! Ranar realized. Instead, he stood still, holding the gaudy, purring motorbike.

One of the errants yelled out suddenly and charged. He might have been followed, if he had made it past D'Ander's welcoming lunge.

D'Ander whipped his sword out of his victim's body before the wounded man fell, moaning, with his arms locked around a stomach wound.

"Next?" D'Ander asked cheerfully, a bright flush on each cheek making his boldly handsome face look painted.

The remaining five wavered.

A car skidded around the corner, screeched to a halt, and disgorged two swift shapes with a syncopated *thud, thud* of closing doors. It was Sert and Kan.

One look at the reinforcements and the five remaining errants lowered their swords. A couple took a step back. Then one by one, they sheathed their weapons.

D'Ander gave curt orders in Gelack, gesturing towards the man he had brought down and two of the cowed errants rushed to help their fallen comrade, one of them pulling out an instrument that looked like a miniature welding iron while the other struggled with the patient to expose the wound. The strange behavior fascinated Ranar. A moment before, D'Ander and the errants had been bent on killing one another, now they were taking his orders.

"No stay!" D'Ander told Ranar in pigeon English, reclaiming the motorbike with a yank. "Lights Up! Must go Fountain Court."

Eva claimed Ranar's attention, and he ran to join her where she stood beside the nervous young woman and her little boy, guarded by the watchful Vrellish.

"Have you told her about Amel?" Ranar asked.

Eva nodded. "She doesn't believe it. But she's afraid, all the same, for little Von."

"That's the child's name?" Ranar asked, meeting the mother's eyes over the tousled head of her son. Kath was staring at him.

"Reetion," she said suddenly, and turned to Eva. A babble of Gelack ensued.

"Von again," Eva summarized. "He told stories, when she was a novice, about Reetions being commoners who ruled themselves without Sevolites. He rather liked the idea." She huffed a mirthless chuckle. "It's just so ... bizarre! A Soul of Light, the heir of Blue Hearth, maybe even heir to the empire. Our Von!" To hold the rest back, she covered her lower face with her hand.

Sert and Kan lost patience suddenly and herded them all into the car. It wasn't until Ranar found himself pressed into the backseat with the two tense women and the excited toddler that he realized he was shaking.

Kan drove like a thrill seeker, indifferent to the distress he caused. By the time they reached the stairs outside the UnderDocks, the passengers were all thoroughly jostled. Before Ranar had time to recover they were out of the car and headed up the stairs. Eva found it easiest. Kath was burdened with Von. By the time they reached the first great landing she was puffing and Ranar had a stitch in his side again.

"Wait!" he gasped to Eva. "Tell them — to wait." He leaned over, bracing his hands on his legs.

"These are only the nobleborn docks," Eva said, swiping back a strand of blond hair. "We need the highborn level."

Ranar bobbed his head. "Just ... a couple of — ahh!"

Sert descended on him so fast he didn't realize what was happening until she had slung him over a shoulder, with a slap on one buttock for good measure. Kan swept up Kath just as effortlessly, forcing her to yield little Von to Eva as he turned her upside down. Neither highborn seemed burdened, but refused to use both hands, leaving their left hands free. Their swords, Ranar noticed, were sheathed on the right side.

Eva put little Von down after about a minute and he trotted along keeping an eye on his mother, slung over Kan's shoulder. Although the Vrellish highborn only used one hand, he had Kath in a grip secure enough she did not try to struggle. Ranar understood that all too well. He kept still, in part, because he did not want to encourage Sert to take further liberties subduing him. He had never experienced anything so undignified and, he admitted, unapologetically practical in his life.

The Vrellish set them down on the next landing, annoyingly untaxed themselves by their brisk passage up the dockside stairs. Even little Von was in better shape than Eva, although he was small enough that he had been forced to alternate between two-legged stepping and a four-limbed scramble to keep up with Kan.

Kath reclaimed the child. Eva caught her breath, listening to Sert rattle off a Gelack comment that ended with a pointed look in Ranar's direction.

"What's she saying?" Ranar prompted.

Eva took a deep breath. "She says you aren't a Sevolite. Or else Reetion Sevolites are less *rel* than the Golden Demish."

"Tell her I am flattered if she compares my vigor to D'Ander's," said Ranar, feeling irritated.

"No," Eva refused flatly, and straightened her clothing, avoiding him. When she did look up at him again it was with fresh concerns about his sanity.

Ranar recognized the landing at the top of the long flight of stairs. He had been here twice before, but had not been able to look around either time. Now he registered a wide platform to their right, on the lip of a cavernous docking floor. The platform screened out much of the view because it was laden with a row of gates decked out in the colors and heraldry of Fountain Court hearths. Ranar recognized what had to be the one for Green Hearth, colored forest green with a sextant device mounted over the barn-sized gates that gave onto the landing, and flanked by a smaller door. Ranar caught himself staring hard, hoping to see Di Mon, and quickly looked away.

To his left, across a short expanse of bare floor, was a great cylinder sunk into the back of a structure composed of many layers and architectural revisions that rose up to the ceiling on one side, merging into bedrock. On the other side, the flat roof of the Citadel was visible. No railing or other protective barrier intervened between the landing and the sheer drop. The only concession to the daunting drop was that the encrustations of commerce on the Plaza were set back about a body's length from the circumference of the Citadel roof.

Sert grunted something in Gelack and they were on the move again, but at least she didn't try to pick Ranar up, nor did Kan lift Kath.

Ranar found himself scanning the pedestrian traffic around them, checking everyone coming off the highborn docks for Di Mon. As a consequence he paid little attention to people trickling out of the arch at the base of the cylinder. It wasn't until he nearly bumped into Eva when she stopped cold that he looked in that direction.

The Vrellish had already stopped a couple of paces back to watch the thickening mass of cloaked travelers heading towards them from the direction of the Plaza. One of the figures flung back his cloak, with impatience for stealth and disguises, to reveal Prince Hendricks D'Astor. Paladin Thoth was the next to disrobe, followed by ten palace errants in the Ava's livery, all wearing swords. A couple of the errants came forward, level with the two Demish highborns while the rest stayed in the back row.

By now other pedestrians had noticed, too, but instead of fleeing or reporting what was happening to someone, they began to drift inward to establish a loose circle around the tableau centered on what Ranar guessed must be the row of Demish highborns confronting their two Vrellish peers. The extra nobleborns seemed less important, and Ranar had no difficulty grasping that in Gelack terms, he and the other commoners did not count at all.

It was much more complex than a mere brutish brawl, but still apt to prove fatal to someone. Ranar moved to screen Kath and her child from Thoth's view, and was touched to find that Eva followed suit.

Prince Hendricks D'Astor declared something formal. Sert snapped back an answer. They exchanged a couple of lines while Ranar strained, unsuccessfully, for the name Monitum. Then Thoth dove into the conversation with his head up, his chin stiff and his arms waving.

For an awful moment, Ranar was afraid the Vrellish would give them up. Then Sert and Kan cleared their swords. The confident slithering of metal sent a thrill of relief and something less defensible down Ranar's spine.

They will not necessarily fight, he decided, thinking, despite himself, of nature documentaries as he soaked up every nuisance of their body language. The Vrellish projected menace. Hendricks D'Astor stood steady, but he looked unhappy. Thoth continued his harangue, looking nervous and excited. The two other Demish highborns on the front line grew pale and did not draw their swords.

"They are arguing about who ought to take the challenge," Eva summarized hurriedly in English. "The two Demish highborns acting for Lady H'Ran's interests don't have the stomach to take on a Vrellish highborn. Thoth thinks D'Astor should do it, but D'Astor's asking questions. Thoth is trying to make him feel responsible for Kath and her child falling into Vrellish hands."

"Tell D'Astor it is Delm who is the threat to Kath and little Von!" Ranar ordered Eva excitedly. "Tell him Delm wants to kill the child!"

"Me?" Eva was aghast. "Tell a Demish prince that Ava Delm — you are mad!" she cried.

"Then tell me how to say it myself!" he insisted, catching Eva's arm. She pulled away, alarmed.

Suddenly there was a ripple of motion and sound coming from the highborn docks. Kan's head snapped up. Ranar whirled to see Di Mon. He was running towards them with his sword drawn.

Sert shot forward, scattering onlookers. Ranar caught his breath as Di Mon deflected her attack, certain neither combatant could survive the cuts and blocks that filled the next few seconds.

Terror ended just as suddenly as the two Vrellish fencers backed away from each other. *Surely they would talk, now*! Ranar hoped, the swords suddenly as real to him as Di Mon's body.

Sert barked an accusation and Di Mon growled something back in answer, looking every bit as wild as Sert. *He wants to fight*! Ranar realized in horror.

"No!" Ranar cried, and was completely ignored except by Eva who dug her fingers hard into his arm. "Don't distract him," she hissed hotly under her breath.

Sert and Di Mon came together: he darting in, she parrying, rebounding, and attempting to slash as she recovered, only narrowly missing his upper arm. It seemed impossible to Ranar that Di Mon had intended to escape by so fine a margin, but Sert pulled off the same kind of miracle by guiding the tip of his sword past her flesh by no more than its own width, before coolly turning her near escape into an attack. Di Mon tipped her sword away awkwardly, and sprang back to recover.

Now they'll stop, Ranar told himself, convinced he had been watching for a long time because the scene was remarkably vivid to him and seemed to take place in slow motion. He didn't think he could endure much more. The audience of erstwhile pedestrians, on the other hand, were shifting to encircle Sert and Di Mon, which interfered with Ranar's line of sight. He was craning to see past them, or to make his feet move, when he heard Eva gasp and looked towards her too late to get a clear look at the men who seized him, simultaneously, by the arms.

More concerned about the duel than himself at the moment, Ranar tried to pull away from his captors and was shoved down. When he got his feet under him again he turned to see if Sert and Di Mon were still fighting and was punched in the chest by one of the Ava's blue clad errants with the graceful white rose on the breast of his uniform. Ranar really couldn't breath now.

I will suffocate! he thought in panic, as he felt himself begin to be dragged. He didn't suffocate but he did very nearly black out, his ears filled with the sound of Kath crying out in desperation.

Ranar came around again in the midst of a dizzying landscape of gray floor, moving legs, and noises. As his head cleared he realized he was being dragged between two Palace errants with his head lolling down. Kath was on one side of him, a man's arm around her waist with one of his big hands clapped over her mouth. Eva was behaving more quietly, but Kath's little son was acting out enough for them all, kicking and hollering like any child having a temper tantrum, although from what Ranar could grasp, his efforts seemed unchildishly deliberate and the grunting sounds he made were those of pain as well as effort, which upset Ranar all over again because hurting a toddler struck his Reetion sensibilities hard. He had never personally felt unselfish enough to want a child of his own. Now, it felt monstrous that he should be responsible for one under such impossible circumstances!

The whole group of them were moving quickly through the cylinder and about to emerge on the Plaza, headed almost certainly for Blue Pavilion and whatever Delm intended for them. The prospect was enough to make Ranar forget, for the moment, about Di Mon.

Kath succeeded in biting her captor. The man yelped, cast her down on the floor, slipped off his sword belt, and raised his sheathed sword to strike her. Eva turned her head aside. She wasn't held, but she seemed to feel helpless. Von shrieked the Gelack version of "Mom-my!" with a defiant infant anger and defeated vulnerability that broke Ranar's heart. He tried to wrench free of the two men restraining him, and was elbowed sharply in the ribs on one side. Too upset to feel the pain, he kicked as hard as he could, and drew a curse from the man he struck. The next thing he knew he was thrown down, but the errants were too busy, all at once, to bother him more than that.

Ranar looked up to find Prince Hendricks D'Astor chivalrously objecting to the mistreatment of the woman and child. Little Von was down again and in his mother's arms and Kath knelt sobbing and hugging the frightened child. Eva stood beside them with the tips of her fingers on the top of the girl's head, looking at D'Astor with tears of gratitude in her eyes.

"Tell him!" Ranar ordered Eva, and gasped as he was shoved down once more by a booted foot.

"Ranar!" he heard Eva cry as the women were moved off once again, under their self-appointed guardian's direct supervision. That was when Ranar discovered Demish chivalry did not extend to making him an object of D'Astor's concern — he was left to his abusive captors.

Ranar fought back inexpertly as the gang of five errants closed in on him. The one he had kicked earlier shoved him into another one who pitched him towards a third. They said things he did not understand, egging each other on, while the highborns left in charge made no move to intervene as Ranar was struck in the stomach and dropped to his knees, doubled over.

The usual crowd of spectators had formed around them. Ranar looked to the audience for help, but all he saw in their faces was fear for his alien appearance and — to his horror, the same morbid fascination he had felt before the violence shaping up before him became personal.

Ranar was yanked up by his hair, and cried out. An errant punched him in the face, almost casually, and he staggered, tasting blood. He was caught again and shoved into the next man in the circle ringing him around.

He tried to stop them again but they were too strong. And he felt something he had never felt in his whole life, until then: he felt inferior; he could be injured and humiliated. He could be killed.

He was vulnerable.

* * *

"Pay for Vretla's soul!" Sert spat at Di Mon, her teeth gritted.

"She will live!" Di Mon fired back just as fiercely.

"Not cleanly!" Sert snarled at him. "They'll change her!"

"Are you sure!" Di Mon demanded. "Do you really think I would do that to her!" His impatience boiled as hot as his anger. Something was going on, beyond Sert, with Ranar. Energy swirled through his body like poison demanding action.

Sert gave a yell of fury and charged, slashing at his head. It took all of his skill to stay alive and it was wonderful! The will to win surged through him, depression burning off like the shell of a star going nova. Their slashing, darting blades made thrilling music as their bodies labored.

When he drew blood he was disappointed. Sert had warded off a trick targeting her bicep and his blade sliced her cheek on the rebound. She thwacked his sword clear the next instant, already retreating, but the blood was there, wet and glistening from ear to jawline. They could smell it.

Kan thrust through the circle of witnesses to put himself at the third point of a triangle formed by Sert and Di Mon. "First blood!" he suggested with force. A scattering of voices from the audience called "To the death!" in response, and the Demish majority took up the cry, hungry for the spectacle or just glad to see Vrellish highborns killing each other. For a moment their excitement felt contagious, then a trio of sleek Vrellish nobleborns elbowed their way through, eliciting grunts from the ring leaders shouting for a death match as they elbowed or punched them going past. Inside, their presence dampened the electric space between Sert and Di Mon. A male went to Sert, pulling out a seamer used for closing wounds. One of the females approached Di Mon while the other prowled the inner perimeter, encouraging the audience to break up. Di Mon ignored the first woman's seductive look, and she gave up with a wistful air, aware of his chilly reputation by Vrellish standards. She switched her attention to Kan, instead. It wasn't every day a Vrellish highborn left Red Reach to visit court and *mekan'stan* relationships were not exclusive. Nor was it mere coincidence that the nobleborn helping Sert was a male. It was the Vrellish way for violence to inspire sexual behavior in its aftermath, discharging its destructive power.

The dynamics grated on Di Mon's newly refreshed nerves. They were so useful and so natural — except for him.

"*Ack Rel*," Kan told him gruffly. "For today."

Sarilous will be grateful, thought Di Mon, then remembered that Sarilous was dead.

A cry claimed his attention, coming from out of sight in the direction of the Palace Shell.

Ranar! he thought, and was horrified for a moment that he might have said it under his breath. He swallowed down the panic and answered Sert's *mekan'st* with a curt nod, then he plunged into the Palace Shell, creating a buzz of commentary in his wake as people recognized him.

Di Mon erupted out onto the Plaza following the trail of the Ava's men left by the knots of gossiping bystanders. They were making for Blue Pavilion, and he knew he couldn't let them get there. Not, especially, if he was right about why Ranar and Eva might be in the company of a girl with a rather pretty, dark-haired toddler.

People pointed at him as he flew past with his sword drawn. Vendors stared from their stalls. Few would go about their business again until they had heard about the duel they had missed, and marveled at how close the ancient house of Monitum had come to losing its last highborn. The thought mocked him, but he could not stop now.

He saw a mass of people and heard destructive laughter. He ran faster.

The first spectator he tore away — the rest melted before him. He slashed the end of his blade down the back of the first palace errant, eliciting a yelp that got everyone's attention. Another errant tried to draw and he opened his forearm for him.

Then the nobleborns pulled back, like lips in a grimace, to reveal one of the Demish highborns with them. Di Mon felt like a runaway ship, bound to swallow more *gap* than he could survive, but he had not stopped calculating. He had not killed any challenge class inferiors, which might entitle his opponents to gang up on him in the eyes of the spectators, so if they tried it they would be hindered by the self-appointed witnesses of honor representing the interests of the Watching Dead. Di Mon had known people who claimed to be literally possessed when they intervened to stop dishonorable violence. Others did it just because they could. It didn't matter.

The Demish played by the rules. Only one highborn went for him.

Killing him was ridiculously easy. The Demish man was still warming up to the idea of fighting, while Di Mon was fresh from fighting Sert and still reacting first and thinking later. His opponent's eyes widened as if he felt betrayed to discover that the tall tales of Vrellish swiftness he had scoffed at with his friends at sparring sessions, were real and lethal.

Di Mon let him get on with dying, and turned to face the second highborn who had been willing to stand by and watch Ranar be beaten by bullying inferiors he should have disciplined. The second man declined to clear his weapon. The death of his comrade had registered.

Di Mon backed off, still holding his sword in a fencer's grip. He waited until he was more than a lunge's width clear of the second Demish highborn before casting about him for Ranar. He knew the Reetion wasn't dead because he had heard him moan earlier, but he didn't seem to be in sight, either.

"He went that way," a spectator informed him, pointing, "after the others."

* * *

Ranar rejected defeat. He was physically weaker, yes. The Sevolites tormenting him could kill him. They might even break him, he acknowledged — shocked to realize that intellect counted for so little in extremity. But they were still an ugly blemish of destructive spite in a larger universe in which he was worth far, far more than any number of them. The worst they could do to his world view was to make him ashamed to be human because they were, so he would prove that being human could be something better.

While Di Mon fought, Ranar got painfully to his feet, fixated on two women and a little boy. No decent Reetion could let a child be murdered by its grandfather, especially not when he had been responsible for Delm's men finding the child's mother. Besides, rescuing Kath and little Von suited him better than witnessing the one Sevolite he both loved and respected commit murder, and he'd had a feeling from the moment Di Mon showed up that somebody was going to die.

Ranar's goals were thoroughly consistent with his Reetion values, and that held him together. His tactics, however, were amateur.

Fleeing the sounds of Di Mon's attack, he stumbled into some of the errants he had just escaped and nearly panicked before he realized they would very likely take him to little Von and the women, which was what he wanted. They seized him and shoved him along ahead of them, but it felt all right now that it was his idea. They were less confident since Di Mon's intrusion and wasted no time getting to Blue Pavilion, where they were stopped by a highborn with a young face, who asked questions.

Ranar was able to grasp a little of the young man's greeting, since many Gelack nouns, especially, were English cognates and he was starting to make sense of common verbs even if pronouns were still a bit challenging. The guard called himself Prince Taran of Princess Reach, and mentioned Prince Hendricks D'Astor. He was earnest and anxious enough that Ranar felt a spasm of sympathy for the young Sevolite, who seemed uneasy to be guarding Blue Pavilion, perhaps for the sake of the traffic that Delm's personal retainers were dragging in. But just like D'Astor, any concern invoked by helpless women with a toddler did not extend to a male, brown-faced Reetion.

Ranar was hustled down spiral stairs amid a press of errant bodies wearing sheathed swords, and into a resplendent space lined in rich draperies and paintings. His missing friends were at the bottom, Eva belatedly taking his advice by making an impassioned plea, in Gelack, to Prince D'Astor, although from D'Astor's expression Ranar feared his most likely conclusion would be to pity Eva her insane delusions. Kath knelt at her feet clutching Von.

Eva spoke Delm's name three times in quick succession, making D'Astor raise his eyebrows and shift his attention to Kath's son. Thoth's face burned with righteous outrage. Before Eva finished, he rushed at her and struck her silent. D'Astor stopped Thoth hitting her again, once she was down, but did no more.

Ranar would have given years of his life, at that moment, to speak Gelack. It made him want to scream to be so powerless despite his conviction that D'Astor might help if he could make him see past his prejudices.

A fat, well-dressed man came up the spiral stairs from a level below Blue Hearth itself. He wore no sword, yet he commanded attention.

Like Sarilous, Ranar conjectured. The new arrival bowed to Prince D'Astor and delivered a message, obsequiously. D'Astor took his sword from its sheath, dropped the belt, and let an errant help him shed his jacket, leaving him in a white shirt. Then he took his sword back from the errant and was gone, with a final wave in the direction of the women accompanied by a curt order.

The fat *gorarelpul* bobbed and mouthed reassuring words, but the instant D'Astor was out of the room, he snapped his own orders to Delm's errants. Kath bolted. Errants seized her and wrenched Von away. Ranar broke away to help them but did not get far. Bruised muscles reasserted their complaints as he was thrown forward onto his knees again. He crawled over to Eva, which was at least possible, and found that she was still breathing but unconscious. She should be treated for concussion! A part of him could not grasp why first responders were not there to help. Emotionally, he half-expected them to appear.

"You would be the Reetion," a mocking, self-important voice declared, speaking English.

Ranar's head jerked up, wincing as he turned. He was still on the floor beside Eva. Kath was standing alone, gone very still.

"So you do speak English," said the *gorarelpul*, sounding delighted. He was seated with Von between his knees, wrapped tightly in a throw rug borrowed from the floor and gagged with a silken handkerchief. The child stared at his mother, eyes bright with tears, and looking frightened, but now and then he wriggled with a show of spirit. Kath stared at the needle gun the *gorarelpul* held in his right hand, his left one engaged in keeping Von under control.

"I speak English," Ranar acknowledged with an irrational flurry of hope.

"How nice!" said the *gorarelpul*. "One so very seldom gets to practice. I learned it, of course, because the Monatese like to think no one else will make the effort, and use it to speak privately in public." He gestured briefly to the two errants still in the room with him, one standing behind the women and one guarding the bottom of the stairs. Then he beamed at Ranar again. "I presume that there are also many Reetion languages?"

"One shared language," Ranar said, "and some pseudo-native ones on affiliated worlds."

"Worlds?"

"Are you conducting research?" Ranar asked him impatiently. "If so, all you need to do is visit. Everything we know is available to every citizen, as knowledge should be, everywhere."

The *gorarelpul* raised manicured eyebrows that were oddly disturbing in such a marred and ugly face. "Feeling defensive?" he remarked, and stroked Von's mop of jet black hair, trusting the rug and his legs to hold the child as he did. Von didn't like it and squirmed harder. Ranar's hands clenched into fists at his side. It might have been futile, but it was involuntary.

"The Demish do the same thing," drawled the *gorarelpul*. "Corner them, and they defend their culture." He sighed. "Sometimes they recite poetry. Which I would not mind," he added, "if it wasn't so sugary. I like verse with some spice to it. I am Balous, by the way. The Royal *Gorarelpul*, bonded to the Ava himself."

"Stop that and release the boy," Ranar ordered.

Balous stopped stroking Von's hair to study Ranar's clenched fists and angry stare. "So," he said, "Reetions are indeed commoners who rule themselves, or else you are uniquely lacking in humility." He sighed again. "It really is a pity I must kill you, since visiting to ask my questions isn't going to be something I can put in my calendar for some years. Not unless H'Reth proves surprisingly capable," he added, taking pleasure in his own wit, and shifted the needle-gun to target Ranar's chest.

Ranar did not doubt that Balous killed people, but he did not believe he was about to die. That possibility was just too unfathomable to register. Not so his fears for others.

"What about the child and his mother?" he insisted, as if Balous had to answer to him.

"I've explained everything to the mother," Balous told him, enjoying himself. "She will do what I say, or the child perishes. I will genotype him myself. If he is not — shall we say — more than he seems, he'll be returned to her. If he is, she will accept a surrogate until it can be publicly genotyped to satisfy honorable fools like Hendricks D'Astor. If she doesn't her own child will suffer."

"You will kill him anyway," Ranar predicted.

Balous smiled like a sphinx. Ranar suspected he was vain about his plots and schemes, and Delm didn't give him enough chance to brag about it. *Can I use that against him?* Ranar asked himself desperately.

"And Eva?" Ranar asked to keep him talking.

"Ah, yes. Liege Monitum's *lyka*." Balous shifted his body to control the struggling two-year-old whose vigor was not boding well for his prospects of proving to be a commoner. "That depends, I suppose, on whether Liege Monitum survives the day himself. I understand that Sert is looking for him, but he hasn't lived this long by being as impulsive as the average Vrellish highborn, so I had best hang on to the *lyka* in case I need her for blackmail or bribery. It's unlikely," Balous acknowledged, "but I suspect the exalted Liege of Monitum, so famous for his most un-Vrellish coolness, may also prove more sentimental than most Vrellish. If not, I will have to find some other way to silence him." He smirked and lectured as if Ranar was a rebellious student. "I cannot let anyone attack my master with the sort of vicious slanders Eva dared to voice here. Not even the liege of the ancient, weak, infertile House of Monitum." He chuckled.

"It is not true," a new voice declared, emotionally, in English.

Ranar and Balous both turned to see Thoth standing before them in the full formal regalia of a Golden Demish paladin. He had come from a room deeper inside Blue Hearth, and preoccupied as they were by the prospect of people entering up or down the spiral stairs, neither Ranar nor Balous had noticed him. Balous blinked, astonished, and Kath — who understood none of the English — began creeping towards Von while he was distracted.

"What the prostitute said is not true!" Thoth insisted with religious fervor, glaring scornfully at Eva's crumpled form. "Delm is a Soul of Light!" He turned his head to Ranar. "No Soul of Light would harm an innocent child," he explained almost patiently. "And Amel was not even Delm's son!"

"Of course not," Balous soothed, but Thoth turned on him angrily.

"I know you," he accused, "you vile, simpering filth! I know by your very tone of voice what you think when you say one thing and mean another. You think you are protecting Delm from his own flesh and blood! You think Delm has lied!"

"Goldens," Balous complained, with a great sigh, studying Thoth with disappointment as he shifted the needle gun to target him instead of Ranar, "They pick up languages so carelessly! A nasty habit."

Balous would have shot Thoth square in the heart then, if two other things hadn't happened. Kath sprang for Von, still held prisoner between the *gorarelpul's* knees, and a body fell down the stairs, colliding with the errant still guarding the bottom.

* * *

Di Mon did not slow down when he reached Blue Pavilion. A Demish prince he recognized stepped forward. He was a highborn, and therefore an obstacle. Di Mon attacked.

Prince Taran failed to block effectively and Di Mon impaled him through the side, almost over-committing to a deflection at the last moment since he did not want to kill the youth outright. The nobleborns might mob him if Taran went down too easily before witnesses had gathered. Taran fell back, in pain but too proud to yield to the invader. Di Mon backed him through the curtained entrance, jabbing and harassing, and finally lunged with bullying intent when the less experienced fighter stood with his back to the stairs. Taran shifted back as he'd been trained, and found no floor behind him. He realized his danger and bravely threw himself forward. Di Mon let their swords collide near their hilts, and they strained against each other, the Demish prince both larger and more desperate, but no match for Di Mon's fifty years of experience in exploiting opportunities and weaknesses. Taran toppled, struck the stairs hard, and fell, head over heels into the errant at the bottom, limbs flopping unnaturally after the initial impact.

Di Mon bounded down the stairs and leaped over the tangle at the bottom, slashing at the errant's face as he tried to get out from under Taran. The errant clutched his eye, wailing.

Delm's *gorarelpul* shook off a commoner girl, only to have Thoth take the child they fought over, knocking Balous to the floor as he succeeded.

Di Mon had no time to care — the second errant in the room was trying to kill Eva and Ranar.

Di Mon body checked Ranar to the floor, knocking him clear of Eva's unconscious body. He followed through without pause, running their attacker through the middle at the cost of a slash on his upper arm. The cut stung, but it did not slice into muscle deeply enough to impair function and that was all that mattered to Di Mon.

Ranar looked at him as if he were a demon. Di Mon was angry at the unspoken criticism, but it sobered him. He reached down to pull Ranar up with his right hand.

"Thoth!" the Reetion cried and pointed. "He took the child! Amel's child! Eva's almost sure! The mother followed!"

A commoner mother, Di Mon thought, grasping how that might escape Sevolite notice. Yet even by a commoner mother, Amel's child would be all he needed to prove Amel a Pureblood.

"Take care of Eva!" he told Ranar, and tore down the stairs to the Octagon, where he passed like a knife through the perturbed Demish milling at the base of the stairs. Thoth had been this way. The commoner girl was trapped in the arms of well-meaning bystanders, struggling and crying out, "Von!

Von!" Presuming that it was the child she called to, the name itself gave Di Mon hope.

The Octagon duplicated the divisions of Fountain Court, each pie-shaped wedge named for the hearth above. Di Mon passed through the back end of Blue Wedge unchallenged to where people thinned out and it narrowed. He could see Kertatt opposite, on Green Wedge, surrounded by his own retainers. There were pitifully few of them compared to the Demish arrayed in banks of comfortable seats on neighboring Silver Wedge. Delm was seated there, rather than among his own household on Blue Wedge, in order to be surrounded by princes and princesses in all of their Demish regalia. There were at least twenty Demish princes and three times that many Demish Highlords who were also in the highborn challenge class. Excluding himself, Di Mon counted four Vrellish highborns: two Nersallians on Black Wedge plus Sert and Kan, surrounded by Vretla's nobleborn vassals from Spiral Hall. The Nersallians were sons of Hangst Nersal. Once that might have made them allies, but Di Mon could no more rely on them, now, than he could count on Sert to back him. He spotted Ses among the nobleborns surrounding them and presumed she must have summoned Branst and Horth Nersal to court after the debacle over Vretla at Den Eva's.

Hendricks D'Astor circled Prince D'Ander on the large, circular challenge floor that occupied the same space on the Octagon as the central fountain on the residential level above.

Clever of Delm, Di Mon acknowledged, *to substitute D'Astor for H'Us*. D'Ander would be loath to kill a Princessian tournament champion with such an unblemished reputation, and Di Mon knew from his own experience how good D'Astor was at defense.

Di Mon tracked one intricate exchange, a rally of feints and parries as they fussed with each others' blades. *The Demish play at swords*, he thought with contempt. They would probably stop at the first disabling wound, and whether

Perry D'Aur lived or died, they would be at it again in a couple of years, over the same business.

Delm sat, enthroned among roses and surrounded by his principal vassals, the H'Usians. The Paladin, Thoth, knelt to offer a child to him, like a character in some Demoran play. The jarring presence in the whole pretty scene was Perry D'Aur, guarded, shackled and gagged like a dangerous animal. Delm had even put her in plain men's clothes, allowing her no claim to rank, family, or femininity that might arouse Demish sympathies. She was watching the duel, but the expression in her eyes was resigned and cynical.

Di Mon padded forward drawing Vrellish stares. They knew something was going to happen, but he could not count on their help. He turned his attention back to Delm, wondering how he would get at the man, layered deep as he was in Demish adulation. He deserved no other protection — no shield of honor.

Thoth rose long enough to place the child on Delm's lap. "Light of Divine, Beauty of Soul," he implored, "I have heard you accused of seeking this child's death — madness in itself! The reason defies hearing, therefore I beg you to genotype him, now, before Sevildom assembled! Dispel the accusations that still haunt you, so unfairly, from that evil time when you were married to Ev'rel, your Vrellish half sister! Ev'rel, who called you things no Soul of Light could endure being! I have never believed what she said!" He ended on a rising note of anguish. "Please, I beg you, prove it is all a wicked fabrication!"

The Ava stared down at the child in his lap, as though wondering how it had got there. Von touched the fur trim of Delm's robe and stroked it, taking comfort in the novel feeling. Then he tipped his face up and said, clearly, with a wavering note of worry, "I want my mommy, please." He even managed to talk up, although he did it simply, without any suffixes.

Delm collected himself and smiled, beaming forgiveness for the error. "Of course," he told little Von sweetly, with that

disarming beauty he exuded like breath. The same beauty
that was echoed in the child's face. *How*, Di Mon thought,
can they not see it?

Ladies in the stands around him murmured with abashed
amusement. Di Mon caught wispy phrases like "So gracious
of the Ava," or "How dear."

"You bless me with your understanding!" Thoth exclaimed in tears, and abased himself at the feet of Delm's
flowery chair.

"Ev'rel did not lie!" Di Mon declared, his voice ringing,
raising gasps for both insulting words and grammar. "That
child on your lap is your grandson, and even if you break his
neck, his genes will still condemn you." He jerked his head
in Perry D'Aur's direction. "She is nothing but a scapegoat
for what you did at Den Eva's to eliminate a child that Von,
the courtesan, had fathered. A child you had to kill because
you had discovered Von was Pureblood Amel, your son!"

The duelists stood clear of each other. Prince H'Us waved
back his highborn henchmen and came forward, looking big,
stiff, and awkward.

"My dear Di Mon," the Silver Demish admiral said with
dismayed concern, shocked white by Di Mon's words, but
more concerned about his contract-friend and ally than the
risk of there being any truth in them: as if he thought the
Vrellish liege was under the influence of some potent, but
temporary, madness. "You've been flying too hard. Ran into
trouble, I expect, eh? Out in Killing Reach?"

Di Mon narrowed his eyes. "Draw or step aside."

H'Us shook his leonine head. "I'll grant you," he told Di
Mon under his breath in a whisper, leaning closer, "Delm's
a wastrel. But attacking Sevolites with flame throwers and
murdering women?" He clapped Di Mon firmly on the arm,
making him start violently and raised his voice to an audible
level again. "We will genotype the child, certainly, if it will
set your mind at rest. Just enough blood shed to wet a testing
strip should do the trick, eh?"

Delm stood, surrounded by roses, with Von in his grip. "Of course," he said, a little shrilly, smiled and cleared his throat. Von stopped toying with Delm's furs and began to wriggle. Delm thrust him at the nearest errant. "But the ladies must retire," Delm insisted. "This is much too upsetting for them. We will reconvene here in an hour. At that time, neutral houses may collect blood samples from this poor child. But in the meantime, he must be allowed to rest. He's frightened." Delm waved to the errant holding Von. "Take him inside and notify Balous to see to him."

Di Mon felt the mood in the room shift, read it in the way all eyes averted from him and returned to Delm. Delm, who read that shift as easily as Di Mon, smiled upon them all as he settled back onto the chair. *They will let him get away with it*, Di Mon realized. *They are too much in awe of him, or what he stands for, to think.*

I am not, Di Mon thought, clearly. His right fist drove into H'Us' stomach. The instant after, his left hand cleared his sword. The big Demish Prince doubled over. Di Mon recoiled from the blow and uncoiled towards Delm. His will skimmed forward, his sword followed. A woman screamed. He heard movement on either side. He shifted neither eye nor blade nor awareness from that patch of white silk and silver thread that covered Delm's beating heart.

An attendant threw himself in front of Delm's chest as a living shield. Di Mon had no problem killing them both, but feared his blade would lodge in the wrong ribs. His point floated upwards, fixed again on a white throat among fur. He took his last step and leaned forward into the air.

His sword drove deep into the wood of the throne with a jar that Di Mon felt through his spine. Delm shrieked and wrenched his head away as a jet of brilliant arterial blood shot sideways. Di Mon let go of the sword and crashed among the roses. Delm kicked out, catching him in the temple, then the Ava's body heaved, with that Sevolite strength he rarely used, and the throne, attendant, and Ava went over with a great crash.

Hands descended on Di Mon as he rolled aside and started to sit up, dazed. He considered fighting back, but saw no point to it now. What he could do, he had done.

Errants and nobility piled in upon the toppled throne and wounded Ava. The thrashing white figure and spurting blood disappeared beneath a heaving mass of liveried backs. Delm's choking shrieks continued to rise over the screams of panic and outrage and the shouted orders to bring help, stand back, look to the ladies, staunch the bleeding, and pleas to the Ava to lie still. Delm's panicked struggles and his strength were hampering his would-be saviors; one of whom — Di Mon thought he recognized Hendricks D'Astor's voice — forgot protocol so far as to bellow, "Hold him *down!*"

Di Mon watched the chaos with indifference as H'Us' men dragged him clear and pinned his arms behind him. H'Us, pale and slightly hunched, set his blade to Di Mon's throat. "You'll die disgraced on Ava's Square for this, you Vrellish animal. I'll only kill you quickly if our Ava lives."

It was only then that Di Mon noticed the Vrellish, forming a half crescent ring in front of him. There were highborns and nobleborns, drawn from Black Hearth and Red, with nearly all his own Greens mixed in: all arrayed against the Demish like a single organism despite the disparity in numbers.

Sert spoke. "You can fight me for the privilege of killing him, later," she told H'Us, "if you're still so inclined, once we know who this wretched child is."

"Show us the child!" Branst Nersal cried excitedly. "Now. Or more blood will spill!" His less emotional shadow, Horth Nersal, stood at his side, inscrutable, and more dangerous.

They all became suddenly aware that the shrieks and shouting had stopped. Several people were sobbing quietly. The crowd around Delm unfolded, no longer white and silver but white and silver and bright red. Prince D'Astor walked unsteadily out of the center of them, white-faced, his hands and sleeves soaked in blood, and blood sprayed in sweeping arcs across his chest. He said, staring at Di Mon, "He's dead. The Ava is dead."

Di Mon inhaled. For the first and perhaps only time in his life, that unmistakable metallic smell was the sweetest scent he had ever known. Now he was ready to die.

"Genotype the child," Prince H'Us said, through gritted teeth, glaring into Di Mon's impassive face.

Di Mon blinked. It took a moment for him to realize what H'Us had just said, and then words came back to him, and wits. "If he proves to be Amel's, he is Monitum's!" Di Mon stated promptly, thinking that if Demish patience failed prematurely, they might just respect his claim in apology. He hoped Tessitatt would have the sense to take Von and insist he came as a gift, without complications of challenge right. Of course if he thought about it, rationally, he had nothing but guesses, rumors and shouted words to assure him the child was Amel's. He would have laughed at the absurdity of it all if the sword at his throat allowed for it.

Ses Nersal was there with the Nersallians. Di Mon met her eyes over Prince H'Us' shoulder.

"Eva and the Reetion," he said, and paused for the sake of the discomfort caused by speaking. A trickle of blood began where the uncompromising sword pressed. "They're in Blue Hearth," Di Mon finished.

Another white faced Demish retainer ran into their midst, from the direction of Blue Wedge, to relay bad news to Hendricks D'Astor, who had joined them. "Prince Taran, your Highnesses. He's dead!" He pointed at Di Mon. "Liege Monitum pushed him down the stairs!"

Di Mon was sorry for that, in a distant way. But that was *Okal Rel*.

D'Ander did not take it so impersonally. He was over beside Perry D'Aur, prevailing on the stunned palace staff to give up custody. At the sound of Taran's name he stopped tearing off Perry's bounds and met Di Mon's eyes with a look of grief that turned to disillusionment.

That's right, Di Mon thought sourly. *We're all Vrellish animals. Even me.* He saw no point, with a sword to his throat, of trying to explain he hadn't meant the young Princessian's fall to be fatal.

* * *

Take care of Eva! Ranar thought to himself testily. If this were Rire, he would be receiving medical attention himself! He had been punched and threatened, frightened and forced to witness murder, and now he was supposed to be looking after Di Mon's *lyka*? It was an unworthy thought, but his first reaction was to wonder if she meant more to Di Mon than he did.

Other explanations were possible: like expecting another man to stand surrogate in defense of a vulnerable woman. Although given what he had seen of Vrellish culture it was more likely Sevolite paternalism towards a commoner, in which case Ranar should be flattered. *Stop analyzing!* Ranar told himself, afraid that he was simply jealous. Gelion seemed intent on making him suffer feelings he could not respect.

Eva was unconscious, he wasn't. *That* was the simple explanation.

Since no first responders had put in an appearance, Ranar knelt with a self-pitying moan and did what he could to assess Eva's condition. An ugly red mark on her face showed where she had been hit. He pulled back an eyelid. He wasn't entirely sure what to look for, but suspected it was a good sign that her pupils looked normal to him. He still wasn't sure if he should move her. What if her neck or spine were injured? Her legs were warm, but he didn't think that proved anything. If she had sprawled over one of the throw rugs he could have pulled her out at minimal risk. But she hadn't.

"Law and Reason," Ranar grumbled in Reetion, and climbed painful back to his feet again. Should he try to get help? If so, from where? His side ached. His knee hurt. Blood was drying on his temple from a cut made by somebody's ring. Shouldn't somebody be looking after him?

"Tell me what happened, Reetion," a voice said in English.

Ranar jerked and spun, feeling his injured knee wobble until he shifted his weight evenly again. Balous, the *gorarelpul*, was sitting up, looking shaken, with the needle gun back in his hand again.

"Tell me!" Balous insisted.

"People have been killed," Ranar said, "as you can see."

"Where is the child?" Balous demanded, and remembered. "Thoth! Where has he taken him?"

The foggy idea Ranar had earlier, became clear.

"You said too much while Thoth was listening," Ranar told him. "You were too eager to brag to me, trusting your English would be incomprehensible to anyone who overheard, and your master is going to pay. You have betrayed Delm."

Balous bubbled out a huffy sound. "You're bluffing," he said. "Besides, what if I do like to brag to my victims? It does Delm no harm. I do not have to like him, just serve. You've no idea how hard it is cleaning up his messes! He wants this woman, that woman, a flag ship, a sperm sample collected, a child murdered!" Balous scowled petulantly. "He's supposed to be a Soul of Light." He frowned. "Such things do not help maintain the image. And who else can I complain to but the victims that I am about to kill?" He sighed. "Now, since I'm feeling much better and you're getting boring —"Balous raised the needle gun and fired. But his hand was shaking, allowing Ranar to throw himself down in time. The bolt zipped over his head and fell harmlessly. Ranar wondered, more than academically, if it was poisoned. Balous cursed him as he loaded another bolt.

Wails and shouts erupted from the stairwell. Cries of disaster and terror.

Balous froze and went pasty white. "No," he whispered, disbelieving. He tried to get up, forgetting about Ranar. A man came pounding up the stairs followed by a thin stampede of ladies, all wide-eyed and whispering in awe-struck voices with handkerchiefs clutched to their faces. A couple were in floods of tears.

"It's the Ava!" the lead man told Balous. "The Ava's been assassinated!"

The needle gun dropped from the *gorarelpul's* fingers. "No," he said again, in fear, and dropped on one knee. "I didn't mean it!" he wailed, clutching at his head. He tried to stagger towards the stairs to get down, gasping and looking — to Ranar's satisfaction — as if his conscience bond was bothering him. The tide was against him. Some people gave way to him, some didn't. More and more of them were pressing in.

Ranar decided Eva would be trampled if he left her on the floor, so he hauled her up, straining. There was nowhere to flee except further into Blue Hearth, or out of it. He picked the latter, choosing the direction that should lead to Fountain Court if the layout of Blue Hearth mirrored Green Hearth. Moving slowly, Eva a limp weight in his arms that he could barely manage, Ranar passed through several rooms without seeing anybody. If there were servants about they had gone to ground in their own quarters.

But there were guards in the Entrance Hall. They looked at him, uncertain about what they should be doing. The door to Fountain Court was just beyond.

Ranar let Eva slump onto a bench along the wall and pointed backward, crying in the very little Gelack he had acquired, "Delm! Octagon!"

The panic in his voice was genuine enough to stampede them, coupled with the shouts echoing down Blue Hearth's Throat.

Ranar heaved up Eva and tried to hurry towards the exit. He passed doors on either side, afraid they would open and spout errants as he went past, and even more afraid each time he put one at this back. Finally he reached the outer doors, but they were bolted closed.

He put Eva down to lift a bar across the inside and work the large, ornate lock with shaking hands. The door swung open. There was Fountain Court — empty. Everyone was on the Octagon to watch the duel. But there was nowhere to go except one of the other Hearths. He spotted Green Hearth directly across from Blue and decided he would try his luck there.

Someone yelled behind him. Ranar turned to see errants at the far end of the hall again. For an instant, he nearly sprinted away, leaving Eva, but he couldn't do it. He picked her up again with a groan, sure she had gotten heavier.

Two of the errants who had returned for him ran forward. One had a black rod the length of a man's forearm that made nasty electrostatic snapping sounds. It didn't look like something Sevolites used on each other.

As the errants caught up, two new shapes flowed in around him. The woman relieved him of Eva and snapped orders, expecting him to follow her. She wore black slacks and shirt with a set of three red slashes on the breast. She wore a sword but didn't have it cleared. The man with her covered their retreat with a drawn sword. One look at him and the errants pursuing Ranar lost their ambitions.

The black-clad highborn backed out, kicked the door closed, and continued to face backwards, toward Blue Hearth, covering their passage around the fountain. Once they had Fountain Court's centerpiece between them and Blue Hearth, he dashed ahead of them.

The woman carried Eva into Black Hearth where she promptly dumped her off on servants. She said something to Ranar, and headed down the hearth's Throat. After a moment's hesitation, Ranar followed.

Black Hearth was austere after the luxury of Blue Hearth's interior. He followed the woman down the internal stairs and across an empty space behind high screens at the bottom. He could feel the presence of people as they neared the Octagon.

They cleared the screens, and there was Di Mon, held by a brawny Demish man with a sword to this throat, and beside him a toppled chair strewn about with blood-sprayed flowers.

* * *

The Demish were murderously angry. Di Mon marveled at how long they could sustain it without slitting his throat. His own intensity was drained out of him. He felt like himself again, free of the anxiety that had peaked with the loss of his heir.

Who probably never was, he thought ironically. Vretla had become pregnant so easily not because of Kertatt's unsuspected potency or blind luck, but by having sex with a Pureblood. He wondered how the Demish would take to an icon who had worked as a courtesan on Fountain Court. Not well, he suspected. If he lived, he would make Ev'rel Ava. It seemed the least he could do to make things up to her. He hoped D'Ander would not prove to have other ideas.

The tension on the Octagon dismayed him. There were times in the empire's history when dozens had perished in melees started by similar stand-offs. It was one of the reasons the empire was running short of highborns. He wondered what Ranar would make of that fact and smiled, privately.

H'Us tipped his blade, lifting Di Mon's chin to lay its flat against the soft skin underneath it. Di Mon was getting tired of holding his head up. He was tired of the Demish princes with their huge, muscled shoulders holding his arms fast behind him.

He said, "Kill me, or let me stand clear while we wait for the results." H'Us obliged him.

Released, he shook himself and straightened his tunic. The cut on his arm had stopped bleeding but his sleeve was stiff. The nick on his throat trickled blood.

He said, "Thank you."

H'Us was too shocked and bitter to answer. The Demish glowered. The Vrellish watched. Everyone waited.

D'Ander had been joined by his daughter, Ayrium. Di Mon watched them exchange words privately, their heads together. Perry D'Aur was with them, unbound and looking shaken, but not wholly daunted. Ayrium met Di Mon's eyes and held his stare. They had made a bond of honor to settle the custody of Amel at their mutual convenience. Something in the pointed way she stared suggested there may be cause to enact that agreement.

Not today, though, thought Di Mon. If he survived this he would not pick up a sword again until he'd had Ranar to himself for an hour, not just to love but to talk to, about anything he wanted to. The notion made him feel almost like laughing.

Heralds emerged from Silver Hearth and Black Hearth. Blue and Green Hearths would have done their own tests, but were excluded by virtue of being the houses in conflict. Red Hearth had no means to do a genotyping but would believe the Nersallians. The heralds conferred and one from Black Hearth went forward.

"We agree," she declared loudly, holding up Von's readout. "This child is Delm's grandson."

A murmur began, swiftly silenced by the herald as she went on. "The child is also the grandson of Ev'rel. His mother is a commoner. His paternal contribution is consistent with a possible profile for Amel, who must, in order for this 50 percent Sevolite child to be the grandson of both Ev'rel and Delm, have been a Pureblood as his mother, Ev'rel, declared to this court at her trial."

H'Us dropped his sword. It fell with a clatter in the sudden silence.

Di Mon spotted Ranar, watching from Black Wedge, and started forward. Ses Nersal intercepted him with a hug. He kissed her to say thank you.

"Vrellishly done," Sert said grudgingly. "You will answer for your Lorel nature later, after I get a look at Vretla."

Di Mon nodded, deciding it was not a propitious time to caution that he had no guarantee Vretla would survive to return to court. He would deal with that contingency if and when he must.

"Where is Tessitatt?" Branst asked, inevitably. Di Mon's niece had always been his prime motivation for pro-Monatese sentiments.

"With Vretla Vrel," Di Mon told the young Nersallian, "on *TouchGate Hospital*."

"Oh," Branst said, and stepped back.

His own Monatese errants were the next to descend on him. "Take the mother and child into Green Hearth, out to the docks and to Monitum," Di Mon told Captain Hesseratt, "before the Demish finish fretting about Amel."

Hesseratt nodded.

"Amel is alive," Ayrium was assuring a circle of astonished Demish. They were all men — the skirted Demish women had evaporated. Ayrium was bold and buxom in flight leathers, face marked with the dark shadows of superficial bruising that suggested she had flown hard to get here, but still looking very capable and wearing a sword like her father. "I've seen him. He's a nice kid."

"But — a courtesan?" A befuddled Demish Highlord asked of no one in particular. They conferred in a buzz of controversy: some not believing it possible to honor an ex-courtesan, some saying, "Yes, but he's Amel!" Di Mon also caught variations of a theme that laid the blame at the feet of Amel's Vrellish influence, through his mother Ev'rel. According to this line of reasoning a true Soul of Light would have perished at the very thought of working at Den Eva's.

"Fear not then!" D'Ander declared, barging in, his face burning with anger. "Amel will not trouble you. I have him —"

Not technically accurate, Di Mon thought dryly, *Ayrium is your daughter, not your vassal.*

" — and I will protect him, as he deserves to be protected," proclaimed D'Ander, "as a Soul of Light, descended from my emperor!"

Uniform outrage greeted that assertion. Di Mon cursed and waded back into the middle of the brewing Demish storm before H'Us and D'Ander had their swords cleared once more.

"Ayrium owes me a duel for possession of Amel," Di Mon asserted loudly, and looked right at her. "We will fight it in our own time by terms yet to be agreed on. I will seek this court's approval of the details," he said, with a placating glance at H'Us, but thinking about Ev'rel. "Agreed?" he demanded of Ayrium, pointedly ignoring D'Ander. If the two of them had any sense, they'd get off the Octagon with Perry D'Aur before the rest of the Demish started thinking clearly. For starters, it was downright provocative for Perry D'Aur to be in possession of the one living highborn with a legitimate genetic claim on the lands she had taken by mutiny, and while the question of whether Perry D'Aur murdered Amel or married him was immaterial to Di Mon, he didn't want more fighting today.

"Agreed," Ayrium told him frankly.

"What!" exclaimed D'Ander.

She began explaining to D'Ander about teaming up with Di Mon in Killing Reach, but once Di Mon decided he could trust her to honor their pact, he lost interest and looked for Ranar.

He found the Reetion watching from Black Wedge. Di Mon went swiftly to meet him, took his elbow, and marched him towards Green Wedge as fast as the Reetion would let him.

"Eva's unconscious but I think she's all right," Ranar reported. "She's in Black Hearth."

"Good," Di Mon said, "she'll be safe there."

"You trust them?"

"The Nersallians?" Di Mon shrugged. He felt cheerful. It was a good feeling. "I trust them to conduct themselves with honor."

"What happened here?" Ranar asked, forced to skip a few steps to keep up. "Are you hurt? What was H'Us doing? Is Delm really dead?"

The few people left out on Green Wedge made way for their liege, bowing. *Not something they always did*, Di Mon thought, bemused. *They must have been impressed.*

He nudged Ranar up the stairs. The Reetion balked and turned. "I am tired of being pushed, picked up, and generally shoved around by Sevolites!" he declared.

Di Mon grinned. Ranar was charming when he lost his temper, but more effective when he kept his head. He was young. He would have time to learn.

"All right," Di Mon said.

Ranar deflated, ambushed by Di Mon's urbane politeness. "You haven't told me anything," he complained instead.

"Later." Di Mon gestured graciously. "Upstairs."

Ranar sighed, looked up, and muttered something in Reetion.

"Pardon?"

"Nothing," Ranar said. "Just — more stairs." But he padded up ahead of Di Mon quietly. Di Mon watched him with appreciation, thinking that, for a Reetion, he had really done quite well surviving Gelion.

Green Hearth was all but abandoned.

"This way," Di Mon said.

"You might thank me, just the once," the Reetion told him as they passed down the Throat, side by side. "It wouldn't utterly destroy your highborn pride."

"Thank you?" Di Mon asked, as they turned down Family Hall.

"Yes!" Ranar insisted, annoyed. "I found the child you were looking for. A child of this Prince Amel. I got the Vrellish out of Green Hearth. And I did look after Eva." The Reetion hesitated. "You are sure she'll be all right next door?"

"Yes," said Di Mon, pushing open the door he had been heading for. Ranar looked in, around Di Mon's shoulder, and drew back again.

"That's your bedroom," the Reetion said.

Di Mon went in, released the sword belt one of his errants had returned to him, and threw the weapon on a chest. Ranar came in and closed the door quietly.

"Lock it," said Di Mon.

"I ... don't know how to lock things," Ranar faltered.

Di Mon did it himself, then he turned Ranar toward him with both hands and kissed him.

"I know you are afraid of this," Ranar said, very still and unresponsive. "You aren't going to just — lose control again, pretend it didn't happen, and send me away somewhere? Alone?"

Di Mon thought it was a silly question. He was making himself perfectly clear.

"We have fifteen minutes," he said, "maybe ten."

"I see." Ranar glanced at the door again. "Will it always be like this?" he asked. "Furtive and frightening? Disguising our love with lies?"

"No," Di Mon assured him, "sometimes it will be worse."

Epilogue

Ann did not forget Von. In her good dreams about him they made love. In the bad ones she pursued H'Reth with a sword, or spent eons in hearings explaining why she had done things and pretending she had been space drunk.

She collected prints of the pleasanter pictures from his time on *Second Contact Station*, and started a diary written to him. There wasn't a lot else she wanted to do as a Supervised Citizen.

Her hearing overlapped with Lurol's and went on for a whole month. Rire took her heroism into account, and all her recent flight exposure. She claimed Von had consented to the erasure of his conscience bond, hoping that might excuse her lie about the Reetion vote, but expert opinion held that was impossible and Ann was charged with lying, again, to cover up. She argued that it happened off the record, while she and Von were being intimate, but Lurol said that would have brought on an attack. There was also the problem of why she hadn't told anyone earlier, when it might have spared everyone a lot of trouble. She mumbled that the message had been sort of cryptic and she didn't realize what he had meant at first. That went down like a lead balloon when she could not come up with details on the spot, and so she let the second lie drop.

In the end the presiding jury overrode arbitration to forgive her all her minor foul ups, in consideration of her bravery and youth, but they upheld the verdict of guilty for willfully misrepresenting the Reetion vote and lying about the off-record consent given by Von. It wasn't helpful that she didn't volunteer for psych probe confirmation of her testimony.

Lurol's trial went better, although public opinion condemned her oversights and celebrated Von's virtues with twenty-twenty hindsight and the leisure to construct humane alternatives from the safety of comfortable living rooms. Lurol was told she should have realized this and done that. She should have disallowed the use made of Von as a resource enabling translation and the extraction of memories directly from his brain without permission once she realized what was going on. She should have checked the status of his human rights when she realized he was Sevolite. Ann would have felt sorry for her if Lurol hadn't grown more unshakeable with each attack, wielding logic like a sturdy club in defense of her better decisions while stoically admitting to her faults. In the end, both Lurol and the visitor probe were excused due to the unprecedented circumstances.

Two things upset Ann about the ruling apart from Lurol getting off while she stewed in another Megan group home. The first was the lack of emphasis on the way Lurol rebalanced Von's psychology — Lurol made that out to be no more than good psychiatry under bad circumstances, but Ann thought there was an ethical problem you could fly a ship through in Lurol's choice of how to tip the balance! The second was the way Von's data acquired a following all its own, beginning with mind scientists like Lurol, but spreading to the general population.

The day she heard about a discussion group called "Friends of Prince Amel," she took all her own pictures down, wiped her cache of his data, and stopped writing in her diary to Von.

Rire knew by then who Prince Amel was to the Gelacks. Court news reached them in a series of communiqués from Ranar, all censored by the Gelack House of Monitum, which was shocking to Rire even though the Monatese confined their intervention to a veto. Anything Ranar was allowed to write, Ranar claimed, would at least be true. Quaintly, writing was what he actually sent, penned on vellum and delivered to *Second Contact Station* by a Monatese nobleborn once every couple of months.

A crisis struck while Ann was still Supervised, which prompted the transformation of *Second Contact* into an early warning outpost and diplomatic station renamed *SkyBlue Station*. Ann applied to serve and received so much attention from Space Service that she grew hopeful, but in the end her Supervision stuck. Rire could not trust a pilot, however talented, who told lies.

Ann spent her twentieth birthday Supervised.

She dissipated her frustration through the ill-considered seduction of a counselor she rather liked, which she felt guilty about when he was yanked and advised to retrain for another specialization. He was so upset he didn't want to see her again. Apart from him, she indulged herself with a few fellow residents, but they had their own problems, which were even more boring than her own. They didn't impress her the way N'Goni had when she was young, and she didn't want them the way that she still wanted Von. But Von was a dream she could possess now only in her heart.

It was time, she decided, to grow up. Intent on getting out, she enrolled in Space Service studies while she was still Supervised and slaked her physicality in exercise. Then, over a year after she had met Von, and months into her new regimen, there came a miracle.

Amel Dem'Vrel, son of Ev'rel Dem'Vrel and Royal Envoy of the Gelacks' new Ava, sent a message to Rire through Purple Alliance contacts to *SkyBlue Station*. It came recorded on Reetion equipment, showing him dressed formally in sword and braided jacket against the incongruous background of a field marked with the muddy tracks of farm machinery. An uncooperative breeze forced him to swipe hair from his face twice and he spoke a little hurriedly in Reetion, saying he had heard Ann was imprisoned and that he understood it concerned her part in seeing to it that his conscience bond was erased. He said he was grateful to Ann for understanding that he had wanted his freedom. Gelack style, for confirmation of identify, he sent the blit in a leather pouch sealed with a plastic chip that held a few cells of his blood.

Ann cried for hours afterwards.

A new hearing ruled in her favor, and Space Service sent her to serve as lead pilot on *SkyBlue*.

Ann half expected Von to be there when she showed up. He was not. No Gelack, thus far, had felt comfortable enough to do more than drop off mail and pick it up, refusing even to dock. The Monatese pilots set up beacons for the Reetions to find Ranar's reports, and the PA stepped in as a middle-man to periodically run mail in the other direction, primarily to Monitum.

Ann did meet Ranar again, though. He was brought by the Monatese to live and work for a while on *SkyBlue* as resident diplomat, which Rire approved because he was the only Reetion with the right kind of experience. He couldn't see Ann at once, and it was hard for Ann to find the discipline to let him sleep his trip off, so she went swimming in *SkyBlue's* recreational pool instead, until she was too tired to do anything more than collapse.

The next morning she made a late start. She was hunched over her breakfast, poking at scrambled eggs, when Ranar introduced himself with, "May I sit down?"

Ann's head snapped up. She dropped her fork. "Of course!"

He sat down and she shifted to the edge of her seat, watching him arrange his plate and cup. He was drinking a steaming infusion that wasn't hot chocolate.

Some sort of tea, she guessed, *probably Gelack*.

"So," she said, "how is, uh, Gelion?"

"Amel is all right, I think," he said at once.

Ann scowled, not liking to be so transparent. "Is he having fun being a prince and stuff? I don't suppose he thinks about me much."

Ranar drove her crazy by placidly eating the mouthful of scrambled eggs already en route to his mouth, and then paused to dab his napkin to his mouth.

"Amel asked me about you the last time I saw him, in fact," Ranar said at last, making Ann's heart thump. "I told him about the hearing. No doubt that's why he sent the message claiming he empowered you to lie about the vote."

Ann brightened. "Yeah?" she said, hoping for details about how Von had looked and whether he had felt sorry for her.

"Very Gelack of him to equate Supervision with imprisonment, I thought," Ranar remarked.

"Oh?" Ann was willing to encourage anything so long as Ranar talked.

"And producing suitable lies to help you out is pure Amel," Ranar continued in a disapproving tone. "I should have anticipated that."

He knows Amel better than I do, Ann realized, feeling miserable. *I am yesterday's news. Someone Prince Amel knew when he was Von.*

Ranar sorted out another mouthful and ate that. "I am very pleased," he said next, "with this station."

He dragged her unwillingly into discussing the *SkyBlue* mission until she could stand it no more.

"Look," she said. "Amel is Royal Envoy, right? That means he does a lot of flying around. Delivering messages for the Ava."

Ranar seemed taken aback, as if he imagined they had exhausted the topic in their first exchange. "More or less, I suppose," Ranar agreed and shrugged, "but he does more, as a rule, than fly around. He's in Golden Reach right now on a diplomatic mission. He left some months ago." He sipped from his glass. "Amel's related to the Golden Demish, of course, which makes him valuable. But the Soul of Light business clashed with his history once the details started getting out. It may be rather an awkward homecoming, given that. And his mixed blood, of course — he's not a blond."

Ann stood up.

Ranar blinked at her. "Ann?"

She inhaled to explain but didn't know how, and hitting him would get her in trouble, so she just left and walked back to her room.

When she got there she looked at the bed and thought, *No. I am not going to throw myself on the bed and sob. Not anymore.*

Beauty, Von, Amel — whoever he was! — was not hers anymore, maybe he never really had been. She was damn well going to value what she had had. How many Reetions got a chance to make love to a court trained, Gelack courtesan?

Ann sniffed, blinking back tears, and got angry. So Amel was rare and precious. So what! She was no slouch. And she wasn't the lame, mooning kid her counselors made her out to be who had to have a perfect and exciting lover. She really, really had to move on.

One thing was for sure: this time she wouldn't start by making a play for Ranar. He still looked okay but he seemed as if he had aged a decade in other ways. One could overdo the maturity thing, too. Besides, this time she was picking someone who would appreciate her!

Three and a half weeks later, she was drinking hot chocolate with a new lover in a lounge looking out on space. The place had picked up the nickname Pit Stop because it was only a short walk from the special, Gelack-friendly rim dock used by *SkyBlue's* PA visitors. Few of the PA pilots making mail runs would linger more than absolutely necessary, but those who did were always welcome in the Pit Stop. The locals made a point of feeding them and pumping them for stories as if they were stray animals or wandering minstrels, which made the arrival of someone in flight leathers something of a holiday occasion.

This time, however, Ann heard people at the tables behind her catch their breath audibly, in violation of the standing directive to treat their guests like ordinary people when they dropped in. She heard a smooth and pleasant voice completing a sentence ending with "... can find Ann?" He must have begun the sentence in the buzz of a half-filled room. There was dead silence by the time he finished his last syllable.

Ann swiveled around, facing away from her table.

It was Von. Or Amel, rather. He looked unaccountably nervous to find himself the center of attention, but he overcame it with a twitch of his pastel lips and tossed his dark hair back. Sweat showed in his hairline. He was fresh from flying, and dressed in Gelack flight leathers that were pure white except for small signs of wear and a beige crest embroidered on his left breast. He didn't have a sword with him, just a kit slung over one shoulder.

He stood very still, looking worried by all the attention, as he scanned the staring faces. His face lit up when he saw hers. "Ann!" he exclaimed, his smile releasing all his inner beauty. He hurried towards her, weaving gracefully between the tables, but checked himself as her date rose to greet him.

"Are you really him?" the guy asked.

Amel's eyes flicked from him to Ann and back. "I'm not sure," he said. "I'm Amel Dem'Vrel. Does that help?"

"You're him, alright!" Ann's boyfriend laughed. "Wow, a real highborn Sevolite!"

Amel looked a bit offended, or embarrassed, or maybe just uncomfortable. The expression was so subtle it was hard to be sure. "There's debate about that, in some quarters of the Empire," he confessed.

Ann couldn't move. She couldn't speak.

"I'm sorry if I'm interrupting," Amel told her, shifting his kit on his shoulder to cover his social uncertainty. "I can translate Gelack thoughts into Reetion pretty well, but I don't really know your protocols," he flushed a little, the way any young man might who was muffing an introduction to a girl he liked. "Sorry, that's a Golden Demish way to put it," he said, and paused unnecessarily to clear his throat. "I was in Killing Reach and I heard you were here. I thought I would sort of drop over, and see how you were."

"Doing five *skim'facs* I'll bet!" enthused Ann's boyfriend. He had captured her attention, on their first date, with his admiration of her own feats in flight. She hadn't realized until now that it was because he belonged to the 'how much, how fast' school of male status calculators.

Amel clearly thought he was an idiot. "Uh, no, actually," he said politely, looking a bit strained.

"What's the hardest you've ever flown?" asked Ann's boyfriend. "I'll bet —"

Ann pounced. She captured Amel's arm and she didn't look back.

"Is he —" Amel began, pointing backwards with a loose gesture of his thumb.

"No," said Ann.

"Oh," Amel said happily. "I thought he was."

She pulled him down beside her at the first empty table and gave him just enough time to deposit his shoulder bag beside him, before capturing his hands and squeezing.

People were staring, and the damned arbiter would be monitoring them. Ann was breathing hard, seriously wanting to just rip his clothes off but afraid that might be a bit too forward.

"I've missed you," she said, staring into his wonderful eyes with their crisp cool, gray facets that somehow projected warmth that melted you.

He stared right back at her, a little short of breath, "I've missed you, too."

Okay, Ann realized, swallowing thickly, *I can't stand this*.

She got up. He rose with her. She threw herself into his arms and they went willingly around her as he kissed her. It was like being home and on an exotic adventure, simultaneously.

"So," she said, hands locked on white leather, staring up just a little, "two years. Wow."

"Yes," he said.

"How have you been?"

"Don't ask," he advised. "You?"

"Out of prison," she grinned at him, delirium bubbling up. "Let's —"

"Yes?"

"Oh, hell, Von —"

His faint smile notified her of the error.

"Sorry! Prince Amel?"

He didn't care. His hands were on her waist and his face had the look of a man thinking about dissolving himself in a woman.

He put his face against hers, breathing very gently in her radiating ear. "You should know. I should warn you ..."

He drew back again, showing every symptom of a need for her as real as hers for him, but he dampened his soft pastel lips and grew troubled. Her stomach began to cramp. But she could see he had to get something out on the table before he could go any further. The faster the better then, as far as she was concerned.

He looked around the room. The arbiter's omniscient surveillance was inhibiting him.

Ann asked gruffly, "Got a ship?"

"What? Oh, yes," he said, catching on. He snatched his bag up. Hand in hand they walked indecently fast out of the Pit Stop, through the archway to the customized Gelack dock. Amel helped her into his envoy class *rel*-skimmer and led her into an empty cargo space behind the cockpit area. It looked as if he slept there himself sometimes. The floor was heaped with surprisingly luxurious cushions with clean white cabinets lining the low walls. They had to stoop to enter and lie down to be comfortable, but she didn't mind that.

He kissed her long and brilliantly, lying warm and firm beside her, before remembering he wanted to talk.

"Ann," he said, stroking her, shifting a leg in a way that made her want to faint and get very energetic at the same time. "I ought to be clear about ..." He petered out again.

"What!" she demanded.

He looked pained. "About me. It isn't safe, I don't think. I mean to be my lover."

"Good!" Ann cried, desperate to shut him up. "Heavens preserve I should get bored!" She added one condition in deference to her greater maturity. "Let's stay in dock this time, though."

He pushed himself up on an elbow, embarrassed. "Oh, Ann, that was such a bad idea, I know. I'm sorry. But I had figured that out on my own. I mean, really, in the end, it was your fault, you know."

Ann didn't see how it could have been her fault when she had been unconscious or delusional the whole time, but she didn't want to talk anymore. Not, at least, until she had had as much of him as she could take and still be able to stand afterwards. So she simply said, "Shut up." And he did.